②

TRIBULATION FORCE

TRIBULATION

THE CONTINUING DRAMA OF THOSE LEFT BEHIND

FORCE

TIM LaHaye
JERRY B. JENKINS

Tyndale House Publishers, Inc.
WHEATON, ILLINOIS

Published in association with the literary agency of Alive Communications, Inc., 1465 Kelly Johnson Blvd., Suite 320, Colorado Springs, CO 80920.

Scripture taken from the New King James Version. Copyright © 1979, 1980, 1982 by Thomas Nelson, Inc. Used by permission. All rights reserved.

ISBN 0-7394-2501-3

Printed in the United States of America

*To those readers of **Left Behind**
who wrote to tell us of its impact*

PROLOGUE

What Has Gone Before...

IN one cataclysmic instant, millions of people all over the world disappeared. They simply vanished, leaving behind everything material: clothes, eyeglasses, contact lenses, hairpieces, hearing aids, fillings, jewelry, shoes, even pacemakers and surgical pins.

Millions vanished. But millions more remained—adults, but no children, and only a few young teens. All babies, including the unborn, disappeared—some during birth.

Worldwide chaos ensued. Planes, trains, buses, and cars crashed, ships sank, homes burned, grieving survivors committed suicide. A transportation and communications gridlock, coupled with the disappearances of many service personnel, left most to fend for themselves until some semblance of order returned.

Some said the world had been invaded by aliens from outer space. Others said the disappearances resulted from an enemy attack. And yet every country on the globe was touched by the disappearances.

Airline captain Rayford Steele and his twenty-year-old daughter Chloe were left behind. Rayford's wife and their twelve-year-old son vanished. Rayford, piloting a 747 over the Atlantic en route to London, told his senior flight attendant, Hattie Durham, that he didn't know what had happened. The terrifying truth was that he knew all too well. His wife had warned him of this very event. Christ had come to take away his own, and the rest, Rayford and Chloe included, had been left behind.

Rayford became consumed with finding the truth and making sure that he and Chloe would not miss any second chance. He felt responsible for her skepticism, for her believe-only-what-you-can-see-and-feel attitude.

His search took him to his wife's church, where a handful of people, including even one on the pastoral staff, had been left behind. Visitation Pastor Bruce Barnes had lost his wife and children, and he, above all others, knew immediately that his weak, phony faith had failed him at the most critical instant of his life. In a single moment, he became the most convinced skeptic on earth—an enthusiastic, unapologetic evangelist.

Under Bruce's tutelage and the influence of a videotape the senior pastor had left for just such a time, first Rayford and then Chloe came to believe in Christ. With their new pastor they formed what they call the Tribulation Force, a core group determined to challenge the forces of evil during the Tribulation period predicted in the Bible.

Meanwhile, Cameron—"Buck"—Williams, a senior staff writer for the prestigious newsmagazine *Global Weekly,* was on a quest of his own. Buck had been aboard Rayford Steele's plane when the Rapture occurred, and he was assigned to make some sense of the worldwide disappearances. His interviewing brought him into contact with one of the most powerful and charismatic personalities ever, the mysterious Romanian leader, Nicolae Carpathia. Within two weeks of the vanishings, Carpathia was swept to international power as head of the United Nations, promising to unite the devastated globe as one peaceful village.

Buck introduced flight attendant Hattie Durham to Carpathia, who quickly made her his personal assistant. After coming to faith in Christ under the influence of Rayford, Chloe, and Bruce, Buck felt responsible for Hattie and became desperate to get her away from Carpathia.

Demoted for allegedly blowing a major assignment, Buck relocated from New York to Chicago, where he joined Rayford, Chloe, and Bruce as the fourth member of the Tribulation Force. Together these four have determined to stand and fight against all odds, to never give in. Representing millions who missed the opportunity to meet Christ in the air, they have resolved not to lose hold of their newfound faith, no matter what the future might bring.

Buck Williams has witnessed the murderous evil power of Nicolae Carpathia, and Bruce Barnes knows from his study of Scripture that dark days lie ahead. The odds are, only one of the four members of the Tribulation Force will survive the next seven years.

But only Bruce has more than a hint of the terror to come. If the others knew, they might not venture so bravely into the future.

ONE

It was Rayford Steele's turn for a break. He pulled the headphones down onto his neck and dug into his flight bag for his wife's Bible, marveling at how quickly his life had changed. How many hours had he wasted during idle moments like this, poring over newspapers and magazines that had nothing to say? After all that had happened, only one book could hold his interest.

The Boeing 747 was on auto from Baltimore to a four o'clock Friday afternoon landing at Chicago O'Hare, but Rayford's new first officer, Nick, sat staring ahead anyway, as if piloting the plane. *Doesn't want to talk to me anymore,* Rayford thought. *Knew what was coming and shut me down before I opened my mouth.*

"Is it going to offend you if I sit reading this for a while?" Rayford asked.

The younger man turned and pulled the left phone away from his own ear. "Say again?"

Rayford repeated himself, pointing to the Bible. It had belonged to the wife he hadn't seen for more than two weeks and probably would not see for another seven years.

"As long as you don't expect me to listen."

"I got that loud and clear, Nick. You understand I don't care what you think of me, don't you?"

"Sir?"

Rayford leaned close and spoke louder. "What you think of me would have been hugely important a few weeks ago," he said. "But—"

"Yeah, I know, OK? I got it, Steele, all right? You and lots of other people think the whole thing was Jesus. Not buying. Delude yourself, but leave me out of it."

Rayford raised his brows and shrugged. "You wouldn't respect me if I hadn't tried."

"Don't be too sure."

But when Rayford turned back to his reading, it was the *Chicago Tribune* sticking out of his bag that grabbed his attention.

The *Tribune,* like every other paper in the world, carried the front-page story: During a private meeting at the United Nations, just before a Nicolae Carpathia press conference, a horrifying murder/suicide had occurred. New U.N. Secretary-General Nicolae Carpathia had just installed the ten new members of the expanded Security Council, seeming to err by inaugurating two men to the same position of U.N. ambassador from the Great States of Britain.

According to the witnesses, billionaire Jonathan Stonagal, Carpathia's friend and financial backer, suddenly overpowered a guard, stole his handgun, and shot himself in the head, the bullet passing through and killing one of the new ambassadors from Britain.

The United Nations had been closed for the day, and Carpathia was despondent over the tragic loss of his two dear friends and trusted advisers.

Bizarre as it might seem, Rayford Steele was one of only four people on the planet who knew the truth about Nicolae Carpathia—that he was a liar, a hypnotic brainwasher, the Antichrist himself. Others might suspect Carpathia of being other than he seemed, but only Rayford, his daughter, his pastor, and his new friend journalist Buck Williams knew for sure.

Buck had been one of the seventeen in that United Nations meeting room. And he had witnessed something entirely different—not a murder/suicide, but a double murder. Carpathia himself, according to Buck, had methodically borrowed the guard's gun, forced his old friend Jonathan Stonagal to kneel, then killed Stonagal and the British ambassador with one shot.

Carpathia had choreographed the murders, and then, while the witnesses sat in horror, Carpathia quietly told them what they had seen—the same story the newspapers now carried. Every witness in that room but one corroborated it. Most chilling, they believed it. Even Steve Plank, Buck's former boss, now Carpathia's press agent. Even Hattie Durham, Rayford's onetime flight attendant, who had become Carpathia's personal assistant. Everyone except Buck Williams.

Rayford had been dubious when Buck told his version in Bruce Barnes's office two nights ago. "You're the only person in the room who saw it your way?" he had challenged the writer.

"Captain Steele," Buck had said, "we all saw it the same way. But then Carpathia calmly described what he wanted us to think we had seen, and everybody but me immediately accepted it as truth. I want to know how he explains that he had the dead man's successor already there and sworn in when the murder took place. But now there's no evidence I was even there. It's as if Carpathia washed me from their memories. People I know now swear I wasn't there, and they aren't joking."

Chloe and Bruce Barnes had looked at each other and then back at Buck. Buck had finally become a believer, just before entering the meeting at the U.N. "I'm absolutely convinced that if I had gone into that room without God," Buck said, "I would have been reprogrammed too."

"But now if you just tell the world the truth—"

"Sir, I've been reassigned to Chicago because my boss believes I missed that meeting. Steve Plank asked why I had not accepted his invitation. I haven't talked to Hattie yet, but you know she won't remember I was there."

"The biggest question," Bruce Barnes said, "is what Carpathia thinks is in your head. Does he think he's erased the truth from *your* mind? If he knows you know, you're in grave danger."

Now, as Rayford read the bizarre story in the paper, he noticed Nick switching from autopilot to manual. "Initial descent," Nick said. "You want to bring her in?"

"Of course," Rayford said. Nick could have landed the plane, but Rayford felt responsible. He was the captain. He would answer for these people. And even though the plane could land itself, he had not lost the thrill of handling it. Few things reminded him of life as it had been just weeks before, but landing a 747 was one of them.

Buck Williams had spent the day buying a car—something he hadn't needed in Manhattan—and hunting for an apartment. He found a beautiful condo, at a place that advertised already-installed phones, midway between the *Global Weekly* Chicago bu-

reau office and New Hope Village Church in Mount Prospect. He
tried to convince himself it was the church that would keep drawing him west of the city, not Rayford Steele's daughter, Chloe.
She was ten years his junior, and whatever attraction he might
feel for her, he was certain she saw him as some sort of a wiz-
ened mentor.

Buck had put off going to the office. He wasn't expected there
until the following Monday anyway, and he didn't relish facing
Verna Zee. When it had been his assignment to find a replacement for veteran Lucinda Washington, the Chicago bureau chief
who had disappeared, he had told the militant Verna she had
jumped the gun by moving into her former boss's office. Now
Buck had been demoted and Verna elevated. Suddenly, she was
his boss.

But he didn't want to spend all weekend dreading the meeting,
and neither did he want to appear too eager to see Chloe Steele
again right away, so Buck drove to the office just before closing.
Would Verna make him pay for his years of celebrity as an award-
winning cover-story writer? Or would she make it even worse by
killing him with kindness?

Buck felt the stares and smiles of the underlings as he moved
through the outer office. By now, of course, everyone knew what
had happened. They felt sorry for him, were stunned by his lapse
of judgment. How could Buck Williams miss a meeting that
would certainly be one of the most momentous in news history,
even if it hadn't resulted in the double death? But they were also
aware of Buck's credentials. Many, no doubt, would still consider
it a privilege to work with him.

No surprise, Verna had already moved back into the big office.
Buck winked at Alice, Verna's spike-haired young secretary, and
peered in. It looked as if Verna had been there for years. She had
already rearranged the furniture and hung her own pictures and
plaques. Clearly, she was ensconced and loving every minute of it.

A pile of papers littered Verna's desk, and her computer screen
was lit, but she seemed to be idly gazing out the window. Buck
poked his head in and cleared his throat. He noticed a flash of
recognition and then a quick recomposing. "Cameron," she said
flatly, still seated. "I didn't expect you till Monday."

"Just checking in," he said. "You can call me Buck."

"I'll call you Cameron, if you don't mind, and—"

"I do mind. Please call—"

"Then I'll call you Cameron even if you *do* mind. Did you let anyone know you were coming?"

"I'm sorry?"

"Do you have an appointment?"

"An appointment?"

"With me. I have a schedule, you know."

"And there's no room for me on it?"

"You're asking for an appointment then?"

"If it's not inconvenient. I'd like to know where I'm going to land and what kind of assignments you have in mind for me, that kind of—"

"Those sound like things we can talk about when we meet," Verna said. "Alice! See if I have a slot in twenty minutes, please!"

"You do," Alice called out. "And I would be happy to show Mr. Williams his cubicle while he's waiting, if you—"

"I prefer to do that myself, Alice. Thank you. And could you shut my door?"

Alice looked apologetic as she rose and moved past Buck to shut the door. He thought she even rolled her eyes. *"You* can call me Buck," he whispered.

"Thanks," she said shyly, pointing to a chair beside her desk.

"I have to wait here, like seeing the principal?"

She nodded. "Someone called here for you earlier. Didn't leave her name. I told her you weren't expected till Monday."

"No message?"

"Sorry."

"So, where *is* my cubicle?"

Alice glanced at the closed door, as if fearing Verna could see her. She stood and pointed over the tops of several partitions toward a windowless corner in the back.

"That's where the coffeepot was last time I was here," Buck said.

"It still is," Alice said with a giggle. Her intercom buzzed. "Yes, ma'am?"

"Would you two mind whispering if you must talk while I'm working?"

"Sorry!" This time Alice did roll her eyes.

"I'm gonna go take a peek," Buck whispered, rising.

"Please don't," she said. "You'll get me in trouble with you-know-who."

Buck shook his head and sat back down. He thought of where he had been, whom he had met, the dangers he had faced in his career. And now he was whispering with a secretary he had to keep out of trouble from a wanna-be boss who had never been able to write her way out of a paper bag.

Buck sighed. At least he was in Chicago with the only people he knew who really cared about him.

———————

Despite his and Chloe's new faith, Rayford Steele found himself subject to deep mood swings. As he strode through O'Hare, passed brusquely and silently by Nick, he suddenly felt sad. How he missed Irene and Raymie! He knew beyond doubt they were in heaven, and that, if anything, they should be feeling sorry for him. But the world had changed so dramatically since the disappearances that hardly anyone he knew had recaptured any sense of equilibrium. He was grateful to have Bruce to teach him and Chloe and now Buck to stand with him in their mission, but sometimes the prospect of facing the future was overwhelming.

That's why it was such sweet relief to see Chloe's smiling face waiting at the end of the corridor. In two decades of flying, he had gotten used to passing passengers who were being greeted at the terminal. Most pilots were accustomed to simply disembarking and driving home alone.

Chloe and Rayford understood each other better than ever. They were fast becoming friends and confidants, and while they didn't agree on everything, they were knit in their grief and loss, tied in their new faith, and teammates on what they called the Tribulation Force.

Rayford embraced his daughter. "Anything wrong?"

"No, but Bruce has been trying to get you. He's called an emergency meeting of the core group for early this evening. I don't know what's up, but he'd like us to try to get hold of Buck."

"How'd you get here?"

"Cab. I knew your car was here."

"Where would Buck be?"

"He was going to look for a car and an apartment today. He could be anywhere."

"Did you call the *Weekly* office?"

"I talked to Alice, the secretary there, early this afternoon. He wasn't expected until Monday, but we can try again from the car.

I mean, you can. You should call him, don't you think? Rather than me?"

Rayford suppressed a smile.

Alice sat at her desk leaning forward, her head cocked, gazing at Buck and trying not to laugh aloud as he regaled her with whispered wisecracks. All the while he wondered how much of the stuff from his palatial Manhattan office would fit into the cubicle he was to share with the communal coffeepot. The phone rang, and Buck could hear both ends of the conversation from the speakerphone. From just down the hall came the voice of the receptionist. "Alice, is Buck Williams still back there?"

"Right here."

"Call for him."

It was Rayford Steele, calling from his car. "At seven-thirty tonight?" Buck said. "Sure, I'll be there. What's up? Hm? Well, tell her I said hi, too, and I'll see you both at the church tonight."

He was hanging up as Verna came to the door and frowned at him. "A problem?" he said.

"You'll have your own phone soon enough," she said. "Come on in."

As soon as he was seated Verna sweetly informed him that he would no longer be the world-traveling, cover-story-writing, star headliner of *Global Weekly*. "We here in Chicago have an important but limited role in the magazine," she said. "We interpret national and international news from a local and regional perspective and submit our stories to New York."

Buck sat stiffly. "So I'm going to be assigned to the Chicago livestock markets?"

"You don't amuse me, Cameron. You never have. You will be assigned to whatever we need covered each week. Your work will pass through a senior editor and through me, and I will decide whether it is of enough significance and quality to pass along to New York."

Buck sighed. "I didn't ask the big boss what I was supposed to do with my works in progress. I don't suppose you know."

"Your contact with Stanton Bailey will now funnel through me as well. Is that understood?"

"Are you asking whether I understand, or whether I agree?"

"Neither," she said. "I'm asking whether you will comply."

"It's unlikely," Buck said, feeling his neck redden and his pulse surge. He didn't want to get into a shouting match with Verna. But neither was he going to sit for long under the thumb of someone who didn't belong in journalism, let alone in Lucinda Washington's old chair and supervising him.

"I will discuss this with Mr. Bailey," she said. "As you might imagine, I have all sorts of recourse at my disposal for insubordinate employees."

"I can imagine. Why don't you get him on the phone right now?"

"For what?"

"To find out what I'm supposed to do. I've accepted my demotion and my relocation. You know as well as I do that relegating me to regional stuff is a waste of my contacts and my experience."

"And your talent, I assume you're implying."

"Infer what you want. But before you put me on the bowling beat, I have dozens of hours invested in my cover story on the theory of the disappearances—ah, why am I talking to you about it?"

"Because I'm your boss, and because it's not likely a Chicago bureau staff writer will land a cover story."

"Not even a writer who has already done several? I dare you to call Bailey. The last time he said anything about my piece, he said he was sure it would be a winner."

"Yeah? The last time I talked to him, he told me about the last time he talked to you."

"It was a misunderstanding."

"It was a lie. You said you were someplace and everybody who was there says you weren't. I'd have fired you."

"If you'd had the power to fire me, I'd have quit."

"You want to quit?"

"I'll tell you what I want, Verna. I want—"

"I expect all my subordinates to call me Ms. Zee."

"You have no subordinates in this office," Buck said. "And aren't you—"

"You're dangerously close to the line, Cameron."

"Aren't you afraid *Ms. Zee* sounds too much like *Missy?*"

She stood. "Follow me." She bristled past him, stomping out of her office and down the long hallway in her sensible shoes.

Buck stopped at Alice's desk. "Thanks for everything, Alice," he said quickly. "I've got a bunch of stuff that's being shipped here that I might need to have you forward to my new apartment."

Alice was nodding but her smile froze when Verna hollered down the hall. *"Now,* Cameron!"

Buck slowly turned. "I'll get back to you, Alice." Buck moved deliberately enough to drive Verna crazy, and he noticed people in their cubicles pretending not to notice but fighting smiles.

Verna marched to the corner that served as the coffee room and pointed to a small desk with a phone and a file cabinet. Buck snorted.

"You'll have a computer in a week or so," she said.

"Have it delivered to my apartment."

"I'm afraid that's out of the question."

"No, Verna, what's out of the question is you trying to vent all your frustration from who knows where in one breath. You know as well as I do that no one with an ounce of self-respect would put up with this. If I have to work out of the Chicago area, I'm going to work at home with a computer and modem and fax machine. And if you expect to see me in this office again for any reason, you'll get Stanton Bailey on the phone right now."

Verna looked prepared to stand her ground right there, so Buck headed back to her office with her trailing him. He passed Alice, who looked stricken, and waited at Verna's desk until she caught up. "Are you dialing, or am I?" he demanded.

———

Rayford and Chloe ate on the way home and arrived to an urgent phone message from Rayford's chief pilot. "Call me as soon as you get in."

With his cap under his arm and still wearing his uniform trench coat, Rayford punched the familiar numbers. "What's up, Earl?"

"Thanks for getting back to me right away, Ray. You and I go back a long way."

"Long enough that you should get to the point, Earl. What'd I do now?"

"This is not an official call, OK? Not a reprimand or a warning or anything. This is just friend to friend."

"So, friend to friend, Earl, should I sit down?"

"No, but let me tell you, buddy, you've got to knock off the proselytizing."

"The—?"

"Talking about God on the job, man."

"Earl, I back off when anyone says anything, and you know I don't let it get in the way of the job. Anyway, what do *you* think the disappearances were all about?"

"We've been through all that, Ray. I'm just telling you, Nicky Edwards is gonna write you up, and I want to be able to say you and I have already talked about it and you've agreed to back off."

"Write me up? Did I break a rule, violate procedure, commit a crime?"

"I don't know what he's going to call it, but you've been warned, all right?"

"I thought you said this wasn't official yet."

"It's not, Ray. Do you want it to be? Do I have to call you back tomorrow and drag you in here for a meeting and a memo for your file and all that, or can I just smooth everybody's feathers, tell 'em it was a misunderstanding, you're cool now, and it won't happen again?"

Rayford didn't respond at first.

"C'mon, Ray, this is a no-brainer. I don't like you having to think about this one."

"Well, I *will* have to think about it, Earl. I appreciate your tipping me off, but I'm not ready to concede anything just yet."

"Don't do this to me, Ray."

"I'm not doing it to you, Earl. I'm doing it to myself."

"Yeah, and I'm the one who has to find a replacement pilot certified for the 'forty-seven and the 'fifty-seven."

"You mean it's that serious! I could lose my job over this?"

"You bet you could."

"I'll still have to think about it."

"You've got it bad, Ray. Listen, in case you come to your senses and we can make this go away, you need to recertify on the 'fifty-seven soon. They're adding a half dozen more within a month or so, and they're going to be running them out of here. You want to be on that list. More money, you know."

"Not that big a deal to me anymore, Earl."

"I know."

"But the idea of flying the 757 *is* attractive. I'll get back to you."

"Don't make me wait, Ray."

———

"I will get Mr. Bailey on the phone if I can," Verna said. "But you realize it's late in New York."

"He's always there, you know that. Use his direct, after-hours number."

"I don't have that."

"I'll write it down for you. He's probably interviewing a replacement for me."

"I'll call him, Cameron, and I will even let you have your say, but I am going to speak to him first, and I reserve the right to tell him how insubordinate and disrespectful you've been. Please wait outside."

Alice was gathering up her stuff as if about ready to leave when Buck emerged with a mischievous look. Others were streaming from the office to the parking lot and the train. "Did you hear all that?" Buck whispered.

"I hear everything," she mouthed. "And you know those new speakerphones, the ones that don't make you wait till the other person is done talking?"

He nodded.

"Well, they don't make it obvious you're listening in, either. You just shut off the transmit button, like this, and then if something happens to hit the speakerphone button, oops, then you can hear a conversation without being heard. Is that cool, or what?"

From the speakerphone on her desk came the sound of the phone ringing in New York.

"Stanton. Who's this?"

"Um, sir, sorry to bother you at this hour—"

"You got the number, you must have something important. Now who is this?"

"Verna Zee in Chicago."

"Yeah, Verna, what's happening?"

"I've got a situation here. Cameron Williams."

"Yeah, I was going to tell you to just stay out of his hair. He's working on a couple of big pieces for me. You got a nice spot there he can work in, or should we just let him work out of his apartment?"

"We have a place for him here, sir, but he was rude and insubordinate to me today and—"

"Listen, Verna, I don't want you to have to worry about Williams. He's been put out to pasture for something I can't figure out, but let's face it, he's still our star here and he's going to be doing pretty much the same thing he's been doing. He gets less money and a less prestigious title, and he doesn't get to work in New York, but he's going to get his assignments from here. You just don't worry yourself about him, all right? In fact, I think it would be better for you and for him if he *didn't* work out of that office."

"But, sir—"

"Something else, Verna?"

"Well, I wish you had let me know this in advance. I need you to back me on this. He was inappropriate with me, and—"

"What do you mean? He came on to you, made a pass at you, what?"

Buck and Alice pressed their hands over their mouths to keep from bursting with laughter. "No, sir, but he made it clear he is not going to be subordinate to me."

"Well, I'm sorry about that, Verna, but he's not, OK? I'm not going to waste Cameron Williams on regional stuff, not that we don't appreciate every inch of copy that comes out of your shop, understand."

"But, sir—"

"I'm sorry, Verna, is there more? Am I not being clear, or what's the problem? Just tell him to order his equipment, charge it to the Chicago account, and work directly for us here. Got that?"

"But shouldn't he apolog—"

"Verna, do you really need me to mediate some personality conflict from a thousand miles away? If you can't handle that job there . . ."

"I can, sir, and I will. Thank you, sir. Sorry to trouble you."

The intercom buzzed. "Alice, send him in."

"Yes, ma'am, and then may I—"

"Yes, you may go."

Buck sensed Alice taking her time gathering her belongings, however, staying within earshot. He strode into the office as if he expected to talk on the phone with Stanton Bailey.

"He doesn't need to talk with you. He made it clear that I'm not expected to put up with your shenanigans. I'm assigning you to work from your apartment."

Buck wanted to say that he was going to find it hard to pass up the digs she had prepared for him, but he was already feeling guilty about having eavesdropped on her conversation. This was something new. Guilt.

"I'll try to stay out of your way," he said.

"I'd appreciate that."

When he reached the parking lot, Alice was waiting. "That was great," she said.

"You ought to be ashamed of yourself." He smiled broadly.

"You listened too."

"That I did. See ya."

"I'm going to miss the six-thirty train," she said. "But it was worth it."

"How about if I drop you off? Show me where it is."

Alice waited while he unlocked the car door. "Nice car."

"Brand-new," he answered. And that was just how he felt.

———

Rayford and Chloe arrived at New Hope early. Bruce was there, finishing a sandwich he had ordered. He looked older than his early thirties. After greeting them, he pushed his wire rims up into his curly locks and tilted back in his squeaky chair. "You get hold of Buck?" he asked.

"Said he'd be here," Rayford said. "What's the emergency?"

"You hear the news today?"

"Thought I did. Something significant?"

"I think so. Let's wait for Buck."

"Then let me tell you in the meantime how I got in trouble today," Rayford said.

When he finished, Bruce was smiling. "Bet that's never been in your personnel file before."

Rayford shook his head and changed the subject. "It seems so strange to have Buck as part of the inner core, especially when he's so new to this."

"We're all new to it, aren't we?" Chloe said.

"True enough."

Bruce looked up and smiled. Rayford and Chloe turned to see Buck in the doorway.

TWO

BUCK didn't know how to respond when Rayford Steele greeted him warmly. He appreciated the warmth and openness of his three new friends, but something nagged at him and he held back a little. He still wasn't quite comfortable with this kind of affection. And what was this meeting about? The Tribulation Force was scheduled to meet regularly, so a specially called meeting had to mean something.

Chloe looked at him expectantly when she greeted him, yet she did not hug him, as Steele and Bruce Barnes had done. Her reticence was his fault, of course. They barely knew each other, but clearly there had been chemistry. They had given each other enough signals to begin a relationship, and in a note to Chloe, Buck had even admitted he was attracted to her. But he had to be careful. Both were brand-new in their faith, and they were only now learning what the future held. Only a fool would begin a relationship at a time like this.

And yet wasn't that exactly what he was—a fool? How could it have taken him so long to learn anything about Christ when he had been a stellar student, an international journalist, a so-called intellectual?

And what was happening to him now? He felt guilty about listening in on the phone while his bosses discussed him. He would never have given eavesdropping a second thought in the past. The tricks and schemes and outright lies he had told just to get a story would have filled a book. Would he be as good a journalist now with God in his life, seeming to prick his conscience over even little things?

• • •

Rayford sensed Buck's uneasiness and Chloe's hesitancy. But mostly he was struck by the nearly instantaneous change in Bruce's countenance. Bruce had smiled at Rayford's story of getting into trouble on the job, and he had smiled when Buck arrived. Suddenly, however, Bruce's face had clouded over. His smile had vanished, and he was having trouble composing himself.

Rayford was new to this kind of sensitivity. Before his wife and son had disappeared, he had not wept in years. He had always considered emotion weak and unmanly. But since the disappearances, he had seen many men weep. He was convinced that the global vanishings had been Christ rapturing his church, but for those who remained behind, the event had been catastrophic.

Even for him and for Chloe, who had become believers because of it, the horror of losing the rest of their family was excruciating. There were days when Rayford had been so grief-stricken and lonely for his wife and son that he wondered if he could go on. How could he have been so blind? What a failure he had been as a husband and father!

But Bruce had been a wise counselor. He too had lost a wife and children, and he, of all people, should have been prepared for the coming of Christ. With Bruce's support and the help of the other two in this room, Rayford knew he could go on. But there was more on Rayford's mind than just surviving. He was beginning to believe that he—and all of them—would have to take action, perhaps at the risk of their very lives.

If there had been a moment's doubt or hesitation about that, it was dispelled when Bruce Barnes finally found his voice. The young pastor pressed his lips together to keep them from quivering. His eyes were filling.

"I, uh, need to talk to you all," he began, leaning forward and pausing to compose himself. "With all the news coming out of New York by the minute these days, I've taken it upon myself to keep CNN on all the time. Rayford, you said you hadn't heard the latest. Chloe?" She shook her head. "Buck, I assume you have access to every Carpathia announcement as it breaks."

"Not today," Buck said. "I didn't get into the office until the end of the day, and I didn't hear a thing."

Bruce seemed to cloud up again, then he gave an apologetic smile. "It isn't that the news is so devastating," he said. "It's just that I feel such a tremendous responsibility for you all. You know

I'm trying to run this church, but that seems so insignificant compared to my study of prophecy. I'm spending most of my days and evenings poring over the Bible and commentaries, and I feel the press of God on me."

"The press of God?" Rayford repeated. But Bruce broke into tears. Chloe reached across the desk and covered one of his hands with hers. Rayford and Buck also reached to touch Bruce.

"It's so hard," Bruce said, fighting to make himself understood. "And I know it's not just me. It's you guys and everybody who comes to this church. We're all hurting, we've all lost people, we all missed the truth."

"But now we've found it," Chloe said, "and God used you in that."

"I know. I just feel so full of conflicting emotions that I wonder what's next," Bruce said. "My house is so big and so cold and so lonely without my family that sometimes I don't even go home at night. Sometimes I just study until I fall asleep, and I go home in the morning only to shower and change and get back here."

Uncomfortable, Rayford looked away. Had he been the one trying to communicate with his friends, he would have wanted someone to change the subject, to get him back to what the meeting was about. But Bruce was a different kind of a guy. He had always communicated in his own way and in his own time.

Bruce reached for a tissue, and the other three sat back. When Bruce spoke again, his voice was still husky. "I feel an enormous weight on me," he said. "One of the things I had never been good at was reading the Bible every day. I pretended to be a believer, a so-called full-time Christian worker, but I didn't care about the Bible. Now I can't get enough of it."

Buck could identify. He wanted to know everything God had been trying to communicate to him for years. That was one reason, besides Chloe, that he didn't mind relocating to Chicago. He wanted to come to this church and hear Bruce explain the Bible every time the doors were opened. He wanted to immerse himself in Bruce's insight and teaching as a member of this little core group.

He still had a job and he was writing important stuff, but learning to know God and listening to him seemed his primary occupation. The rest was just a means to an end.

Bruce looked up. "Now I know what people meant when they said they feasted on the Word. Sometimes I sit drinking it in for

hours, losing track of time, forgetting to eat, weeping and praying. Sometimes I just slip from my chair and fall to my knees,
calling out to God to make it clear to me. Most frightening of all,
he's doing just that."

Buck noticed Rayford and Chloe nodding. He was newer at
this than they were, but he felt that same hunger and thirst for
the Bible. But what was Bruce getting at? Was he saying that God
had revealed something to him?

Bruce took a deep breath and stood. He stepped to the corner
of the desk and sat on it, towering over the other three. "I need
your prayers," he said. "God is showing me things, impressing
truths on me that I can barely contain. And yet if I say them publicly, I will be ridiculed and maybe put myself in danger."

"Of course we'll pray," Rayford said. "But what does this have
to do with today's news?"

"It has everything to do with the news, Rayford." Bruce shook
his head. "Don't you see? We know Nicolae Carpathia is the Antichrist. Let's assume for the sake of argument that Buck's story
of Carpathia's supernatural hypnotic power and the murder of
those two men is ridiculous. Even so, there's plenty of evidence
that Carpathia fits the prophetic descriptions. He's deceptive. He's
charming. People are flocking to support him. He has been thrust
to power, seemingly against his own wishes. He's pushing a one-
world government, a one-world currency, a treaty with Israel,
moving the U.N. to Babylon. That alone proves it. What are the
odds that one man would promote all those things and *not* be the
Antichrist?"

"We knew this was coming," Buck said. "But has he gone public with all that?"

"All today."

Buck let out a low whistle. "What did Carpathia say?"

"He announced it through his media guy, your former boss,
what's his name?"

"Plank."

"Right. Steve Plank. They held a press conference so he could
inform the media that Carpathia would be unavailable for several
days while he conducted strategic high-level meetings."

"And he said what the meetings were about?"

"He said that Carpathia, while not seeking the position of leadership, felt an obligation to move quickly to unite the world in a
move toward peace. He has assigned task forces to implement the
disarming of the nations of the world and to confirm that it has

been done. He is having the 10 percent of the weaponry that is not destroyed from each nation shipped to Babylon, which he has renamed New Babylon. The international financial community, whose representatives were already in New York for meetings, has been charged with the responsibility of settling on one currency."

"I never would have believed it." Buck frowned. "A friend tried to tell me about this a long time ago."

"That's not all," Bruce went on. "Do you think it was coincidental that leaders of the major religions were in New York when Carpathia arrived last week? How could this be anything but the fulfillment of prophecy? Carpathia is urging them to come together, to agree on some all-inclusive effort at tolerance that would respect their shared beliefs."

"Shared beliefs?" Chloe said. "Some of those religions are so far apart they would never agree."

"But they *are* agreeing," Bruce said. "Carpathia is apparently making deals. I don't know what he's offering, but an announcement is expected by the end of the week from the religious leaders. I'm guessing we'll see a one-world religion."

"Who'd fall for that?"

"Scripture indicates that many will."

Rayford's mind was reeling. It had been hard for him to concentrate on anything since the day of the disappearances. At times he still wondered if this was all a crazy nightmare, something he would wake up from and then change his ways. Was he Scrooge, who needed such a dream to see how wrong he'd been? Or was he George Bailey, Jimmy Stewart's character from *It's a Wonderful Life*, who got his wish and then wished he hadn't?

Rayford actually knew two people—Buck and Hattie—who had personally met the Antichrist! How bizarre was that? When he allowed himself to dwell on it, it sent a dark shiver of terror deep inside him. The cosmic battle between God and Satan had crashed into his own life, and in an instant he had gone from skeptical cynic, neglectful father, and lustful husband with a roving eye, to fanatical believer in Christ.

"Why has the news today set you off so much, Bruce?" Rayford asked. "I don't think any of us doubted Buck's story or had any lingering question about whether Carpathia was the Antichrist."

"I don't know, Rayford." Bruce returned to his chair. "All I know is that the closer I get to God, the deeper I get into the Bible, the heavier the burden seems on my shoulders. The world needs to know it is being deceived. I feel an urgency to preach Christ everywhere, not just here. This church is full of frightened people, and they're hungry for God. We're trying to meet that need, but more trouble is coming.

"The news that really got to me today was the announcement that the next major order of business for Carpathia is what he calls 'an understanding' between the global community and Israel, as well as what he calls 'a special arrangement' between the U.N. and the United States."

Buck sat up straighter. "What do you make of that?"

"I don't know what the U.S. thing is, because as much as I study I don't see America playing a role during this period of history. But we all know what the 'understanding' with Israel will be. I don't know what form it will take or what the benefit will be to the Holy Land, but clearly this is the seven-year treaty."

Chloe looked up. "And that actually signals the beginning of the seven-year period of tribulation."

"Exactly." Bruce looked at the group. "If that announcement says anything about a promise from Carpathia that Israel will be protected over the next seven years, it officially ushers in the Tribulation."

Buck was taking notes. "So the disappearances, the Rapture, didn't start the seven-year period?"

"No," Bruce said. "Part of me hoped that something would delay the treaty with Israel. Nothing in Scripture says it has to happen right away. But once it does, the clock starts ticking."

"But it starts ticking toward Christ setting up his kingdom on earth, right?" Buck asked. Rayford was impressed that Buck had learned so much so quickly.

Bruce nodded. "That's right. And that's the reason for this meeting. I need to tell you all something. I am going to have a two-hour meeting, right here in this office, every weeknight from eight to ten. Just for us."

"I'll be traveling a lot," Buck said.

"Me too," Rayford added.

Bruce held up a hand. "I can't force you to come, but I urge you. Anytime you're in town, be here. In our studies we're going to outline what God has revealed in the Scriptures. Some of it you've already heard me talk about. But if the treaty with Israel comes within the next few days, we have no time to waste. We need to be starting new churches, new cell groups of believers. I want to go to Israel and hear the two witnesses at the Wailing Wall. The Bible talks about 144,000 Jews springing up and traveling throughout the world. There is to be a great soul harvest, maybe a billion or more people, coming to Christ."

"That sounds fantastic," Chloe said. "We should be thrilled."

"I *am* thrilled," Bruce said. "But there will be little time to rejoice or to rest. Remember the seven Seal Judgments Revelation talks about?" She nodded. "Those will begin immediately, if I'm right. There will be an eighteen-month period of peace, but in the three months following that, the rest of the Seal Judgments will fall on the earth. One fourth of the world's population will be wiped out. I don't want to be maudlin, but will you look around this room and tell me what that means to you?"

Rayford didn't have to look around the room. He sat with the three people closest to him in the world. Was it possible that in less than two years, he could lose yet another loved one?

Buck closed his notebook. He was not going to record the fact that someone in that room might be dead soon. He recalled that during his first day at college he had been asked to look to his right and to his left. The professor had said, "One of the three of you will not be here in a year." That was almost funny compared to this.

"We don't want to simply survive, though," Buck said. "We want to take action."

"I know," Bruce said. "I guess I'm just grieving in advance. This is going to be a long, hard road. We're all going to be busy and overworked, but we must plan ahead."

"I was thinking about going back to college," Chloe mused. "Not to Stanford, of course, but somewhere around here. Now I wonder, what's the point?"

"You can go to college right here," Bruce said. "Every night at eight. And there's something else."

"I thought there might be," Buck said.

"I think we need a shelter."

"A shelter?" Chloe said.

"Underground," Bruce said. "During the period of peace we can build it without suspicion. When the judgments come, we wouldn't be able to get away with anything like that."

"What are you talking about?" Buck asked.

"I'm talking about getting an earthmover in here and digging out a place we can escape to. War is coming—famine, plagues, and death."

Rayford held up a hand. "But I thought we weren't going to turn tail and run."

"We're not," Bruce said. "But if we don't plan ahead, if we don't have a place to retreat to, to regroup, to evade radiation and disease, we'll die trying to prove we're brave."

Buck was impressed that Bruce had a plan, a real plan. Bruce said he would order a huge water tank and have it delivered. It would sit at the edge of the parking lot for weeks, and people would assume it was just some sort of a storage tank. Then he would have an excavator dig out a crater big enough to house it.

Meanwhile, the four of them would stud up walls, run power and water lines into the hole, and generally get it prepared as a hideout. At some point Bruce would have the water tank taken away. People who saw that would assume it was the wrong size or defective. People who didn't see it taken away would assume it had been installed in the ground.

The Tribulation Force would attach the underground shelter to the church through a hidden passageway, but they would not use it until they had to. All their meetings would be in Bruce's office.

The meeting that night ended with prayer, the three newest believers praying for Bruce and his weight of leadership.

Buck urged Bruce to go home and get some sleep. On his way out, Buck turned to Chloe. "I'd show you my new car, but it doesn't seem like that big a deal anymore."

"I know what you mean." She smiled. "It looks nice, though. You want to join us for some dinner?"

"I'm not really hungry. Anyway, I've got to get started moving into my new place."

"Do you have furniture yet?" she asked. "You could stay with us until you get some. We've got plenty of room."

He thought about the irony of that. "Thanks," he said. "It's furnished."

Rayford came up from behind. "Where'd you land anyway, Buck?"

Buck described the condo, halfway between church and the *Weekly.*

"That's not far."

"No," Buck said. "I'll have everybody over once I get settled."

Rayford had opened his car door, and Chloe waited at the passenger door. The three of them stood silent and awkward in the dim light from the streetlamps. "Well," Buck said, "I'd better get going." Rayford slid into the car. Chloe still stood there. "See ya."

Chloe gave a little wave, and Buck turned away. He felt like an idiot. What was he going to do about her? He knew she was waiting, hoping for some sign that he was still interested. And he was. He was just having trouble showing it. He didn't know if it was because her father was there or because too much was happening in their lives right now.

Buck thought about Chloe's comment that there wasn't much use in going to college. That applied to romance as well, he thought. Sure, he was lonely. Sure, they had a lot in common. Sure, he was attracted to her, and it was clear she felt the same about him. But wasn't getting interested in a woman right now a little trivial, considering all Bruce had just talked about?

Buck had already fallen in love with God. That had to be his passion until Christ returned again. Would it be right, let alone prudent, to focus his attention on Chloe Steele at the same time? He tried to push her from his mind.

Fat chance.

———

"You like him, don't you?" Rayford said as he pulled the car out of the parking lot.

"He's all right."

"I'm talking about Buck."

"I know who you're talking about. He's all right, but he hardly knows I exist anymore."

"There's a lot on his mind."

"I get more attention from Bruce, and he's got more on his mind than any of us."

"Let Buck get settled in and he'll come calling."

"He'll come calling?" Chloe said. "You sound like Pa on *Little House on the Prairie.*"

"Sorry."

"Anyway, I think Buck Williams is through calling."

———

Buck's apartment was antiseptic without his own stuff in it. He kicked off his shoes and called his voice mail in New York. He

wanted to leave a message with Marge Potter, his former secretary there, asking when he could expect his boxes from the office.
She beat him to the punch. The first of his three messages was
from Marge. "I didn't know where to ship your stuff, so I over-
nighted it to the Chicago bureau office. Should be there Monday
morning."

The second message was from the big boss, Stanton Bailey.
"Give me a call sometime Monday, Cameron. I want to get your
story by the end of next week, and we need to talk."

The third was from his old executive editor, Steve Plank, now
Nicolae Carpathia's spokesman. "Buck, call me as soon as you
can. Carpathia wants to talk to you."

Buck sniffed and chuckled and erased his messages. He recorded a thanks to Marge and an I-got-your-message-and-will-call-
you to Bailey. He merely made a note with Steve's phone number
and decided to wait to call him. *Carpathia wants to talk to you.*
What a casual way to say, *The enemy of God is after you.* Buck
could only wonder whether Carpathia knew he had not been
brainwashed. What would the man do, or try to do, if he knew
Buck's memory had not been altered? If he realized Buck knew he
was a murderer, a liar, a beast?

Rayford sat watching the television news, hearing commentators
pontificate on the meaning of the announcements coming out of
the United Nations. Most considered the scheduled move of the
U.N. to the ruins of Babylon, south of Baghdad, a good thing.
One said, "If Carpathia is sincere about disarming the world and
stockpiling the remaining 10 percent of the hardware, I'd rather
he store it in the Middle East, in the shadow of Tehran, than on
an island off New York City. Besides, we can use the soon-to-be-
abandoned U.N. building as a museum, honoring the most atro-
cious architecture this country has ever produced."

Pundits predicted frustration and failure in the proposed out-
comes of the meetings between both the religious leaders and the
financial experts. One said, "No single religion, as attractive as
that sounds, and no one-world currency, as streamlined as that
would be. These will be Carpathia's first major setbacks, and perhaps then the masses will become more realistic about him. The
honeymoon will soon be over."

"Want some tea, Dad?" Chloe called from the kitchen. He declined, and she came out a minute later with her own. She sat on the other end of the couch from him, her slippered feet tucked up under her robe. Her freshly washed hair was wrapped in a towel.

"Got a date this weekend?" Rayford asked when the news broke for a commercial.

"Not funny," she said.

"It wasn't meant to be. Would that be so strange, someone asking you out?"

"The only person I want to ask me out has apparently changed his mind about me."

"Nonsense," Rayford said. "I can't imagine all that must be on Buck's mind."

"I thought *I* was on his mind, Dad. Now I sit here like a schoolgirl, wondering and hoping. It's all so stupid. Why should I care? I just met him. I hardly know him. I just admire him, that's all."

"You admire him?"

"Sure! Who wouldn't? He's smart, articulate, accomplished."

"Famous."

"Yeah, a little. But I'm not going to throw myself at him. I just thought he was interested, that's all. His note said he was attracted to me."

"How did you respond to that?"

"To him, you mean?"

Rayford nodded.

"I didn't. What was I supposed to do? I was attracted to him, too, but I didn't want to scare him off."

"Maybe he thinks he's scared you off. Maybe he thinks he came on too strong too soon. But you didn't feel that way?"

"In a way I did, but down deep it was right. I thought just being open to him and staying friendly would make the point."

Dad shrugged. "Maybe he needs more encouragement."

"He's not going to get it from me. Not my style. You know that."

"I know, hon," Rayford said, "but a lot has changed about you recently."

"Yeah, but my style hasn't." That made even her laugh. "Daddy, what am I going to do? I'm not ready to give up on him, but couldn't you see it wasn't the same? He should have asked me out for something to eat, but he didn't even accept our invitation."

"*Our* invitation? *I* was in on that?"

"Well, it wouldn't have been appropriate for me to ask him out by myself."

"I know. But maybe he didn't want to go out with me around."

"If he felt about me the way I thought he did, he would have. In fact, he would have asked me first and left you out of it. I mean . . . I didn't mean it that way, Dad."

"I know what you meant. I think you're being a little too gloomy too soon about this. Give him a day. See what a difference a night's sleep makes."

The news came back on, and Chloe sipped her tea. Rayford felt privileged that she would talk to him about things like this. He didn't remember that she had even talked to Irene much about guys. He knew he was her only port in a storm, but still he enjoyed her confidence. "I don't have to watch this if you want to talk some more," he told her. "There's nothing new here since what Bruce told us."

"No," she said, standing. "Frankly, I'm sick of myself. Sitting here talking about my love life, or lack of it, seems pretty juvenile at this point in history, don't you think? It's not like there's nothing to fill my time even if I don't go back to school. I want to memorize Ezekiel, Daniel, and Revelation for starters."

Rayford laughed. "You're kidding!"

"Of course! But you know what I mean, Dad? I never would have dreamed the Bible would even interest me, but now I'm reading it like there's no tomorrow."

Rayford fell silent, and he could tell Chloe was struck by her own unintentional irony. "I am too," he said. "I already know more about end-times prophecy than I ever knew existed. We're living it, right here, right now. There aren't many tomorrows left, are there?"

"Certainly not enough to waste pining away over a guy."

"He's a pretty impressive guy, Chlo'."

"You're a big help. Let me forget him, will you?"

Rayford smiled. "If I don't mention him, you'll forget him? Should we get him kicked out of the Tribulation Force?"

Chloe shook her head. "And anyway, how long has it been since you called me *Chlo'*?"

"You used to like that."

"Yeah. When I was nine. 'Night, Dad."

"'Night, sweetheart. I love you."

Chloe had been heading toward the kitchen, but she stopped

and turned and hurried back, bending to embrace him, careful not to spill her tea. "I love you too, Dad. More than ever and with all my heart."

———————

Buck Williams lay on his stomach in his new bed for the first time. It felt strange. His was a nice place in a good building, but suburban Chicago was not New York. It was too quiet. He had brought home a bag of fresh fruit, ignored it, watched the news, and turned on soft music. He decided to read the New Testament until he fell asleep.

Buck had been soaking up whatever he could from Bruce Barnes about what was to come next, but he found himself turning to the Gospels rather than the Old Testament or the Revelation prophecies. What a revolutionary Jesus turned out to be. Buck was fascinated with the character, the personality, the mission of the man. The Jesus he had always imagined or thought he knew about was an impostor. The Jesus of the Bible was a radical, a man of paradoxes.

Buck set the Bible on the nightstand and rolled onto his back, shielding his eyes from the light. *If you want to be rich, give your money away,* he told himself. *That's the gist of it. If you want to be exalted, humble yourself. Revenge sounds logical, but it's wrong. Love your enemies, pray for those who put you down. Bizarre.*

His mind wandered to Chloe. What was he doing? She wasn't blind. She was young, but she was not stupid. He couldn't lead her on and then change his mind, not without being up front. But *was* he changing his mind? Did he really want to just forget about her? Of course not. She was a wonderful person, fun to talk to. She was a fellow believer and compatriot. She would be a good friend, regardless.

So it had already come to that? He would give her the let's-be-friends line? Was that what he wanted?

God, what am I supposed to do? he prayed silently. *To tell you the truth, I'd love to be in love. I'd love to start a relationship with Chloe. But is she too young? Is this the wrong time to even be thinking about such a thing? I know you have a lot for us to do. What if we did fall in love? Should we get married? What would we do about children, if you're coming back in seven years? If there was ever a time to wonder about bringing children into this world, it's now.*

Buck pulled his arm away from his eyes and squinted at the light. Now what? Was God supposed to answer him aloud? He knew better than that. He swung his legs over the side and sat on the bed, his head in his hands.

What had gotten into him? All he wanted to know was whether he should keep pursuing Chloe. He started praying about it, and all of a sudden he was thinking about marriage and children. Craziness. *Maybe that's how God works,* he thought. *He leads you to logical, or illogical, conclusions.*

Based on that, he thought he had better not encourage Chloe anymore. She was interested, he could see that. If he showed the same interest, it would lead only one direction. In the new chaotic world they lived in, they would eventually grow desperate for each other. Should he allow that?

It didn't make sense. How could he let anything compete with his devotion to God? And yet he couldn't just ignore her, start treating her like a sister. No, he would do the right thing. He would talk to her about it. She was worth it, that was for sure. He would set an informal date, and they would have a chat. He would tell her straight out that, left to his own wishes, he would want to get to know her better. That would make her feel good, wouldn't it? But would he have the courage to follow through and tell her what he really thought—that neither of them should pursue a romantic relationship now?

He didn't know. But he was sure of one thing: if he didn't set it up right now, he probably never would. He looked at his watch. A little after ten-thirty. Would she still be up? He dialed the Steeles.

Rayford heard the phone on his way up the stairs. He heard Chloe stir, but her light was off. "I'll get it, hon," he said. He hurried to his bed table and answered.

"Mr. Steele, it's Buck."

"Hey, Buck, you've got to quit calling me *Mister*. You're making me feel old."

"Aren't you old?" Buck said.

"Cute. Call me Ray. What can I do for you?"

"I was wondering if Chloe was still up."

"You know, I don't think she is, but I can check and see if she's still awake."

"No, that's all right," Buck said. "Just have her call me at her convenience, would you?" He gave Rayford his new number.

"Dad!" Chloe said a few minutes later. "You knew I was awake!"

"You didn't answer when I said I'd get it," he said. "I wasn't sure. Don't you think this is for the best? Let him wait till morning?"

"Oh, Dad!" she said. "I don't know. What do you think he wanted?"

"I have no idea."

"Ooh, I hate this!"

"I love it."

"You would."

THREE

SATURDAY morning Buck drove to New Hope Village Church, hoping to catch Bruce Barnes in his office. The secretary told him Bruce was finishing up his sermon preparation, but that she also knew he would want to see Buck. "You're part of Bruce's inner circle, aren't you?" she said.

Buck nodded. He guessed he was. Should it have been an honor? He felt so new, like such a baby, as a follower of Christ. Who would ever have predicted this for him? And yet who would have dreamed the Rapture would take place? He shook his head. *Only the millions who were ready,* he decided.

With the announcement that Buck was waiting, Bruce immediately swung open his door and embraced him. That was something new for Buck, too, all this hugging, especially among men. Bruce looked haggard. "Another long night?" Buck asked.

Bruce nodded. "But another long feast on the Word. I'm making up for lost time, you know. I've had these resources on hand for years and never took advantage of them. I'm trying to decide how to tell the congregation, probably within the next month, that I feel called to travel. People here are going to have to step up and help lead."

"You're afraid they'll feel abandoned?"

"Exactly. But I'm not leaving the church. I'll be here as much as I can. As I told you and the Steeles yesterday, this is a weight I feel God has put on me. There's joy in it—I'm learning so much. But it's scary, too, and I know I'm not up to it, apart from the Spirit's power. I think it's just another price I have to pay for having missed the truth the first time. But you didn't come to hear me complain."

"I just have two quick things, and then I'll let you get back to your study. First, and I've been pushing this from my mind the last few days, but I feel terrible about Hattie Durham. Remember her? Rayford's flight attendant—"

"The woman you introduced to Carpathia? Sure. The one Rayford almost had a fling with."

"Yeah, I suppose he feels bad about her too."

"I can't speak for him, Buck, but as I recall, you tried to warn her about Carpathia."

"I told her she might wind up being his plaything, yes, but at the time I had no idea who he really was."

"She went to New York on her own. It was her choice."

"But, Bruce, if I hadn't introduced them, he wouldn't have asked to see her again."

Bruce sat back and folded his arms. "You want to rescue her from Carpathia, is that it?"

"Of course."

"I don't see how you could do it without putting yourself in danger. She's no doubt enamored with her new life already. She's gone from being a flight attendant to being the personal assistant to the most powerful man in the world."

"Personal assistant and who knows what else."

Bruce nodded. "Probably so. I don't imagine he chose her for her clerical skills. Still, what do you do? Call her and tell her her new boss is the Antichrist and that she should leave him?"

Buck said, "That's why I'm here. I don't know what to do."

"And you think I do."

"I was hoping."

Bruce smiled wearily. "Now I know what my former senior pastor, Vern Billings, meant when he said people think their pastor should know everything."

"No advice then?"

"This is going to sound trite, Buck, but you have to do what you have to do."

"Meaning?"

"Meaning if you've prayed about it and feel a real leading from God to talk with Hattie, then do it. But you can imagine the consequences. The next person to know about it will be Carpathia. Look what he's done to you already."

"That's the issue," Buck said. "Somehow I have to find out

how much Carpathia knows. Does he think he wiped from my memory that I was at that meeting, the way he wiped it from everyone else's? Or does he know I know what went on and that's why he got me in trouble, demoted, relocated, and all that?"

"And you wonder why I'm weary?" Bruce said. "My gut feeling is that if Carpathia knew you were a believer now and that you had been protected from his brainwashing, he'd have you killed. If he thinks he still has power over you, as he does over people without Christ in their lives, he'll try to use you."

Buck sat back and stared at the ceiling. "Interesting you should say that," he said. "That leads me to the second thing I wanted to talk with you about."

Rayford spent the morning on the phone finalizing arrangements for his recertification on the Boeing 757. Monday morning he was to fly as a passenger from O'Hare to Dallas, where he would practice takeoffs and landings on military runways a few miles from the Dallas–Fort Worth airport.

"I'm sorry, Chloe," he said when he was finally off the phone. "I forgot you wanted to call Buck back this morning."

"Correction," she said. "I wanted to call him back last night. In fact, I wanted to talk to him when he called."

Rayford held up both hands in surrender. "My mistake," he said. "Guilty. The phone is yours."

"No thanks."

Rayford raised his brows at his daughter. "What? Now you're going to punish Buck because of me? Call him!"

"No, the truth is I think this worked out for the best. I wanted to talk to him last night, but you were probably right. I would have seemed too eager, too forward. And he said I should call him back at my convenience. Well, first thing in the morning wouldn't be that convenient. In fact, I'll see him in church tomorrow, right?"

Rayford shook his head. "Now you're going to play games with him? You were worried about obsessing over him like a schoolgirl, and now you're acting like one."

Chloe looked hurt. "Oh, thanks, Dad. Just remember, letting him wait was your idea."

"That was just overnight. Don't involve me in this if it's going to get silly."

"Well, Buck, here's your chance to check in on Hattie," Bruce Barnes said. "What do *you* think Carpathia wants?"

Buck shook his head. "No idea."

"Do you trust this Steve Plank?"

"Yeah, I trust him. I worked for Steve for years. The scary thing is, he welcomed me to Carpathia's pre–press conference meeting, told me where to sit, told me who the various people were. Then later he asked why I hadn't shown up. Told me Carpathia was a little put out that I wasn't there."

"And you know him well enough to know whether he's being straight with you."

"Frankly, Bruce, he's the main reason I believe that Carpathia is the fulfillment of these prophecies we're studying. Steve is a hard-nosed journalist from the old school. That he could be talked into leaving legitimate news coverage to be spokesman for a world politician shows Carpathia's power of persuasion. Even I turned down that job. But to sit through that carnage and then forget that I was even there, that's just . . ."

"Unnatural."

"Exactly. I'll tell you what was weird, though. Something in me wanted to believe Carpathia when he explained what had happened. Pictures began forming in my mind of Stonagal shooting himself and killing Todd-Cothran in the process."

Bruce shook his head. "I confess that when you first told us that story, I thought you had gone mad."

"I would have agreed with you, except for one thing."

"What's that?"

"Well, all those other people saw it happen and remembered it one way. I remembered it entirely differently. If Steve had just told me I hadn't seen it right, maybe I would have thought I was going crazy and had myself committed. But instead he told me I wasn't even there! Bruce, *no one* remembers I was there! Well, tell me I'm in denial, but that's hogwash. I was back in my office recording every detail into my computer by the time the news media got Carpathia's version. If I wasn't there, how did I know that Stonagal and Todd-Cothran would be carried out of there in body bags?"

"You don't have to persuade me, Buck," Bruce said. "I'm on your side. The question now is, what does Carpathia want? Do you think if he talks to you in private he'll reveal his true self? or threaten you? or let you know he's aware that you know the truth?"

"For what purpose?"

"To intimidate you. To use you."

"Maybe. Maybe all he wants to do is try to read me, try to determine whether he succeeded in brainwashing me, too."

"It's pretty dangerous business, that's all I've got to say."

"I hope that's *not* all you've got to say, Bruce. I was hoping for a little more counsel."

"I'll pray about it," Bruce said. "But right now I don't know what to tell you."

"Well, at least I have to call Steve back. I don't know whether Carpathia wants to talk by phone or in person."

"Can you wait until Monday?"

"Sure. I can tell him I assumed he wanted me to call him back during business hours, but I can't guarantee he won't call me in the meantime."

"He has your new number?"

"No. Steve calls my voice mail in New York."

"Easy enough to ignore."

Buck shrugged and nodded. "If that's what you think I should do."

"Since when have I become your adviser?"

"Since you became my pastor."

When Rayford returned from running errands that morning, he realized from her body language and terse comments that he had offended Chloe. "Let's talk," he said.

"About what?"

"About how you have to cut me some slack. I was never very good at this parenting thing, and now I'm having trouble treating you like the adult that you are. I'm sorry I called you a school-girl. You handle Buck any way you think is right, and ignore me, all right?"

Chloe smiled. "I was ignoring you already. I don't need your permission for that."

"Then you forgive me?"

"Don't worry about me, Dad. I can't stay mad at you for long anymore. Seems to me we need each other. I called Buck, by the way."

"Really?"

She nodded. "No answer. I guess he wasn't waiting by the phone."

"Did you leave a message?"

"No machine yet, I guess. I'll see him at church tomorrow."

"Will you tell him you called?"

Chloe smiled mischievously. "Probably not."

Buck spent the rest of the day tweaking his cover story for *Global Weekly* on the theories behind the disappearances. He felt good about it, deciding it might be the best work he had ever done. It included everything from the tabloidlike attack by Hitler's ghost, UFOs, and aliens, to the belief that this was some sort of cosmic evolutionary cleansing, a survival-of-the-fittest adjustment in the world's population.

In the middle of the piece, Buck had included what he believed was the truth, of course, but he did not editorialize. It was, as usual, a third-person, straight news-analysis article. No one but his new friends would know that he agreed with the airline pilot and the pastor and several others he interviewed—that the disappearances had been a result of Christ's rapture of his church.

Most interesting to Buck was the interpretation of the event on the part of other churchmen. A lot of Catholics were confused, because while many remained, some had disappeared—including the new pope, who had been installed just a few months before the vanishings. He had stirred up controversy in the church with a new doctrine that seemed to coincide more with the "heresy" of Martin Luther than with the historic orthodoxy they were used to. When the pope had disappeared, some Catholic scholars had concluded that this was indeed an act of God. "Those who opposed the orthodox teaching of the Mother Church were winnowed out from among us," Peter Cardinal Mathews of Cincinnati, a leading archbishop, had told Buck. "The Scripture says that in the last days it will be as in the days of Noah. And you'll recall that in the days of Noah, the good people remained and the evil ones were washed away."

"So," Buck concluded, "the fact that we're still here proves we're the good guys?"

"I wouldn't put it so crassly," Archbishop Mathews had said, "but, yes, that's my position."

"What does that say about all the wonderful people who vanished?"

"That perhaps they were not so wonderful."

"And the children and babies?"

The bishop had shifted uncomfortably. "That I leave to God," he said. "I have to believe that perhaps he was protecting the innocents."

"From what?"

"I'm not sure. I don't take the Apocrypha literally, but there are dire predictions of what might be yet to come."

"So you would not relegate the vanished young ones to the winnowing of the evil?"

"No. Many of the little ones who disappeared I baptized myself, so I know they are in Christ and with God."

"And yet they are gone."

"They are gone."

"And we remain."

"We should take great solace in that."

"Few people take solace in it, Excellency."

"I understand that. This is a very difficult time. I myself am grieving the loss of a sister and an aunt. But they had left the church."

"They had?"

"They opposed the teaching. Wonderful women, most kind. Most earnest, I must add. But I fear they have been separated as chaff from wheat. Yet those of us who remain should be confident in our standing with God as never before."

Buck had been bold enough to ask the archbishop to comment on certain passages of Scripture, primarily Ephesians 2:8-9: "For by grace you have been saved through faith, and that not of yourselves; it is the gift of God, not of works, lest anyone should boast."

"Now you see," the archbishop said, "this is precisely my point. People have been taking verses like that out of context for centuries and trying to build doctrine on them."

"But there are other passages just like those," Buck said.

"I understand that, but, listen, you're not Catholic, are you?"

"No, sir."

"Well, see, you don't understand the broad sweep of the historical church."

"Excuse me, but explain to me why so many non-Catholics are still here, if your hypothesis is right."

"God knows," Archbishop Mathews had said. "He knows hearts. He knows more than we do."

"That's for sure," Buck said.

Of course Buck left his personal comments and opinions out of the article, but he was able to work in the Scripture and the arch-bishop's attempt to explain away the doctrine of grace. Buck planned to transmit the finished article to the *Global Weekly* of-fices in New York on Monday.

As he worked, Buck kept an ear open for the phone. Very few people had his new number. Only the Steeles, Bruce, and Alice, Verna Zee's secretary. He expected his answering machine, his desktop computer, fax machine, and other office equipment, along with files from the office, to arrive at the Chicago bureau Mon-day. Then he would feel more at home and equipped to work out of the second bedroom.

Buck had half expected to hear from Chloe. He thought he had left it with Rayford that she would call at her convenience. Maybe she was the type who didn't call men, even when she had missed their call. On the other hand, she was not quite twenty-one yet, and he admitted he had no idea about the customs and mores of her generation. Maybe she saw him as a big brother or even a father figure and was repulsed by the idea that he might be interested in her. That didn't jibe with her look and her body lan-guage from the night before, but he hadn't been encouraging then, either.

He simply wanted to do the right thing, to talk with her—to clarify that the timing was bad for them, and that they should be-come close friends and compatriots in the common cause. But then he felt foolish. What if she had not even considered anything more than that? He would be explaining away something that wasn't even there.

But maybe she had phoned when he was with Bruce that morn-ing. He would just call her. Invite her to see his new place when she had time, and then they would have their talk. He would play it by ear, trying to determine what her expectations had been, and then either let her down easy or ignore a subject that didn't need to be raised.

Rayford answered the phone. "Chloe!" he called out. "Buck Williams for you!"

He could hear her voice in the background. "Could you tell

him I'll call him back? Better yet, I'll see him in church tomorrow."

"I heard that," Buck said. "Fair enough. See you then."

Apparently she's not wasting any energy worrying about us, Buck decided. He dialed his voice mail in New York. The only message was from Steve Plank.

"Buck, what's the deal? How long does it take to get settled? Do I have to call the Chicago bureau? I've left messages there, but old man Bailey told me you'd be working out of your own place.

"Did you get my message that Carpathia wants to talk to you? People don't make a habit of making him wait, my friend. I'm stalling him, telling him you're in transit, relocating, and all that. But he had sort of hoped to see you this weekend. I honestly don't know what he wants, except that he's still high on you. He's not holding a grudge over your standing him up on his invitation to that meeting, if you're worried about that.

"Tell you the truth, Buck, the newsman in you would have wanted to be there and should have been there. But you'd have been as rattled by it as I have been. A violent suicide before your eyes is no easy thing to forget.

"Listen, call me so I can get you two together. Bailey tells me you're putting the finishing touches on the theory article. If you can get with Carpathia soon enough, you can include his ideas. He's made no secret of them, but an exclusive quote or two wouldn't hurt either, right? You know where to reach me any time of the day or night."

Buck stored the message. What was he supposed to do? It sounded as if Carpathia wanted a private face-to-face. Not many days before, Buck would have jumped at the chance. To interview the leading personality in the world on the eve of the delivery of your most important cover story? Still, Buck was a new believer, convinced that Carpathia was the Antichrist himself. He had seen the man's power. And Buck was just getting started in his faith. He didn't know much about the Antichrist. Was the man omniscient like God? Could he read Buck's mind?

Carpathia obviously could manipulate people and brainwash minds. But did that mean he knew what people were thinking, too? Was Buck able to resist Carpathia only because he had the Spirit of Christ within him? He wished there was something in the Bible that specifically outlined the powers of the Antichrist. Then he would know what he was dealing with.

At the very least, Carpathia had to be curious about Buck. He must have wondered, when Buck slipped away from the conference room where the murders had been committed, whether there had been some glitch in his own mind-control powers. Otherwise, why erase from everyone else's mind not only the murders, replacing them with a picture of a bizarre suicide, but also the memory that Buck had been there at all?

Clearly, Nicolae had tried to cover himself by making everyone else forget Buck was there. If such a move was supposed to make Buck doubt his own sanity, it hadn't worked. God had been with Buck that day. He saw what he saw, and nothing could shake that. There was no second-guessing, no twinge of wondering if he was merely in denial. One thing was sure, he would not tell Carpathia what he knew. If Carpathia was certain Buck had not been tricked, he would have no recourse but to have him eliminated. If Buck could keep Carpathia thinking he had succeeded, it would give them one small advantage in the war against the forces of evil. What Buck or the Tribulation Force might do with that advantage, he could not fathom.

But he did know one thing. He would not return Steve Plank's call until Monday.

Rayford was glad he and Chloe had decided to go early to church. The place was jammed every week. Rayford smiled at his daughter. Chloe looked the best he had seen her since coming home from college. He wanted to tease her, to ask her if she was dressing for Buck Williams or for God, but he let it go.

He took one of the last spots in the parking lot and saw cars lined up around the block, looking for places on the street to park. People were grieving. They were terror-stricken. They were looking for hope, for answers, for God. They were finding him here, and the word was spreading.

Few people who sat under the earnest and emotional teaching of Bruce Barnes could come away doubting that the vanishings had been the work of God. The church had been snatched away, and they had all been left behind. Bruce's message was that Jesus was coming again in what the Bible called "the glorious appearing" seven years after the beginning of the Tribulation. By then, he said, three-fourths of the world's remaining population would be wiped out, and probably a larger percentage of believers in

Christ. Bruce's exhortation was not a call to the timid. It was a challenge to the convinced, to those who had been persuaded by God's most dramatic invasion of human life since the incarnation of Jesus Christ as a mortal baby.

Bruce had already told the Steeles and Buck that a quarter of the earth's population would die during the second, third, and fourth judgments from the Seven-Sealed Scroll of Revelation. He cited Revelation 6:8, where the apostle John had written, "So I looked, and behold, a pale horse. And the name of him who sat on it was Death, and Hades followed with him. And power was given to them over a fourth of the earth, to kill with sword, with hunger, with death, and by the beasts of the earth."

But what was to come after that was even worse.

A minute or two after they had settled in their seats, Rayford felt a tap on the shoulder. He turned just as Chloe did. Buck Williams sat directly behind them in the fourth row and had touched them simultaneously. "Hey, strangers," he said. Rayford stood and embraced Buck. That alone told him how much had changed in him in just a matter of weeks. Chloe was cordial, shaking Buck's hand.

After they were seated again, Buck leaned forward and whispered, "Chloe, the reason I was calling was that I wondered—"

But the music had begun.

Buck stood to sing with everyone else. Many seemed to know the songs and the words. He had to follow as the words were projected on the wall and try to pick up the melodies. The choruses were simple and catchy, but they were new to him. Many of these people, he decided, had had plenty of exposure to church—more than he had. How had they missed the truth?

After a couple of choruses, a disheveled Bruce Barnes hurried to the pulpit—not the large one on the platform, but a small lectern at floor level. He carried his Bible, two large books, and a sheaf of papers he was having trouble controlling. He smiled sheepishly.

"Good morning," he began. "I realize a word of explanation is in order. Usually we sing more, but we don't have time for that today. Usually my tie is straighter, my shirt fully tucked in, my suit coat buttoned. That seems a little less crucial this morning. Usually we take up an offering. Be assured we still need it, but please find the baskets on your way out at noon, if indeed I let you out that early.

"I want to take the extra time this morning because I feel an urgency greater even than the last few weeks. I don't want you to worry about me. I haven't become a wild-eyed madman, a cultist, or anything other than what I have been since I realized I had missed the Rapture.

"I have told my closest advisers that God has weighed heavily upon me this week, and they are praying with me that I will be wise and discerning, that I will not go off half-cocked and shooting at some new and strange doctrine. I have read more, prayed more, and studied more this week than ever, and I am eager to tell you what God has told me.

"Does God speak to me audibly? No. I wish he would. I wish he had. If he had, I probably would not be here today. But he wanted me to accept him by faith, not by his proving himself in some more dramatic way than simply sending his Son to die for me. He has left us his Word, and it gives us all we need to know."

Buck felt a lump in his throat as he watched his new friend beg and plead and cajole his listeners to hear, to understand, to make themselves available to God for the instruction God wanted them to have. Bruce told his own story yet again, how he had lived a phony life of pietism and churchianity for years, and how when God came to call, he had been found wanting and had been left behind, without his wife and precious children. Buck had heard the story more than once, yet it never failed to move him. Some sobbed aloud. Those hearing it for the first time got Bruce's abbreviated version. "I never want to stop telling what Christ has done for me," he said. "Tell your stories. People can identify with your grief and your loss and your loneliness. I will never again be ashamed of the gospel of Christ. The Bible says that the Cross offends. If you are offended, I am doing my job. If you are attracted to Christ, the Spirit is doing his work.

"We've already missed the Rapture, and now we live in what will soon become the most perilous period of history. Evangelists used to warn parishioners that they could be struck by a car or die in a fire and thus they should not put off coming to Christ. I'm telling you that should you be struck by a car or caught in a fire, it may be the most merciful way you can die. Be ready this time. Be ready. I will tell you how to get ready.

"My sermon title today is 'The Four Horsemen of the Apocalypse,' and I want to concentrate on the first, the rider of the white horse. If you've always thought the Four Horsemen of the

Apocalypse was a Notre Dame football backfield, God has a lesson for you today."

Buck had never seen Bruce so earnest, so inspired. As he spoke he referred to his notes, to the reference books, to the Bible. He began to perspire and often wiped sweat from his brow with his pocket handkerchief, which he took time to admit he knew was a faux pas. It seemed to Buck that the congregants, as one, merely chuckled with him as encouragement to keep on. Most were taking notes. Nearly everyone followed along in a Bible, their own or one provided in the pews.

Bruce explained that the book of Revelation, John's account of what God had revealed to him about the last days, spoke of what was to come after Christ had raptured his church. "Does anyone here doubt we're in the last days right now?" he thundered. "Millions disappear, and then what? Then what?"

Bruce explained that the Bible predicts first a treaty between a world leader and Israel. "Some believe the seven-year tribulation period has already begun and that it began with the Rapture. We feel the trials and tribulations already from the disappearance of millions, including our friends and loved ones, don't we? But that is nothing compared to the tribulation to come.

"During these seven years, God will pour out three consecutive sets of judgments—seven seals in a scroll, which we call the Seal Judgments; seven trumpets; and seven bowls. These judgments, I believe, are handed down for the purposes of shaking us loose from whatever shred of security we might have left. If the Rapture didn't get your attention, the judgments will. And if the judgments don't, you're going to die apart from God. Horrible as these judgments will be, I urge you to see them as final warnings from a loving God who is not willing that any should perish.

"As the scroll is opened and the seals are broken, revealing the judgments, the first four are represented by horsemen—the Four Horsemen of the Apocalypse. If you have ever been exposed to such imagery and language before, you probably considered it only symbolic, as I did. Is there anyone here who still considers the prophetic teaching of Scripture mere symbolism?"

Bruce waited a dramatic moment. "I thought not. Heed this teaching. The Seal Judgments will take us about twenty-one months from the signing of the treaty with Israel. In the coming weeks I will teach about the fourteen remaining judgments that will carry us through the end of the seven-year period, but for now, let's concentrate on the first four of the seven seals."

As Bruce plunged ahead, Buck was struck that the last speaker he had heard who was so captivating was Nicolae Carpathia. But Carpathia's impression had been choreographed, manipulated. Bruce wasn't trying to impress anyone with anything but the truth of the Word of God. Would he tell this body that he believed he knew who the Antichrist was? In a way Buck hoped he would. But that might be considered slander, to publicly finger someone as the archenemy of almighty God.

Or would Bruce simply tell what the Bible said and let the people come to their own conclusions? The news was already full of rumors about some impending agreement between Carpathia—or at least the Carpathia-led U.N.—and Israel. If Bruce predicted a pact that was borne out over the next few days, who could doubt him?

Rayford was more than fascinated. He was stunned. In many ways, Bruce was reading his mind. Not long ago he would have scoffed at such teaching, at such a literal take on so clearly a poetic and metaphoric passage. But what Bruce said made sense. The young man hadn't been preaching more than a few weeks. That had not been his calling or his training. But this wasn't preaching as much as teaching, and Bruce's passion, the immersion of his soul into the subject, made it all the more compelling.

"I don't have time to get into the second and third and fourth horsemen this morning," Bruce said, "except to say that the rider on the red horse signifies war, the black horse famine, and the pale horse death. Just a little something to look forward to," he added wryly, and some chuckled nervously. "But I warned you this is not for the faint of heart."

He sped toward his point and his conclusion by reading from Revelation 6:1-2: "Now I saw when the Lamb opened one of the seals; and I heard one of the four living creatures saying with a voice like thunder, 'Come and see.' And I looked, and behold, a white horse. He who sat on it had a bow; and a crown was given to him, and he went out conquering and to conquer."

Bruce dramatically moved back a step and began clearing off the small lectern. "Don't worry," he said, "I'm not finished." To Rayford's surprise, people began to applaud. Bruce said, "Are you clapping because you want me to finish, or because you want me to go on all afternoon?"

And the people clapped all the more. Rayford wondered what was happening. He applauded too, and Chloe and Buck were doing the same. They were drinking this in, and they wanted more and more. Clearly Bruce had been in tune with what God was showing him. He had said over and over that this was not new truth, that the commentaries he cited were decades old and that the doctrine of the end times was much, much older than that. But those who had relegated this kind of teaching to the literalists, the fundamentalists, the closed-minded evangelicals, had been left behind. All of a sudden it was all right to take Scripture at its word! If nothing else convinced people, losing so many to the Rapture finally reached them.

Bruce stood before the bare lectern now with only his Bible in his hand. "I want to tell you now what I believe the Bible is saying about the rider of the white horse, the first horseman of the Apocalypse. I will not give my opinion. I will not draw any conclusion. I will simply leave it to God to help you draw any parallels that need to be drawn. I will tell you only this in advance: This millenniums-old account reads as fresh to me as tomorrow's newspaper."

FOUR

BUCK sat in the pew behind Rayford and Chloe Steele and glanced at his watch. More than an hour had flown by since he had last checked. His stomach told him he was hungry, or at least that he could eat. His mind told him he could sit there all day, listening to Bruce Barnes explain from the Bible what was happening today and what would happen tomorrow. His heart told him he was on a precipice. He knew where Bruce was going with this teaching, with this imagery from the book of Revelation. Not only did he know who the rider of the white horse was, Buck knew the rider personally. He had experienced the power of the Antichrist.

Buck had spent enough time with Bruce and the Steeles, poring over the passages, to know beyond doubt that Nicolae Carpathia embodied the enemy of God. And yet he could not jump to his feet and corroborate Bruce's message with his own account. Neither could Bruce reveal that he knew precisely who the Antichrist was, or that someone in this very church had met him.

For years Buck had been an inveterate name-dropper. He had run in high circles for so long that it was not uncommon for him to be able to say, "Met him," "Interviewed her," "Know him," "Was with her in Paris," "Stayed in their home."

But that self-centeredness had been swept away by the disappearances and his experiences on the front lines of supernatural events. The old Buck Williams would have welcomed the prospect of letting on that he was a personal acquaintance of not only the leading personality in the world, but also the very Antichrist foretold in Scripture. Now he simply sat riveted as his friend preached on.

"Let me clarify," Bruce was saying, "that I don't believe it is God's intent to convey individual personality through the imagery of these horsemen, but rather world conditions. They don't all refer to specific people, because, for instance, the fourth horseman is called Death.

"Ah, but the first horseman! Notice that it is the Lamb who opens the first seal and reveals that horseman. The Lamb is Jesus Christ, the Son of God, who died for our sins, was resurrected, and recently raptured his church.

"In Scripture the first in a succession is always important—the firstborn, the first day of the week, the first commandment. The first rider, the first of the four horses of the first seven judgments, is important! He sets the tone. He is the key to understanding the rest of the horsemen, the rest of the Seal Judgments, indeed, the rest of all of the judgments.

"Who is this first horseman? Clearly he represents the Antichrist and his kingdom. His purpose is 'conquering and to conquer.' He has a bow in his hand, a symbol of aggressive warfare, and yet there is no mention of an arrow. So how will he conquer? Other passages indicate that he is a 'willful king' and that he will triumph through diplomacy. He will usher in a false peace, promising world unity. Will he be victorious? Yes! He has a crown."

In one way, this was all new to Rayford, and he knew it was to Chloe as well. But they had been so immersed in this teaching with Bruce since they had come to faith in Christ that Rayford anticipated every detail. It seemed he was becoming an instant expert, and he could not recall having ever picked up on a subject so quickly. He had always been a good student, especially in science and math. He had been a quick study in aviation. But this was cosmic. This was life. This was the real world. It explained what had happened to his wife and son, what he and his daughter would endure, and what would happen tomorrow and for the next several years.

Rayford admired Bruce. The young man had instantly realized that his phony brand of Christianity had failed him at the most pivotal point in human history. He had immediately repented and dedicated himself to the task of rescuing everyone possible. Bruce Barnes had surrendered himself to the cause.

Under other circumstances, Rayford might have worried about

Bruce, fearing he was wearing himself out, stretching himself too thin. But Bruce seemed energized, fulfilled. He would need more sleep, sure, but for now he was brimming with the truth and eager to share it. And if the others were like Rayford, they could think of nothing they would rather do than sit here under that instruction.

"We'll talk next week and following about the next three horsemen of the Apocalypse," Bruce was saying, "but let me just leave you with something to watch for. The rider of the white horse is the Antichrist, who comes as a deceiver promising peace and uniting the world. The Old Testament book of Daniel—chapter 9, verses 24 through 27—says he will sign a treaty with Israel.

"He will appear to be their friend and protector, but in the end he will be their conqueror and destroyer. I must close for this week, but we'll talk more about why this happens and what will come of it. Let me close by telling you how you can be sure *I* am not the Antichrist."

That got people's attention, including Rayford's. There was embarrassed laughter.

"I'm not implying that you suspect me," Bruce said, to more laughs. "But we may get to the point where every leader is suspect. Remember, however, that you will never hear peace promised from this pulpit. The Bible is clear that we will have perhaps a year and a half of peace following the pact with Israel. But in the long run, I predict the opposite of peace. The other three horsemen are coming, and they bring war, famine, plagues, and death. That is not a popular message, not a warm fuzzy you can cling to this week. Our only hope is in Christ, and even in him we will likely suffer. See you next week."

Rayford sensed a restlessness in the crowd as Bruce closed in prayer, as if others felt the same way he did. He wanted to hear more, and he had a million questions. Usually the organist began playing near the end of Bruce's prayer and Bruce immediately headed to the back of the church where he shook hands with people as they left. But today Bruce didn't get as far as the aisle before he was stopped by people who embraced him, thanked him, and began asking questions.

Rayford and Chloe were in one of the rows closest to the front, and though Rayford was aware that Buck was talking to Chloe, he also heard what people were asking Bruce.

"Are you saying that Nicolae Carpathia is the Antichrist?" one asked.

"Did you hear me say that?" Bruce said.

"No, but it was pretty clear. They're already talking on the news about his plans and some sort of deal with Israel."

"Keep reading and studying," Bruce said.

"But it can't be Carpathia, can it? Does he strike you as a liar?"

"How does he strike you?" Bruce said.

"As a savior."

"Almost like a messiah?" Bruce pressed.

"Yeah!"

"There is only one Savior, one Messiah."

"I know, spiritually, but politically I mean. Don't tell me Carpathia's not what he seems to be."

"I'll tell you only what Scripture says," Bruce said, "and I will urge you to listen carefully to the news. We must be wise as serpents and gentle as doves."

"That's how I would have described Carpathia," a woman said.

"Be careful," Bruce said, "about ascribing Christlike attributes to anyone who doesn't align himself with Christ."

As the service ended, Buck took Chloe's arm, but she seemed less responsive than he might have hoped. She turned slowly to see what he wanted, and her expression bore no sign of that expectant look she'd had Friday night. Clearly, he had somehow wounded her. "I'm sure you're wondering what I was calling about," he began.

"I figured you'd tell me eventually."

"I just wondered if you wanted to see my new place." He told her where it was. "Maybe you could drop over late tomorrow morning and see it, and then we could get some lunch."

"I don't know," Chloe said. "I don't think I can do lunch, but if I'm over that way maybe I'll stop by."

"OK." Buck was deflated. Apparently it wasn't going to be difficult to let her down gently. It certainly wasn't going to break her heart.

As Chloe slipped into the crowd, Rayford reached to shake Buck's hand. "So how are you, my friend?"

"I'm doing all right," Buck said. "Getting settled in."

A question gnawed at Rayford. He looked at the ceiling and then back at Buck. In his peripheral vision he saw hundreds of people milling about, wanting their individual moments with Bruce Barnes. "Buck, let me ask you something. Do you ever regret introducing Hattie Durham to Carpathia?"

Buck pressed his lips together and shut his eyes, rubbing his forehead with his fingers. "Every day," he whispered. "I was just talking to Bruce about that."

Rayford nodded and knelt on the pew seat, facing Buck. Buck sat. "I wondered," Rayford said. "I have a lot of regrets about her. We were friends, you know. Coworkers, but friends, too."

"I gathered," Buck said.

"We never had a relationship or anything like that," Rayford assured him. "But I find myself caring about what happens to her."

"I hear she's taken a thirty-day leave of absence from Pan-Con."

"Yeah," Rayford said, "but that's just window dressing. You know Carpathia's going to want to keep her around, and he'll find the money to pay her more than she's making with us."

"No doubt."

"She's got to be enamored of the job, not to mention him. And who knows where that relationship might go?"

"Like Bruce says, I don't think he hired her for her brain," Buck said.

Rayford nodded. So they agreed. Hattie Durham was going to become one of Carpathia's diversions. If there had ever been hope for her soul, it would be remote as long as she was in his orbit every day.

"I worry about her," Rayford continued, "and yet because of our friendship I don't feel I'm in a position to warn her. She was one of the first people I tried to tell about Christ. She was not receptive. Before that I had implied more of an interest in her than I had a right to have, and naturally she's not real positive about me just now."

Buck leaned forward. "Maybe I'll get a chance to talk to Hattie sometime soon."

"But what will you say?" Rayford asked. "For all we know they may already be intimate. She'll tell him everything she knows. If she tells him you've become a believer and that you're trying to rescue her, he'll know he had no impact on your mind when he was brainwashing everyone else."

Buck nodded. "I've thought about that. But I feel responsible for her being there. I *am* responsible for her being there. We can pray for her, but I'm going to feel pretty useless if I can't do something concrete to get her out of there. We've got to get her back here where she can learn the truth."

"I wonder if she's already moved to New York," Rayford said. "Maybe we'll find a reason for Chloe to call her apartment in Des Plaines."

As they separated and made their way out of the church, Rayford began wondering how much he should encourage the relationship between Chloe and Buck. He liked Buck a lot, what little he knew of him. He believed him, trusted him, considered him a brother. He was bright and insightful for a young guy. But the idea that his daughter might date or even fall in love with a man on speaking terms with the Antichrist . . . it was too much to fathom. He would have to be frank with them both about it, if it appeared their relationship was going anywhere.

But once he joined Chloe in the car he realized that was not something he needed to fret about just yet.

"Don't tell me you've invited Buck to join us for lunch," she said.

"Didn't even think of it. Why?"

"He's treating me like a sister, and yet he wants me to drop in and see his place tomorrow."

Rayford wanted to say "So what?" and ask her if she didn't think she was reading too much into the words and actions of a man she barely knew. For all she knew, Buck could be madly in love with her and not know how to broach it. Rayford said nothing.

"You're right," she said. "I'm obsessing."

"I didn't say a word."

"I can read your mind," she said. "Anyway, I'm mad at myself. I come away from a message like that one, and all I can think about is a guy I've somehow let slip away. It's not important. Who cares?"

"You do, apparently."

"But I shouldn't. Old things are passed away and all things have become new," she said. "Worrying about guys should definitely be an old thing. There's no time for trivia now."

"Suit yourself."

"That's just what I don't want to do. If I suited myself I'd see Buck this afternoon and find out where we stand."

"But you're not going to?"

She shook her head.

"Then would you do me a favor? Would you try to reach Hattie Durham for me?"

"Why?"

"Actually, I'm just curious to know whether she's already moved to New York."

"Why wouldn't she have? Carpathia's hired her, hasn't he?"

"I don't know. She's on a thirty-day leave. Just call her apartment. If she's got a machine running, then she's not made up her mind yet."

"Why don't *you* call her?"

"I think I've intruded enough in her life."

———————————

Buck stopped for Chinese carryout on the way home and sat eating alone, staring out the window. He turned on a ball game but ignored it, keeping the sound low. His mind was full of conflict. His story was ready to be transmitted to New York, and he would be eager for a reaction from Stanton Bailey. He also looked forward to getting his office machines and files, which should arrive at the Chicago bureau office in the morning. It would be good to pick those up and get organized.

He couldn't shake Bruce's message, either. It wasn't so much the content as Bruce's passion. He needed to get to know Bruce better. Maybe that would be a cure for his loneliness—and Bruce's. If Buck himself were this lonely, it had to be much worse for a man who had had a wife and children. Buck was used to a solitary life, but he'd had a network of friends in New York. Here, unless he heard from the office or someone else in the Tribulation Force, the phone was not going to ring.

He certainly wasn't handling the Chloe situation well. When he had been demoted, Buck had considered the relocation from New York to Chicago a positive turn—he would get to see more of her, he'd be in a good church, get good training, have a core of friends. But he also felt he had been on the right track when he began to slow his pursuit of her. The timing was bad. Who pursues a relationship during the end of the world?

Buck knew—or at least believed—that Chloe was not toying with him. She wasn't playing hard to get just to keep him interested. But whether she was doing it on purpose or not, it was working, and he felt foolish to be dwelling on it.

Whatever had happened, however she was acting, and for

whatever reason, he owed it to her to have it out. He might regret the let's-be-friends routine, but he didn't see that he had any
other choice. He owed it to her and to himself to just pursue the
friendship and see what came of it. For all he knew, she wouldn't
be interested in more than that anyway.

He reached for the phone, but when he put it to his ear, he
heard a strange tone, and then a recorded voice. "You have a
message. Please push star two to hear it."

A message? I never ordered voice mail. He pushed the buttons.
It was Steve Plank.

"Buck, where the devil are you, man? If you're not going to answer your voice mail, I'm going to quit leaving messages there. I
know you're unlisted there, but if you think Nicolae Carpathia is
someone to trifle with, ask yourself how I got your phone number. You'll wish you had these resources as a journalist. Now,
Buck, friend to friend, I know you check your messages often,
and you know Carpathia wants to talk to you. Why didn't you
call me? You're making me look bad. I told him I'd track you
down and that you'd come and see him. I told him I didn't understand your not accepting his invitation to the installation meeting,
but that I know you like a brother and you wouldn't stand him
up again.

"Now he wants to see you. I don't know what it's all about or
even whether I'll sit in on it. I don't know if it's on the record,
but you can certainly ask him for a few quotes for your article.
Just get here. You can hand deliver your article to the *Weekly,*
say hi to your old friend Miss Durham, and find out what Nicolae wants. There's a first-class ticket waiting for you at O'Hare
under the name of McGillicuddy for a nine o'clock flight tomorrow morning. A limo will meet your plane, and you'll have lunch
with Carpathia. Just do it, Buck. Maybe he wants to thank you
for introducing him to Hattie. They seem to be hitting it off.

"Now, Buck, if I don't hear from you, I'm going to assume
you'll be here. Don't disappoint me."

"What's the scoop?" Rayford asked.

Chloe imitated the recorded voice. " 'The number you have dialed has been disconnected. The new number is . . .' "

"Is what?"

She handed him a scrap of paper. The area code was for New York City. Rayford sighed. "Do you have Buck's new number?"

"It's on the wall by the phone."

Buck called Bruce Barnes. "I hate to ask you this, Bruce," he said. "But could we get together tonight?"

"I'm about to take a nap," Bruce said.

"You should sleep through. We can do it another time."

"No, I'm not going to sleep through. You want the four of us to meet, or just you and me?"

"Just us."

"How about I come to your place then? I'm getting tired of the office and the empty house."

They agreed on seven o'clock, and Buck decided he would take his phone off the hook after one more call. He didn't want to risk talking to Plank, or worse, Carpathia, until he had talked over and prayed about his plans with Bruce. Steve had said he would assume Buck was coming unless he heard back, but it would be just like Steve to check in with him again. And Carpathia was totally unpredictable.

Buck called Alice, the Chicago bureau secretary. "I need a favor," he said.

"Anything," she said.

He told her he might be flying to New York in the morning but he didn't want Verna Zee knowing about it. "I also don't want to wait any longer for my stuff, so I'd like to bring you my extra key before I head for the airport. If you wouldn't mind bringing that stuff over here for me and locking back up, I'd really appreciate it."

"No problem. I have to be going that way late morning anyway. I'm picking up my fiancé at the airport. Verna doesn't have to know I'm delivering your stuff on the way."

"You want to go to Dallas with me tomorrow morning, Chlo'?" Rayford asked.

"I don't think so. You're going to be in 757s all day anyway, right?"

Rayford nodded.

"I'll stay around here. Maybe I'll take Buck up on his offer to see his place."

Rayford shook his head. "I can't keep up with you," he said. "Now you *want* to go over there and see the guy who treats you like a sister?"

"I wouldn't be going to see him," she said. "I'd be going to see his place."

"Ah," Rayford said. "My mistake."

———————

"You hungry?" Buck asked before Bruce had even gotten in the door that evening.

"I could eat," Bruce said.

"Let's go out," Buck suggested. "You can see the place when we get back."

They settled into a booth in a dark corner of a noisy pizza place, and Buck filled Bruce in on the latest from Steve Plank. "You thinking about going?" Bruce asked.

"I don't know what to think, and if you knew me better, you'd know that's pretty bizarre for me. My instincts as a journalist say yes, of course—go, no question. Who wouldn't? But I know who this guy is, and the last time I saw him he put a bullet through two men."

"I'd sure like to get Rayford's and Chloe's input on this."

"I thought you might," Buck said. "But I'd like to ask you to hold off on that. If I go, I'd rather they not know."

"Buck, if you go, you're going to want all the prayer support you can get."

"Well, you can tell them after I'm gone or something. I should be having lunch with Carpathia around noon or a little after, New York time. You can just tell them I'm on an important trip."

"If that's what you want. But you have to realize, this is not how I see the core group."

"I know, and I agree. But they both might see this as pretty reckless, and maybe it is. If I do it, I don't want to disappoint them until I've had a chance to debrief them and explain myself."

"Why not do that in advance?"

Buck cocked his head and shrugged. "Because I haven't sorted it out myself yet."

"It sounds to me like you've already made up your mind to go."

"I suppose I have."

"Do you want me to talk you out of it?"

"Not really. Do you want to?"

"I'm as much at a loss as you are, Buck. I can't see anything positive coming from it. He's a dangerous man and a murderer. He could wipe you out and get away with it. He did it before with a roomful of witnesses. On the other hand, how long can you dodge him? He gets access to your unlisted phone number two days after you move in. He can find you, and if you avoid him you'll certainly make him mad."

"I know. This way I can just tell him I was busy moving in and getting settled—"

"Which you were."

"—Which I was, and then I'm there on time, on his ticket, wondering what he wants."

"He'll be trying to read you, to find out how much you remember about what he did."

"I don't know what I'll say. I didn't know what I'd do at the installation meeting either. I sensed the evil in that room, but I also knew God was with me. I didn't know what to say or how to react, but as I look back on it, God led me perfectly just to be silent and let Carpathia come to whatever conclusion he wanted to."

"You can depend on God this time, too, Buck. But you should have some sort of plan, go over in your mind what you might say or not say, that sort of thing."

"In other words, instead of sleeping tonight?"

Bruce smiled. "I don't suppose there's much prospect of that."

"I don't suppose."

By the time Buck gave Bruce the quick tour of his place, Buck had decided to go to New York in the morning.

"Why don't you just call your friend . . . ," Bruce began.

"Plank?"

"Yeah, Plank, and tell him you're coming. Then you can quit dreading his call and leave your phone open for me or whoever else might want to talk to you."

Buck nodded. "Good idea."

But after leaving a message for Steve, Buck got no more calls that night. He thought about calling Chloe to tell her not to come by the next morning, but he didn't want to have to tell her why or make up something, and he was convinced she wasn't coming anyway. She certainly hadn't sounded interested that morning.

———

Buck slept fitfully. Fortunately, the next morning he didn't see Verna until after he had dropped off his key to Alice and was driving out of the lot. Verna was driving in, and she did not see him.

Buck had no identification with the name *McGillicuddy* on it. At O'Hare he picked up an envelope under the phony name and realized that not even the young woman at the counter would have known a ticket was inside.

At the gate he checked in about half an hour before boarding was to begin. "Mr. McGillicuddy," the middle-aged man at the counter said, "you are free to preboard if you wish."

"Thanks," Buck said.

He knew that first-class passengers, frequent flyers, the elderly, and people with small children boarded first. But as Buck went to sit in the waiting area, the man asked, "You don't wish to board right away?"

"I'm sorry?" Buck said. "Now?"

"Yes, sir."

Buck looked around, wondering if he had missed something. Few people were even in line yet, let alone preboarding.

"You have the exclusive privilege of boarding at your leisure, but of course it's not required. Your choice."

Buck shrugged. "Sure, I'll board now."

Only one flight attendant was on the plane. The coach section was still being cleaned. Nevertheless, the flight attendant offered him champagne, juice, or a soft drink and allowed him to look at a breakfast menu.

Buck had never been a drinker, so he declined the champagne, and he was too keyed up to eat. The flight attendant said, "Are you sure? An entire bottle has been set aside for you." She looked at her clipboard. " 'Compliments of N. C.' "

"Thanks anyway." Buck shook his head. Was there no end to what Carpathia could—or would—do?

"You don't want to take it with you?"

"No, ma'am. Thanks. Would you like it?"

The attendant gave him a stunned look. "Are you kidding? It's Dom Pérignon!"

"Feel free."

"Really?"

"Sure."

"Well, would you sign that you accepted it so I don't get in trouble for taking it?" Buck signed the clipboard. What next?

"Um, sir?" the attendant said. "What is your name?"

"I'm sorry," Buck said. "I wasn't thinking." He took the clipboard, crossed out his own name, and signed "B. McGillicuddy."

Normally coach passengers would steal glances at those in first class, but now even the other first-class passengers checked Buck out. He had tried not to be showy, but clearly he was getting preferential treatment. He was waiting on board when they arrived, and during the flight the attendants hovered felicitously around him, topping off his drink and asking if he wanted anything else. Whom had Carpathia paid for this treatment, and how much?

At Kennedy International, Buck did not have to look for someone holding a placard with his name on it. A uniformed driver strode directly to him as he appeared at the end of the jetway, reached for his carry-on, and asked if he had checked any bags.

"No."

"Very good, sir. Follow me to the car, please."

Buck was a world traveler and had been treated like both a king and a pauper over the years. Yet even he found this routine unsettling. He followed the driver meekly through the airport to a black stretch limo at the curb. The driver opened the door, and Buck stepped from the sun into the dark interior.

He had not told the driver his name and had not been asked. He assumed this was all part of Carpathia's hospitality. But what if he had been mistaken for someone else? What if this was just a colossal blunder?

As his eyes adjusted to the low light and the tinted windows, Buck noticed a man in a dark suit sitting with his back to the driver, staring at him. "You with the U.N.," Buck asked, "or do you work directly for Mr. Carpathia?"

The man did not respond. Nor did he move. Buck leaned forward. "Excuse me!" he said. "Do you—"

The man put a finger to his lips. *Fair enough,* Buck thought. *I don't need to know.* He was curious, though, whether he was meeting Carpathia at the U.N. or at a restaurant. And it would have been nice to know whether Steve Plank would be there.

"You mind if I talk to the driver?" Buck said. No reaction. "Excuse me, driver?"

But there was Plexiglas between the front seat and the rest of the chassis. The man who looked like a bodyguard still sat staring, and Buck wondered if this would be his last ride. Strangely, he didn't experience the dread that had overwhelmed him that last time. He didn't know if this was from God, or if he was just naïve. For all he knew, he could be on his way to his own execution. The only record of his trip was a mistaken signature on the flight attendant's clipboard, and he had crossed that out.

Rayford Steele sat in the cockpit of a Boeing 757 on the military runway in the shadow of Dallas–Fort Worth. A certifying examiner in the first officer's seat had already clarified that he was there only to take notes. Rayford was to run through the proper preflight checklist, communicate to the tower, wait for clearance, take off, follow tower instructions for the proper flight path, enter a holding pattern, and land. He was not told how many times he might have to repeat that entire sequence, or whether anything else would be required.

"Remember," the examiner said, "I'm not here to teach you a thing or to bail you out. I answer no questions, and I touch no controls."

The preflight check went off without a hitch. Taxiing the 757 was different from the huge, bulky feel of the 747, but Rayford managed. When he received clearance, he throttled up and felt the unusually responsive thrust from the aerodynamic wonder. As the plane hurtled down the runway like a racehorse eager to run, Rayford said to the examiner, "This is like the Porsche of airplanes, isn't it?"

The examiner didn't even look at him, let alone answer.

The takeoff was powerful and true, and Rayford was reminded of flying the powerful but much smaller fighter planes from his military days. "More like a Jaguar?" he asked the examiner, and that at least elicited a tiny smile and a slight nod.

Rayford's landing was picture-perfect. The examiner waited until he had taxied back into position and shut down the engines. Then he said, "Let's do that two more times and get you on your way."

Buck Williams' limo was soon stuck in traffic. Buck wished he'd brought something to read. Why did this have to be so mysterious? He didn't understand the point of his treatment on both ends of the plane ride. The only other time someone had suggested he use an alias was when a competing magazine was making an offer they hoped he couldn't refuse, and they didn't want *Global Weekly* to get wind he was even considering it.

Buck could see the United Nations headquarters in the distance, but he still didn't know whether that was his destination until the driver swept past the appropriate exit. He hoped they were headed somewhere nice for lunch. Besides the fact that he had skipped breakfast, he also liked the prospect of eating more than that of dying.

As Rayford was escorted to the Pan-Con courtesy van for his ride to DFW airport, his examiner handed him a business-size envelope. "So did I pass?" Rayford said lightly.

"You won't know that for about a week," the man said.

Then what's this? Rayford wondered, entering the van and tearing open the envelope. Inside was a single sheet of United Nations stationery, already embossed with *Hattie Durham, Personal Assistant to the Secretary-General.* The handwritten message read simply:

Captain Steele,
I assume you know that the brand-new Air Force One is a 757.
Your friend,
Hattie Durham

FIVE

BUCK began to feel more confident that he wasn't in mortal danger. Too many people had been involved in getting him from Chicago to New York and now to midtown. On the other hand, if Nicolae Carpathia could get away with murder in front of more than a dozen eyewitnesses, he could certainly eliminate one magazine writer.

The limo eventually wound its way to the docks, where it stopped on the circle drive in front of the exclusive Manhattan Harbor Yacht Club. As the doorman approached, the chauffeur lowered the front passenger window and waved a finger at him, as if warning him to stay away from the car. Then the bodyguard got out, holding the car door, and Buck stepped into the sunshine. "Follow, please," the bodyguard said.

Buck would have felt right at home in the Yacht Club except that he was walking with a suited man who conspicuously guided him past a long line of patrons waiting for tables. The maître d' glanced up and nodded as Buck followed his escort to the edge of the dining room. There the man stopped and whispered, "You will dine with the gentleman in the booth by the window."

Buck looked. Someone waved vigorously at him, drawing stares. Because the sun was to the man's back, Buck saw only the silhouette of a smallish, stooped man with wild wisps of hair. "I will be back for you at one-thirty sharp," the bodyguard said. "Don't leave the dining room without me."

"But—"

The bodyguard slipped away, and Buck glanced at the maître d', who ignored him. Still self-conscious, Buck made his way through the crowd of tables to the booth by the window, where he was exuberantly greeted by his old friend Chaim Rosenzweig. The man knew enough to whisper in public, but his enthusiasm was boundless.

"Cameron!" the Israeli exulted in his thick accent. "How good to see you! Sit down, sit down! This a lovely place, no? Only the best for friends of the secretary-general."

"Will he be joining us, sir?"

Rosenzweig looked surprised. "No, no! Much too busy. Hardly ever able to get away. Entertaining heads of state, ambassadors, everyone wants a piece of him. I hardly see him more than five minutes a day myself!"

"How long will you be in town?" Buck asked, accepting a menu and allowing the waiter to drape a linen napkin on his lap.

"Not much longer. By the end of this week Nicolae and I are to finish preparations for his visit to Israel. What a glorious day it will be!"

"Tell me about it, Doctor."

"I will! I will! But first we must catch up!" The old man suddenly grew serious and spoke in a somber voice. He reached across the table and covered Buck's hand with both of his. "Cameron, I am your friend. You must tell me straight out. How could you have missed such an important meeting? I am a scientist, yes, but I also consider myself somewhat of a diplomat. I worked hard behind the scenes with Nicolae and with your friend, Mr. Plank, to be sure you were invited. I don't understand."

"I don't understand either," Buck said. What else could he say? Rosenzweig, creator of a formula that made the Israeli deserts bloom like a greenhouse, had been his friend ever since Buck profiled him as *Global Weekly's* Newsmaker of the Year more than a year before. Rosenzweig was the one who had first mentioned the name Nicolae Carpathia to Buck. Carpathia had been a low-level politico from Romania who had asked for a private audience with Rosenzweig after the formula had become famous.

Heads of state from all over the world had tried to curry favor with Israel to get access to the formula. Many countries sent diplomats to sweet-talk Rosenzweig himself when they got nowhere with the Israeli prime minister. Oddly, Carpathia was the one who most impressed Rosenzweig. He had arranged the visit himself and come on his own, and at the time he seemed to have no power to make any deals, even if Rosenzweig had been open to one. All Carpathia had sought from Rosenzweig was his good will. And he got it. Now, Buck realized, it was paying off.

"Where were you?" Dr. Rosenzweig asked.

"That's the question of the ages," Buck said. "Where are any of us?"

Rosenzweig's eyes twinkled, though Buck felt like a fool. He was talking gibberish, but he didn't know what else to say. He couldn't tell the man, *I was there! I saw the same thing you saw, but you were brainwashed by Carpathia because he's the Antichrist!*

Rosenzweig was a bright, quick man with a love for intrigue. "So, you don't want to tell me. All right. Not being there was your loss. Of course, you were spared the horror it turned into, but what a historic meeting nonetheless. Get the salmon. You'll love it."

Buck had always, *always* made it a habit to ignore recommendations in restaurants. It probably was one of the reasons for his nickname. He realized how rattled he was when he ordered what Rosenzweig suggested. And he loved it.

"Let me ask *you* something now, Dr. Rosenzweig."

"Please! Please, *Chaim.*"

"I can't call you Chaim, sir. A Nobel Prize winner?"

"Please, you will honor me. Please!"

"All right, Chaim," Buck said, barely able to get the name out. "Why am I here? What is this all about?"

The old man pulled the napkin from his lap, wiped his whole bearded face with it, balled it up, and plopped it onto his plate. He pushed the plate aside, sat back, and crossed his legs. Buck had seen people warm to a subject before, but never with as much relish as Chaim Rosenzweig.

"So, the journalist in you comes out, eh? Let me begin by telling you that this is your lucky day. Nicolae has in mind for you an honor that is such a privilege I cannot tell you."

"But you will tell me, won't you, sir?"

"I will tell you what I have been instructed to tell you, and no more. The rest will come from Nicolae himself." Rosenzweig glanced at his watch, a plastic-banded twenty-dollar toy that seemed incongruous with his international status. "Good. We have time. He has allotted thirty minutes for your visit, so please keep that in mind. I know you are friends and you may want to apologize for missing his meeting, but just remember that he has a lot to offer you and not much time to do it. He flies to Washington late this afternoon for a meeting with the president. By the way, the president offered to meet in New York, if you can imagine, but Nicolae, humble as he is, would hear nothing of it."

"You find Carpathia humble?"

"Probably as humble as any leader I have ever met, Cameron. Of course, I know many public servants and private people who are humble and have a right to be! But most politicians, heads of state, world leaders, they are full of themselves. Many of them have much to be proud of and in many ways it is their egos that allow them to accomplish what they accomplish. But never have I seen a man like this."

"He's pretty impressive," Buck admitted.

"That's not the half of it," Dr. Rosenzweig insisted. "Think about it, Cameron. He has not sought these positions. He rose from a low position in the Romanian government to become president of that nation when an election was not even scheduled. He resisted it!"

I'll bet, Buck thought.

"And when he was invited to speak at the United Nations not a month ago, he was so intimidated and felt so unworthy, he almost declined. But you were there! You heard the speech. I would have nominated him for prime minister of Israel if I thought he would have taken it! Almost immediately the secretary-general stepped down and insisted Nicolae replace him. And he was elected unanimously, enthusiastically, and he has been endorsed by nearly every head of state around the world.

"Cameron, he has ideas upon ideas! He is the consummate diplomat. He speaks so many languages that he hardly ever needs an interpreter, even for the chiefs of some of the remote tribes in South America and Africa! The other day he shared a few phrases understood only by an Australian Aborigine!"

"Let me just stop you for a second, Chaim," Buck said. "You know, of course, that in exchange for stepping down from the secretary-generalship of the U.N., Mwangati Ngumo was promised access to your formula for use in Botswana. It wasn't quite so selfless and altruistic as it seemed, and—"

"Of course, Nicolae has told me all about that. But it was not part of any agreement. It was a gesture of his personal gratitude for what President Ngumo has done for the United Nations over the years."

"But how can he show his personal gratitude by giving away *your* formula, sir? No one else anywhere has access to it, and—"

"I was more than happy to offer it."

"You were?" Buck's mind reeled. Was there no limit to Carpathia's persuasive power?

The old man uncrossed his legs and leaned forward, his elbows on the table. "Cameron, it all ties together. This is part of why you're here. The agreement with the former secretary-general was an experiment, a model."

"I'm listening, Doctor."

"It's too early to tell, of course, but if the formula works as well as it has in Israel, Botswana will immediately become one of the most fertile countries in all of Africa, if not the world. Already President Ngumo has seen his stature rise within his own nation. Everyone agrees he was distracted from his duties at the U.N. and that the world is better now for the new leadership."

Buck shrugged, but apparently Rosenzweig didn't notice. "And so Carpathia plans to do more of this, brokering your formula for favors?"

"No, no! You're missing the point. Yes, I have persuaded the Israeli government to license use of the formula to the secretary-general of the United Nations."

"Oh, Chaim! For what? Billions of dollars that Israel no longer needs? It makes no sense! Having the formula made you the richest nation on earth for its size and solved myriad problems, but it was the exclusivity that made it work! Why do you think the Russians attacked you? They don't need your land! There's no oil to be found! They wanted the formula! Imagine if all the vast reaches of that nation were fertile!"

Dr. Rosenzweig held up a hand. "I understand that, Cameron. But money has nothing to do with this. I need no money. Israel needs no money."

"Then what could Carpathia offer that is worthy of the trade?"

"What has Israel prayed for since the beginning of her existence, Cameron? And I am not talking about her rebirth in 1948. From the beginning of time as the chosen people of God, what have we prayed for?"

Buck's blood ran cold, and he could only sit there and nod resignedly. Rosenzweig answered his own question. "*Shalom.* Peace. 'Pray for the peace of Israel.' We are a fragile, vulnerable land. We know God Almighty supernaturally protected us from the onslaught of the Russians. Do you know that there was so much death among their troops that the bodies had to be buried in a common grave, a crater gouged from our precious soil by one of their bombs, which God rendered harmless? We had to burn some of their bodies and bones. And the debris from their weapons of destruction was so massive that we have used it as a raw resource and are refabricating it into marketable goods. Cameron," he added ominously, "so many of their planes crashed—well, all of them, of course. They still had burnable fuel, enough that we estimate we will be able to use it for five to eight more years. Can you see why peace is so attractive to us?"

"Chaim, you said yourself that God Almighty protected you. There could be no other explanation for what happened the night of that invasion. With God on your side, why do you need to barter with Carpathia for protection?"

"Cameron, Cameron," Rosenzweig said wearily, "history has shown our God to be capricious when it comes to our welfare. From the children of Israel wandering forty years in the desert to the Six-Day War to the Russian invasion to now, we do not understand him. He lends us his favor when it suits his eternal plan, which we cannot comprehend. We pray, we seek him, we try to curry his favor. But in the meantime we believe that God helps those who help themselves. You know, of course, that this is why you are here."

"I know nothing," Buck said.

"Well, it's part of why you're here. You understand that such an agreement takes a lot of homework—"

"What agreement are we talking about?"

"I'm sorry, Cameron, I thought you were following. You do not think it was easy even for me, despite my stature within my own country, to persuade the powers to release a license to the formula even to a man as attractive as Nicolae."

"Of course not."

"And you are right. Some of the meetings went long into the night, and every time I felt I had convinced someone, another was brought in. Every new ear had to be convinced. Many times I nearly gave up in despair. But finally, finally, with many conditions, I was empowered to hammer out an arrangement with the United Nations."

"With Carpathia, you mean."

"Of course. Make no mistake. He is the United Nations now."

"You got that right," Buck said.

"Part of the agreement is that I become part of his senior staff, an adviser. I will cochair the committee that decides where the formula will be licensed."

"And no money changes hands?"

"None."

"And Israel gets protection from her neighbors from the United Nations?"

"Oh, it is much more complex than that, Cameron. You see, the formula is now tied into Nicolae's global disarmament policy. Any nation even suspected of resisting the destruction of 90 percent of its weapons and the surrender of the remaining 10 percent to Nicolae—or I should say to the U.N.—will never be allowed to even be considered as an applicant for a license. Nicolae has pledged that he—and I will be there to ensure this, of course—will be more than judicious in licensing our nearest neighbors and most dangerous enemies."

"There has to be more than that."

"Oh, there is, but the crux of it is this, Cameron. Once the world has been disarmed, Israel should not have to worry about protecting her borders."

"That's naïve."

"Not as naïve as it might appear, because if there is one thing Nicolae Carpathia is not, it is naïve. Knowing full well that some nations may hoard or hide weapons or produce new ones, the full agreement between the sovereign state of Israel and Security Council of the United Nations—with the personal signature of Nicolae Carpathia—makes a solemn promise. Any nation that threatens Israel will suffer immediate extinction, using the full complement of weaponry available to the U.N. With every country donating 10 percent, you can imagine the firepower."

"What I cannot imagine, Chaim, is an avowed pacifist, a rabid global-disarmament proponent for his entire political career, threatening to blow countries off the face of the earth."

"It's only semantics, Cameron," Rosenzweig said. "Nicolae is a pragmatist. There is a good bit of the idealist in him, of course, but he knows that the best way to keep the peace is to have the wherewithal to enforce it."

"And this agreement lasts for—?"

"As long as we want it. We offered ten years, but Nicolae said he would not require the freedom to license the formula for that long. He said he would ask for only seven years, and then the full rights to the formula return to us. Most generous. And if we want to renew the agreement every seven years, we are free to do that, too."

You won't have any need for a peace treaty in seven years,

Buck thought. "So, what does this have to do with me?" he asked.

"That's the best part," Rosenzweig said. "At least for me, because it honors you. It is no secret that Nicolae is aware of your status as the most accomplished journalist in the world. And to prove that he bears no ill will for your snub of his last invitation, he is going to ask you to come to Israel for the signing of the treaty."

Buck shook his head.

"I know it is overwhelming," Rosenzweig said.

Rayford's plane hit the ground at O'Hare at one o'clock Chicago time. He called home and got the answering machine. "Yeah, Chloe," he said, "I'm back earlier than I thought. Just wanted you to know I'll be there within the hour and—"

Chloe grabbed the phone. She sounded awful. "Hi, Dad," she mumbled.

"You under the weather?"

"No. Just upset. Dad, did you know that Buck Williams is living with someone?"

"What!?"

"It's true. And they're engaged! I saw her. She was carrying boxes into his condo. A skinny little spike-haired girl in a short skirt."

"Maybe you had the wrong place."

"It was the right place."

"You're jumping to conclusions."

"Dad, listen to me. I was so mad I just drove around a while, then sat in a parking lot and cried. Then around noon I went to see him at the *Global Weekly* office, and there she was, getting out of her car. I said, 'Do you work here?' and she said, 'Yes, may I help you?' and I said, 'I think I saw you earlier today,' and she said, 'You might have. I was with my fiancé. Is there someone here you need to see?' I just turned and left, Dad."

"You didn't talk to Buck then?"

"Are you kidding? I may never talk to him again. Just a minute. Someone's at the door."

A minute later Chloe came back on. "I can't believe it. If he thinks this makes any difference . . ."

"What?"

"Flowers! And of course they're anonymous. He had to have seen me driving by and knew how I'd feel. Unless you want these, you'll find them in the trash when you get home."

At a few minutes after two in New York, Buck waited with Chaim Rosenzweig in the opulent waiting room outside the office of the secretary-general of the United Nations. Chaim was merrily going on about something, and Buck pretended to pay attention. He was praying silently, not knowing if his foreboding sense of evil was psychological because he knew Nicolae Carpathia was nearby, or if the man truly emitted some sort of demonic aura detectable to followers of Christ. Buck was warmed by the knowledge that Bruce was praying for him right then, and he was having second thoughts about not informing Rayford and Chloe of his trip. His return ticket was for the 5 P.M. flight, so he knew he'd be back in time for the first of the 8 P.M. study sessions Bruce had planned. Buck looked forward to it already. He might even see if Chloe wanted to have a late dinner, just the two of them, before the meeting. "So what do you think about that?" Dr. Rosenzweig said.

"I'm so sorry, Doctor," Buck said. "My mind was elsewhere."

"Cameron, don't be nervous. Nicolae was upset, yes, but he has only good things in store for you."

Buck shrugged and nodded.

"Anyway, I was saying. My dear friend Rabbi Tsion Ben-Judah has finished his three-year study, and it wouldn't surprise me if he wins a Nobel Prize for it."

"His three-year study?"

"You weren't listening at all, were you, my friend?"

"I'm sorry."

"You must do better when you are with Nicolae, promise me."

"I will. Forgive me."

"It's all right. But listen, Rabbi Ben-Judah was commissioned by the Hebrew Institute of Biblical Research to do a three-year study."

"A study of what?"

"Something about the prophecies relating to Messiah so we Jews will recognize him when he comes."

Buck was stunned. The Messiah had come, and the Jews left behind had missed him. When he had come the first time most did not recognize him. What should Buck say to his friend? If he declared himself a "Tribulation saint," as Bruce liked to refer to new believers since the Rapture, what might he be doing to himself? Rosenzweig was a confidant of Carpathia's. Buck wanted to say that a legitimate study of messianic prophecies could lead only to Jesus. But he said only, "What *are* the major prophecies pointing to the Messiah?"

"To tell you the truth," Dr. Rosenzweig said, "I don't know. I was not a religious Jew until God destroyed the Russian Air Force, and I can't say I'm devout now. I always took the messianic prophecies the way I took the rest of the Torah. Symbolic. The rabbi at the temple I attended occasionally in Tel Aviv said himself that it was not important whether we believed that God was a literal being or just a concept. That fit with my humanist view of the world. Religious people, Jewish or otherwise, seldom impressed me any more than the atheist with a good heart.

"Dr. Ben-Judah was a student of mine twenty-five years ago. He was always an unabashed religious Jew, Orthodox but short of a fundamentalist. Of course he became a rabbi, but certainly not because of anything I taught him. I liked him and always have. He recently told me he had finished the study and that it was the most fulfilling and rewarding work he has ever done." Rosenzweig paused. "I suppose you are wondering why I tell you this."

"Frankly, yes."

"I'm lobbying for Rabbi Ben-Judah's inclusion on Nicolae Carpathia's staff."

"As?"

"Spiritual adviser."

"He's looking for one?"

"Not that he knows of!" Rosenzweig said, roaring with laughter and slapping his knee. "But so far he has trusted my judgment. That's why you're here."

Buck lifted an eyebrow. "I thought it was because Carpathia thinks I'm the best journalist in the world."

Dr. Rosenzweig leaned forward and whispered conspiratorially, "And why do you think he believes that?"

Rayford had had trouble reaching Chloe from his car phone, but he finally got through. "Wondered if you wanted to go out with your old man tonight," he suggested, thinking she needed to be cheered up.

"I don't know," she said. "I appreciate it, Dad, but we're going to Bruce's eight o'clock meeting, aren't we?"

"I'd like to," Rayford said.

"Let's stay in. I'm all right. I was just on the phone with Bruce. I wanted to know if he knew whether Buck was coming tonight."

"And?"

"He wasn't entirely sure. He hoped so. I hope not."

"Chloe!"

"I'm just afraid of what I'll say, Dad. No wonder he's been cool toward me with that, that, whatever-you-call-her in his life. But the flowers! What was that all about?"

"You don't even know they were from him."

"Oh, Dad! Unless they were from you, they were from Buck."

Rayford laughed. "I wish I'd thought of it."

"So do I."

Hattie Durham approached Buck and Chaim Rosenzweig, and they both stood. "Mr. Williams!" she said, embracing him. "I haven't seen you since I took this job."

Yes, you have, Buck thought. *You just don't remember.*

"The secretary-general and Mr. Plank will see you now," she told Buck. She turned to Dr. Rosenzweig. "Doctor, the secretary-general asks that you be prepared to join the meeting in about twenty-five minutes."

"Certainly," the old man said. He winked at Buck and squeezed his shoulder.

Buck followed Hattie past several desks and down a mahogany-appointed hallway, and he realized he had never seen her out of uniform. Today she wore a tailored suit that made her look like a classy, wealthy, sophisticated woman. The look only enhanced her stunning beauty. Even her speech seemed more cultured than he remembered. Her exposure to Nicolae Carpathia seemed to have improved her presence.

Hattie tapped lightly on the office door and poked her head in. "Mr. Secretary-General and Mr. Plank, Cameron Williams of *Global Weekly.*" Hattie pushed the door open and slipped away as Nicolae Carpathia advanced, reaching for Buck's hand with

both of his. Buck seemed strangely calmed by the man and his
smile. "Buck!" he said. "May I call you Buck?"

"You always have," Buck said.

"Come! Come! Sit! You and Steve know each other, of
course."

Buck was more struck with Steve's appearance than with Carpathia's. Nicolae had always dressed formally, with perfectly co-
ordinated accessories, suit coat buttoned, everything in place. But
Steve, despite his position as executive editor of one of the most
prestigious magazines in the world, had not always dressed the
way you might expect a journalist to dress. He had always worn
the obligatory suspenders and long-sleeved shirts, of course, but
he was usually seen with his tie loosened and his sleeves rolled
up, looking like a middle-aged yuppie or an Ivy League student.

Today, however, Steve looked like a clone of Carpathia. He
carried a thin, black-leather portfolio and from head to toe
looked as if he had come off the cover of a Fortune 500 edition
of *GQ*. Even his hairstyle had a European flair—razor cut, blow-
dried, styled, and moussed. He wore new, designer-frame glasses,
a charcoal suit just this side of pitch-black, a white shirt with a
collar pin and tie that probably cost what he used to pay for a
sports coat. The shoes were soft leather and looked Italian, and if
Buck wasn't mistaken, there was a new diamond ring on Steve's
right hand.

Carpathia pulled an extra chair from his conference table,
added it to the two before his desk, and sat with Buck and Steve.
Right out of a management book, Buck thought. *Break down the
barrier between the superior and the subordinate.*

Yet despite the attempt at an equal playing field, it was clear
the intent of the meeting was to impress Buck. And he was impressed. Hattie and Steve had already changed enough to be
nearly unrecognizable. And every time Buck looked at Carpathia's
strong, angular features and quick, seemingly genuine disarming
smile, he wished with everything in him that the man was who he
appeared to be and not who Buck knew him to be.

He never forgot, never lost sight of the fact that he was in the
presence of the slickest, most conniving personality in history. He
only wished he knew someone as charming as Carpathia who was
real.

Buck felt for Steve, and yet he had not been consulted before
Steve had left *Global Weekly* for Carpathia's staff. Now, much as
Buck wanted to tell him about his newfound faith, he could trust

no one. Unless Carpathia had the supernatural ability to know everything, Buck hoped and prayed he would not detect that Buck was an enemy agent within his camp. "Let me begin with a humorous idiom," Carpathia said, "and then we will excuse Steve and have a heart-to-heart, just you and me, hmm?"

Buck nodded.

"Something I have heard only since coming to this country is the phrase 'the elephant in the room.' Have you heard that phrase, Buck?"

"You mean about people who get together and don't talk about the obvious, like the fact that one of them has just been diagnosed with a terminal illness?"

"Exactly. So, let us talk about the elephant in the room and be done with it, and then we can move on. All right?"

Buck nodded again, his pulse increasing.

"I confess I was confused and a little hurt that you did not attend the private meeting where I installed the new ambassadors. However, as it turned out, it would have been as traumatic for you as it was for the rest of us."

It was all Buck could do to keep from being sarcastic. One thing he could not and would not do was apologize. How could he say he was sorry for missing a meeting he had not missed?

"I wanted to be there and wouldn't have missed it for anything," Buck said. Carpathia seemed to look right through him and sat as if waiting for the rest of the thought. "Frankly," Buck added, "that whole day seems a blur to me now." A blur with vivid details he would never forget.

Carpathia seemed to loosen up. His formal pose melted and he leaned forward, elbows on his knees, and looked from Buck to Steve and back. He looked peeved. "So, all right," he said, "apparently there is no excuse, no apology, no explanation."

Buck glanced at Steve, who seemed to be trying to communicate with his eyes and a slight nod, as if to say, *Say something, Buck! Apologize! Explain!*

"What can I say?" Buck said. "I feel badly about that day." That was as close as he would come to saying what they wanted him to say. Buck knew Steve was innocent. Steve truly believed Buck had not been there. Carpathia, of course, had masterminded and choreographed the whole charade. Acting upset that he wasn't getting an apology or an explanation was the perfect move, Buck thought. Clearly, Carpathia was fishing for some evidence that Buck knew what had happened. All Buck could do

was play dumb and be evasive and pray that God would somehow blind Carpathia to the truth that Buck was a believer and
that he had been protected from susceptibility to Carpathia's
power.

"All right," Carpathia said, sitting back and composing himself
again. "We all feel bad, do we not? I grieve the loss of two compatriots, one a dear friend for many years." Buck felt his stomach
turn. "Now, Buck, I want to talk to you as a journalist, and we
will excuse our friend Mr. Plank."

Steve stood and patted Buck on the shoulder, leaving quietly.
Buck became painfully aware that now it was just him and God
sitting knee-to-knee with Nicolae Carpathia.

But it wasn't knee-to-knee for long. Nicolae suddenly rose and
went back around his desk to the executive chair behind it. Just
before he sat, he touched the intercom button, and Buck heard
the door open behind him.

Hattie Durham whispered, "Excuse me," took the extra chair
from in front of the desk, and put it back at the conference table.
As she was leaving, she adjusted and straightened the chair Steve
had used. Just as quietly, she slipped out. Buck thought that very
strange, this seemingly scripted arrangement of the entire meeting,
from the formal announcement of his presence, to the staging of
who would be there and where they would sit. With the office
now back to the way it was when Buck entered and Carpathia
ensconced behind his massive desk, all pretense of equalizing the
power base was gone.

Yet Carpathia still had the charm turned all the way up. He
intertwined his fingers and stared at Buck, smiling. "Cameron
Williams," he said slowly. "How does it feel to be the most cele-
brated journalist of your time?"

What kind of a question was that? It was precisely because
Buck didn't ask such questions that he *was* a respected journalist.
"Right now I'm just a demoted hack," he said.

"And humble besides," Carpathia said, grinning. "In a moment
I am going to make clear to you that even though your stock may
have fallen at *Global Weekly,* it has not fallen in the eyes of the
rest of the world, and certainly not with me. I should have been
more upset by your missing my meeting than your publisher was,
and yet he overreacted. We can put these things behind us and
move on. One mistake does not negate a lifetime of achievement."

Carpathia paused as if he expected Buck to respond. Buck was becoming more and more fond of silence. It seemed to be the right choice with Carpathia, and it certainly was the way God had led him during the murderous meeting when Carpathia had polled everyone to assess what they had seen. Buck believed silence had saved his life.

"By the way," Carpathia said when it was clear Buck had nothing to say, "do you have with you your cover story on the theories behind the vanishings?"

Buck couldn't hide his surprise. "As a matter of fact, I do."

Carpathia shrugged. "Steve told me about it. I would love to see it."

"I'm afraid I wouldn't be able to show it to anyone until the *Weekly* gets the final draft."

"Surely they have seen your working copy."

"Of course."

"Steve said you might want a quote or two from me."

"Frankly, unless you have something new, I think your views have already been so widely broadcast that they would be old to our readers."

Carpathia looked hurt.

"I mean," Buck said, "you still hold to the nuclear reaction with natural forces idea, right? That lightning may have triggered some spontaneous interaction between all the stockpiled nuclear weapons, and—"

"You know your friend Dr. Rosenzweig also subscribes to that theory."

"I understand that, yes sir."

"But it will not be represented in your article?"

"Sure it will. I thought the question was whether I needed a fresh quote from you. Unless your view has changed, I do not."

Carpathia looked at his watch. "As you know, I am on a tight schedule. Your trip was all right? Accommodations acceptable? A good lunch? Dr. Rosenzweig filled you in some?"

Buck nodded to every question.

"Assuming he told you about the U.N. treaty with Israel and that the signing will be a week from today in Jerusalem, let me extend a personal invitation to you to be there."

"I doubt the *Weekly* would send a Chicago staff writer to an international event of that magnitude."

"I am not asking that you join the press corps of thousands from around the world who will be seeking credentials as soon as the announcement is made. I am inviting you to be part of my delegation, to sit at the table with me. It will be a privilege no other media person in the world will have."

"*Global Weekly* has a policy that its journalists are not to accept any favors that might—"

"Buck, Buck," Carpathia said. "I am sorry to interrupt, but I will be very surprised if you are still an employee of *Global Weekly* a week from today. Very surprised."

Buck raised his eyebrows and looked skeptically at Carpathia. "Do you know something I don't know?" And as soon as it was out of his mouth, Buck realized he had unintentionally asked the core question of this meeting.

Carpathia laughed. "I know of no plans to fire you, no. I think the punishment for your blown assignment has already been meted out. And though you turned down an offer of employment from me before, I truly believe I have an opportunity for you that will change your mind."

Don't count on it, Buck thought. But he said, "I'm listening."

"BEFORE I get into that," Carpathia said, stalling, a maddening trait of his that never failed to annoy Buck, "let me just reflect on something. Do you remember when I assured you that I could make a problem go away for you?"

Did Buck remember? Up to the day of the murders, it had been his most chilling look at Carpathia. An informant of Buck's, a Welshman with whom he had gone to college, had turned up dead after getting too close to an international banking scheme involving his own boss, Joshua Todd-Cothran, head of the London Exchange.

Buck had flown to England to investigate with a Scotland Yard friend, only to be nearly killed himself when the Yard agent died in a car bombing. Buck determined that what had been ruled the suicide of his Welsh friend had actually been a homicide, and Buck had had to escape Britain under a phony name. When he got back to New York, none other than Nicolae Carpathia promised him that if Todd-Cothran had been involved in anything underhanded, Carpathia himself would take care of it. Not long after, Todd-Cothran died before Buck's eyes at Carpathia's hand in a double murder that only Buck seemed to recall.

"I remember," Buck said flatly, the understatement of his life.

"I made clear that I would not tolerate insincerity or deviousness in my administration of the U.N. And the Todd-Cothran situation took care of itself, did it not?"

Took care of itself? Buck remained silent.

"Do you believe in luck, Mr. Williams?"

"No."

"You do not believe that luck comes to those who do the right things?"

"No."

"I do. I always have. Oh, the occasional bumbler or even criminal gets lucky once in a while. But usually the better someone does his job, the luckier he seems to be. You follow?"

"No."

"Let me simplify. You were in dire danger. People around you were dying. I told you I would take care of that, and yet obviously I could have nothing personally to do with it. I confess that when I so boldly assured you that I could make your problems go away, I was not sure how I would effect that. Not being a religious person, I have to say that in this case, good karma was with me. Would you not agree?"

"To be perfectly honest with you, sir, I have no idea what you're saying."

"And you wonder why I like you so much?" Carpathia smiled broadly. "You are a person I need! What I am saying is that you and I both had a problem. You were on someone's hit list, and I had two people in my trust who were involved in serious crimes. By committing suicide and killing Todd-Cothran in the process, my old friend Jonathan Stonagal took care of the problems we both had. That is good karma, if I understand my Eastern friends."

"So while you say you're grieving over the deaths of your friends, in reality you're glad they're both dead."

Carpathia sat back, looking impressed. "Precisely. Glad for your sake. I grieve their loss. They were old friends and once trusted advisers, even mentors. But when they went bad, I was going to have to do something about it. And make no mistake, I would have. But Jonathan did it for me."

"Imagine that," Buck said. Carpathia's eyes bored into him as he seemed to examine Buck's mind.

"I never cease to be amazed," Nicolae continued, "at how quickly things change."

"I can't argue with that."

"Not a month ago I served in the Romanian senate. The next minute I was president of the country, and an hour later I became secretary-general of the United Nations."

Buck smiled at Carpathia's attempt at hyperbole, and yet his ascent to power had seemed almost that fast. Buck's smile faded when Carpathia added, "It is almost enough to make an atheist believe in God."

"But you ascribe it to good karma," Buck said.

"Frankly," Carpathia said, "it merely humbles me. In many ways it does seem this has been my destiny, but I never would have dreamed it or imagined it, let alone planned it. I have sought no office since I ran for the Romanian senate, and yet this has been thrust upon me. I can do nothing less than give it my all and hope I act in a manner worthy of the trust that has been placed in me."

A month earlier, Buck would have cursed the man to his face. He wondered if his sentiment showed. Apparently it did not.

"Buck," Carpathia continued, "I need you. And this time I am not going to take no for an answer."

———————

Rayford hung up his car phone after talking with Bruce Barnes. Rayford had asked if he could come a few minutes early that night to show Bruce something, but he did not tell him what it was. He pulled the note from Hattie from his breast pocket and spread it across the steering wheel. What in the world did it mean, and how did she, or obviously her boss, know where to find him?

His car phone rang. He pushed a button and spoke into the speaker embedded in the visor in front of him. "Ray Steele," he said.

"Daddy, have you been on the phone?"

"Yeah, why?"

"Earl's been trying to reach you."

"What's up?"

"I don't know. Sounds serious though. I told him you were on the way home and he was surprised. He said something about nobody ever keeping him informed about anything. He thought you were coming back from Dallas later and—"

"So did I."

"Anyway, he had been hoping to catch you at O'Hare before you left."

"I'll call him. See you tonight. I'm going to go a little early to talk with Bruce. You can come with me and wait in the outer office, or we can take two cars."

"Yeah, right, Dad. I'm so sure I'll wait in the outer office and have to face Buck alone. I don't think so. You go ahead. I'll be a few minutes late."

"Oh, Chloe."

"Don't start, Dad."

Buck felt bold. Curious, but bold. Certainly he wanted to hear what Carpathia had in mind, but it seemed the man was most impressed when Buck spoke his mind. Buck wasn't ready to tell him all that he knew and what he really thought, and he probably never would, but he felt he owed it to himself to speak up now.

"I probably shouldn't have come without knowing what you wanted," Buck said. "I almost didn't. I took my time getting back to Steve."

"Oh, let us be frank and serious," Carpathia said. "I am a diplomat, and I am sincere. You must know me well enough by now to know that." He paused as if waiting for Buck to assure him it was true. Buck did not even nod. "But, come, come. You do not apologize or explain why you ignored my last invitation, and yet I hold no grudge. You could not have afforded to snub me again."

"I couldn't? What would have happened to me?"

"Perhaps it would have gotten back to Stanton Bailey again, and you would have been demoted even further. Or fired. Disgraced either way. I am not naïve, Buck. I know the origin of your nickname, and it is part of what I admire so much about you. But you cannot keep bucking me. It is not that I consider myself anything special, but the world and the news media do. People ignore me at their peril."

"So I should be afraid of you, and that's why I should look favorably on whatever role you're about to offer me?"

"Oh, no! Afraid of ignoring me, yes, but only for the obvious, practical reasons I just outlined. But that fear should motivate you only to come when I ask and provide your way. It should never be the basis on which you decide to work with me. It will not take fear to persuade you on that score." Buck wanted to ask what it would take, but it was clear that was what Nicolae wanted him to ask, so he again said nothing.

"What is that old phrase from the movies you Americans are so fond of? 'An offer you cannot refuse'? That is what I have for you."

"Rayford, I hate to do this to you, but we've got to talk face-to-face, and this afternoon."

"Earl, I'm almost home."

"I'm sorry. I wouldn't ask you if it wasn't important."

"What's up?"

"If I could tell you over the phone, I wouldn't be apologizing about insisting on the face-to-face, would I?"

"You want me to head back there right now?"

"Yes, and I'm sorry."

"There are laws and there are rules," Carpathia was saying. "Laws I obey. Rules I do not mind ignoring if I can justify it. For instance, in your country you are not allowed to bring your own food into a sporting arena. Something about wanting to keep all the concession money for management. Fine. I can see why they would have such a rule, and if I were the owner, I would probably try to enforce the same. But I would not consider it a criminal act to smuggle in my own snack. You follow me?"

"I guess."

"There is a rule that pertains to heads of state and official bodies, like the United Nations. It is understood that only in a repressive dictatorship would the ruler have any ownership or financial interest in a major news media outlet."

"Absolutely."

"But is it a law?"

"In the United States it is."

"But internationally?"

"Not uniformly."

"There you go."

Carpathia clearly wanted Buck to ask where he was going, but Buck would not. "You are fond of the term *bottom line*," Nicolae said. "I have heard you use it. I know what it means. The bottom line here is that I am going to purchase major media, and I want you to be part of it."

"Part of what?"

"Part of the management team. I will become sole owner of the great newspapers of the world, the television networks, the wire services. You may run for me any one of those you wish."

"The secretary-general of the U.N. owning major media? How could you ever possibly justify that?"

"If laws need to be changed, they will change. If ever the time was right to have a positive influence on the media, Buck, it is now. Do you not agree?"

"I do not."

"Millions have vanished. People are scared. They are tired of war, tired of bloodshed, tired of chaos. They need to know that peace is within our grasp. The response to my plan to disarm the world has been met with almost unanimous favor."

"Not by the American militia movement."

"Bless them," Carpathia said, smiling. "If we accomplish what I have proposed, do you really think a bunch of zealots running around in the woods wearing fatigues and shooting off popguns will be a threat to the global community? Buck, I am merely responding to the heartfelt wishes of the decent citizens of the world. Of course there will still be bad apples, and I would never forbid the news media to give them fair coverage, but I do this with the purest of motives. I do not need money. I have a sea of money."

"The U.N. is that flush?"

"Buck, let me tell you something that few others know, and because I trust you, I know you will keep my confidence. Jonathan Stonagal named me the sole beneficiary of his estate."

Buck could not hide his surprise. That Carpathia might be named in the multibillionaire's will would have shocked no one, but sole beneficiary? That meant Carpathia now owned the major banks and financial institutions in the world.

"But, but, his family . . . ," Buck managed.

"I have already settled out of court with them. They pledge to keep silence and never again contest the will, and they get 100 million dollars each."

"That would silence me," Buck said. "But how much did they sacrifice by not getting their fair share?"

Carpathia smiled. "And you wonder why I admire you? You know that Jonathan was the wealthiest man in history. To him money was simply a commodity. He did not even carry a wallet. In his own charming way, he was frugal. He would let a lesser man pick up a dinner check, and in the next breath buy a company for hundreds of millions. It was just numbers to him."

"And what will it be for you?"

"Buck, I say this from the bottom of my heart. What this tremendous resource gives me is the opportunity to achieve my lifelong dream. I want peace. I want global disarmament. I want the peoples of the world to live as one. The world should have seen itself as one village as soon as air travel and satellite communications brought us all together decades ago. But it took the vanishings—which may have been the best thing that ever happened to this planet—to finally bring us together. When I speak, I am heard and seen nearly all over the world.

"I am not interested in personal wealth," Nicolae continued. "My history proves that. I know the value of money. I do not mind using it as a form of persuasion, if it is what motivates a person. But all I care about is mankind." Buck was sick to his stomach, and his mind was flooded with images. Carpathia staged Stonagal's "suicide" and manufactured more witnesses than any court would ever need. Now was the man trying to impress him with his altruism, his largesse?

Buck's mind flew to Chicago, and he suddenly missed Chloe. What was this? Something in him longed to simply talk with her. Of all the times for it to become crystal clear that he did not want to be "just friends," this was the worst. Was it merely Carpathia's shocking admission that made him long for something or someone comfortable and safe? There was a purity, a freshness about Chloe. How had he mistaken his feelings for her as mere fascination with a younger woman?

Carpathia stared at him. "Buck, you will never tell a living soul what I have told you today. No one must ever know. You will work for me, and you will enjoy privileges and opportunities beyond your imagination. You will think about it, but you will say yes in the end."

Buck fought to keep his mind on Chloe. He admired her father, and he was developing a deep bond with Bruce Barnes, a person with whom he would never have had anything in common before becoming a follower of Christ. But Chloe was the object of his attention, and he realized that God had planted these thoughts to help him resist the hypnotic, persuasive power of Nicolae Carpathia.

Did he love Chloe Steele? He couldn't say. He hardly knew her. Was he attracted to her? Of course. Did he want to date her, to begin a relationship with her? Absolutely.

"Buck, if you could live anywhere in the world, where would it be?"

Buck heard the question and stalled, pursing his lips to appear to be thinking about it. All he could think of was Chloe. What would she think if she knew this? Here he sat as the most-talked-about man in the world offered him a blank check, and all he could think about was a twenty-year-old college dropout from Chicago.

"Where, Buck?"

"I'm living there now," Buck said.

"Chicago?"

"Chicago."

In truth, he suddenly couldn't imagine living apart from Chloe. Her body language and responses the last couple of days told him he had alienated her somehow, but he had to believe it was not too late to turn that around. When he showed interest, she had too. When he gave an unclear signal, so did she. He would clarify his interest and hope for the best. There were still serious questions to consider, but for now all he knew was that he missed her terribly.

"Why would anyone want to live in Chicago?" Carpathia asked. "I know the airport is central, but what else does it offer? I am asking you to expand your horizons, Buck. Think Washington, London, Paris, Rome, New Babylon. You have lived here for years, and you know it is the capital of the world—at least until we relocate our headquarters."

"You asked me where I would like to live if I could live anywhere," Buck said. "Frankly, I *could* live anywhere. With the Internet and fax machines, I can file a story from the North Pole. I did not choose Chicago, but now I would not want to leave there."

"What if I offered you millions to relocate?"

Buck shrugged and chuckled. "You have a corner on the wealth of the world, and you say you are not motivated by money. Well, I have very little, and I am truly not motivated by it."

"What motivates you?"

Buck prayed quickly and silently. God, Christ, salvation, the Tribulation, love, friends, lost souls, the Bible, learning, preparing for the Glorious Appearing, New Hope Village Church, Chloe. Those were the things that motivated him, but could he say that? Should he? *God, give me the words!*

"I am motivated by truth and justice," Buck said flatly.

"Ah, and the American way!" Carpathia said. "Just like Superman!"

"More like Clark Kent," Buck said. "I'm just a reporter for a great metropolitan weekly."

"All right, you want to live in Chicago. What would you like to do, if you could do anything you wanted?"

Suddenly Buck snapped back to reality. He wished he could retreat to his private thoughts of Chloe, but he felt the pressure of the clock. This trip, strange as it had been, had been worth the grief just for that morsel about Carpathia's inheritance from Stonagal. He didn't like sparring with Nicolae, and he worried about the minefield represented by this latest question.

"Anything I wanted? I suppose I used to see myself one day in a publisher's role, you know, when I'm a little long in the tooth to be running all over the world chasing down stories. It would have been fun to have a great team of talented people and assign them, coach them, and put together a publication that showcased their abilities. I'd miss the legwork though, the research, the interviewing, and the writing."

"What if you could do both? Have the authority and the staff and the publication, and also give yourself some of the best assignments?"

"I suppose that would have been the ultimate."

"Buck, before I tell you how I can make that happen, tell me why you talk about your dreams in the past tense, as if you no longer have them."

Buck had not been careful. When he had relied on God for an answer, he had been given one. When he ventured out on his own, he had slipped. He knew the world had only seven more years, once the treaty was signed between Carpathia and Israel.

"I guess I just wonder how long this old world has," Buck said. "We're still digging out from the devastation of the disappearances, and—"

"Buck! You insult me! We are closer to world peace now than we have been in a hundred years! My humble proposals have found such receptive ears that I believe we are about to usher in an almost utopian global society! Trust me! Stay with me! Join me! You can fulfill all your dreams! You are not motivated by money? Good! Neither am I. Let me offer you resources that will allow you to never think or worry about money again.

"I can offer you a position, a publication, a staff, a headquarters, and even a retreat, that will allow you to do all you have ever wanted to do and even live in Chicago."

Carpathia paused, as he always did, waiting for Buck to bite. And Buck bit.

"This I've got to hear," he said.

"Excuse me one moment, Buck," Carpathia said, and he buzzed Hattie. Apparently he signaled her in a different way than usual, because rather than answering on the intercom, she appeared at the door behind Buck. He turned to acknowledge her, and she winked at him.

"Ms. Durham," Carpathia said, "would you inform Dr. Rosenzweig, Mr. Plank, and President Fitzhugh that I am running a bit behind schedule. I am estimating ten more minutes here, another ten with Chaim and Steve, and then we will be in Washington by five."

"Very good, sir."

Rayford parked at O'Hare and hurried through the terminal to the underground control center and Earl Halliday's office. Earl had been his chief pilot for years, and Rayford had grown from being one of his best young pilots to one of his veteran stars. Rayford felt fortunate to be at a place now where he and Earl could speak in shorthand, cutting through the bureaucratic red tape and getting to the heart of matters.

Earl was waiting outside his office door and looking at his watch when Rayford approached. "Good," Earl said. "C'mon in."

"Nice to see you, too," Rayford said, tucking his cap under his arm as he sat.

Earl sat in the only other chair in his cluttered office, the one behind his desk. "We've got a problem," he began.

"Thanks for easing into it," Rayford said. "Did Edwards write me up for, what did you call it, proselytizing?"

"That's only one part of the problem. If it wasn't for that, I'd be sitting here giving you some incredible news."

"Such as?"

"First tell me if I misunderstood you. When I first came down on you about talking about God on the job, you said you had to think about it. I said if you'd just assure me you'd back off, I'd make the write-up by Edwards go away. Right?"

"Right."

"Now, when you agreed to go to Dallas today to recertify, shouldn't I have been able to assume that meant you were going to play ball?"

"Not entirely. And I suppose you're wondering how my recert went."

"I already know how it went, Ray!" Earl snapped. "Now answer my question! Are you saying you went down there to get your papers on the 'five-seven and all the while you had no intention of backing off from sounding so religious on the job?"

"I didn't say that."

"Say what you mean, then, Ray! You've never played games with me, and I'm too old for this. You hit *me* with all that church and Rapture stuff, and *I* was polite, wasn't I?"

"A little too polite."

"But I took it as a friend, just like you listen to me when I brag about my kids, right?"

"I wasn't bragging about anything."

"No, but you were excited about it. You found something that gave you comfort and helped explain your losses, and I say, great, whatever makes your boat float. You started pressing me about coming to church and reading my Bible and all that, and I told you, kindly I hope, that I considered that personal and that I would appreciate it if you'd lay off."

"And I did. Though I still pray for you."

"Well, hey, thanks. I also told you to watch it on the job, but no, you were still too new to it, still flush with the novelty of it, high as a guy who's just found the latest get-rich-quick scheme. So what do you do? You start pushing Nick Edwards, of all people. He's a comer, Ray, and people in high places here like him."

"I like him, too. That's why I care about him and his future."

"Yeah, all right, but he made it pretty clear he didn't want to hear any more, just like I did. You let up on me, so why couldn't you let up on him?"

"I thought I did."

"You thought you did." Earl pulled a file from his drawer and fingered his way to a certain page. "Then you deny telling him, and I quote, 'I don't care what you think of me'?"

"That's a little out of context, but, no, I wouldn't deny the spirit of that. All I was saying was that—"

"I know what you were saying, Ray, all right, because you said it to me, too! I told you I didn't want to see you become one of these wild-eyed fanatics who thinks he's better than everybody else and tries to get 'em saved. You said you just cared about me, which I appreciate, but I said you were getting close to losing my respect."

"And I said I didn't care."

"Well, can't you see how insulting that is?"

"Earl, how can I insult you when I care enough about your eternal soul to risk our friendship? I told Nick the same thing I told you, that what people feel about me isn't that important anymore. Part of me still cares, sure. Nobody wants to be seen as a fool. But if I don't tell you about Christ just because I'm worried about what you'll think of me, what kind of friend would I be?"

Earl sighed and shook his head, staring at the file again. "So, you contend that Nick took you out of context, but everything you just said is right here in this report."

"It is?"

"It is."

Rayford cocked his head. "What do you know about that? He heard me. He got the point."

"He certainly must not have agreed with the point. Otherwise, why this?" Earl shut the folder and slapped it.

"Earl, I was right where you and Nick are the night before the disappearances. I—"

"I've heard all this," Earl said.

"I'm just saying I understand your position. I was almost estranged from my wife because I thought she had become a fanatic."

"You told me."

"But my point now is that she *had* become a fanatic. She was right! She was proven right!"

"Rayford, if you want to preach, why don't you get out of aviation and into the ministry?"

"Are you firing me?"

"I hope I don't have to."

"Do you want me to apologize to Nicky, tell him I realized I pushed him too far but that my intentions were good?"

"I wish it was that easy."

"Isn't that what you offered the other day?"

"Yes! And I upheld my end of the bargain. I have not copied this file to Personnel or to my superiors, and I told Nicky I wouldn't. I said I would keep it, that it would become a permanent part of my personal file on you as my subordinate—"

"Which means nothing."

"Of course, you and I know that, and Nick is no dummy either. But it seemed to satisfy him. I assumed that your going to Dallas for recert was your way of telling me you heard what I was saying and that we were helping each other out."

Rayford nodded. "I had planned to be more judicious and try to be sure I didn't get you into trouble defending me for my actions."

"I didn't mind doing this, Ray. You're worth it. But you turned around and pulled the same stunt this morning. What were you thinking?"

Rayford flinched and sat back. He set his hat on the desk and held out both hands, palms up. "This morning? What are you talking about? I thought it went well, perfect in fact. Didn't I pass?"

Earl leaned across the desk and scowled. "You didn't pull the same thing with your examiner this morning that you've pulled with me and Nick and every other first officer you've worked with for the past few weeks?"

"Talk to him about God, you mean?"

"Yes!"

"No! In fact, I felt a little guilty about it. I said hardly anything to him. He was pretty severe, giving me the usual prattle about what he was and wasn't there for."

"You didn't preach at him?"

Rayford shook his head, trying to remember if he had done or said anything that could be misconstrued. "No. I didn't hide my Bible. Usually it's in my flight bag, but I had it out when I first met him, because I'd been reading it in the van. Hey, are you sure this complaint didn't come from the van driver? He saw me reading and asked about it, and we discussed what had happened."

"Your usual."

Rayford nodded. "But I didn't get any negative reaction from him."

"Neither did I. This complaint comes from your examiner."

"I don't understand it," Rayford said. "You believe me, don't you, Earl?"

"I wish I did," Earl said. "Now don't give me that look. I know we've been friends a long time, and I never once thought you lied to me. Remember that time you voluntarily grounded yourself because you didn't think your flight was going out and you'd had a few drinks?"

"I even offered to pay for another pilot."

"I know. But what am I supposed to think now, Ray? You say you didn't hassle this guy. I want to believe you. But you've done it to me and to Nick and to others. I gotta think you did it this morning, too."

"Well, I'm going to have to talk with this guy," Rayford said.

"No, you're not."

"What, I can't confront my accuser? Earl, I didn't say a word to the man about God. I wish I had, especially if I'm going to have to take grief for it. I want to know why he said that. It had to be a misunderstanding, some secondhand complaint from the van driver, but like I say, I didn't sense any resistance from him. He must have said something to the examiner, though. Otherwise, where would the examiner even get the idea that I've done this before, unless the Bible just set him off?"

"I can't imagine the van driver having any contact with the examiner. Why would he, Ray?"

"I'm at a loss, Earl. I'm not sure I would have apologized if I had legitimately been in trouble for this, so I sure can't apologize for something I didn't do."

Buck recalled Rosenzweig telling him how the president had offered to come to New York to meet with Carpathia, but out of his vast humility, Nicolae had insisted on going to Washington. Now Carpathia casually has his personal assistant send word that he'll be late? Had he planned this? Was he systematically letting everyone know where they stood with him?

A few minutes later Hattie knocked and entered.

"Mr. Secretary-General," she said, "President Fitzhugh is sending *Air Force One* for you."

"Oh, tell him that will not be necessary," Carpathia said.

"Sir, he said it's already in the air and that you should come at your leisure. The pilot will let the White House know when you're on your way."

"Thank you Ms. Durham," Carpathia said. And to Buck, "What a nice man! You have met him?"

Buck nodded. "My first Newsmaker of the Year subject."

"His first or second time winning?"

"His second." Buck marveled anew at the encyclopedic memory

of the man. Was there any doubt who the subject of this year's Newsmaker would be? It was an assignment Buck did not relish.

———————

Earl shifted nervously. "Well, let me tell you, this comes at the worst possible time. The new *Air Force One,* which is scheduled to go into service next week, is a seven-five-seven."

Rayford was nonplussed. The note from Hattie Durham, saying the same thing, was still in his pocket.

SEVEN

RAYFORD shifted in his chair and watched his chief pilot's face. "I had heard that, yes," he hedged. "Is there anyone in America who hasn't heard about the new plane? I wouldn't mind seeing it, with everything they say is in it."

"It's top of the line, for sure," Earl said. "Absolute latest in technology, communications, security, and accommodations."

"You're the second person who's reminded me about that plane today. What's the point?"

"The point is, the White House has contacted our brass. Seems they think it's time their current pilot be put out to pasture. They want us to recommend a new guy. The people in Dallas narrowed a list to a half dozen senior pilots, and it came to me because your name is on it."

"Not interested."

"Not so fast! How can you say that? Who wouldn't want to fly one of the most advanced planes in the world, one outfitted like that, for the most powerful man on earth? Or I guess I should say the *second* most powerful, now that we've got this Carpathia guy at the U.N."

"Simple. I'd have to move to Washington."

"What's keeping you here? Is Chloe going back to school?"

"No."

"Then she's mobile too. Or does she have a job?"

"She's looking for one."

"Then let her find one in Washington. The job pays twice what you're making now, and you're already in the top 5 percent at Pan-Con."

"Money doesn't mean that much to me," Rayford said.

"Get off it!" Earl snapped. "Who calls me first when new numbers are in the air?"

"It's just not true of me anymore, Earl. And you know why."

"Yeah, spare me the sermon. But, Ray, the financial freedom to get a bigger, nicer place, run in different circles—"

"It's the circle I'm running in that's keeping me in Chicago. My church."

"Ray, the salary—"

"I don't care about the money. It's just Chloe and me now, remember?"

"Sorry."

"If anything, we ought to be downsizing. We've got more house than we need, and I've certainly got more money than I can spend."

"Then do it for the challenge! No regular route, a staff of first officers and navigators. You'll fly all over the world, a different place every time. It's an accomplishment, Ray."

"You said there were five other names."

"There are, and they're all good men. But if I lobby for you, you've got it. The problem is, I can't lobby for you with this Nick Edwards thing in the file."

"You said it was only in your file."

"It is, but with this morning's snafu, I can't risk hiding it. What if I get you the White House assignment and that examiner squawks? As soon as that gets out, Edwards sees it and corroborates the story. No assignment for you, and I look like an idiot for burying the complaint and championing you. End of story."

"It's the end of the story anyway," Rayford said. "I can't move."

Earl stood. "Rayford," he said slowly, "calm down and listen to me. Open your mind a little. Let me tell you what I'm hearing, and then just give me one chance to persuade you."

Rayford started to protest, but Earl cut him off.

"Please! I can't make your decision for you, and I won't try. But you have to let me finish. Even though I don't agree with your take on the disappearances, I'm happy for you that you've found some comfort in religion."

"It's not—"

"Ray, I know. I know. I've listened to you and I've heard you. To you it's not religion, it's Jesus Christ. Did I listen well, or what? I admire that you've given yourself to this. You're devout. I don't doubt you. But you don't just thumb your nose at an assignment that a thousand pilots would die for. Frankly, I'm not entirely sure you'd have to relocate. How often do you see a president of the United States traveling on a Sunday? Surely not more than you fly Sundays now."

"Because of seniority, I hardly ever fly Sundays."

"You can assign someone else to fly Sundays for you. You'll be the captain, the senior guy, in charge, the boss. You won't have me to answer to anymore."

"I'll do it!" Rayford said, smiling. "I'm kidding."

"Of course, it would make more sense for you to live in Washington, but I'll bet if your only condition is living in Chicago, they'd do it."

"No possible way."

"Why?"

"Because my church is not just about Sundays. We meet frequently. I'm close to the pastor. We meet almost every day."

"And you can't see living without that."

"I can't."

"Ray, what if this is a phase? What if you eventually lose your zeal? I'm not saying you're a phony or that you're going to turn your back on what you've found. I'm just saying the novelty might wear off, and you might be able to work somewhere else if you can get back to Chicago on the weekends."

"Why is this so important to you, Earl?"

"You don't know?"

"I don't."

"Because it's something I've dreamed of all my life," Earl said. "I kept up on all the latest certifications all my years in this position, and I've applied for the pilot's job with every new president."

"I never knew that."

"Of course you didn't. Who would admit that and let the world know he got his guts ripped out every four or eight years, seeing other guys get the job? Your getting it would be the next best thing. I could enjoy it vicariously."

"For that reason alone I wish I was free to take it."

Earl sat back down. "Well, thanks for that table scrap."

"I didn't mean it that way, Earl. I'm serious."

"I know you are. Truth is, I know a couple of the other yokels on the list, and I wouldn't let them drive my car."

"I thought you said they were good men."

"I'm just trying to tell you that if you don't take this, someone else will."

"Earl, I really don't think—"

Earl held up a hand. "Ray, do me a favor, will you? Will you not decide right now? I mean, I know you've pretty much already decided, but would you hold off telling me officially until you've slept on it?"

"I'll pray about it," Rayford conceded.

"I thought you might."

"Are you forbidding me from calling that examiner?"

"Absolutely. You want to file a grievance, do it on paper, through channels, the right way."

"You sure you want to recommend a guy you don't believe for a job like this?"

"If you tell me you didn't pressure the guy, I have to believe you."

"I didn't even broach the subject, Earl."

"This is crazy." Earl shook his head.

"Who did the complaint go to?"

"My secretary."

"From?"

"From his secretary, I guess."

"Can I see it?"

"I shouldn't."

"Let me see it, Earl. What do you think, I'm going to turn you in?"

Earl buzzed his secretary. "Francine, bring me your notes on the complaint you got from Dallas this morning." She brought him a single typed sheet. Earl read it and slid it across the desk to Rayford. It read:

Took a call at 11:37 A.M. from a woman who identified herself as Jean Garfield, secretary to Pan-Con Certification Examiner Jim Long of Dallas. Asked how to go about lodging a complaint of religious harassment against Rayford Steele due to his pressuring Long during his recert this A.M. Told her I would get back to her. She did not leave a number, but said she would call back later.

Rayford held up the paper. "Earl, you're a better detective than this."

"What do you mean?"

"This smells."

"You don't think it's legit?"

"First of all, my guy had a two-syllable last name on his ID badge. And when was the last time you remember an examiner having a secretary?"

Earl made a face. "Good call."

"Speaking of calls," Rayford said, "I'd like to know where that call came from. How hard would that be to determine?"

"Not hard. Francine! Call security for me, please."

"Would you mind asking her to check something else for me?" Rayford said. "Ask her to call Personnel and see if we have a Jim Long or a Jean Garfield working for Pan-Con."

"If you do not mind," Carpathia said, "I would now like to ask your friends to join us."

Now, already? Buck wondered. *Just in time for the big news, whatever it is?*

"This is your show," Buck said, surprised at Carpathia's pained expression. "Your meeting, I mean. Sure, invite them in."

Buck didn't know whether it was just his imagination, but it seemed both Steve Plank and Chaim Rosenzweig had bemused, knowing looks when they entered, trailed by Hattie. She set a chair from the conference table on the other side of Buck, and the men sat. Hattie left again.

"Mr. Williams has a prerequisite," Carpathia announced, to the low murmur from Plank and Rosenzweig. "He must be headquartered in Chicago."

"That just helps narrow it down," Dr. Rosenzweig said. "Does it not?"

"It does indeed," Carpathia said. Buck glanced at Plank, who was nodding. The secretary-general turned toward Buck. "Here is my offer: You become president and publisher of the *Chicago Tribune,* which I shall acquire from the Wrigley family within the next two months. I will rename it *The Midwest Tribune* and publish it under the auspices of Global Community Enterprises. The headquarters will remain Tribune Tower in Chicago. Along with your job comes a limousine with driver, a personal valet, whatever staff you deem necessary, a home on the North Shore with domestic help, and a retreat home on Lake Geneva in southern Wisconsin. Beyond naming the publication and the publishing

company, I will not intrude on your decision making. You will
have complete freedom to run the paper any way you wish." His
voice took a tone of sarcasm. "With your twin towers of truth
and justice undergirding every word."

Buck wanted to laugh aloud. It didn't surprise him that Carpathia could afford such a purchase, but there was no way a man
so visible could hide behind a publishing company name and
break every rule of journalistic ethics by owning a major media
outlet while serving as secretary-general of the United Nations.

"You'll never get away with it," Buck said. He kept silent
about the real issue: that Carpathia would never give anyone in
his charge complete freedom unless he believed he had total control of their mind.

"That will be *my* problem," Carpathia said.

"But with complete freedom," Buck said, "I would be your
problem too. I am devoted to the tenet that the public has a right
to know. So the first investigative piece I assign, or write myself,
would be about ownership of the publication."

"I would welcome the publicity," Carpathia said. "What would
be wrong with the United Nations owning a paper dedicated to
news of the global community?"

"You wouldn't own it personally?"

"That is semantics. If it would be more appropriate for the
U.N. to own it than for me, I would donate the money, or buy it
and donate the company to the U.N."

"But then the *Tribune* becomes a house organ, an in-house
sheet promoting the interests of the U.N."

"Which makes it legal."

"But which also makes it impotent as an independent news
voice."

"That will be up to you."

"Are you serious? You would allow your own publication to
criticize you? To take issue with the United Nations?"

"I welcome the accountability. My motives are pure, my goals
are peaceful, and my audience is global."

Buck turned in frustration to Steve Plank, knowing full well
that Steve was one who had already proven susceptible to Carpathia's power. "Steve, you're his media adviser! Tell him there's no
credibility in such a venture! It would not be taken seriously."

"It wouldn't be taken seriously at first by other news media,
Buck," Steve acknowledged. "But it won't be long before Global
Community Publishing owns those media services too."

"So by monopolizing the publishing industry, you eliminate the competition and the public doesn't know the difference?"

Carpathia nodded. "That is one way to phrase it. And if my motives were anything but ideal, I would have a problem with it too. But what is wrong with controlling global news when we are headed toward peace and harmony and unity?"

"Where is the power to think for oneself?" Buck asked. "Where is the forum for diverse ideas? What happens to the court of public opinion?"

"The court of public opinion," Steve said, "is calling for more of what the secretary-general has to offer."

Buck was defeated, and he knew it. He couldn't expect Chaim Rosenzweig to understand the ethics of journalism, but when a veteran like Steve Plank could support a puff sheet for a benevolent dictator, what hope was there?

"I can't imagine being involved in such a venture," Buck said.

"I love this man!" Carpathia exulted, and Plank and Rosenzweig smiled and nodded. "Think about it. Mull it over. Somehow I will make it legal enough to be acceptable even to you, and then I will not take no for an answer. I want the paper, and I am going to get it. I want you to run it, and I am going to get you. Freedom, Buck Williams. Total freedom. The day you believe I am intruding, you may quit with full pay."

———

Having thanked Earl Halliday for his confidence and promising not to declare himself just yet—though Rayford could not imagine taking the job—he stood in the terminal at an otherwise deserted bank of pay phones. Francine, Earl's secretary, had confirmed that there was no Jean Garfield working for Pan-Con. And while there were no fewer than six James Longs, four of them were baggage handlers and the other two were midlevel bureaucrats. None worked in Dallas, none was an examiner, and none had a secretary.

"Who's out to get you?" Earl had asked.

"I can't imagine."

Francine reported that the call she took that morning had been traced to New York. "It'll take them a few hours to get an exact phone number," she said, but Rayford knew in a flash who it was. He couldn't be sure *why* she would do it, but only Hattie Durham would pull a stunt like that. Only she would have access to Pan-Con people who would know where he was and what he was doing that morning. And what was that business about *Air Force One?*

He called information and got the number for the United Nations. After reaching the switchboard and then the administrative offices, he finally got Hattie, the fourth person to pick up the phone.

"Rayford Steele here," he said flatly.

"Oh, hi, Captain Steele!" The brightness in her voice made him cringe.

"I give up," Rayford said. "Whatever you're doing, you win."

"I don't follow."

"C'mon, Hattie, don't play dumb."

"Oh! My note! I just thought it was funny, because I was talking to a friend in Pan-Con traffic the other day, and she mentioned that my old friend was recerting on the 757 this morning in Dallas. Wasn't it funny that I had mail waiting for you? Wasn't that just the funniest?"

"Yeah, hilarious. What does it mean?"

"The message? Oh, nothing. Surely you knew that, right? Everybody knows the new *Air Force One* is going to be a 'fifty-seven, don't they?"

"Yeah, so why remind me?"

"It was a joke, Rayford. I was kidding you about recertifying as if you were going to be the president's new pilot. Don't you get it?"

Was it possible? Could she be that naïve and innocent? Could she have done something that vapid and have been so coincidentally lucky? He wanted to ask how she knew he would be offered the job, but if she didn't know it, he certainly did not want to tell her.

"I get it. Very funny. So what was the phony complaint all about?"

"The phony complaint?"

"Don't waste my time, Hattie. You're the only person who knew where I was and what I was doing, and I come back to some bogus charge about religious harassment."

"Oh, that!" she laughed. "That was just a wild guess. You had an examiner, didn't you?"

"Yes, but I didn't—"

"And you had to give him the big pitch, didn't you?"

"No."

"Come now, Rayford. You gave it to me, to your own daughter, to Cameron Williams, to Earl Halliday, to just about everybody you've worked with since. Really? You didn't preach to the examiner?"

"As a matter of fact, I didn't."

"Well, OK, so I guessed wrong. But it's still funny, don't you think? And the odds were with me. What would you have thought if you *had* come on strong with him and then came back to a complaint? You would have apologized to him, and he would have denied it. I love practical jokes! C'mon, give me some credit."

"Hattie, if you're trying to get back at me for how I treated you, I suppose I deserve it."

"No, Rayford, it's not that! I'm over it. I'm over you. If we'd had a relationship, I would never be where I am today, and believe me, I never want to be anywhere else. But this wasn't revenge. It was just supposed to be funny. If it doesn't amuse you, I'm sorry."

"It got me into trouble."

"Oh, come on! How long would it take to check out a story like that?"

"All right, you win. Any more surprises for me?"

"Don't think so, but stay on your toes."

Rayford didn't buy a word of it. Carpathia had to know about the White House offer. Hattie's note and that offer, and what her little joke almost did to scotch the deal, were too coincidental to be her lame attempt at a practical joke. Rayford was not in a good mood when he returned to the parking garage. He only hoped Chloe was not still upset. If she was, maybe both of them could cool down before the meeting that night.

Chaim Rosenzweig put a gnarled hand on Buck's knee. "I urge you to accept this most prestigious position. If you do not accept it, someone else will, and it will not be as good a paper."

Buck was not about to argue with Chaim. "Thank you," he said. "I have a lot to think about." But accepting the offer was not something he was going to consider. How he longed to talk about this, first to Chloe and then to Bruce and Rayford.

When Hattie Durham interrupted apologetically and moved to the desk to speak quietly with Carpathia, Steve began to whisper something to Buck. But Buck was blessed with the ability to discern what was worth listening to and what was worthy of ignoring. Right now he decided it would be more profitable to eavesdrop on Hattie and Nicolae than to pay attention to Steve. He leaned toward Steve, pretending to listen.

Buck knew Steve would be trying to sell him on the job, to assure him that it was Steve himself who lobbied for it, to admit that as a journalist it sounded crazy at first, but that this was a new world, blah, blah, blah. And so Buck nodded and maintained some eye contact, but he was listening to Hattie Durham and Carpathia.

"I just took a call from the target," she said.

"Yes? And?"

"It didn't take him long to figure it out."

"And *Air Force One?*"

"I don't think he has a clue."

"Good work. And the other?"

"No response yet."

"Thank you, dear."

The target. That didn't sound good. The rest of it he assumed had something to do with Carpathia's ride that afternoon on the president's plane.

Carpathia turned his attention back to his guest. "At the very least, Buck, talk this over with the people who care about you. And if you think of more specific dreams you would accomplish if resources were no object, remember that you are in the driver's seat right now. You are in a seller's market. I am the buyer, and I will get the man I want."

"You make me want to turn you down, just to show I cannot be bought."

"And as I have said so many times, that is the very reason you are the man for the job. Do not make the mistake of passing up the opportunity of a lifetime just to prove a small point."

Buck felt caught. On one side of him was a man he had admired and worked with for years, a journalist with principle. On the other was a man he loved like a father, a brilliant scientist who was in many ways naïve enough to be the perfect foil, one of the pawns in an end-of-the-world chess game. Outside the door was an acquaintance he had met on an airplane when God had invaded the world. He had introduced her to Nicolae Carpathia just to show off, and look where they were now.

Directly in front of him, smiling that handsome, disarming

smile, was Carpathia himself. Of the four people Buck was dealing with that afternoon, Carpathia was the one he understood the
most. He also understood that Carpathia was the one with whom
he had the least influence. Was it too late to plead with Steve, to
warn him of what he had gotten into? Too late to rescue Hattie
from the stupidity of his introduction? Was Chaim too enamored
with the geopolitical possibilities to listen to reason and truth?

And if he did confide in any of them, would that be the end of
any hope that he could keep the truth from Carpathia—that Buck
himself was protected from his power by God?

Buck couldn't wait to get back to Chicago. His condo was
brand-new and didn't seem familiar. His friends were new too,
but there was no one in the world he trusted more. Bruce would
listen and study and pray and offer counsel. Rayford, with that
scientific, analytical, pragmatic mind, would make suggestions,
never forcing opinions.

But it was Chloe he missed the most. Was this of God? Had
God impressed her upon Buck's mind at his most vulnerable moment with Carpathia? Buck hardly knew the woman. Woman?
She was barely more than a girl, but she seemed . . . what? Mature? More than mature. Magnetic. When she listened to him, her
eyes seemed to drink him in. She understood, empathized. She
could give advice and feedback without saying a word.

There was a comfort zone with her, a feeling of safety. He had
barely touched her twice. Once to wipe from her mouth a dab of
chocolate from a cookie, and in church the morning before, just
to get her attention. And yet now, a two-hour plane ride from
her, he felt an overwhelming need to embrace her.

He couldn't do that, of course. He scarcely knew her and didn't
want to scare her away. And yet in his mind he looked forward
to the day when they felt comfortable enough to hold hands or
draw close to each other. He imagined them sitting somewhere,
just enjoying each other's company, her head on his chest, his
arm around her.

And he realized how desperately lonely he had become.

Rayford found Chloe miserable. He had decided not to tell her
yet of the events of his day. It had been too weird, and she had
apparently had a doozy of a day herself. He held her and she

wept. Rayford noticed a huge bouquet of flowers sticking out of a wastebasket.

"Those made it worse, Dad. At least my reaction showed me something—how much I cared for Buck."

"That sounds pretty analytical for you," Rayford said, regretting it as soon as it was out of his mouth.

"I can't be analytical because I'm a woman, is that it?"

"Sorry! I shouldn't have said it."

"I'm sitting here crying, so my whole response to this is emotional, right? Don't forget, Dad, five semesters on the dean's list. That's not emotional; that's analytical. I'm more like you than like Mom, remember?"

"Don't I know it. And because we are the way we are, we're still here."

"Well, I'm glad we've got each other. At least I was until you accused me of being a typical woman."

"I never said that."

"It's what you were thinking."

"Now you're a mind reader, too?"

"Yeah, I'm an emotional fortune-teller."

"I surrender," Rayford said.

"Oh, come on, Dad. Don't give up so soon. Nobody likes an easy loser."

On the plane, again coddled in first class, Buck had trouble not chuckling aloud. Publisher of the *Tribune!* In twenty years, maybe, if it wasn't owned by Carpathia and Christ wasn't returning first. Buck felt as if he had won the lottery in a society where money was useless.

After dinner he settled back and gazed at the setting sun. It had been many, many years since he had been drawn to a city because of a person. Would he be back in time to see her before tonight's meeting? If the traffic wasn't too bad, he might have enough time to talk the way he really wanted to.

Buck didn't want to scare Chloe off by being too specific, but he wanted to apologize for his waffling. He didn't want to push anything. Who knew? Maybe she had no interest. He was certain only that he did not want to be the one to close the door on any possibility. Maybe he should call her from the plane.

"Bruce offered me a job today," Chloe said.

"You're kidding," Rayford said. "What?"

"Something right up my alley. Study, research, preparation, teaching."

"Where? What?"

"At the church. He wants to 'multiply his ministry.' "

"A paid position?"

"Yep. Full time. I could work at home or at the church. He would give me assignments, help me develop curriculum, all that. He wants to go slow on the teaching part, since I'm so new at this. A lot of the people I'd be teaching have spent their lives in church and Sunday school."

"What would you teach?"

"The same things he's teaching. My research would help in his lesson preparation, too. I would eventually teach Sunday school classes and small groups. He's going to ask you and Buck to do the same, but of course he doesn't know yet what Buck's up to with his little fiancée."

"And you were prudent enough not to tell him."

"For now," Chloe said. "If Buck doesn't realize it's wrong— and maybe he doesn't—somebody needs to tell him."

"And you're signing up for the job."

"I will if no one else will. I'm the only one who knows first-hand right now."

"But don't you have just a little conflict of interest?"

"Dad, I had no idea how much I hoped that something would develop with Buck. Now I wouldn't want him if he threw himself at me."

The phone rang. Rayford answered it, then covered the mouthpiece. "Here's your chance to prove that," he said. "Buck calling from an airplane."

Chloe squinted as if trying to decide whether to be available. "Give me that," she said.

Buck was certain Rayford Steele would have told his daughter who was calling. But her hello sounded flat, and did not include his name, so he felt obligated to identify himself.

"Chloe, it's Buck! How are you?"

"I've been better."

"What's up? You sick?"

"I'm fine. Did you want something?"

"Um, yeah, I kind of wanted to see you tonight."

"Kind of?"

"Well, yeah, I mean I do. Can I?"

"I'll be seeing you at the meeting at eight, right?" she said.

"Yeah, but I was wondering if you'd have a little time before that."

"I don't know. What did you want?"

"Just to talk with you."

"I'm listening."

"Chloe, is something wrong? Am I missing something? You seem upset."

"The flowers are in the trash, if that's any hint," she said.

The flowers are in the trash, he repeated in his mind. That was an expression he hadn't heard. It must mean something to someone from her generation. He might be a famous writer, but he had sure missed that one.

"I'm sorry?" he said.

"It's a little too late for that," she said.

"I mean, I'm sorry—I missed what you were saying."

"You didn't hear me?"

"I heard you, but I don't get your meaning."

"What about 'the flowers are in the trash' do you not understand?"

Buck had been a little distant from her Friday night, but what was this? Well, she was worth the work. "Let's start with the flowers," he said.

"Yes, let's," she said.

"What flowers are we talking about?"

Rayford motioned with both hands for Chloe to take it easy. He was afraid she was going to blow, and whatever was going on, she sure wasn't giving Buck an inch. If there was any truth to what Chloe was alleging, she wasn't going to help restore him this way. Maybe Buck *hadn't* thrown off all the trappings of his former life. Maybe there *were* some areas that would have to be dealt with forthrightly. But wasn't that true of all four of them in the Tribulation Force?

"I'll see you tonight, OK?" Chloe concluded. "No, not before the meeting. I don't know if I'll have time afterward or not. . . . Well, it depends on what time we get out, I guess. . . . Yes, he said eight to ten, but, Buck, do you get it that I don't really want to talk to you right now? And I don't know if I'll want to talk later. . . . Yes, see you then."

She hung up. "Ooh, that man is persistent! I'm seeing a side of him I never imagined."

"Still wish something would develop?" Rayford said.

She shook her head. "Whatever was there has been snuffed out now."

"But it still hurts."

"It sure does. I just didn't realize how much I was getting my hopes up."

"I'm sorry, honey."

She sank to the couch and rested her face in her hands. "Dad, I know we didn't owe each other anything, but don't you think he and I talked enough and connected enough that I should have known if there was someone in his life?"

"Seems like it, yes."

"Did I just totally misread him? Does he think it's OK to say he's attracted to me without telling me he's unavailable?"

"I can't imagine."

Rayford didn't know what else to say. If there was anything to what Chloe was saying, he was beginning to lose respect for Buck too. He seemed like such a good guy. Rayford only hoped they could help him.

———————

Buck was wounded. He still longed to see Chloe, but it was not the idealistic dream he had imagined. He had done something or not done something, and it was going to take more than a little apology over mixed signals to get to the bottom of it.

The flowers are in the trash, he thought. Whatever in the world that meant.

EIGHT

Buck's condo door nudged a stack of boxes when he entered. He'd have to send Alice a thank-you note. He only wished he had time to start arranging his home office, but he had to get going if he hoped to catch Chloe before the meeting.

He arrived at New Hope about half an hour early and saw Rayford's car parked next to Bruce's. *Good,* he thought, *everybody's here.* He glanced at his watch. Had he forgotten the time change? Was he late? He hurried into the office and knocked on Bruce's door as he stepped in. Bruce and Rayford looked up awkwardly. It was just the two of them.

"I'm sorry, I guess I'm a little early."

"Yeah, Buck," Bruce said. "We'll be a little while and we'll see you at eight, all right?"

"Sure. I'll just talk with Chloe. She here?"

"She'll be along a little later," Rayford said.

"OK, I'll just wait for her out here."

"Well, first of all," Bruce told Rayford, "congratulations. Regardless of what you decide to do, that is a fantastic honor and an accomplishment. I can't imagine many pilots turning down that offer."

Rayford sat back. "Truthfully, I haven't spent much time thinking of it that way. I guess I should be grateful."

Bruce nodded. "I guess you should. Did you want advice, or just an ear? Obviously, I'll pray with you about it."

"I'm open to advice."

"Well, I feel so inadequate, Rayford. I appreciate that you want to stay here in Chicago, but you also have to consider whether this opportunity is from God. I want to stay around here too, but I feel him leading me to travel, to start more small groups, to visit Israel. I know you're not staying here just for me, but—"

"That's part of it, Bruce."

"And I appreciate that, but who knows how long I'll be here?"

"We need you, Bruce. I think it's clear God has you here for a reason."

"I suppose Chloe told you that I'm looking for more teachers."

"She did. And she's excited about it. And I'm willing to learn."

"Normally a church wouldn't put brand-new believers in the positions of leaders or teachers, but there's no alternative now. I'm virtually a new believer myself. I know you'd make a good teacher, Rayford. The problem is, I can't shake the thought that this opportunity with the president is a unique one you should seriously consider. Imagine the impact you might have on the president of the United States."

"Oh, I don't think the president and his pilot interact much, if at all."

"He doesn't interview a new pilot?"

"I doubt it."

"You'd think he'd want to get to know the man who has his life in his hands every time that plane leaves the ground."

"I'm sure he trusts the people who make that decision."

"But surely there will be occasions when you might interact."

Rayford shrugged. "Maybe."

"President Fitzhugh, strong and independent as he is, must be as personally frightened and searching as any private citizen. Think of the privilege of telling the leader of the free world about Christ."

"And losing my job over it," Rayford said.

"You'd have to pick your spots, of course. But the president lost several relatives in the Rapture. What was it he said when asked what he made of it? Something about being sure it wasn't God's doing, because he had always believed in God."

"You're talking about this as if I'm naturally going to take the job."

"Rayford, I can't make your decisions for you, but I need you to remember: Your loyalty now is not to this church or to the Tribulation Force or to me. Your loyalty is to Christ. If you decide not to pursue this opportunity, you had better be dead sure it's not of God."

It was just like Bruce, Rayford thought, to put a whole new spin on this. "Do you think I should say anything to Chloe or Buck?"

"We're all in this together," Bruce said.

"Meanwhile," Rayford said, "let me bounce something else off you. How do you feel about romance during this point of history?"

Bruce suddenly looked uncomfortable. "Good question," he said. "Frankly, I know why you're asking." Rayford doubted that. "I know the loneliness you must feel. At least you have Chloe for companionship, but you must have that same aching emptiness that I feel after losing my wife. I've thought about whether I'm to go on alone through the next seven or so years. I don't like the prospect, but I know I'll be busy. To be very transparent with you, I suppose I harbor some hope that God might bring someone into my life. Right now is too soon, of course. I'll grieve and mourn my wife for a long time, as if she were dead. I know she's in heaven, but she's dead to me. There are days when I feel so alone I can hardly breathe."

This was as self-revelatory as Bruce had been since telling his own story of having missed the Rapture, and Rayford was stunned that he had been the one to instigate it. He had merely been asking for Chloe's sake. She had become enamored of Buck, and if that wasn't going to work out, should she put herself in a situation where someone else might come along, or was that inappropriate, given the few years left before Christ's return again?

"I'm just curious about the logistics," Rayford explained. "If two people fell in love, what should they do about it? Does the Bible say anything about marriage during this period?"

"Not specifically," Bruce said, "as far as I can tell. But it doesn't prohibit it, either."

"And kids? Would it be prudent for a couple to bring children in this world now?"

"I haven't thought about that," Bruce said. "Would you want another child at your age?"

"Bruce! *I'm* not looking to marry again. I'm thinking of Chloe. I'm not saying she has any prospects, but if she did . . ."

Bruce squeaked back in his chair. "Imagine having a baby now," he said. "You wouldn't have to think about junior high school, let alone high school or college. You would be raising that child, preparing him or her for the return of Christ in just a few years."

"You'd also be guaranteeing a child a life of fear and danger and a 75 percent chance of dying during the judgments to come."

Bruce rested his chin in his hand, elbow on the desk. "True enough," he said. "I'd have to advise a lot of caution, prayer, and soul-searching before considering that."

Buck had never been good at waiting. He browsed the shelves of the sitting area outside Bruce's office. Apparently this was where the former pastor had stored his less frequently used reference works. There appeared to be dozens of books on esoteric Old Testament themes. Buck leafed through a few of them, finding them dry.

Then he came across a church photo directory dated two years earlier. There, under the B's, was a picture of a younger, longer-haired Bruce Barnes. He looked a bit fuller in the face, wore a pasted-on smile, and surrounding him were his wife and children. What a treasure Bruce had lost! His wife was pleasant looking and plump, with a weary but genuine smile.

On the next page was Dr. Vernon Billings, the now-departed senior pastor. He looked at least in his midsixties and was shown with his petite wife and three children and their respective spouses. Bruce had already said that the entire family had been raptured. Pastor Billings had a Henry Fonda-ish quality, with deep crow's feet and a crinkly smile. He looked like a man Buck would have enjoyed knowing.

Buck flipped to the other end of the directory and found the Steeles. There was Rayford in his pilot's uniform, looking pretty much the same as he did today with perhaps slightly less gray in the hair and a little more definition in his face. And Irene. It was the first picture of her he had seen. She looked bright and cheery, and if you could believe the faddish study of photo-psychology, she appeared more devoted to her husband than he did to her. Her body leaned toward him. He sat rigid, straight up.

Also in the picture was Rayford Junior, identified in the caption as "Raymie, 10." He and his mother had asterisks by their names. Rayford did not. And neither did Chloe, who was listed as "18, Freshman, Stanford University, Palo Alto, California (not pictured)."

Buck flipped to the legend, which explained that an asterisk in-dicated a church member. The rest, he assumed, were mere at-tenders.

Buck looked at his watch. Ten to eight. He peered out the window to the parking lot. The Steeles' second car was there, next to Rayford's and Buck's and Bruce's. He put his hand on the glass to cut the glare and could make out Chloe behind the wheel. Ten minutes was hardly enough time to talk, but he could at least greet her and walk her inside.

As soon as Buck stepped out the door, Chloe emerged from the car and hurried toward the church. "Hey!" he said.

"Hello, Buck," she said, clearly without enthusiasm.

"Flowers still in the trash?" he tried, hoping for some clue to what was up with her.

"As a matter of fact they are," she said, brushing past him and opening the door herself. He followed her up the stairs, through the foyer, and into the offices.

"I don't think they're ready for us yet," he said, as she went directly to Bruce's door and knocked.

Apparently Bruce told her the same thing, and she backed out with an apology. Obviously Chloe would rather be anywhere but there and looking at anything but him. She had been crying, and her face was red and blotchy. He ached to reconnect with her. Something told him this was not just a mood, a part of her personality he would have to get used to. Something specific was plainly wrong, and Buck was in the middle of it. There was nothing he would rather do right then than get to the bottom of it. But that would have to wait.

Chloe sat with her arms and legs crossed, her top leg swinging.

"Look what I found," Buck said, thrusting the old church directory under her nose. She didn't even reach for it.

"Um-hm," she said.

Buck opened it to the B's and showed her Bruce's and Dr. Billings's families. Suddenly she softened, took the directory, and studied it. "Bruce's wife," she said softly. "And look at those children!"

"Your family is in there too," Buck said.

Chloe took her time getting to the S's, studying page after page of pictures as if looking for anyone else she recognized. "Went to high school with him," she said idly. "She and I were in the same fourth grade. Mrs. Schultz was my freshman P.E. teacher."

When she finally got to her own family she was overcome. Her face contorted and she stared, the tears coming. "Raymie when he was ten," she managed. Buck instinctively put a hand on her shoulder, and she stiffened. "Please don't do that."

"Sorry," he said, and the office door opened.

• • •

"Ready," Rayford said. He noticed that Buck looked sheepish and Chloe looked terrible. He hoped she hadn't started in on him already.

"Daddy, look," she said, standing and handing him the directory.

Rayford's throat tightened and he sucked in a huge breath when he saw the photo. He sighed painfully. It was almost too much to take.

He closed the directory and handed it to Buck, but at the same time he heard Bruce's chair squeak. "What're you guys looking at?"

"Just this," Buck said, showing him the cover and trying to replace it in the bookshelf. But Bruce reached for it. "It's a couple of years old," Buck added.

"About a month after we started coming here," Rayford said.

Bruce flipped right to the picture of his family, stood studying it for several seconds, and said, "You're in here, Rayford?"

"Yes," Rayford said simply, and Buck noticed him trying to get Chloe to move into the office.

Bruce turned to the Steele picture and nodded, smiling. He brought the directory back into the office with him, tucked it under his Bible and notebook, and opened the meeting in prayer.

Bruce started a little emotionally, but he soon warmed to his topic. He was flipping from Revelation to Ezekiel and Daniel and back again, comparing the prophetic passages to what was happening in New York and the rest of the world.

"Any of you hear the news about the two witnesses in Jerusalem today?"

Buck shook his head, and Rayford did the same. Chloe did not respond. She was not taking notes either or asking any questions. "A reporter said that a little band of a half dozen thugs tried to charge the two, but they all wound up burned to death."

"Burned?" Buck said.

"No one knew where the fire came from," Bruce said. "But we know, don't we?"

"Do we?"

"Look at Revelation 11. The angel tells the apostle John, " 'And I will give power to my two witnesses, and they will prophesy one thousand two hundred and sixty days, clothed in sackcloth. These are the two olive trees and the two lampstands standing before the God of the earth. And if anyone wants to harm them, fire proceeds from their mouth and devours their enemies. And if anyone wants to harm them, he must be killed in this manner.' "

"They breathed fire on them like dragons?"

"It's right here in the book," Bruce said.

"I'd like to see that on CNN," Buck said.

"Keep watching," Bruce said. "We'll see more than that."

Rayford wondered if he would ever get used to the things God was revealing to him. He could hardly fathom how far he'd come, how much he had accepted in less than a month. There was something about the dramatic invasion of God into humankind and into himself specifically that had changed the way he thought. From being a man who had to have everything documented, he suddenly found himself believing without question the most ludicrous news accounts, as long as they were corroborated by Scripture. And the opposite was also true: He believed everything in the Bible. Sooner or later the news would carry the same story.

Bruce turned to Buck. "How did your day go?" To Rayford, it seemed like an inside question.

"More to talk about than I can get into here," Buck said.

"No kidding," Chloe snapped. It was the first thing she had said.

Buck glanced at her and said, "I'll debrief you tomorrow, Bruce, and then we can talk about it here tomorrow night."

"Oh, let's talk about it now," Chloe said. "We're all friends here."

Rayford wished he could shush his own daughter, but she was an adult. If she wanted to press an issue, regardless of how she came across, that was her prerogative.

"You don't even know where I was today," Buck told her, clearly puzzled.

"But I know who you were with."

Rayford saw the glance Buck shot at Bruce, but he didn't understand it. Obviously, something had transpired between the two of them that wasn't public knowledge yet. Could he have told Chloe that Buck met with Carpathia?

"Did you—?" Bruce shook his head.

"I don't think you know, Chloe," Buck said. "Let me discuss it with Bruce tomorrow, and I'll bring it up for prayer in our meeting tomorrow night."

"Yeah, sure," Chloe said. "But I have a question and a prayer request for tonight."

Bruce looked at his watch. "OK, shoot."

"I'm wondering what you think about dating relationships during this time."

"You're the second person who's asked me that today," Bruce said. "We must be lonely people." Chloe snorted, then scowled at Buck.

She must assume it was Buck who asked Bruce that earlier, Rayford thought.

"Let me make that a topic for one of our sessions," Bruce said.

"How about the next one?" Chloe pressed.

"All right. We can discuss it tomorrow night."

"And can you add to it what the rules are for morality for new believers?" Chloe said.

"Excuse me?"

"Talk about how we're supposed to live, now that we call ourselves followers of Christ. You know, like morals and sex and all of that."

Buck winced. Chloe didn't sound like herself. "All right," Bruce said. "We can cover that. But I don't think it'll come as any great shock to you to know that the rules that applied before the Rapture still apply. I mean, this could be a short lesson. We're called to purity, and I'm sure it won't surprise you—"

"It might not be so obvious to all of us," Chloe said.

"We'll deal with it tomorrow night then," Bruce said. "Anything else for right now?"

Before anyone said anything or even offered closing prayer requests, Chloe said, "Nope. See you tomorrow night then." And she left.

The three men prayed, and the meeting ended awkwardly, none of them wanting to talk, as Nicolae Carpathia had put it, about the elephant in the room.

Buck arrived home frustrated. He was not used to being unable to fix something, and most maddening, he didn't even know what was wrong. He changed out of his traveling clothes and into hiking boots, khakis, denim shirt, and leather jacket. He phoned the Steeles. Rayford answered but after a few minutes came back to the phone to say that Chloe was unavailable. Buck was only guessing, but it sounded as if Rayford was as frustrated with her as he was.

"Rayford, is she standing right there?"

"That's correct."

"Do you have any idea what her problem is?"

"Not totally."

"I want to get to the bottom of it," Buck said.

"I concur with that."

"I mean tonight."

"Affirmative. Absolutely. You can try her again tomorrow."

"Rayford, are you telling me it's all right for me to come there right now?"

"Yes, you're right. I can't promise she'll be here, but try again tomorrow."

"So if I came there right now, I would not be offending you."

"Not at all. We'll expect your call tomorrow then."

"I'm on my way."

"OK, Buck. Talk to you then."

Rayford didn't like deceiving Chloe. It was almost like lying. But he had enjoyed the coded banter with Buck. He remembered a little tiff he'd had when dating Irene years before. She was very upset with him over something and told him she didn't want him to call her until he heard from her, and she stormed off.

He hadn't known what to do, but his mother gave him some advice. "You go to her right now, find her, and put the ball in her court. She can walk away from you once, but if she sends you away when you're coming after her, then you'll know she's serious. She may not know her own mind, but down deep, if I know women, I know she'd rather you pursue her than let her run."

And so, in a way, he had encouraged Buck's instinct to do the same with Chloe. He knew they weren't an item yet, but he thought they both wanted it that way. He had no idea what this other woman in Buck's life was all about, but he was sure that if Buck forced the issue, Chloe would confront him about her and find out. If Buck was living with someone, that was a problem for Rayford and Bruce as well as for Chloe. But Chloe's evidence seemed thin at best.

"So he's going to try to call me tomorrow?" Chloe said.

"That's what I told him."

"How did he react?"

"He was just clarifying."

"You sounded pretty clear."

"I tried to be."

"I'm going to bed," she said.

"Why don't we talk awhile first?"

"I'm tired, Dad. And I'm talked out." She moved toward the stairs.

Rayford stalled her. "So, will you take his call tomorrow, you think?"

"I doubt it. I want to see how he reacts to Bruce's teaching tomorrow night."

"How do you think he'll react?"

"Dad! How would I know? All I know is what I saw this morning. Now let me go to bed."

"I just want to hear you out on this, hon. Talk to me."

"I'll talk to you tomorrow."

"Well, would you stay up and talk to me if I talked about me and my job situation instead of you and Buck?"

"Don't put me and Buck in the same sentence, Dad. And no, unless you're getting fired or switching jobs or something, I'd really rather do it another time."

Rayford knew he could snag her attention with what had happened to him that day, from the note from Hattie to the bogus harassment charge to the meeting with Earl Halliday. But he was more in a mood to talk about all that than she was. "Want to help me tidy up the kitchen?"

"Daddy, the kitchen is spotless. Anything you need done around here I'll do tomorrow, all right?"

"Coffee timer set for the morning?"

"Programmed since the beginning of time, Dad. What's with you?"

"I'm just feeling a little lonely. Not ready to turn in yet."

"If you need me to stay up with you I will, Dad. But why don't you just watch some TV and relax?"

Rayford couldn't delay her any longer. "I'll do that," he said. "I'll be right down here in the living room with the TV on, OK?"

She gave him a funny look and matched his tone. "And I'll be right up in my room at the top of the stairs with my light off, OK?"

He nodded.

She shook her head. "Now that we have both reported in and we know where the other will be and what we'll be doing, am I excused?"

"You're excused."

Rayford waited until Chloe started up the stairs to turn on the front porch light. Buck knew the address and the general area, but he had not been there before.

The news was ending and only talk shows coming on, but Rayford didn't care. He was sitting there only as a diversion anyway. He glanced through the curtains, looking for Buck's car. "Dad?" Chloe called down. "Could you turn that down a little? Or watch in your room?"

"I'll turn it down," he said, as headlights briefly flooded the living room and came up the drive. Before he adjusted the volume, he hurried to the door and intercepted Buck before he rang the bell. "I'm going upstairs to bed," he whispered. "Give me a second and then ring the bell. I'll be in the shower, and she'll have to answer it."

Rayford shut and deadbolted the door. He turned the television off and went upstairs.

As he passed Chloe's room he heard, "Daddy, you didn't have to turn it off. Just down."

"It's all right," he said. "I'm going to take a shower and get to bed."

" 'Night, Dad."

" 'Night, Chlo'."

Rayford stood in the shower with the water off and the master bath door open. As soon as he heard the doorbell, he turned on the water. He heard Chloe call, "Dad! Someone's at the door!"

"I'm in the shower!"

"Oh, Dad!"

This was a great idea! Buck thought, impressed that Rayford Steele trusted him enough to let him talk to his daughter when she obviously had something against him.

He waited a moment and rang the bell again. From inside he heard, "Just a minute, I'm coming!"

Chloe's face appeared in the tiny window in the middle of the ornate door. She rolled her eyes. "Buck!" she called through the closed door. "Call me tomorrow, will you? I was already in bed!"

"I need to talk to you!" Buck said.

"Not tonight."

"Yes, tonight," he said. "I'm not leaving till you talk to me."

"You're not?" she said.

"No, I'm not."

Chloe called his bluff. The porch light went out, and he heard her trotting up the stairs. He couldn't believe it. She was tougher than he thought. But he had said he wasn't leaving, and so he could not. If nothing else, Buck was a man of his word. Stubborn was more like it. But that had made him the journalist he was.

He still hadn't shaken the longing for Chloe that had come over-him that afternoon in New York. He'd wait her out, he decided. He'd be on her stoop in the morning when she got up, if that's what it took.

Buck moved to the step at the edge of the porch and sat with his back to the front door, leaning on one of the stately pillars. He knew she would be able to see him if she came back to check. She'd probably be listening for his car, and she wouldn't hear a thing.

"Daddy!" Chloe called from Rayford's bedroom door. "Are you about done?"

"Not really! What's up?"

"Buck Williams is at the door, and he won't leave!"

"What do you want me to do about it?"

"Get rid of him!"

"You get rid of him! He's your problem!"

"You're my dad! It's your duty!"

"Did he harm you? Has he threatened you?"

"No! Now, Dad!"

"*I* don't want him to leave, Chloe! If *you* do, *you* send him away."

"I'm going to bed!" she said.

"So am I!"

Rayford turned off the shower and heard Chloe slam his bed-room door. Then hers. Would she really go to bed and leave Buck on the porch? Would Buck stay? Rayford tiptoed to his door and opened it far enough to be able to keep tabs on Chloe. Her door was still shut. Rayford slipped into bed and didn't move, listen-ing. It was all he could do to keep from chuckling aloud. He had been put on the short list of candidates to be the new pilot for the president of the United States, and here he was, eavesdropping on his own daughter. It was the most fun he'd had in weeks.

Buck hadn't realized how chilly the night was until he had sat next to that cold pillar for a few minutes. His jacket squeaked when he moved, and he raised the fur-lined collar around his neck. The smell reminded him of the many places in the world he had dragged this old bomber jacket. More than once he had thought he'd die in the thing.

Buck stretched his legs in front of him and crossed them at the ankles, suddenly realizing how tired he was. If he had to sleep on this porch, he would.

Then, in the stillness, he heard the faint creaking of the steps inside. Chloe was creeping down to see if he was still there. If it had been Rayford, the steps would have been louder and more sure. Rayford would probably have told him to give it up and go home, that they would try to deal with the problem later. Buck heard the floor near the door creak. Just for effect, he tilted his head toward the pillar and rearranged his posture as if settling in for a snooze.

The footsteps back up the stairs were not so muffled. What now?

Rayford had heard Chloe open her door and make her way down the stairs in the darkness. Now she was on her way back up. She whipped her door open and slapped at the light switch. Rayford leaned so he could see her emerge, which she did a moment later just before she turned out the light. Her hair was pinned atop her head, and she wore her floor-length terry cloth robe. She turned on the light at the top of the stairs and descended with a purpose. If Rayford had to guess, he didn't think she was running the man off.

Buck saw his shadow on the lawn and knew a light was on behind him, but he didn't want to appear either overconfident or too eager. He stayed right where he was, as if already asleep. The door was unlocked and opened, but he heard nothing else. He sneaked a peek. That, apparently, was her invitation to come in. *I've come this far,* Buck thought. *That's not good enough.* He resumed his position, his back to the door.

Half a minute later he heard Chloe stomping to the door again. She swung open the storm door and said, "What do you want, an engraved invitation?"

"Wha—?" Buck said, pretending to be startled and turning around. "Is it morning already?"

"Very funny. Get in here. You've got ten minutes."

He stood to go in, but Chloe let the storm door slap shut as she went to sit on one end of the couch in the living room. Buck let himself in. "That's all right," he said, "I'll keep my coat."

"This visit was your idea, not mine," she said. "Forgive me if I don't treat you as if you were invited."

Chloe sat with her feet tucked under her, arms crossed, as if granting him an extremely reluctant audience. Buck draped his jacket across an easy chair and slid the footstool in front of Chloe. He sat there, staring at her, as if trying to think of where to begin.

"I'm hardly dressed for visitors," she said.

"You look great no matter what you're wearing."

"Spare me," she said. "What do you want?"

"Actually, I wanted to bring you flowers," he said. "Seeing as how yours are in the trash."

"Did you think I was kidding?" she said, pointing past him. He turned and looked. Sure enough, a huge bouquet of flowers was jammed in a wastebasket.

"I didn't think you were kidding," Buck said. "I just thought you were being figurative, and I hadn't heard the expression."

"What are you talking about?"

"When you told me the flowers were in the trash, I thought it was some sort of phrase I'd never heard. It had the flavor of 'the cat is out of the bag' or 'the water is under the bridge.' "

"I said the flowers were in the trash, and that's what I meant. I mean what *I* say, Buck."

Buck was at a loss. They seemed to be on different pages, and he wasn't even sure it was the same script. "Um, could you tell me why the flowers are in the trash? Maybe that would help clarify things for me."

"Because I didn't want them."

"Oh, silly me. Makes sense. And you didn't want them because . . ." He stopped and shook his head, as if she should fill in the blank.

"They insult me because of where they came from."

"And where did they come from?"

"OK, then because of *who* they came from."

"And they came from whom?"

"Oh, Buck, really! I don't have time for this and I'm not in the mood."

Chloe moved to stand and suddenly Buck was angry. "Chloe, wait just a minute." She sat back down and folded up again, looking perturbed. "You owe me an explanation."

"No, you owe *me* an explanation."

Buck sighed. "I'll explain anything you want, Chloe, but no

more games. It was clear we were attracted to each other, and I know I gave off some less-than-interested signals Friday night, but today I realized—"

"This morning," she interrupted, obviously fighting tears, "I discovered why you seemed to have lost interest all of a sudden. You were feeling guilty about not telling me everything, and if you think those flowers fixed anything—"

"Chloe! Let's talk about real problems! I had nothing to do with those flowers."

For once, Chloe was silent.

NINE

CHLOE sat looking skeptically at Buck. "You didn't?" she managed finally.

He shook his head. "Apparently you have another admirer."

"Yeah, right," she said. "Another? As if that makes two?"

Buck spread his hands before him. "Chloe, there's obviously been a lack of communication here."

"Obviously."

"Call me presumptuous, but I was under the impression that we sort of hit it off from the moment we met." He paused and waited for a response.

She nodded. "Nothing serious," she said. "But yes, I thought we liked each other."

"And I was with you on the plane when you prayed with your dad," he said.

She nodded slightly.

"That was a special time," he continued.

"OK," she agreed.

"Then I went through my ordeal and couldn't wait to get back here to tell all of you about it."

Chloe's lip quivered. "That was the most incredible story I had ever heard, Buck, and I didn't doubt you for a second. I knew you were going through a lot, but I thought we had connected."

"I didn't know what to call it," Buck said, "but as I told you in my note that Sunday, I was attracted to you."

"Not only to me, apparently."

Buck was speechless. "Not only to you?" he repeated.

"Just go on with your speech."

Speech? She thinks this is a speech? And she thinks there's some-one else? There hasn't been anyone else in years! Buck was de-flated and thought of giving up, but he decided she was worth it. Misguided, jumping to strange conclusions for some reason, but worth it.

"Between Sunday and Friday night I did a lot of thinking about us."

"Here it comes," she said, tearing up again. What did she think? That he was prepared to sleep on her porch just to dump her for someone else when she finally let him in?

"I realize that Friday night I was giving you mixed signals," he said. "Well, maybe not so mixed. I was pulling away."

"There wasn't much to pull away from."

"But we were getting there, weren't we?" Buck said. "Didn't you think we were going to progress?"

"Sure. Until Friday night."

"I'm a little embarrassed to admit this—" he said hesitantly.

"You should be," she said.

"—but I realized I was being pretty premature, given how re-cently we had met, and your age, and—"

"So, there it is. It's not your age that's the problem, is it? It's my age."

"Chloe, I'm sorry. The issue was not your age or my age. The issue was the *difference* in our ages. Then I realized that with only about seven more years ahead of us, that becomes a nonis-sue. But I was all mixed up. I was thinking about our future, you know, what might come of our relationship, and we don't even have a relationship yet."

"And we're not going to, Buck. I'm not going to share you. If there was a future for us, it would be an exclusive relationship, and—oh, never mind. Here I go talking about stuff neither of us even considered before."

"Apparently we did," Buck said. "I just said I did, and it sounds like you've been looking ahead a little, too."

"Not any more, not since this morning."

"Chloe, I'm going to have to ask you something, and I don't want you to take it the wrong way. This may sound a little con-descending, even parental, and I don't mean it to be." She sat stiffly, as if expecting a reprimand. "I'm going to ask you not to say anything for a minute, all right?"

"Pardon me?" she said. "I'm not allowed to speak?"

"That's not what I'm saying."

"It's what you just said."

Buck came just short of raising his voice. He knew his look and tone were stern, but he had to do something. "Chloe, you're not listening to me. You're not letting me finish a thought. There's some subtext here I know nothing about, and I can't defend myself against mysteries and fantasies. You keep talking about not sharing me—is there something you need to ask me or accuse me of before I can go on here?"

Rayford, who had been lying still and nearly holding his breath trying to listen, had heard very little of the conversation until Buck raised his voice. Rayford heard that and silently cheered. Chloe increased her volume, too. "I want to know about anybody else in your life before I even think—oh, Buck, what are we talking about? Aren't there a lot more important things to be thinking about right now?"

Rayford couldn't hear Buck's whispered response, and he was tired of trying. He moved to the doorway and called down to them. "Could you two either speak up or just whisper? If I can't hear, I'm going to sleep!"

"Go to sleep, Dad!" Chloe said.

Buck smiled. Chloe was also suppressing a grin.

"Chloe, all weekend I've been thinking about all the 'more important things' we have to think about. I almost had myself talked into giving you the let's-be-friends routine . . . until I was sitting in that office this afternoon and you came over me."

"*I* came over you? You saw me at the *Global Weekly* office?"

"The *Global Weekly* office? What are you talking about?"

Chloe hesitated. "Well, what office were you talking about?"

Buck grimaced. He hadn't planned to talk about his meeting with Carpathia. "Can we save that until we're back on even ground here? I was saying I was suddenly overwhelmed with the need to see you, to talk to you, to get back to you."

"Back from where? Or back from whom, I should ask."

"Well, I'd rather not get into that until I think you're ready to hear it."

"I'm ready, Buck, because I already know."

"How do you know?"

"Because I was there!"

"Chloe, if you were at the Chicago bureau office, then you

know I wasn't there today, I mean, except for early this morning."

"So you *were* there."

"I was just dropping off some keys to Alice."

"Alice? That's her name?"

Buck nodded, lost.

"What's her last name, Buck?"

"Her last name? I don't know. I've always just called her Alice. She's new. She replaced Lucinda's secretary, who disappeared."

"You want me to believe you really don't know her last name?"

"Why should I lie about that? Do you know her?"

Chloe's eyes bored into him. Buck knew they were finally getting somewhere. He just didn't know where. "I can't say I know her, exactly," Chloe said. "I just talked to her, that's all."

"You talked to Alice," he repeated, trying to make it compute.

"She told me you and she were engaged."

"Oh, she did not!" Buck shouted, then quieted, peeking up the stairs. "What are you talking about?"

"We're talking about the same Alice, aren't we?" Chloe said. "Skinny, spiky dark hair, short skirt, works at *Global Weekly?*"

"That's her." Buck nodded. "But don't you think I'd know her last name if we were engaged? Plus, that would be mighty big news to her fiancé."

"So she's engaged, but not to you?" Chloe said, sounding doubtful.

"She told me something about picking up her fiancé today," he said. Chloe looked stricken. "Do you mind if I ask how you happened to be at the *Weekly* and talking to her? Were you looking for me?"

"As a matter of fact, I was," Chloe said. "I had seen her earlier, and I was surprised to see her there."

"Like I said, Chloe, I wasn't there today."

"Where were you?"

"I asked you first. Where had you seen Alice?"

Chloe spoke so softly Buck had to lean forward to hear. "At your condo."

Buck sat back, everything coming into focus. He wanted to laugh, but poor Chloe! He fought to stay serious. "It's my fault," he said. "I invited you, my plans changed, and I never told you."

"She had your keys," Chloe whispered.

Buck shook his head sympathetically. "I gave them to her so

she could deliver some equipment I was expecting at the office. I had to be in New York today."

Buck's frustration with Chloe melted into sympathy. She couldn't maintain eye contact, and she was clearly on the verge of tears. "So you really didn't send the flowers," she whispered.

"If I'd known I needed to, I would have."

Chloe uncrossed her arms and buried her face in her hands. "Buck, I'm so embarrassed," she moaned, and the tears came. "I have no excuse. I was worried after Friday night, and then I just made a big thing out of nothing."

"I didn't know you cared that much," Buck said.

"Of course I cared. But I can't expect you to understand or to forgive me after I've been such a, such a—oh, if you don't even want to see me again, I'd understand." She was still hiding her face. "You'd better go," she added. "I wasn't presentable when you got here, and I'm certainly not now."

"Is it all right if I sleep on your porch? 'Cause I'd like to be here when you are presentable."

She peeked at him through her hands and smiled through her tears. "You don't have to do this, Buck."

"Chloe, I'm just sorry I contributed to this by not telling you about my trip."

"No, Buck. It was all my fault, and I'm so sorry."

"OK," he said. "You're sorry, and I forgive you. Can that be the end of it?"

"That's just going to make me cry more."

"What'd I do now?"

"You're just being too sweet about this!"

"I can't win!"

"Give me a minute, will you?" Chloe sprang from the couch and hurried up the stairs.

Ever since asking them to either speak up or quiet down, Rayford had been sitting just out of sight at the top of the stairs. He tried to get up and sneak back into the master bedroom, but he was just rising when Chloe nearly ran into him.

"Dad!" she whispered. "What are you doing?!"

"Eavesdropping. What does it look like?"

"You're awful!"

"*I'm* awful? Look what you did to Buck! Way to hang a guy before he's tried."

"Dad, I was such a fool."

"It was just a comedy of errors, hon, and like Buck said, it only shows how much you cared."

"Did you know he was coming?"

Rayford nodded.

"Tonight? You knew he was coming tonight?"

"Guilty."

"And you made me answer the door."

"So shoot me."

"I ought to."

"No, you ought to thank me."

"That's for sure. You can go to bed now. I'm going to change and see if Buck wants to take a walk."

"So you're saying I can't come along? Or even follow from a distance?"

Buck heard whispering upstairs, then water running and drawers opening and shutting. Chloe came back down in jeans and a sweatshirt, a jacket, a cap, and tennis shoes. "Do you have to go?" she said. "Or do you want to take a walk?"

"You're not kicking me out after all?"

"We need to talk somewhere else so Dad can get to sleep."

"We were keeping him up?"

"Sort of."

Rayford heard the front door shut, then knelt by his bed. He prayed Chloe and Buck would be good for each other, regardless of what the future held for them. Even if they became only good friends, he would be grateful for that. He crawled into bed, falling into a light, fitful sleep, listening for Chloe's return and praying about the opportunity that had been presented him that day.

The night was nippy but clear as midnight approached. "Buck," Chloe said as they turned a corner to wend their way through the fashionable Arlington Heights subdivision, "I just want to say again how—"

Buck stopped and snagged Chloe's jacket sleeve. "Chloe, don't. We've got only seven years. We can't live in the past. We've both stumbled this weekend, and we've apologized, so let's be done with it."

"Really?"

"Absolutely." They continued walking. "'Course, I'm gonna need to find out who's sending you flowers."

"I've been thinking about that, and I have a suspicion."

"Who?"

"It's kind of embarrassing, because that might have been my fault too."

"Your old boyfriend?"

"No! I told you when we first met, we dated when I was a freshman and he was a senior. He graduated and I never heard from him again. He's married."

"Then it had better not be him. Any other guys at Stanford who wish you would come back?"

"Nobody with the style to send flowers."

"Your dad?"

"He already denied it."

"Who does that leave?"

"Think about it," Chloe said.

Buck squinted and thought. "Bruce!? Oh, no, you don't think . . . ?"

"Who else is there?"

"How would you have encouraged him?"

"I don't know. I like him a lot. I admire him. His honesty moves me, and he's so passionate and sincere."

"I know, and he has to be lonely. But it's only been a few weeks since he lost his family. I can't imagine it would be him."

"I tell him I enjoy his messages," Chloe said. "Maybe I'm being more friendly than I need to be. It's just that I never thought of him that way, you know?"

"Could you? He's a sharp young guy."

"Buck! He's older than you!"

"Not much."

"Yeah, but you're on the very end of the age spectrum I'd even consider."

"Well, thank you so much! How soon before you have to have me back to the home?"

"Oh, Buck, it's so embarrassing! I need Bruce as a friend and as a teacher!"

"You're sure you wouldn't consider more?"

She shook her head. "I just can't see it. It's not that he's unattractive, but I can't imagine ever thinking of him that way. You know, he asked me to work for him, full-time. I never even thought there might be an ulterior motive."

"Now don't jump to conclusions, Chloe."

"I'm good at that, aren't I?"

"You're asking the wrong person."

"What am I going to do, Buck? I don't want to hurt him. I can't tell him I don't think of him in that way. You know this all has to just be a reaction to his loss. Like he's on the rebound."

"I can't imagine what it would be like to lose a wife," Buck said.

"And kids."

"Yeah."

"You told me once that you were never serious about anyone."

"Right. Well, a couple of times I thought I was, but I had jumped the gun. One girl, a year ahead of me in grad school, dumped me because I was too slow to make a move on her."

"No!"

"Guess I'm a little old-fashioned that way."

"That's encouraging."

"I lost whatever feeling I had for her real quick."

"I can imagine. So you weren't the typical college guy?"

"You want the truth?"

"I don't know. Do I?"

"Depends. Would you rather hear that I have all kinds of experience because I'm such a cool guy, or that I'm a virgin?"

"You're going to tell me whatever I want to hear?"

"I'm going to tell you the truth. I just wouldn't mind knowing in advance which you'd want to hear."

"Experienced or a virgin," Chloe repeated. "That's a no-brainer. Definitely the latter."

"Bingo," Buck said softly, more from embarrassment than from braggadocio.

"Wow," Chloe said. "That's something to be proud of these days."

"I have to say I'm more grateful than proud. My reasons were not as pure as they would be today. I mean, I know it would have been wrong to sleep around, but I didn't abstain out of any sense of morality. When I had opportunities, I wasn't interested. And I was so focused on my studies and my future, I didn't have that many opportunities. Truth is, people always assumed I got around because I ran in pretty fast circles. But I was backward when it came to stuff like that. Kind of conservative."

"You're apologizing."

"Maybe. I don't mean to be. It's kind of embarrassing to be my age and totally inexperienced. I've always been sort of ahead of my generation in other ways."

"That's an understatement," Chloe said. "You think God was protecting you, even before you were aware of him?"

"I never thought of it that way, but it very well could be. I've never had to worry about disease and all the emotional stuff that goes with intimate relationships."

Buck self-consciously rubbed the back of his neck.

"This is embarrassing you, isn't it?" Chloe said.

"Yeah, a little."

"So I suppose you'd rather not hear about my sexual experience or lack of it."

Buck grimaced. "If you don't mind. See, I'm only thirty and I feel like an old-timer when you even use the word . . . *sex*. So maybe you should spare me."

"But Buck, what if something comes of our relationship? Aren't you going to be curious?"

"Maybe I'll ask you then."

"But what if by then you're already madly in love with me, and you find out something you can't live with?"

Buck was ashamed of himself. It was one thing to admit to a woman that you're a virgin when it seemed to put you in one of the smaller minorities in the world. But she was so straightforward, so direct. He didn't want to talk about this, to hear about it, to know, especially if she was more "experienced" than he. And yet she had a point. She seemed more comfortable talking about their future than he did, but he was the one who had decided to pursue a relationship. Rather than respond to her question, he just shrugged.

"I'll spare you the mystery," Chloe said. "My boyfriends in high school, and my boyfriend my freshman year at Stanford and I were not models of, what did my mother call it, propriety? But I'm happy to say we never had sex. That's probably the reason I never lasted with any of them."

"Um, Chloe, that's good news, but could we talk about something else?"

"You *are* an old codger, aren't you?"

"I guess." Buck blushed. "I can interview heads of state, but this kind of frankness is new to me."

"C'mon, Buck, you hear this and a lot worse on talk shows everyday."

"But I don't put you in the category of a talk-show guest."

"Am I too blunt?"

"I'm just not used to it and not good at it."

Chloe chuckled. "What are the odds that two unmarried people are taking a walk at midnight in America and both of them are virgins?"

"Especially after all the Christians were taken away."

"Amazing," she said. "But you want to talk about something else."

"Do I!"

"Tell me why you had to go to New York."

It was after one o'clock when Rayford stirred at the sound of the front door. It opened but did not close. He heard Chloe and Buck chatting from just inside the door. "I've really got to get going," Buck said. "I'm expecting a response from New York on my article tomorrow morning, and I want to be awake enough to interact."

After Buck left, Rayford heard Chloe close the door. Her footsteps on the stairs seemed lighter than they had earlier in the evening. He heard her tiptoe to his door and peek in. "I'm awake, hon," he said. "Everything all right?"

"Better than all right," she said, coming to sit on the edge of the bed. "Thanks, Dad," she said in the darkness.

"You have a good talk?"

"Yeah. Buck is incredible."

"He kiss you?"

"No! Dad!"

"Hold hands?"

"No! Now stop it! We just talked. You wouldn't believe the offer he got today."

"Offer?"

"I don't have time to get into it tonight. You flying tomorrow?"

"No."

"We'll talk about it in the morning."

"I want to tell you about an offer I got today, too," Rayford said.

"What was it?"

"Too involved for tonight. I'm not going to take it anyway. We can talk about it in the morning."

"Dad, tell me one more time you didn't send those flowers just to cheer me up. I'll feel awful if you did and I trashed them."

"I didn't, Chlo'."

"That's good, I guess. But it wasn't Buck, either."

"You're sure?"

"Positive this time."

"Uh-oh."

"You thinking what I'm thinking, Dad?"

"I've been wondering about Bruce ever since I heard Buck tell you it wasn't him."

"What am I going to do, Dad?"

"If you're going to work with the man, you'll have to have a talk with him."

"Why is it my responsibility? I didn't start this! I didn't encourage it—at least I didn't mean to."

"Well, you could ignore it. I mean, he sent them anonymously. How were you supposed to know who they were from?"

"Yeah! I don't really know, do I?"

"Of course not."

"I'm supposed to see him tomorrow afternoon," she said, "to talk about this job."

"Then talk about the job."

"And ignore the flowers?"

"You sort of already did that, didn't you?"

Chloe laughed. "If he's got the guts to own up to sending them, then we can talk about what it all means."

"Sounds good."

"But, Dad, if Buck and I keep seeing each other, it's going to become obvious."

"You don't want people to know?"

"I don't want to shove it in Bruce's face, knowing how he feels about me."

"But you *don't* know."

"That's right, isn't it? If he doesn't tell me, I don't know."

"G'night, Chloe."

"But it's going to be awkward working for him or with him, won't it, Dad?"

"'Night, Chloe."

"I just don't want to—"

"Chloe! It's tomorrow already!"

"'Night, Dad."

Buck was awakened midmorning Tuesday by a call from Stanton
Bailey. "Cameron!" he shouted. "You awake?"

"Yes, sir."

"You don't sound like it!"

"Wide-awake, sir."

"Late night?"

"Yes, but I'm awake now, Mr.—"

"You always were honest to a fault there, Cam. That's why I
still don't understand your insisting you were at that meeting
when—ah, that's behind us. You're exiled; I'm wishing you were
replacing Plank here, but hey, what's done is done, huh?"

"Yes, sir."

"Well, you've still got it."

"Sir?"

"Still got the touch. How does it feel to write another award-
winner?"

"Well, I'm glad you like it, Mr. Bailey, but I didn't write it for
an award."

"We never do, do we? Ever craft one just to make it fit a category in some contest? Me neither. I've seen guys try it, though.
Never works. They could take a lesson from you. Thorough, long
but tight, all the quotes, all the angles, fair to every opinion. I
thought it was real good of you not to make the alien kooks and
the religious wackos look stupid. Everybody's got a right to his
own opinion, right? And these represent the heartland of America,
whether they believe it was something green from Mars or Jesus
on a horse."

"Sir?"

"Or whatever imagery that is. You know what I mean. Anyway, this thing's a masterpiece, and I appreciate your usual great
job and not letting this other business get you down. You keep up
the good work, stay there in Chicago for an appropriate amount
of time so it still looks like I've got some control over my star
guy, and you'll be back in New York before you know it. When's
your lease up?"

"A year, but actually I like it here, and—"

"Very funny. Just talk to me when they start pushing you on
that lease, Cameron, and we'll get you back here. I don't know
about executive editor, because we've got to fill that before then
and it probably wouldn't make much sense, you going from the
wilderness to the saddle. But we'll at least get your salary back up

where it belongs, and you'll be back here doing what you do best."

"Well, thanks."

"Hey, take the day off! This thing'll hit the stands a week from yesterday and you'll be the talk of the town for a few days."

"I just might take you up on that."

"And listen, Cameron, stay out of that little gal's hair there. What's her name?"

"Verna Zee?"

"Yeah, Verna. She'll do all right, but just leave her alone. You don't even have to be over there unless you need to be for some reason. What's next on your plate?"

"Steve's trying to get me to go to Israel next week for the signing of the treaty between Israel and the U.N."

"We've got a slew of people going, Cameron. I was going to put the religion editor on the cover story."

"Jimmy Borland?"

"Problem?"

"Well, first, I don't see it as a religious story, especially with the one-world religion meeting going on in New York at the same time, the Jews talking about rebuilding the temple, and the Catholics voting on a new pope. And this is going to sound self-serving, but do you really think Jimmy can handle a cover story?"

"Probably not. It just seemed like a good fit. He's been over there so many times on his beat, and just about anything Israel does can be considered religious, right?"

"Not necessarily."

"I've always liked that you talk to me straight, Cameron. Too many yes people around here. So you don't think this is a religious thing just because it's happening in the so-called Holy Land."

"Anything Carpathia is involved in is geopolitical, even if it has some religious ramifications. A great religious angle over there, besides the temple thing, is those two preachers at the Wailing Wall."

"Yeah, what's with those crazies? Those two said it wasn't going to rain in Israel for three and a half years, and so far it hasn't! That's a dry land as it is, but if they go that long without rain, everything's gonna dry up and blow away. How dependent is that scientist guy's—uh, Rosenzweig's—formula on rain?"

"I'm not sure, sir. I know it requires less rain than if you tried to grow without it, but I think there still has to be water from somewhere to make it work."

"I'd like to see Jimmy get an exclusive with those two," Bailey said, "but they're dangerous, aren't they?"

"Sir?"

"Well, two guys tried to kill them and wound up dropping dead on the spot, and what was this thing the other day? A bunch of guys got burned up. People said those two called down fire from heaven!"

"Others were saying they breathed fire on them."

"I heard that too!" Bailey said. "That's some kind of halitosis problem, eh?"

Bailey was laughing, but Buck couldn't fake it. He believed the fire-breathing story because it was right out of Scripture, and neither did he put people who believed the Rapture in the same category as the UFO wackos.

"Anyway," Bailey continued, "I haven't told Borland he's got the cover, but I think rumor has it that he's in line for it. I could put you on it, and I'd rather, but somebody else would have to get bumped from the trip, because we're maxed out budgetwise. Maybe I could send one less photographer."

Buck was eager for a photographer to get some supernatural evidence on film. "No, don't do that," he said. "Plank is offering to let me fly over there as part of the U.N. contingency." There was a long silence. "Sir?"

"I don't know about that, Cameron. I'm impressed that they've apparently forgiven you for stiffing them last time, but how do you maintain objectivity when you're on their dime?"

"You have to trust me, sir. I have never traded favors."

"I know you haven't, and Plank knows you haven't. But does Carpathia understand journalism?"

"I'm not sure he does."

"Neither am I. You know what I'm afraid of."

"What's that?"

"That he'll try stealing you away."

"Not much chance of my going anywhere," Buck said.

"Still, I would have thought he'd be more upset at you than I was, and now he wants you to ride along on this deal-signing thing?"

"He actually wants me to sit in on the signing as part of his delegation."

"That would be totally inappropriate."

"I know."

"Unless you could make it clear that you're not part of the delegation. What a great spot! The only media person at the table!"

"Yeah, but how would I do that?"

"It could be something simple. Maybe you wear a patch on your jacket that makes it obvious you're with *Weekly*."

"I could do that."

"You could carry it with you and slap it on once everyone's in place."

"That sounds a little underhanded."

"Oh, don't kid yourself, son. Carpathia's a politician's politician, and he has all kinds of reasons for wanting you there with him. Not the least of which would be greasing the skids so you could slide out of *Global Weekly*."

"I have no such plans, sir."

"Well, I know you don't. Listen, do you think you could still get in on the signing, I mean be right there when it happens, with the involved parties instead of the press corps, even if you didn't ride with the U.N. delegation?"

"I don't know. I could ask."

"Well, ask. Because I'll spring for an extra ticket on a commercial flight before I'll see you go over there at U.N. expense. I don't want you owing Carpathia any favors, but there's not much I wouldn't do to see you peeking over his shoulder when he signs that treaty."

TEN

Buck liked the idea of taking the day off, not that he had anything ambitious planned anyway. He puttered around in the spare bedroom, setting up his office. Once everything was plugged in and tested, he checked his E-mail and found one long message from James Borland, religion editor of *Global Weekly*.

Uh-oh, he thought.

> I'd get on the phone and have it out with you voice to voice. But I think better on paper and want to vent a little here before I get your usual excuses. You knew full well that I was in line for the treaty signing cover story. The thing's happening in the religious capital of the world, Cameron. Who did you think would handle it?
>
> Just because I'm not your typical cover-story writer and haven't done one before doesn't mean I couldn't handle it. I might have come to you for advice on it anyway, but you probably would have wanted to share the byline, your name first.
>
> The old man tells me that your writing it was his idea, but don't think I can't envision you talking your way into this one and me out of it. Well, I'm going to be in Israel, too. I'll stay out of your hair if you'll stay out of mine.

Buck immediately phoned Borland. "Jimmy," he said, "it's Buck."

"You got my E-mail?"

"I did."

"I have nothing more to say."

"I imagine not," Buck said. "You were pretty clear."

"Then what do you want?"

"Just to set the record straight."

"Yeah, you're going to convince me that your story lines up with Bailey's, that you didn't even ask for the assignment."

"To tell you the truth, Jim, I did tell Bailey I saw it as more of a political than a religious story, and I even wondered aloud whether you were up to it."

"And you don't think that constitutes running me off the story so you can write it?"

"I may have, Jim, but it wasn't intentional. I'm sorry, and if it means that much to you, I'll insist that you do it."

"Right. What's the catch?"

"That I get your stories, and one new one."

"You want my beat?"

"Just for a few weeks. In my mind, you've got the most enviable job on the *Weekly*."

"Why don't I trust you, Buck? You sound like Tom Sawyer trying to get me to paint your fence."

"I'm dead serious, Jim. You let me cover the one-world religion story, the rebuilding of the temple story, the two preachers at the Wailing Wall story, the vote for a new pope story, and another one in your bailiwick I haven't told anyone about yet, and I'll see to it you get to do the cover story on the treaty."

"I'll bite. What's the big scoop on my beat that I've missed?"

"You didn't miss it. I just have a friend who was in the right place at the right time."

"Who? What?"

"I won't reveal my source, but I happen to know that Rabbi Tsion Ben-Judah—"

"I know him."

"You do?"

"Well, I know of him. Everybody does. Pretty impressive guy."

"Have you heard what he's up to?"

"Some research project, isn't it? Something typically musty?"

"So that's another one you don't want. It sounds like I'm asking for Baltic and Mediterranean and offering Boardwalk and Park Place."

"That's exactly what it sounds like, Buck. You think I'm stupid?"

"I sure don't, Jimmy. That's one thing you don't understand. I'm not your enemy."

"Just my competitor, keeping the cover stories for yourself."

"I just offered you one!"

"Something doesn't wash, Buck. The one-world religion meeting is dry as dust, and the thing will never work anyway. Nothing's going to stand in the way of the Jews rebuilding their temple because no one but the Jews care. I'll grant you that those two guys at the Wailing Wall would be a great story, but more than a half-dozen people who've tried to get near them wound up dead. I have to think every journalist in the world has asked for an exclusive, but no one's had the guts to go in there. Everybody knows who the new pope's gonna be. And who in the world cares about the rabbi's research?"

"Whoa, back up a second there, Jim," Buck said. "Now, see, you've got a leg up on me on the pope thing because I have no idea who the new one will be."

"Oh, come on, Buck. Where have you been? All the smart money is on Archbishop Mathews out of—"

"Cincinnati? Really? I interviewed him for the—"

"I know, Buck. I saw it. Everybody around here has seen your next Pulitzer."

Buck was silent. Did the depths of jealousy know no bounds?

Borland must have sensed he'd gone too far. "Truthfully, Buck, I've got to hand it to you. That's going to be one good read. But you got no hint that he's got the inside track on the papacy?"

"None."

"He's a pretty crafty guy. He's got support coming out his ears, and I think he's a shoo-in. So do a lot of other people."

"So, since I know him and I think he trusts me, you won't mind that story being part of the trade?"

"Oh, you just assume we're making this trade now, is that it?" Jimmy said.

"Why not? How bad do you want the cover?"

"Buck, you think I don't know you're going to be part of the U.N. contingent at the signing and that you're going to be wearing a *Global Weekly* blazer or hat or something to get us a little play?"

"So make it part of your cover story. 'Substitute Religion Editor Gets to Stand Next to Secretary-General.' "

"Not funny. No way Plank gives you that plum and then settles for someone else writing the piece."

"I'm telling you, Jim, I'll insist on it."

"You weren't supposed to have any more bargaining power after missing that Carpathia meeting before. What makes you think Bailey will listen to you? You're just a Chicago bureau writer now."

Buck felt his old ego kick in, and the words were out before he could measure them. "Yeah, just a Chicago bureau writer who wrote next week's cover story and has been assigned the following week's too."

"Touché!"

"I'm sorry, Jim. That was out of line. But I'm serious about this. I'm not just bluffing to make you think your beat is a bigger deal than a cover story. I'm convinced things are breaking religiously that make much more interesting stories than the treaty signing."

"Wait a minute, Buck. You're not one of the suckers buying into the prophetic, apocalyptic, all-this-has-been-foretold-in-the-Bible theories, are you?"

That's exactly what I am, Buck thought, but he couldn't afford to go public yet. "How widespread is that view?" Buck asked.

"You ought to know. You wrote the cover story."

"My story gives voice to all the opinions."

"Yeah, but you ran into the Rapture nuts. They'd love to see some spin on all these stories you want to do that shoehorns them into God's plan."

"You're the religion editor, Jim. Do they have a point?"

"Doesn't sound to me like something God would have done."

"You're allowing that there is a God."

"In a manner of speaking."

"What manner?"

"God is in all of us, Buck. You know my view."

"Your view hasn't changed since the disappearances?"

"Nope."

"Was God in the people who disappeared?"

"Sure."

"So now part of God is gone?"

"You're way too literal for me, Buck. Next you're going to tell me the treaty proves Carpathia's the Antichrist."

How I'd love to convince you, Buck thought. *And someday I'll try.* "I know the treaty is a big deal," he said. "Probably bigger than most people realize, but the signing is just the show. The fact that there's an agreement was the story, and that story has been told."

"The signing may just be show, but it's worth a cover, Buck. Why wouldn't you think I could handle it?"

"Tell me I can have the other stuff, and I'll see that you get it."

"Deal."

"You're serious?"

"'Course I'm serious. I'm sure you think you've pulled one over on me, but I'm no kid anymore, Buck. I don't care where this cover ranks with all the ones you've done. I'd like to have it for my scrapbook, my grandkids, all that."

"I understand."

"Yeah, you understand. You've got your whole life ahead of you, and you'll do twice as many covers as you've already done."

"Chloe! Come down here!"

Rayford stood in the living room, too stunned to even sit. He had just flipped on the TV and heard the special news bulletin.

Chloe came hurrying down the stairs. "I've got to get to the church," she said. "What's up?"

Rayford shushed her and they watched and listened. A CNN White House correspondent spoke. "Apparently this unusual gesture came as a result of a meeting early last evening between U.N. Secretary-General Nicolae Carpathia and President Gerald Fitzhugh. Fitzhugh has already led the way among heads of state in his unwavering support of the administration of the new secretary-general, but this lending of the new presidential aircraft sets a whole new standard.

"The White House sent the current *Air Force One* to New York late yesterday afternoon to collect Carpathia, and today comes this announcement that the maiden flight of the new *Air Force One* will carry Carpathia and not the president himself."

"What?" Chloe asked.

"The treaty signing in Israel," Rayford said.

"But the president is going, isn't he?"

"Yes, but on the old plane."

"I don't get it."

"Neither do I."

The CNN reporter continued, "Skeptics suspect a behind-the-scenes deal, but the president himself made this statement from the White House just moments ago."

CNN ran a tape. President Fitzhugh looked perturbed. "Naysayers and wholly political animals can have a field day with this gesture," the president said, "but peaceloving Americans and everyone tired of politics-as-usual will celebrate it. The new plane is beautiful. I've seen it. I'm proud of it. There's plenty of room on it for the entire United States and United Nations delegations, but I have decided it is only right that the U.N. contingency have the plane to themselves for this maiden voyage.

"Until our current *Air Force One* becomes *Air Force Two,* we will christen the new 757 *'Global Community One'* and offer it to Secretary-General Carpathia with our best wishes. It's time the world rallies round this lover of peace, and I am proud to lead the way by this small gesture.

"I also call upon my colleagues around the globe to seriously study the Carpathia disarmament proposal. Strong defense has been a sacred cow in our country for generations, but I'm sure we all agree that the time for a true, weaponless peace is long past due. I hope to have an announcement soon on our decisions in this regard."

"Dad, does this mean you would—?"

But Rayford silenced Chloe again with a gesture as CNN cut to New York for a live response from Carpathia.

Nicolae gazed directly into the camera, appearing to look right into the eyes of each viewer. His voice was quiet and emotional. "I would like to thank President Fitzhugh for this most generous gesture. We at the United Nations are deeply moved, grateful, and humbled. We look forward to a wonderful ceremony in Jerusalem next Monday."

"Man, is he slick." Rayford shook his head.

"That's the job you told me about. You'd be flying that plane?"

"I don't know. I suppose. I didn't realize the old *Air Force One* was going to become *Air Force Two,* the vice president's plane. I wonder if they're really retiring the current pilot. It's like musical chairs. If the current pilot stays with the 747 when it becomes *AF2,* what happens to the current *AF2* pilot?"

Chloe shrugged. "You're sure you don't want the job flying the new plane?"

"Surer now than ever. I don't want to have anything to do with Carpathia."

Buck took a call from Alice at the Chicago office. "You'd better get two lines into there," she said, "if you're going to keep working from home."

"I've got two lines," Buck said. "But one of 'em's for my computer."

"Well, Mr. Bailey's been trying to reach you, and he's been getting a busy signal."

"What did he call there for? He has to know I'm here."

"He didn't call here. Marge Potter was on with Verna about something else and told her."

"Bet Verna loved that."

"She sure did. She all but danced. She thinks you're in trouble with the big boss again."

"I doubt it."

"Know what she's guessing?"

"I can't wait."

"That Bailey didn't like your cover story and he's firing you."

Buck laughed.

"Not true?" Alice said.

"Quite the opposite," Buck said. "But do me a favor and don't tell Verna."

Buck thanked her for the deliveries the day before, spared her the story about Chloe having thought Alice was his fiancée, and got off so he could call Bailey. He got to Marge Potter first.

"Buck, I miss you already," she said. "What in the world happened?"

"Someday I'll lay it all out for you," he said. "I hear the boss has been trying to reach me."

"Well, I've been trying for him. Right now he's got Jim Borland in there, and I hear raised voices. Don't think I've ever heard Jim raise his voice before."

"You've heard Bailey raise his?"

Marge laughed. "Not more than twice a day," she said. "Anyway, I'll have him call you."

"You might want to interrupt them, Marge. Their meeting may be the reason he was trying to reach me."

Almost immediately Stanton Bailey was on the line. "Williams, you've got a lot of nerve acting like the executive editor you're not."

"Sir?"

"It's not your place to be assigning cover stories, telling Borland I originally had him in mind for the treaty piece, then kissing

up to him by offering to take his garbage stories and letting him
have your cover article."

"I didn't do that!"

"He didn't do that!" Borland hollered.

"I can't keep up with you two," Bailey said. "Now, what's the
deal?"

With Chloe gone to see about her new job at the church, Rayford
thought about calling his chief pilot. Earl Halliday wanted to hear
from him as soon as possible and would likely call him if Rayford
didn't get back to Earl soon.

Today's news was the very kind of development that would
seal Rayford's decision. He couldn't deny the prestige that would
accompany being the president's pilot. And being Carpathia's
might be even noisier. But Rayford's motives and dreams had
swung 180 degrees. Being known as the pilot of *Air Force One*—
or even *Global Community One*—for seven years was simply not
on his wish list.

The size of his own house had sometimes embarrassed Rayford,
even when four people were living there. At other times he had
been proud of it. It evidenced his status, his station in life, the
level of his achievement. Now it was a lonely place. He was so
grateful to have Chloe home. Though he would not have said a
word if she had returned to college, he didn't know what he
would have done with himself during his off-hours. It was one
thing to busy your mind with all that is necessary to transport
hundreds of people safely by air. But to have virtually nothing to
do at home but eat and sleep would have made the place unbearable.

Every room, every knickknack, every feminine touch reminded
him of Irene. Occasionally something would jump out and flood
his mind with Raymie, too. He found a piece of Raymie's favorite
candy under a cushion on the couch. A couple of his books. A
toy was hiding behind a potted plant.

Rayford was growing emotional, but he didn't mind as much
any more. His grief was more melancholic than painful now. The
closer he grew to God, the more he looked forward to being with
him and with Irene and Raymie after the Glorious Appearing.

He allowed his memories to bring his loved ones closer in his
mind and heart. Now that he shared their faith, he understood

them and loved them all the more. When regret crept in, when he felt ashamed of the husband and father he had been, he merely prayed for forgiveness for having been so blind.

Rayford decided to cook for Chloe that night. He would prepare one of her favorite dishes—shrimp scampi with pasta and all the trimmings. He smiled. In spite of him and all the negative traits she had inherited, she had grown to be a wonderful person. If there was one clear example of how Christ could change a person, she was it. He wanted to tell her that, and dinner would be one expression. It was easy to buy things for her and take her out. He wanted to do something himself.

Rayford spent an hour at the grocery store and another hour and a half in the kitchen before he had everything cooking in anticipation of her arrival. He found himself identifying with Irene, remembering the hopeful expression on her face almost every night. He had said his thank-yous and complimented her enough, he supposed. But it wasn't until now that he realized she must have been doing that work for him out of the same love and devotion he felt for Chloe.

He had never grasped that, and his paltry attempts at compliments must have been seen as perfunctory as they were. Now there was no way to make it up to Irene, except to show up in the kingdom himself, with Chloe alongside.

Buck hung up from the call with Stanton Bailey and Jim Borland wondering why he didn't just accept Carpathia's offer to manage the *Chicago Tribune* and be done with it. He had convinced them both that he was sincere and finally got the old man's gruff approval, but he wondered if it was worth being in the doghouse again. His goal was to tie the religious stories together so neatly that Borland would get an idea how his job should be done and Bailey would get a picture of what he needed in an executive editor.

Buck didn't want that job any more than he had when Steve Plank left and Buck had been talked into it. But he sure hoped Bailey found someone who would make it fun to work there again.

He banged out some notes on his computer, in essence outlining the assignments he had acquired in the trade with Jimmy Borland. He had made the same initial assumptions Borland did about all the breaking stories. But that was before he had studied prophecy, before he knew where Nicolae Carpathia fit into the sweep of history.

Now he was hoping all these things would break at essentially the same time. It was possible he was sitting on the direct fulfillment of centuries-old prophecies. Cover stories or not, these developments would have as much impact on the short remaining history of mankind as the treaty with Israel.

Buck called Steve Plank. "Any word yet?" Steve said. "Anything I can tell the secretary-general?"

"Is that what you call him?" Buck said, astonished. "Not even you can call him by name?"

"I choose not to. It's a matter of respect, Buck. Even Hattie calls him 'Mr. Secretary-General,' and if I'm not mistaken, they spend almost as much time together off the job as on the job."

"Don't rub it in. I know well enough that I introduced them."

"You regret it? You provided a world leader with someone he adores, and you changed Hattie's life forever."

"That's what I'm afraid of," Buck said, realizing he was dangerously close to showing his true colors to a Carpathia confidant.

"She was a nobody from nowhere, Buck, and now she's on the front page of history." That was not what Buck wanted to hear, but then he wasn't planning to tell Steve what he wanted to hear either. "So, what's the story, Buck?"

"I'm no closer to a decision today," Buck said. "You know where I stand."

"I don't understand you, Buck. Where's the glitch? What's going to make this not work? It's everything you've ever wanted."

"I'm a journalist, Steve, not a public relations guy."

"Is that what you're calling me?"

"That's what you are, Steve. I don't fault you for it, but don't pretend to be something you're not."

Clearly, Buck had offended his old friend. "Yeah, well, whatever," Steve said. "You called me, so what did you want?"

Buck told him of the deal he had made with Borland.

"Big mistake," Steve said, still clearly steamed. "You'll recall I never assigned him a cover story."

"This shouldn't be a cover story. The other pieces, the ones he's letting me handle, are the big stories."

Steve's voice rose. "This would have been the biggest cover

story you've ever had! This will be the most widely covered event in history."

"You say that and tell me you're not a PR guy now?"

"Why? What?"

"The U.N. signs a peace treaty with Israel and you think it's bigger than the disappearances of billions all over the globe?"

"Well, yeah, that. Of course."

" 'Well, yeah, that. Of course,' " Buck mimicked. "Good grief, Steve. The story is the treaty, not the ceremony. You know that."

"So you're not coming?"

"Of course I'm coming, but I'm not riding along with you guys."

"You don't want to be on the new *Air Force One?*"

"What?"

"C'mon, Mister International Journalist. Keep the news on, man."

———

Rayford looked forward to Chloe's arrival, but he also looked forward to the meeting of the core group that night. Chloe had told him Buck had been as much against accepting a job with Carpathia as Rayford was against accepting a job with the White House. But you never knew what Bruce would say. Sometimes he had a different view of things, and he often made a lot of sense. Rayford couldn't imagine how such changes could figure in to their new lives, but he was eager to talk about it and pray about it. He looked at his watch. His dinner should be done in half an hour. And that was when Chloe had said she'd be home.

———

"No," Buck said, "I wouldn't want to go over there on the new or the old *Air Force One.* I appreciate the invitation to be part of the delegation, and I'll still take you up on being at the table for the signing, but even Bailey agrees that *Global Weekly* ought to send me."

"You *told* Bailey about our offer?!"

"Not the job offer, of course. But about riding along, sure."

"Why do you think the trip to New York was so clandestine, Buck? You think we wanted the *Weekly* to know about this?"

"I figured you didn't want them to know I was being offered a job, which they don't know. But how was I supposed to explain showing up in Israel and being in on the signing?"

"We hoped it wouldn't make any difference to your former employer by then."

"Just don't make any assumptions, Steve," Buck said.

"You, either."

"Meaning?"

"Don't expect the offer of a lifetime to stay on the table if you're going to thumb your nose at an invitation like you did last time."

"So the job is tied to playing ball on the PR trip."

"If you want to put it that way."

"You're not making me feel any better about the idea, Steve."

"You know, Buck, I'm not sure you're cut out for politics and journalism at this level."

"I agree it's sunk to a new low."

"That's not what I meant. Anyway, remember your big-shot predictions about a new one-world currency? That it would never happen? Watch the news tomorrow, pal. And remember that it was all Nicolae Carpathia's doing, diplomacy behind the scenes."

Buck had seen Carpathia's so-called diplomacy. It was likely the same way he got the president of the United States to hand over a brand-new 757, not to mention how he got eyewitnesses to a murder to believe they'd seen a suicide.

It was time to tell Bruce about his trip.

"Rayford, can you come in?"

"When, Earl?"

"Right now. Big doings with the new *Air Force One*. Have you heard?"

"Yes, it's all over the news."

"You say the word, and you'll be flying that plane to Israel with Nicolae Carpathia on board."

"Not ready to decide yet."

"Ray, I need you in here. Can you come or not?"

"Not today, Earl. I'm in the middle of something here, and I'll have to see you tomorrow."

"What's so important?"

"It's personal."

"What, you've got another deal cooking?"

"I'm cooking, but not another deal. I happen to be preparing dinner for my daughter."

Rayford heard nothing for a moment. Finally: "Rayford, I'm all for family priorities. Heaven knows we've got enough pilots with bad marriages and messed-up kids. But your daughter—"

"Chloe."

"Right, she's college age, right? She'd understand, wouldn't she? Couldn't she put off dinner with Dad for a couple hours, knowing he might get the best flying job in the world?"

"I'll see you tomorrow, Earl. I've got that Baltimore run late morning, back late afternoon. I can see you before that."

"Nine o'clock?"

"Fine."

"Rayford, let me just warn you: If the other guys on the short list ever wanted this job, they're going to be drooling over it now. You can bet they're calling in all their chips, lining up their endorsements, trying to find out who knows who, all that."

"Good. Maybe one of them will get it and I won't have to worry about it anymore."

Earl Halliday sounded agitated. "Now, Rayford—," he began, but Rayford cut him off.

"Earl, after tomorrow morning let's agree not to waste any more of each other's time. You know my answer, and the only reason I haven't made it final yet is because you asked me not to for the sake of our friendship. I'm thinking about it, I'm praying about it, and I'm talking about it with people who care for me. I'm not going to be badgered or shamed into it. If I turn down a job that everyone else wants, and later I regret it, that'll be my problem."

———

Buck was pulling into the parking lot at New Hope Village Church just as Chloe was pulling out. They drew up even with each other and rolled down their windows. "Hey, little girl," Buck said, "you know anything about this church?"

Chloe smiled. "Just that it's crowded every Sunday."

"Good. I'll try it. So, are you taking the job?"

"I could ask you the same question."

"I've already got a job."

"Looks like I have one, too," she said. "I learned more today than I learned in college last year."

"How'd it go with Bruce? I mean, did you tell him you knew he sent the flowers?"

Chloe looked over her shoulder, as if afraid Bruce might hear. "I'll have to tell you all about it," she said. "When we have time."

"After the meeting tonight?"

She shook her head. "I was up too late last night. Some guy, you know."

"Really?"

"Yeah. Couldn't get rid of him. Happens to me all the time."

"Later, Chloe."

Buck couldn't blame Bruce for whatever level of interest he had in Chloe. It just felt strange, competing with your new friend and pastor for a woman.

———

"Is that what it smells like?" Chloe exulted as she came in from the garage. "Shrimp scampi?" She entered the kitchen and gave her dad a kiss. "My favorite! Who's coming over?"

"The guest of honor just arrived," he said. "Would you rather eat in the dining room? We could move in there easily."

"No, this will be perfect. What's the occasion?"

"Your new job. Tell me all about it."

"Dad! What possessed you?"

"I just got in touch with my feminine side," he said.

"Oh, please!" she groaned. "Anything but that!"

During dinner she told him of Bruce's assignments and all the research and study she had done already.

"So, you're going to do this?"

"Learn and study and get paid for it? I think that's an easy call, Dad."

"And what about Bruce?"

She nodded. "What *about* Bruce?"

ELEVEN

BY the time Rayford and Chloe were doing the dishes, Rayford had heard all about her awkward encounter with Bruce. "So he never owned up to sending the flowers?" Rayford said.

"It was so strange, Dad," she said. "I kept trying to get the subject back onto loneliness and how much we all meant to each other, all four of us, and he seemed not to pick up on it. He would agree we all had needs, and then he would shift back to the subject of study or some other thing he wanted me to look up. I finally said I was just curious about romantic relationships during this period of history, and he said he might talk about it tonight. He said others had raised the same subject with him recently and that he had some questions too, so he had been studying it."

"Maybe he'll come clean tonight."

"It isn't a matter of coming clean, Dad. I don't expect him to tell me in front of you and Buck that he sent me the flowers. But maybe we'll be able to read between the lines and find out why he did it."

Buck was still in Bruce's office when Rayford and Chloe arrived. Bruce began the nightly meeting of the Tribulation Force by getting everyone's permission to put on the table everything that was happening in each life. Everyone nodded.

After outlining the offers that Buck and Rayford had received, Bruce said he felt the need to confess his own sense of inadequacy for the role of pastor of a church of new believers. "I still deal with shame every day. I know I have been forgiven and restored, but living a lie for more than thirty years wears on a person, and even though God says our sins are separated as far as the east is from the west, it's hard for me to forget." He also admitted his loneliness and fatigue. "Especially," he said, "as I think about this pull toward traveling and trying to unite the little pockets of what the Bible calls 'tribulation saints.' "

Buck wanted to come right out and ask why he hadn't simply signed a card on Chloe's flowers, but he knew it wasn't his place. Bruce moved on to both Rayford's and Buck's new job opportunities. "This may shock all of you, because I have not expressed an opinion yet, but Buck and Rayford, I think both of you should seriously consider accepting these jobs."

That threw the meeting into an uproar. It was the first time the four of them had spoken so forcefully on such personal subjects. Buck maintained that he would never be able to live with himself if he sold out his journalistic principles and allowed himself to manipulate the news and be manipulated by Nicolae Carpathia. He was impressed that Rayford did not seem to have his head turned by such a choice job offer, but he found himself agreeing with Bruce that Rayford should consider it.

"Sir," Buck said, "the very fact that you're not angling for it is a good sign. If you wanted it, knowing what you know now, we would all be worried about you. But think of the opportunity to be near the corridors of power."

"What's the advantage?" Rayford said.

"Maybe little to you personally," Buck said, "except for the income. But don't you think it would be of great benefit to us to have that kind of access to the president?"

Rayford told Buck he thought they all had a mistaken notion that the pilot of the president's plane would have more real knowledge than anyone who read the daily papers.

"That might be true now," Buck said. "But if Carpathia really buys up the major media outlets, someone next to the president would be one of the few who knows what's really going on."

"All the more reason for *you* to work for Carpathia," Rayford said.

"Maybe I should take your job and you should take mine," Buck said, and finally they were able to laugh.

"You see what's happening here," Bruce said. "We all see each other's situations more clearly and with more level heads than we see our own."

Rayford chuckled. "So you're saying we're both in denial."

Bruce smiled. "Maybe I am. It's possible God has sent these things your way just to test your motives and your loyalties, but they seem too huge to ignore."

Buck wondered if Rayford was wavering as much as he was now. Buck had been dead sure he would never consider such an offer from Carpathia. Now he didn't know what he thought. Chloe broke the logjam. "I think you should both take the jobs."

Buck found it strange that Chloe would wait until a meeting of the four of them to make such an announcement, and it was clear her father felt the same. "You said I should at least keep an open mind, Chlo'," Rayford said. "But you seriously think I should take this?"

Chloe nodded. "This isn't about the president. It's about Carpathia. If he is who we think he is, and we all know that he is, he'll quickly become more powerful than the president of the United States. One or both of you should get as close to him as possible."

"I *was* close to him once," Buck said. "And that's more than enough."

"If all you care about is your own sanity and safety," Chloe pressed. "I'm not discounting the horror you went through, Buck. But without someone on the inside, Carpathia is going to deceive everyone."

"But as soon as I tell what's really happening," Buck said, "he'll eliminate me."

"Maybe. But maybe God will protect you too. Maybe all you'll be able to do is tell us what's happening so we can tell the believers."

"I'd have to sell out every journalistic principle I have."

"And those are more sacred than your responsibilities to your brothers and sisters in Christ?"

Buck didn't know how to respond. This was one of the things he liked so much about Chloe. But independence and integrity had been so ingrained in him since the beginning of his journalism career that he could hardly get a mental handle on pretending to be something he was not. The idea of posing as a publisher while actually on Carpathia's payroll was too much to imagine.

Bruce jumped in and focused on Rayford. Buck was glad to have the spotlight off himself, but he could understand how Rayford must have felt. "I think yours is actually the easier decision, Rayford," Bruce said. "You put some major conditions on it, like being allowed to live here if it's that important to you, and see how serious they are."

Rayford was shaken. He looked at Buck. "If we were voting, would you make it three-to-one?"

"I could ask you the same," Buck said. "Apparently we're the only ones who don't think we should take these jobs."

"Maybe you should," Rayford said, only half kidding.

Buck laughed. "I'm open to considering that I've been blind, or at least shortsighted."

Rayford didn't know what he was open to considering, and he said so. Bruce suggested they pray on their knees—something each had done privately, but not as a group. Bruce brought his chair to the other side of the desk, and the four of them turned and knelt. Hearing the others pray always moved Rayford deeply. He wished God would just tell him audibly what to do, but when he prayed, he simply asked that God would make it plain to all of them.

As Rayford knelt there, he realized he needed to surrender his will to God—again. Apparently this would be a daily thing, giving up the logical, the personal, the tightfisted, closely held stuff.

Rayford felt so small, so inadequate before God, that he could not seem to get low enough. He crouched, he squatted, he tucked his chin to his chest, and yet he still felt proud, exposed. Bruce had been praying aloud, but he suddenly stopped, and Rayford heard him weeping quietly. A lump formed in his own throat. He missed his family, but he was deeply grateful for Chloe, for his salvation, for these friends.

Rayford knelt there in front of his chair, his hands covering his face, praying silently. Whatever God wanted was what he wanted, even if it made no sense from a human standpoint. The overwhelming sense of unworthiness seemed to crush him, and he slipped to the floor and lay prostrate on the carpet. A fleeting thought of how ridiculous he must look assailed him, but he quickly pushed it aside. No one was watching, no one cared. And anyone who thought the sophisticated airplane pilot had taken leave of his senses would have been right.

Rayford stretched his long frame flat on the floor, the backs of his hands on the gritty carpet, his face buried in his palms. Occasionally one of the others would pray aloud briefly, and Rayford realized that all of them were now facedown on the floor.

Rayford lost track of the time, knowing only vaguely that minutes passed with no one saying anything. He had never felt so vividly the presence of God. So this was the feeling of dwelling on holy ground, what Moses must have felt when God told him to remove his shoes. Rayford wished he could sink lower into the carpet, could cut a hole in the floor and hide from the purity and infinite power of God.

He was not sure how long he lay there, praying, listening. After a while he heard Bruce get up and take his seat, humming a hymn. Soon they all sang quietly and returned to their chairs. All were teary-eyed. Finally Bruce spoke.

"We have experienced something unusual," he said. "I think we need to seal this with a recommitment to God and to each other. If there is anything between any of us that needs to be confessed or forgiven, let's not leave here without doing that. Chloe, last night you left us with some implications that were strong but unclear."

Rayford glanced at Chloe. "I apologize," she said. "It was a misunderstanding. Cleared up now."

"We don't need a session on sexual purity during the Tribulation?"

She smiled. "No, I think we're all pretty clear on that subject. There is something I would like clarified though, and I'm sorry to ask you this in front of the others—"

"That's all right," Bruce said. "Anything."

"Well, I received some flowers anonymously, and I want to know if they came from anyone in this room."

Bruce glanced away. "Buck?"

"Not me." Buck grimaced. "I've already suffered for being suspected."

When Bruce looked at him, Rayford just smiled and shook his head.

"That leaves me then," Bruce said.

"You?" Chloe said.

"Well, doesn't it? Didn't you just limit your suspects to those in this room?"

Chloe nodded.

"I guess you'll have to widen your search." Bruce said, blushing. "It wasn't me, but I'm flattered to be suspected. I only wish I'd thought of it."

Rayford's and Chloe's surprise must have showed, because Bruce immediately launched into an explanation. "Oh, I didn't mean what you think I mean," Bruce said. "It's just that . . . well, I think flowers are a wonderful gesture, and I hope they encouraged you, whoever they were from."

Bruce seemed relieved to change the subject and return to his teaching. He let Chloe tell some of what she had researched that day. At ten o'clock, when they were getting ready to leave, Buck turned to Rayford. "As wonderful as that prayer time was, I didn't get any direct leading about what to do."

"Me either."

"You must be the only two." Bruce glanced at Chloe, and she nodded. "It's pretty clear to us what you should do. And it's clear to each of you what the other should do. But no one can make these decisions for you."

Buck walked Chloe out of the church.

"That was amazing," she said.

He nodded. "I don't know where I'd be without you people."

"Us people?" She smiled. "You couldn't have left the last word off that sentence, could you?"

"How could I say that to someone who has a secret admirer?"

She winked at him. "Maybe you'd better."

"Seriously, who do you think it is?"

"I don't even know where to begin."

"That many possibilities?"

"That few. In fact, none."

Rayford was beginning to wonder whether Hattie Durham had had anything to do with Chloe's flowers, but he wasn't going to suggest that to his daughter. What kind of crazy idea would have gone through Hattie's mind to spur such an act? Another example of her idea of a practical joke?

Wednesday morning in Earl Halliday's office at O'Hare, Rayford was surprised to find the president of Pan-Con himself, Leonard Gustafson. He had met Gustafson twice before. Rayford should have known something was up when he got off the elevator on the lower level. The place looked different. Desks were neater, neckties were tied, people looked busier, clutter and mess had been swept out of sight. People raised their eyebrows knowingly at Rayford as he strode toward Earl's office.

Gustafson, former military, was shorter than Rayford and thinner than Earl, but his mere presence was too big for Earl's little office. Another chair had been dragged in, but as Rayford entered, Gustafson leaped to his feet, his trench coat still draped over one arm, and pumped Rayford's hand.

"Steele, man, how are you?" he said, pointing to a chair as if this were his office. "I had to come through Chicago today on another matter, and when I found out you were coming to see Earl, well, I just wanted to be here and congratulate you and release you and wish you the best."

"Release me?"

"Well, not fire you, of course, but to set your mind at ease. You can rest assured there'll be no hard feelings here. You've had a remarkable, no, a stellar career with Pan-Con, and we'll miss you, but we're proud of you."

"Is the news release already written?" Rayford said.

Gustafson laughed a little too loudly. "That can be done right away, and of course we'll want to make the announcement. This will be a feather in your cap, just like it is in ours. You're our guy, and now you'll be his guy. You can't beat that, huh?"

"The other candidates have dropped out?"

"No, but suffice it to say we have inside information that the job is yours if you want it."

"How does that work? Somebody owed some favors?"

"No, Rayford, that's the crazy thing. You must have friends in high places."

"Not really. I've had no contact with the president, and I don't know anyone on his staff."

"Apparently you were recommended by the Carpathia administration. You know him?"

"Never met him."

"Know anyone who knows him?"

"As a matter of fact I do," Rayford muttered.

"Well, you played that card at the right time," Gustafson said. He clapped Rayford on the shoulder. "You're perfect for the job, Steele. We'll be thinking good thoughts about you."

"So I couldn't turn this down if I wanted to?"

Gustafson sat, leaning forward, elbows on his knees. "Earl told me you had some misgivings. Don't make the biggest mistake of your life, Rayford. You want this. You know you want this. It's here for the taking. Take it. I'd take it. Earl would take it. Anyone else on the list would die for it."

"It's too late to make the biggest mistake of my life," Rayford said.

"What's that?" Gustafson said, but Rayford saw Earl touch his arm, as if reminding him he was dealing with a religious fanatic who believed he had missed a chance to be in heaven. "Oh, yeah, that. Well, I mean since then," Gustafson added.

"Mr. Gustafson, how does Nicolae Carpathia tell the president of the United States who should pilot his plane?"

"I don't know! Who cares? Politics is politics, whether it's the Dems and the Repubs in this country or Labor and the Bolsheviks somewhere else."

Rayford thought the analogy a little sloppy, but he couldn't argue the logic. "So somebody's trading something for something, and I'm just the hired hand."

"Isn't that the truth with all of us?" Gustafson said. "But everybody loves Carpathia. He seems above all the politics. If I had to guess, I'd say the president is letting him use the new 'five-seven just because he likes him."

Yeah, Rayford thought, *and I'm the Easter bunny.*

"So will you take the job?"

"I've never been pushed out of a job before."

"You're not being pushed, Rayford. We love you here. We just wouldn't be able to justify not having one of our top guys get the best job in the world in his profession."

"What about my record? A complaint has been lodged against me."

Gustafson smiled knowingly. "A complaint? I know nothing of a complaint? Do you, Earl?"

"Nothing's come across my desk, sir," he said. "And if it did, I'm sure it could be expedited beyond danger in a very short time."

"By the way, Rayford," Gustafson said, "are you familiar with a Nicholas Edwards?"

Rayford nodded.

"Friend of yours?"

"First officer a couple of times. I'd like to think we're friends, yes."

"Did you hear he had been promoted to captain?"

Rayford shook his head. *Politics,* he thought glumly.

"Nice, huh?" Gustafson said.

"Real nice," Rayford said, his head spinning.

"Anything else standing in your way?" Gustafson said.

Rayford could see his choices disappearing. "At the very least, and I'm still not saying I'll take it, I would have to be headquartered in Chicago."

Gustafson grimaced and shook his head. "Earl told me that. I don't get it. I would think you'd want to be out of here, away from the memories of your wife and other daughter."

"Son."

"Yeah, the college boy."

Rayford didn't correct him, but he saw Earl wince.

"Anyway," Gustafson said, "you could get your daughter away from whoever might be stalking her, and—"

"Sir?"

"—and you could get yourself a nice place outside D.C."

"Stalking her?"

"Well, maybe it's not that obvious yet, Rayford, but I sure as blazes wouldn't want my daughter to be hearing from somebody anonymously. I don't care what they were sending."

"But how did you—?"

"I mean, Rayford, you'd never forgive yourself if something happened to that little girl and you had a chance to get her away from whoever is threatening her."

"My daughter is not being stalked or threatened! What are you talking about?"

"I'm talking about the roses, or whatever the bouquet was. What was the deal with that?"

"That's what I'd like to know. As far as I know, only three people, besides whoever sent those, even know she got them. How did *you* find out?"

"I don't remember. Somebody just mentioned that sometimes a person has a reason to leave just as much as he has a reason to like the new opportunity."

"But if you're not pushing me out, I have no reason to leave."

"Not even if your daughter is getting hassled by someone?"

"Anyone who wanted to hassle her could find her in Washington just as easily as here," Rayford said.

"But still . . ."

"I don't like the idea that you know all this."

"Well, don't turn down the job of a lifetime over an insignificant mystery."

"It's not insignificant to me."

Gustafson stood. "I'm not accustomed to begging people to do what I ask."

"So if I don't take this, I'm history with Pan-Con?"

"You ought to be, but I suppose we'd have a tough time with a suit from you after we encouraged you to take the job of piloting the president."

Rayford had no intention of filing a suit, but he said nothing.

Gustafson sat again. "Do me a favor," he said. "Go to Washington. Talk to the people, probably the chiefs of staff. Tell them you'll make the run to Israel for the peace-treaty signing. Then decide what you want to do. Would you do that for me?"

Rayford knew Gustafson would never tell him where he'd heard about Chloe's flowers, and he figured his best bet was to pry it out of Hattie. "Yes," Rayford said at last. "I'll do that."

"Good!" Gustafson said, shaking hands with both Rayford and Earl. "I think we're halfway home. And Earl, make this run to Baltimore today Rayford's last before the trip to Israel. In fact, he's going to be so close to Washington, let's get somebody else to fly his plane back so he can meet with people at the White House today. Can we arrange that?"

"It's already done, sir."

"Earl," Gustafson said, "if you were ten years younger, you'd be the man for the job."

Rayford noticed the pain on Earl's face. Gustafson couldn't know how badly Halliday had wanted that very job. On the way to his plane, Rayford checked his mail slot. There, among the packages and interoffice memos, was a note. It read simply, "Thanks for your endorsement on my early promotion. I really appreciate it. And good luck to you. Signed, Captain Nicholas Edwards."

Several hours later Rayford left the cockpit of his 747 in Baltimore and was met by a Pan-Con operative who presented him with credentials that would get him into the White House. Upon his arrival, he was quickly whisked through the gate. A guard welcomed him by name and wished him luck. When he finally got to the office of an assistant to the chief of staff, Rayford made clear that he was agreeing only to fill in as pilot for the trip to Israel the following Monday.

"Very good," he was told. "We have already begun the character and reference check, the FBI probe, and the Secret Service interviewing. It will take a bit longer to complete anyway, so you'll be in a position to impress us and the president without being responsible for him until you've passed all checkpoints."

"You can authorize me to fly the U.N. secretary-general with less clearance on me than you'd need for the president?"

"Precisely. Anyway, you've already been approved by the U.N."

"I have?"

"You have."

"By whom?"

"By the secretary-general himself."

Buck was on the phone to Marge Potter at *Global Weekly* headquarters in New York when he heard the news. The entire world would go to dollars for currency within one year, the plan to be initiated and governed by the United Nations, funded by a one-tenth of one percent tax to the U.N. on every dollar.

"That doesn't sound unreasonable, does it?" Marge asked.

"Ask the financial editor, Marge," Buck said. "It'll be gazillions a year."

"And just how much is a gazillion?"

"More than either of us can count." Buck sighed. "You were going to do some checking, Marge, about finding someone to help arrange these religion interviews."

He could hear her shuffling papers. "You can catch your one-world religion guys here in New York." she said. "They're heading out Friday, but very few of them will be in Israel. Your temple guys will be in Jerusalem next week. We'll try to get in touch with those two kooks you want at the Wailing Wall, but the smart money here says not to count on it."

"I'll take my chances."

"And where would you like us to send your remains?"

"I'll survive."

"No one else has."

"But I'm not threatening them, Marge. I'm helping them broadcast their message."

"Whatever that is."

"You see why we need a story on them?"

"It's your life, Buck."

"Thank you."

"And you'd better get to this Cardinal Mathews on your way here. He's shuttling back and forth between the one-faith meetings in New York and the Cincinnati archdiocese, and he's heading to the Vatican for the papal vote right after the treaty signing next Monday."

"But he *will* be in Jerusalem?"

"Oh, yes. There's some rumor floating around that in case he's the next pope he's making contacts in Jerusalem for some major shrine or something. But the Catholics would never leave the Vatican, would they?"

"You never know, Marge."

"Well, that's for sure. I hardly get time to think about these things, being gofer for you and everyone else around here who can't do his own legwork."

"You're the best, Marge."

"Flattery will get you, Buck."

"Get me what?"

"It'll just get you."

"What about my rabbi?"

"Your rabbi says he's refusing all news contacts until after he presents his findings."

"And when is that?"

"Word just came today that CNN is giving him an hour of uninterrupted time on their international satellite. Jews will be able to see it all over the world at the same time, but of course it will be in the middle of the night for some of them."

"And when is this?"

"Monday afternoon, after the signing of the treaty. Signing is at 10 A.M. Jerusalem time. Rabbi Ben-Judah goes on the air for an hour at two in the afternoon."

"Pretty shrewd, going on while the world's press elite is crowding Jerusalem."

"All these religious types are shrewd, Buck. The guy who'll probably be the next pope will be at the treaty signing, schmoozing the Israelis. This rabbi thinks he's so all-fired important that the treaty signing will be upstaged by the reading of his research paper. Be sure I'm right on my TV schedule there, Buck. I want to be absolutely certain I miss that one."

"Aw, c'mon, Marge. He's going to tell you how to spot the Messiah."

"I'm not even Jewish."

"Neither am I, but I'd sure want to be able to recognize the Messiah. Wouldn't you?"

"You want me to get serious and tell you the truth one time here, Buck? I think I've seen the Messiah. I think I recognize him. If there's really supposed to be somebody sent from God to save the world, I think he's the new secretary-general of the United Nations."

Buck shivered.

Rayford was priority listed as a first-class passenger for the next flight to Chicago out of Baltimore. He called Chloe from the airport to let her know why he would be later than expected.

"Hattie Durham's been trying to reach you."

"What does she want?"

"She's trying to set up a meeting with you and Carpathia before you become his pilot."

"I'm going to fly him round-trip to Tel Aviv. Why do I have to meet him?"

"More likely he feels he has to meet you. Hattie told him you were a Christian."

"Oh, great! He'll never trust me."

"Probably wants to keep an eye on you."

"I want to talk to Hattie in person, anyway. When does he want to see me?"

"Tomorrow."

"My life's getting too busy all of a sudden. What's new with you?"

"Something more from my secret admirer today," she said. "Candy this time."

"Candy!" Rayford said, spooked by the fears Leonard Gustafson had planted. "You didn't eat any of it, did you?"

"Not yet. Why?"

"Just don't touch that stuff till you know who it's from."

"Oh, Dad!"

"You never know, hon. Please, just don't take any chances."

"All right, but these are my favorites! They look so good."

"Don't even open them until we know, OK?"

"All right, but you're going to want some too. They're the same ones you always bring me from New York, from that one little department-store chain."

"Windmill Mints from Holman Meadows?"

"Those are the ones."

That was the height of insult. How many times had Rayford mentioned to Hattie that he had to get those mints from that store during layovers in New York. She had even accompanied him more than once. So Hattie wasn't even trying to hide that she was sending the mysterious gifts. What was the point? It didn't seem to fit as vengeance for the cavalier way he had treated her. What did it have to do with Chloe? And was Carpathia aware of—or even behind—something so pedestrian?

Rayford would find out, that was sure.

Buck felt alive again. His life had been in such turmoil since the disappearances, he had wondered if it would ever settle back into the hectic norm he so enjoyed. His spiritual journey had been one thing, his demotion and relocation another. But now he seemed back in the good graces of the brass at *Global Weekly,* and he had used his instincts to trade for what he considered the top-breaking stories in the world.

He sat in his new makeshift home office, faxing, E-mailing, phoning, working with Marge and with reporters at *Weekly,* and making contacts for himself as well. He had a lot of people to interview in a short time, and all the developments seemed to be breaking at once.

Though part of him was horrified at what had happened, Buck enjoyed the rush of it. He desperately wanted to convince his own family of the truth. His father and brother would hear none of it, however, and if he had not been busy with challenging, exciting work, that fact alone would have driven him crazy.

Buck had just a few days to get his work done before and after the treaty signing. It seemed his whole life was on fast-forward now, trying to cram as much into seven years as he could. He didn't know what heaven on earth would be like, though Bruce was trying to teach him and Rayford and Chloe. He longed for the Glorious Appearing and the thousand-year reign of Christ on the earth. But in his mind, until he learned and knew more, anything normal he wanted to accomplish—like investigative reporting and writing, falling in love, getting married, maybe having a child—all had to be done soon.

Chloe was the best part of this new life. But did he have the time to do justice to a relationship that promised to be more than anything he had ever experienced? She was different from any woman he had known, and yet he couldn't put a finger on that difference. Her faith had enriched her and made her a new person, and yet he had been attracted to her before either of them had received Christ.

The idea that their meeting might have been part of some divine plan boggled his mind. How he wished they had met years before and had been ready together for the Rapture! If he was going to get any time with her before starting his trip to Israel, it would have to be that very day.

Buck looked at his watch. He had time for one more call, then he would reach Chloe.

Rayford dozed with his earphones on in first class. Images from the news filled the screen in front of him, but he had lost interest in reports of record crime waves throughout the United States. The name Carpathia finally roused him. The United Nations Security Council had been meeting several hours every day, finalizing plans for the one-world currency and the massive disarmament plan the secretary-general had instituted. Originally, the idea was to destroy 90 percent of weapons and donate the remaining 10 percent to the U.N. Now each contributing country would also invest its own soldiers in the U.N. peacekeeping forces.

Carpathia had asked the president of the United States to head up the verification committee, a highly controversial move. Enemies of the U.S. claimed Fitzhugh would be biased and untrustworthy, making certain they destroyed their weapons while the U.S. hoarded its own.

Carpathia himself addressed these issues in his customarily direct and sympathetic way. Rayford shuddered as he listened. Undoubtedly, he would have trusted and supported this man if Rayford hadn't been a Christian.

"The United States has long been a keeper of the peace," Carpathia said. "They will lead the way, destroying their weapons of destruction and shipping to New Babylon the remaining 10 percent. Peoples of the world will be free to come and inspect the work of the U.S., assuring themselves of full compliance and then following in like manner.

"Let me just add this," the secretary-general said. "This is a massive, major undertaking that could take years. Every country could justify month after month of procedural protocol, but we must not let this occur. The United States of America will set the example, and no other country will take longer than they do to destroy their weapons and donate the rest. By the time the new United Nations headquarters is completed in New Babylon, the weapons will be in place.

"The era of peace is at hand, and the world is finally, at long last, on the threshold of becoming one global community."

Carpathia's pronouncement was met with thunderous applause, even from the press.

Later, on the same newscast, Rayford saw a brief special on the new *Air Force One,* a 757 which would be delivered to Washington's Dulles Airport and then flown to New York to await its official maiden voyage under the control of "a new captain to be announced shortly. The new man has been culled from a list of top pilots from the major airlines."

In other news, Carpathia was quoted as saying that he and the ecumenical council of the meeting of religious leaders from around the world would have an exciting announcement by the next afternoon.

―――――――

Buck reached the assistant to Archbishop Peter Cardinal Mathews in Cincinnati. "Yes, he's here, but resting. He leaves tomorrow morning for New York for the final meeting of the ecumenical council, and then he'll be on to Israel and the Vatican."

"I would come anywhere, anytime, at his convenience," Buck said.

"I'll get back to you with an answer, one way or the other, within thirty minutes."

Buck phoned Chloe. "I've got only a few minutes right now," he said, "but can we get together, just the two of us, before the meeting tonight?"

"Sure, what's happening?"

"Nothing specific," he said. "It's just that I'd like to spend sometime with you, now that you know I'm available."

"Available? That's what you are?"

"Yes, ma'am! And you?"

"I guess I'm available too. That means we've got something in common."

"Did you have plans this evening?"

"Nope. Dad's going to be a little late. He was interviewed at the White House today."

"He's taking the job then?"

"He's going to make the maiden voyage and then decide."

"I could have been on that flight."

"I know."

"Pick you up at six?" Buck said.

"I'd love it."

TWELVE

As promised, Cardinal Mathews's assistant called Buck back, and the news was good. The cardinal had been so impressed with Buck's interview of him for the soon-to-appear cover story that he said Buck could ride with him to New York the following morning.

Buck booked the last flight out of O'Hare to Cincinnati that evening. He surprised Chloe by showing up at six with Chinese food. He told her of his plans for the evening trip and added, "I didn't want to waste talking time trying to find a place to eat."

"My dad's going to be jealous when he gets home," she said. "He loves Chinese."

Buck reached deep into the big sack, pulled out an extra order, and grinned. "Gotta keep the dad happy."

Buck and Chloe sat in the kitchen, eating and talking for more than an hour. They talked about everything—their respective childhoods, families, major events of their lives, hopes, fears, and dreams. Buck loved to hear Chloe talk, not just what she said, but even her voice. He didn't know whether she was the best conversationalist he had ever met, or if he was simply falling for her. *Probably both,* he decided.

Rayford arrived to find Buck and Chloe at Raymie's computer, which had not been turned on since the week of the disappearances. Within a few minutes, Buck had Chloe connected to the Internet and set up with an E-mail address. "Now you can reach me anywhere in the world," he said.

Rayford left Buck and Chloe at the computer and examined the mints from Holman Meadows. The candies were still shrink-

wrapped and had been delivered by a reputable company. They
had been addressed to Chloe, but with no message. Rayford decided they had not been tampered with, and even if they had
come from Hattie Durham for some inexplicable reason, there
was no sense in not enjoying them.

"Whoever's in love with your daughter sure has good taste,"
Buck said.

"Thank you," Chloe said.

"I mean good taste in chocolate mints."

Chloe blushed. "I know what you meant," she said.

At Rayford's insistence, Buck had agreed to leave his car in the
Steele's garage during his trip. Buck and Chloe left the Tribulation Force meeting early to get to the airport. Traffic was lighter
than he expected, and they arrived more than an hour before his
flight. "We could have stayed longer at the church," he said.

"Better to be safe, though, don't you think?" she said. "I hate
always running on the edge of lateness."

"Me too," he said, "but I usually do. You can just drop me at
the curb."

"I don't mind waiting with you if you don't mind paying for
the parking."

"You going to be all right going back to the car this time of
night?"

"I've done it lots of times," she said. "There are a lot of security guards."

She parked and they strolled through the massive terminal. He
lugged his leather over-the-shoulder case with his whole world in
it. Chloe seemed awkward, but Buck had nothing for her to
carry, and they weren't at the hand-holding stage yet, so they just
kept moving. Every time he turned so she could hear him, his bag
shifted and the strap slipped off his shoulder, so they eventually
settled into a silent trek to the gate.

Buck checked in and found that it was going to be a nearly
empty flight. "Wish you could come with me," he said lightly.

"I wish—," she began, but apparently thought better of saying
it.

"What?"

She shook her head.

"You wish you could come with me too?"

She nodded. "But I can't and I won't, so let's not start with any of that."

"What would I do with you?" he said. "Put you in my bag?"

She laughed.

They stood at the windows, watching baggage handlers and ground traffic controllers in the night. Buck pretended to look out the window as he stared at Chloe's reflection a few inches from his own. A couple of times he sensed her focus had shifted from the tarmac to the glass as well, and he imagined he was holding her gaze. *Wishful thinking,* he decided.

"We're going to be delayed twenty minutes," the woman at the counter announced.

"Don't feel obligated to stay, Chloe," Buck said. "You want me to walk you back to the car?"

She laughed again. "You're really paranoid about that big old parking garage, aren't you? No, see, the deal is that I bring you here, wait with you at your gate so you won't feel lonely, and then I stay until you're safely on the plane. I wave as it takes off, pretend to be rooted to the spot, and only when the jet trail fades out of sight do I venture out to the car."

"What, do you make this stuff up as you go along?"

"Of course. Now sit down and relax and pretend you're a frequent worldwide traveler."

"I wish for once I could pretend I'm not."

"And then you'd be nervous about the flight and need me here?"

"I need you here anyway."

She looked away. *Slow down,* he told himself. This was the fun part, the parrying stage, but it was also maddeningly uncertain. He didn't want to say things to her just because he would be gone for a few days that he wouldn't say otherwise.

"I need you here too," she said lightly, "but you're leaving me."

"That is something I would never do."

"What, leave me?"

"Absolutely." He kept a humorous tone in an effort not to scare her off.

"Well, that's encouraging. Can't have any of this leaving stuff."

Rayford kept an ear out for Chloe while packing for his quick trip to New York the next afternoon. Earl had called, wanting to know if Carpathia's office had reached him.

"And is that the same Hattie Durham who used to work for us?" Earl asked.

"One and the same."

"She's Carpathia's secretary?"

"Something like that."

"Small world."

———————

"I guess it would be silly to tell you to be careful in Cincinnati and New York and Israel, considering all you've been through," Chloe said.

Buck smiled. "Don't start your good-byes until you're ready to leave."

"I'm not leaving till your plane is out of sight," she said. "I told you that."

"We have time for a cookie," he said, pointing at a vendor in the corridor.

"We already had dessert," she said. "Chocolates and a cookie."

"Fortune cookies don't count," he said. "Come on. Don't you remember our first cookie?"

The day they had met, Chloe had eaten a cookie and he had dabbed a tiny piece of chocolate from the corner of her mouth with his thumb. Not knowing what to do with it, he had licked it off.

"I remember I was a slob," she said. "And you tried a very old joke."

"You feel like a cookie?" he said, setting her up the way she had him in New York that first day.

"Why, do I look like one?"

Buck laughed, not because the joke was any funnier than the first time, he decided, but because it was theirs and it was stupid.

"I'm really not hungry," she said as they peered through the glass as a bored teenager waited for their order.

"Me either," Buck said. "These are for later."

"Tonight later or tomorrow later?" she asked.

"Whenever we synchronize our watches."

"We're going to eat them together? I mean, at the same time?"

"Doesn't that sound exciting?"

"Your creativity never ceases."

Buck ordered two cookies in two bags.

"Can't do that," the teenager said.

"Then I want one cookie," he said, handing over the money and slipping some to Chloe.

"And I want one cookie," she said, money in hand.

The teenager made a face, bagged the cookies for each of them, and made change.

"More than one way to skin a cat," Buck said.

They moseyed back to the gate. A few more passengers had gathered, and the woman at the counter announced that their plane had finally arrived. Buck and Chloe sat watching as the arriving passengers filed past, looking tired.

Buck carefully folded his cookie sack and laid it in his carry-on bag. "I'll be on a plane to New York at eight tomorrow morning," he said. "I'll have this with coffee and think of you."

"That'll be seven o'clock my time," Chloe said. "I'll still be in bed, anticipating my cookie and dreaming of you."

We're still playing around the edges, Buck thought. *Neither of us will say anything serious.*

"I'll wait till you're up, then," he said. "Tell me when you're going to eat your cookie."

Chloe studied the ceiling. "Hmm," she mused. "When will you be in your most important, most formal meeting?"

"Probably sometime late morning at a big hotel in New York. Carpathia is coming for some joint announcement with Cardinal Mathews and other religious leaders."

"Whenever that is, I'll eat my cookie," Chloe said. "And I dare you to eat yours then, too."

"You'll learn not to dare me." Buck smiled, but he was only half kidding. "I know no fear."

"Ha!" she said. "You're afraid of the parking garage here, and you're not even the one walking through it alone!"

Buck reached for her cookie sack.

"What're you doing?" she said. "We're not hungry, remember?"

"Just smell this," he said. "Fragrance is such a memory enhancer."

He opened her cookie sack and held it up to his face. "Mmm," he said. "Cookie dough, chocolate, nuts, butter, you name it."

He tilted it toward her, and she leaned to sniff it. "I do love that smell," she said.

Buck reached with his other hand and cupped her cheek in his palm. She didn't pull away but held his look. "Remember this moment," he said. "I'll be thinking of you while I'm gone."

"Me too," she said. "Now close that bag. That cookie has to stay fresh so the smell will remind me."

Rayford awoke earlier than Chloe and padded down to the kitchen. He lifted the small cookie bag from the counter. *One left,* he thought, and was tempted. Instead he wrote Chloe a note. "Hope you don't mind. I couldn't resist." On the back he wrote, "Just kidding," and laid the note atop the bag. He had coffee and juice, then changed into his workout clothes and went for a run.

Buck sat in first class with Cardinal Mathews on the Cincy to New York morning flight. Mathews was in his late fifties, a beefy, jowly man with close-cropped black hair that appeared to be his own natural color. Only his collar evidenced his station. He carried an expensive briefcase and laptop computer, and Buck noticed from his ticket sleeve that he had checked four bags.

Mathews traveled with an aide, who merely deflected other people and said little. The aide moved to a seat in front of them so Buck could sit next to the archbishop. "Why didn't you tell me you were a candidate for the papacy?" Buck began.

"So, we're just going to jump right into it, are we?" Mathews said. "Don't you like a little champagne in the morning?"

"No thanks."

"Well, you won't mind if I have a little pick-me-up."

"Suit yourself. Tell me when you're available to chat."

Mathews's aide heard the conversation and signaled the flight attendant, who immediately brought the cardinal a glass of champagne. "The usual?" she said.

"Thank you, Caryn," he said, as if to an old friend. Apparently she was. When she was gone he whispered, "The Litewski family, from my first parish. Baptized her myself. She's worked this flight for years. Now where were we?"

Buck did not respond. He knew the cardinal had heard and remembered the question. If he wanted it repeated for his own ego, he could repeat it himself.

"Oh, yes, you were wondering why I didn't mention the papacy. I guess I thought everyone knew. Carpathia knew."

I'll bet he did, Buck thought. *Probably engineered it.* "Is Carpathia hoping you'll get it?"

"Off the record," Mathews whispered, "there is no hoping anymore. We have the votes."

"We?"

"That's the editorial *we.* We, us, me, I have the votes. Understand?"

"How can you be so sure?"

"I've been a member of the college of cardinals for more than ten years. I have never yet been surprised by a papal vote. You know what Nicolae calls me? He calls me P. M."

Buck shrugged. "He calls you by your initials? Is there some significance?"

Mathews's aide peeked back between the seats and shook his head. *So, I should know,* Buck surmised. But he had never been afraid of asking a dumb question.

"Pontifex Maximus," Mathews beamed. "Supreme Pope."

"Congratulations," Buck said.

"Thank you, but I trust you know that Nicolae has much more in mind for my papacy than merely leadership of the Holy Roman Catholic Mother Church."

"Tell me."

"It'll be announced later this morning, and if you do not quote me directly, I'll give you the first shot at it."

"Why would you do that?"

"Because I like you."

"You hardly know me."

"But I know Nicolae."

Buck sank in his seat. "And Nicolae likes me."

"Exactly."

"So this little ride-along was not really entirely the result of my legwork."

"Ah, no," Mathews said. "Carpathia endorsed you. He wants me to tell you everything. Just don't make me look bad or self-serving for what I tell you."

"Will the announcement make you appear that way?"

"No, because Carpathia himself will make that announcement."

"I'm listening."

"Secretary-General Carpathia's office, Ms. Durham speaking."

"Rayford Steele here."

"Rayford! How are—"

"Let me get to the point, Hattie. I want to come early this afternoon so I can speak with you privately for a few minutes."

"That would be wonderful, Captain Steele. I should tell you in advance, however, that I am seeing someone."

"That's not funny."

"I didn't intend it to be."

"Will you have time?"

"Certainly. Secretary-General Carpathia can see you at four. Shall I look for you at three-thirty?"

Rayford hung up the phone as Chloe came into the kitchen, dressed for work at the church. She saw his note. "Oh, Dad! You didn't!" she said, and he thought she was on the verge of tears. She grabbed the bag and shook it. A relieved look came over her as she turned the note over and laughed. "Grow up, Dad. For once in your life, act your age."

He was getting ready to head to the airport and she for work when CNN broadcast a press conference live from the meeting of international religious leaders in New York. "Watch this, Dad," she said. "Buck is there."

Rayford set his carry-on bag on the floor and went to stand next to Chloe, who held a mug of coffee in both hands. The CNN correspondent intoned an explanation of what was to come. "We're expecting a joint statement from the coalition of religious leaders and the United Nations, represented by new Secretary-General Nicolae Carpathia. He seems the man of the hour here, having helped hammer out propositions and pulling together representatives of widely varying systems of belief. Since he has been in office, not a day has passed without some major development.

"Speculation here is that the religions of the world are going to make some fresh attempt at addressing global issues in a more cohesive and tolerant way than ever before. Ecumenism has failed in the past, but we'll soon see if this time around there is some new wrinkle that can finally make it work. Stepping to the podium is Archbishop Peter Cardinal Mathews, prelate of the Cincinnati archdiocese of the Roman Catholic Church and widely seen as a potential successor to Pope John XXIV who served only a controversial five months before being listed among the missing in the disappearances just weeks ago."

The camera panned to the press conference platform, where

more than two dozen religious leaders from around the world, all dressed in their native garb, jockeyed for position. As Archbishop Mathews worked his way through to the bank of microphones, Rayford heard Chloe squeal.

"There's Buck, Dad! Look! Right there!"

She pointed to a reporter who was not in the crowd with the rest of the journalists but seemed to teeter on the back edge of the raised platform. Buck appeared to be trying to keep his balance. Twice he stepped down only to step back up again.

As Mathews droned on about international cooperation, Rayford and Chloe stared at Buck in the back corner. No one else would have even noticed him. "What's he got?" Rayford said. "Is that some sort of a notebook or tape recorder?"

Chloe looked close and gasped. She ran to the kitchen and returned with her cookie sack. "It's his cookie!" she said. "We're going to eat our cookies at the same time!"

Rayford was lost, but he was sure glad he hadn't eaten that cookie. "What—?" he began, but Chloe shushed him.

"It smells just like last night!" she said.

Rayford snorted. "Just what did last night smell like?" he said.

"Shhh!"

And sure enough, as they watched, Buck quickly and quietly reached into his little sack, surreptitiously and almost invisibly slid out the cookie, put it to his mouth, and took a bite. Chloe matched him gesture for gesture, and Rayford noticed she was smiling and crying at the same time.

"You've got it bad," he said, and he left for the airport.

Buck had no idea whether his little antic had been seen by anyone, let alone Chloe Steele. What was this girl doing to him? He had somehow gone from international star journalist to lovestruck romantic doing silly things for attention. But, he hoped, not too much attention. Few people ever noticed anyone on the edge of a TV shot. For all he knew, Chloe could have been watching and not have seen him at all.

More important than his efforts was the major story that broke from what might otherwise have been labeled a typical international confab. Somehow Nicolae Carpathia, either by promising support for Mathews's papacy or by his uncanny ability to charm anyone, had gotten these religious leaders to produce a proposition of incredible significance.

They were announcing not only an effort to cooperate and be more tolerant of each other but also the formation of an entirely new religion, one that would incorporate the tenets of all.

"And lest that sound impossible to the devout members of each of our sects," Mathews said, "we are all, every one of us, in total unanimity. Our religions themselves have caused as much division and bloodshed around the world as any government, army, or weapon. From this day forward we will unite under the banner of the Global Community Faith. Our logo will contain sacred symbols from religions that represent all, and from here on will encompass all. Whether we believe God is a real person or merely a concept, God is in all and above all and around all. God is in us. God is us. We are God."

When the floor was opened to questions, many astute religion editors zeroed in. "What happens to the leadership of, say, Roman Catholicism? Will there be the need for a pope?"

"We will elect a pope," Mathews said. "And we expect that other major religions will continue to appoint leaders in their usual cycles. But these leaders will serve the Global Community Faith and be expected to maintain the loyalty and devotion of their parishioners to the larger cause."

"Is there one major tenet you all agree on?"

This was met with laughter by the participants. Mathews called on a Rastafarian to answer. Through an interpreter he said, "We believe two things concretely. First, in the basic goodness of humankind. Second, that the disappearances were a religious cleansing. Some religions saw many disappear. Others saw very few. Many saw none. But the fact that many were left from each proves that none was better than the other. We will be tolerant of all, believing that the best of us remain."

Buck moved around to the front and raised his hand. "Cameron Williams, *Global Weekly,*" he said. "Follow-up question for the gentleman at the microphone or Mathews or whomever. How does this tenet of the basic goodness of humankind jibe with the idea that the bad people have been winnowed out? How did they miss possessing this basic goodness?"

No one moved to answer. The Rastafarian looked to Mathews, who stared blankly at Buck, clearly not wishing to act upset but also wanting to communicate that he felt ambushed.

Mathews finally took the microphone. "We are not here to debate theology," he said. "I happen to be one of those who believes that the disappearances constituted a cleansing, and that the basic goodness of humankind is the common denominator of those who remain. And this basic goodness is found in greater measure in no one other than United Nations Secretary-General Nicolae Carpathia. Welcome him, please!"

The platform erupted with religious leaders cheering. Some of the press clapped, and for the first time Buck became aware of a huge public contingent behind the press. Due to the spotlights, he had not seen them from the platform, and he had not heard them until Carpathia appeared.

Carpathia was his typical masterful self, giving all the credit to the leadership of the ecumenical body and endorsing this "historic, perfect idea, whose time is long overdue."

He took a few questions, including what would happen to the rebuilding of the Jewish temple in Jerusalem. "That, I am happy to say, will proceed. As many of you know, much money has been donated to this cause for decades, and some prefabrication of the temple in other sites has been underway for years. Once the reconstruction begins, completion should be without delay."

"But what happens to the Islamic Dome of the Rock?"

"I am so glad you asked that question," Carpathia said, and Buck wondered if he hadn't planted it. "Our Muslim brothers have agreed to move not only the shrine but also the sacred section of the rock to New Babylon, freeing the Jews to rebuild their temple on what they believe is the original site.

"And now, if you will indulge me for a moment longer, I would like to say that we clearly are at the most momentous juncture in world history. With the consolidation to one form of currency, with the cooperation and toleration of many religions into one, with worldwide disarmament and commitment to peace, the world is truly becoming one.

"Many of you have heard me use the term Global Community. This is a worthy name for our new cause. We can communicate with one another, worship with one another, trade with one another. With communications and travel advancements, we are no longer a conglomeration of countries and nations, but one complete global community, a village made up of equal citizens. I thank the leaders here who have assembled this piece of the beautiful mosaic, and I would like to make an announcement in their honor.

"With the move of the United Nations headquarters to New

Babylon will come a new name for our great organization. We will become known as the Global Community!" When applause finally subsided, Carpathia concluded, "Thus the name of the new one-world religion, Global Community Faith, is precisely appropriate."

Carpathia was being whisked away as camera and sound crews began tearing down the press conference site. Nicolae saw Buck and broke stride, telling his bodyguards he wanted to talk with someone. They formed a human wall around him as Carpathia embraced Buck. It was all Buck could do to not recoil. "Be careful of what you're doing to my journalistic independence," he whispered in Carpathia's ear.

"Any good news for me yet?" Carpathia asked, holding Buck at arm's length and looking into his eyes.

"Not yet, sir."

"I will see you in Jerusalem?"

"Of course."

"You will keep in touch with Steve?"

"I will."

"You tell him what it will take, and we will do it. That is a promise."

Buck sidled over to a small group where Peter Mathews was holding court. Buck waited until the archbishop noticed him; then he leaned forward and whispered, "What'd I miss?"

"What do you mean? You were there."

"You said Carpathia would make some announcement about an expanded role for the next pope, something bigger and more important even than the Catholic Church."

Mathews stood shaking his head. "Perhaps I had you overrated, friend. I am not the pope yet, but couldn't you tell from the secretary-general's statement that there will be need for a head of the new religion? What better place to headquarter it than the Vatican? And who better to lead it than the new pope?"

"So you'll be the pope of popes."

Mathews smiled and nodded. "P. M.," he said.

Two hours later, Rayford Steele arrived at the United Nations. He had been praying silently since he phoned Bruce Barnes just before he boarded his flight. "I feel like I'm going to meet the devil," Rayford said. "Not much in this life scares me, Bruce. I've always taken pride in that. But I've got to tell you, this is awful."

"First, Rayford, only if you were encountering the Antichrist in the second half of the Tribulation would you actually be dealing with the person who was possessed by Satan himself."

"So what is Carpathia? Some second-rate demon?"

"No, you need prayer support. You know what happened in Buck's presence."

"Buck is ten years younger, and in better shape," Rayford said. "I feel as if I'll fall apart in there."

"You won't. Stay strong. God knows where you are, and he has perfect timing. I'll be praying, and you know Chloe and Buck will be too."

That was of great comfort to Rayford, and it was particularly encouraging to know that Buck was in town. Just knowing he was in close proximity made Rayford feel less alone. Yet in his anxiety over meeting Carpathia face-to-face, he did not want to look past the ordeal of confronting Hattie Durham.

Hattie was waiting when he stepped off the elevator. He had hoped to have a moment to get the lay of the land, to freshen up, to take a deep breath. But there she stood in all her youthful beauty, more stunning than ever because of a tan and expensively tailored clothes on a frame that needed no help. He did not expect what he saw, and he sensed evil in the place when a flash of longing for her briefly invaded his mind.

Rayford's old nature immediately reminded him why she had distracted him during a wintry season of his marriage. He prayed silently, thanking God for sparing him from having done something he would have regretted forever. And as soon as Hattie opened her mouth, he was brought back to reality. Her diction and articulation were more refined, but this was still a woman without a clue, and he could hear it in her tone.

"Captain Steele," she gushed. "How wonderful to see you again! How is everyone else?"

"Everyone else?"

"You know, Chloe and Buck and everybody."

Chloe and Buck are *everybody*, he thought, but he didn't say so.

"Everybody's fine."

"Oh, that's wonderful."

"Is there a private place we can talk?"

She led him to her work area, which was disconcertingly open.

No one was around to overhear them, but the ceilings were at least twenty feet high. Her desk and tables and file cabinets were set in a cavernous area, much like a railway station, with no confining walls. Footsteps echoed, and Rayford had the distinct impression that they were a long way from the offices of the secretary-general.

"So, what's new with you since I saw you last, Captain Steele?"

"Hattie, I don't want to be unkind, but you can stop with the 'Captain Steele' and the pretending to not know what's new. What's new is that you and your new boss have invaded my job and my family, and I seem powerless to do anything about it."

THIRTEEN

STANTON Bailey gripped the armrests of his big chair and rocked back, studying Buck Williams.

"Cameron," he said, "I have never been able to figure you. What was that sack lunch business all about?"

"It was just a cookie. I was hungry."

"I'm always hungry," Bailey roared, "but I don't eat on TV!"

"I wasn't sure I could be seen."

"Well, now you know. And if Carpathia and Plank still let you at the signing table in Jerusalem, no sack lunches."

"It was a cookie."

"No cookies either!"

After years as Hattie Durham's captain, Rayford now felt like her subordinate, sitting across from her impressive desk. Apparently his coming straight to the point had sobered her.

"Rayford, listen," she said, "I still like you in spite of how you dumped me, all right? I would never do anything to hurt you."

"Trying to get a complaint about me into my personnel file is not going to hurt me?"

"That was just a joke. You saw right through it."

"It brought me a lot of grief. And the note waiting for me in Dallas about the new *Air Force One* being a 757."

"Same thing, I told you. A joke."

"Not funny. Too coincidental."

"Well, Rayford, if you can't take a little teasing, then fine, I won't bother. I just thought, friend to friend, a little fun wouldn't hurt."

"Come on, Hattie. You think I'm buying this? This is not your style. You don't pull practical jokes on your friends. It's just not you."

"OK, I'm sorry."

"That's not good enough."

"Well, excuse me, but I don't answer to you anymore."

Somehow Hattie Durham had the capacity to rattle Rayford more than anyone else did. He took a deep breath and fought for composure. "Hattie, I want you to tell me about the flowers and candy."

Hattie was the worst bluffer in the world. "Flowers and candy?" she repeated after a guilty pause.

"Stop with the games," Rayford said. "Just accept that I know it was you and tell me why."

"I only do what I'm told, Rayford."

"See? This is beyond me. I should be asking the most powerful man in the world why he sent my daughter, someone he has never met, flowers and candy? Is he pursuing her? And if he is, why doesn't he sign his name?"

"He's not pursuing her, Rayford! He's seeing someone."

"What does that mean?"

"He has a relationship."

"Anybody we know?" Rayford gave her a disgusted look.

Hattie seemed to be fighting a grin. "It's safe to say we're an item, but the press doesn't know, so we'd appreciate it—"

"I'll make a deal with you. You quit with the anonymous gifts to Chloe, tell me what the point was, and I'll keep your little secret—how's that?"

Hattie leaned forward conspiratorially. "OK," she said, "here's what I think, all right? I mean, I don't know. Like I said, I just do what I'm told. But that's one brilliant mind in there."

Rayford didn't doubt that. He just wondered why Nicolae Carpathia was spending time on such trivia.

"Go on."

"He really wants you as his pilot."

"OK," Rayford said tentatively.

"You'll do it?"

"Do what? I'm just saying I follow you, though I'm not sure I really do. He wants me as his pilot, and so . . . ?"

"But he knows you're happy where you are."

"Still with you, I think."

"He wants to provide not just a job that might lure you away, but also something on your end that might push you from where you are."

"My daughter being pursued by him would push me toward him?"

"No, silly. You weren't supposed to find out who it was!"

"I see. I would be worried that it was someone from Chicago, so I would be inclined to move and take another job."

"There you go."

"I've got lots of questions, Hattie."

"Shoot."

"Why would someone pursuing my daughter make me want to run? She's almost twenty-one. It's time she was pursued."

"But we did it anonymously. That should have seemed a little dangerous, a little upsetting."

"It was."

"Then we did our job."

"Hattie, did you think I wouldn't put two and two together when you sent Chloe's favorite mints, available only at Holman Meadows in New York?"

"Hmph," she said, "maybe that wasn't too swift."

"OK, let's say it worked. I think my daughter's being stalked or pursued by someone who seems sinister. As close as Carpathia is to the president, doesn't he know they're after me to pilot *Air Force One?*"

"Rayford! Duh! *That's* the job he wants you to take."

Rayford slumped and sighed. "Hattie, for the love of all things sacred, just tell me what's going on. I get hints from the White House and Pan-Con that it's Carpathia who wants me in there. I'm approved sight unseen to fly the U.N. delegation to Israel. Carpathia wants me as his pilot but first he wants me to be the captain of *Air Force One?*"

Maddeningly, Hattie turned a tolerant and condescending smile on him. "Rayford Steele," she said in a schoolmarmish tone, "you just don't get it yet, do you? You don't really know who Nicolae Carpathia is."

Rayford was stunned for a second. He knew better than she did who Nicolae Carpathia really was. The question was whether *she* had any inkling. "Tell me," he said. "Help me understand."

Hattie looked behind her, as if expecting Carpathia at any moment. Rayford knew no one could sneak up on them in this echoing, marble-floored edifice. "Nicolae is not going to give back the plane."

"Excuse me?"

"You heard me. It's already been flown to New York. You're going to see it today. It's being painted."

"Painted?"

"You'll see."

Rayford's mind reeled. The plane would have been painted in Seattle before being flown to D.C. Why would it be painted again?

"How's he going to get away with not returning it?"

"He's going to thank the president for the gift, and—"

"He already did that the other day. I heard him."

"But this time he will make it obvious he's thanking the president for a *gift*, not for a *loan*. You get hired by the White House first, and you come with the plane, on the president's salary budget. What can the president do, look betrayed? Say Nicolae is lying? He'll just have to find a way to look as generous as Nicolae makes him out to be. Is that brilliant?"

"It's boorish. It's thievery. Why would I want to work for a man like that? Why would *you?*"

"I'll work with and for Nicolae for as long as he'll let me, Rayford. I have never learned so much in so short a time. This is not thievery at all. Nicolae says the United States is looking for ways to support the U.N. now, and here is a way. You know the world is coming together, and someone is going to lead the new one-world government. Getting this plane is one way to show that President Fitzhugh defers to Secretary-General Carpathia."

Hattie sounded like a parrot. Carpathia had taught her well, if not to understand, at least to believe.

"OK," Rayford summarized, "Carpathia somehow gets Pan-Con and the White House to put me at the top of the list of pilots for *Air Force One*. He has you agitate me at home so I'll want to move. I take the job, he gets the plane and never gives it back. I'm the pilot, but I'm paid by the U.S. government. And this all ties in with Carpathia eventually becoming the leader of the world."

Hattie rested her chin in her entwined fingers, elbows on the desk. She cocked her head. "That wasn't so complicated, was it?"

"I don't get why I'm so important to him."

"He asked who was the best pilot I ever worked for and why."

"And I won," Rayford said.

"You won."

"Did you tell him we almost had a fling?"

"Did we?"

"Never mind."

"Of course I didn't tell him that, and neither will you if you want to keep a good job."

"But you told him I was a Christian."

"Sure, why not? You tell everyone else. I think *he's* a Christian, anyway."

"Nicolae Carpathia?"

"Of course! At least he lives by Christian principles. He's always concerned for the greater good. That's one of his favorite phrases. Like this airplane deal. He knows the U.S. wants to do this, even if they didn't think of it. They might feel a little put out for a while, but since it is for the greater good of the world, they'll eventually see that and be glad they did it. They'll look like generous heroes, and he's doing that for them. That's Christian, isn't it?"

Buck was scribbling furiously. He had left his tape recorder in his bag at the hotel, expecting to get it when he returned from the *Global Weekly* office to interview Rabbi Marc Feinberg, one of the key proponents of rebuilding the Jewish temple. But when Buck had entered the hotel lobby, he had nearly run into Feinberg, who was pulling a large trunk on wheels. "I'm sorry, my friend. I was able to get an earlier flight, and I'm going. Walk with me."

Buck had dug his notebook from one pocket and pen from the other. "How do you feel about the pronouncements?" Buck asked.

"Let me say this: Today I have become a bit of a politician. Do I believe God is a concept? No! I believe God is a person! Do I believe that all the religions of the world can work together and become one? No, probably not. My God is a jealous God and will share his glory with no other. However, can we tolerate each other? Certainly.

"But, you may ask, why do I say I have become a politician? Because I will compromise for the sake of rebuilding the temple. As long as I do not have to sacrifice my belief in the one true God of Abraham, Isaac, and Jacob, I will tolerate and cooperate

with anyone with a good heart. I do not agree with them or with
their methods, many of them, but if they want to get along, I
want to get along. Above all, I want the temple rebuilt on its
original site. This was virtually done as of today. I predict the
temple will be constructed within the year."

The rabbi burst through the front doors and asked the doorman to hail him a cab. "But, sir," Buck said, "if the head of the
new one-world religion considers himself a Christian—"

Feinberg waved Buck off. "Ach! We all know it will be Mathews, and that he will likely be the next pope, too! *Considers*
himself a Christian? He *is* a Christian through and through! He
believes Jesus was Messiah. I'd sooner believe Carpathia is Messiah."

"You're serious?"

"Believe me, I have considered it. Messiah is to bring justice
and lasting peace. Look what Carpathia has done in just weeks!
Does he fit all the criteria? We'll find out Monday. Are you aware
that my colleague Rabbi Tsion Ben-Judah is—"

"Yes, I'll be watching." There were plenty of other sources
Buck could talk to about Carpathia, and he wanted to speak with
Ben-Judah personally. What he wanted from Feinberg was the
temple story. He redirected the subject. "What is so important
about the rebuilding of the temple?"

Rabbi Feinberg stepped and spun, watching the line of cabs,
obviously worried about the time. But though he did not maintain
eye contact with Buck, he continued to expound. He gave Buck
the short course, as if teaching a class of Gentiles interested in
Jewish history.

"King David wanted to build a temple for the Lord," he said.
"But God felt David had shed too much blood as a man of war,
so he let David's son Solomon build it. It was magnificent. Jerusalem was the city where God would place his name and where his
people would come to worship. The glory of God appeared in the
temple, and it became a symbol of the hand of God protecting the
nation. The people felt so secure that even when they turned from
God, they believed Jerusalem was impregnable, as long as the
temple stood."

A cab pulled up and the doorman loaded the large valise into
the trunk. "Pay the man and ride with me," Feinberg said. Buck
had to smile as he pulled a bill from his pocket and pressed it
into the doorman's hand. Even if he had to pay for the cab ride,
it would be a cheap interview.

"Kennedy," Feinberg told the driver.

"Do you have a phone?" Buck asked the driver.

The driver handed him a cellular phone. "Credit-card calls only."

Buck asked to see Feinberg's bill so he could get the number of the hotel. He called the concierge and told her he would need his bag stored longer than he had expected. "Sir, someone took that bag for you."

"Someone what?"

"Took that bag for you. Said he was your friend and would see that you got it."

Buck was stunned. "You let my bag be taken by a stranger who claimed to be a friend of mine?"

"Sir, it's not as bleak as all that. I think the man could easily be located if necessary. He's on the news every night."

"Mr. Carpathia?"

"Yes, sir. One of his people, a Mr. Plank, promised he would deliver it to you."

Feinberg seemed pleased when Buck finally got off the phone. "Back to the temple!" he shouted, and the driver pulled his foot off the gas. "Not you!" Feinberg said. "Us!"

Buck wondered what a man with such unbounded energy and enthusiasm might do in another profession. "You'd have been a killer racquetball player," he said.

"I *am* a killer racquetball player!" Feinberg said. "I'm an A-minus. What are you?"

"Retired."

"And so young!"

"Too busy."

"Never too busy for physical exercise," the rabbi said, smacking himself on his flat, hard stomach. "Ah, the temple," he said. The cab was soon stuck in traffic, and Buck kept scribbling.

When Hattie excused herself to answer the phone on her desk, Rayford slipped his New Testament and Psalms from his pocket. He had been memorizing verses from the Psalms, and as his anxiety over meeting Carpathia grew, he turned to those favorites and ran them over in his mind.

He found Psalm 91 and read verses he had underlined: "He who dwells in the secret place of the Most High shall abide under

the shadow of the Almighty. I will say of the Lord, 'He is my ref-
uge and my fortress; My God, in Him I will trust.' A thousand
may fall at your side, and ten thousand at your right hand; but it
shall not come near you. No evil shall befall you, nor shall any
plague come near your dwelling; for He shall give His angels
charge over you, to keep you in all your ways."

When he looked up, Hattie was off the phone and looking at
him expectantly. "Sorry," he said, closing the Bible.

"That's all right," she said. "The secretary-general is ready for
you."

———

With the cabby's assurance that the rabbi was not going to miss
his plane, Feinberg warmed to his subject. "The temple and the
city of Jerusalem were destroyed by King Nebuchadnezzar. Sev-
enty years later a decree was given to rebuild the city and eventually the temple. The new temple, under the direction of
Zerubbabel and Joshua, the high priest, was so inferior to the
temple of Solomon that some of the elders wept when they saw
the foundation.

"Still, that temple served Israel until it was desecrated by Antio-
chus Epiphanes, a Greco-Roman ruler. About 40 B.C., Herod the
Great had the temple destroyed piece by piece and rebuilt. That
became known as Herod's Temple. And you know what became
of that."

"I'm sorry, I don't."

"You're a religion writer and you don't know what happened
to Herod's Temple?"

"I'm actually a pinch hitter for the religion writer on this
story."

"A pinch hitter?"

Buck smiled. "You're an A-minus racquetball player and you
don't know what a pinch hitter is?"

"It's not a racquetball term, I know that," Rabbi Feinberg said.
"And other than football, which you call soccer, I don't care
about other sports. Let me tell you what happened to Herod's
Temple. Titus, a Roman general, laid siege to Jerusalem, and even
though he gave orders that the temple not be destroyed, the Jews
did not trust him. They burned it rather than allow it to fall into
pagan hands. Today the Temple Mount, the site of the old Jewish

temple, is occupied by the Mohammedans and houses the Muslim mosque called the Dome of the Rock."

Buck was curious. "How were the Muslims persuaded to move the Dome of the Rock?"

"That proves the magnificence of Carpathia," Feinberg said. "Who but Messiah could ask devout Muslims to move the shrine that in their religion is second in importance only to Mecca, the birthplace of Mohammed? But you see, the Temple Mount, the Dome of the Rock, is built right over Mount Moriah, where we believe Abraham expressed his willingness to God to sacrifice his son Isaac. Of course we do not believe Mohammed to be divine, so as long as a Muslim mosque occupies the Temple Mount, we believe our holy place is being defiled."

"So this is a great day for Israel."

"A great day! Since the birth of our nation, we have collected millions from around the world for the rebuilding of the temple. Work has begun. Many prefabricated walls are finished and will be shipped in. I will live to see the reconstruction of the temple, and it will be even more spectacular than in the days of Solomon!"

"At last we meet," Nicolae Carpathia said, rising and coming around his desk to shake hands with Rayford Steele. "Thank you, Ms. Durham. We will sit right here."

Hattie left and shut the door. Nicolae pointed to a chair and sat down across from Rayford. "And so our little circle is connected."

Rayford felt strangely calmed. He was being prayed for, and his mind was full of the promises from the Psalms. "Sir?"

"It is interesting to me how small the world is. Perhaps that is why I believe so strongly that we are becoming truly a global community. Would you believe I met you through an Israeli botanist named Chaim Rosenzweig?"

"I know the name, of course, but we have never met."

"Indeed you have not. But you will. If not while you are here, then Saturday on the plane to Israel. He introduced me to a young journalist who had written about him. That journalist met your flight attendant, Ms. Durham, while on your plane, and eventually introduced her to me. She is now my assistant, and she introduced you to me. A small world."

Earl Halliday had said the same thing when he'd heard that Hattie Durham, a former Pan-Con employee, was working for the man who wanted Rayford as pilot of *Air Force One*. Rayford did not respond to Carpathia. He didn't believe they had met coincidentally. It was not such a small world. It was possible all had been where God had wanted them to be so Rayford could be sitting where he was today. This wasn't something he wanted or had sought, but he was finally open to it.

"So, you want to be the pilot of *Air Force One*."

"No, sir, that was not my desire. I am willing to fly her to Jerusalem with your delegation, at the request of the White House, and then decide about the request to become the pilot."

"You did not seek the position?"

"No, sir."

"But you are willing."

"To give it a try."

"Mr. Steele, I want to make a prediction. I want to presume that you will see this plane, experience the latest technology, and want never to fly anything less."

"That may very well be." *But not for that reason,* Rayford thought. *Only if it's what God wants.*

"I also want to let you in on a little secret, something that has not been announced yet. Ms. Durham has assured me that you are a man who can be trusted, a man of your word, and as of recently also a religious man."

Rayford nodded, unwilling to say anything.

"Then I will trust you to keep my confidence until this is announced. *Air Force One* is being lent to the United Nations as a gesture of support by the president of the United States."

"That's been on the news, sir."

"Of course, but what has not been announced is that the plane will then be given to us, along with the crew, for our exclusive use."

"How nice of President Fitzhugh to offer that."

"How nice indeed," Carpathia said. "And how generous."

Rayford understood how people could be charmed by Carpathia, but sitting across from him and knowing he was lying made it easier to resist his charm.

"When do you fly back?" Carpathia said.

"I left it open. I'm at your disposal. I do need to be home before we leave Saturday, however."

"I like your style," Carpathia said. "You are at my disposal.

That is nice. You realize, of course, that should you get this job—and you will—that this is not a platform for proselytizing."

"Meaning?"

"Meaning that the United Nations, which shall become known as Global Community, and I in particular, are proactively nonsectarian."

"I am a believer in Christ," Rayford said. "I attend church. I read my Bible. I tell people what I believe."

"But not on the job."

"If you become my superior and that becomes a directive, I will be obligated to obey."

"I will and it will and you will," Carpathia said. "Just so we understand each other."

"Clearly."

"I like you, and I believe we can work together."

"I don't know you, sir, but I believe I can work with anybody." Where had that come from? Rayford almost smiled. If he could work with the Antichrist, who couldn't he work with?

As the cab pulled up to the curb at Kennedy International, Rabbi Marc Feinberg said, "I'm sure you won't mind including my trip in your total, as you did interview me."

"Certainly," Buck said. "*Global Weekly* is more than happy to provide you a trip to the airport, provided we don't have to fly you to Israel."

"Now that you mention it—," the rabbi said with a twinkle, but he did not finish the thought. He merely waved, retrieved his valise from the cabby, and hurried into the terminal.

Nicolae Carpathia pressed the intercom button. "Ms. Durham, have you arranged for a car to the hangar?"

"Yes, sir. Rear entrance."

"We are ready."

"I'll buzz you when security arrives."

"Thank you." Nicolae turned to Rayford. "I want you to see the plane."

"Certainly," Rayford said, though he would rather have started toward home. Why on earth had he said he was at Carpathia's disposal?

———

"Back to the hotel, sir?"

"No," Buck said. "The U.N. building, please. And let me use your cell phone again, would you?"

"Credit—"

"Card calls only, I know." He phoned Steve Plank at the U.N. "What's the idea of absconding with my bag?"

"Just trying to do you a favor, old buddy. You at the Plaza? I'll bring it to you."

"That's where I'm staying, but let me come to you. That's what you intended anyway, wasn't it?"

"Yup."

"Be there in an hour."

"Carpathia may not be here."

"I'm not coming to see him. I'm coming to see you."

———

When Hattie buzzed, Carpathia stood and his door opened. Two security guards flanked Nicolae and Rayford as they made their way through the corridors to a freight elevator, down to the first floor below ground level, and into a parking dock, where a limousine waited. The driver leaped out to open the door for Carpathia. Rayford was walked around to the other side, where his door was opened.

Rayford found it strange that though he had been offered no refreshment at the office, Carpathia now insisted on showing him everything available in the limo, from whiskey to wine, to beer and soft drinks. Rayford accepted a Coke.

"Are you not a drinker?"

"Not anymore."

"Used to be?"

"Never a hard drinker, but occasionally unwise. I haven't touched a drop since I lost my family."

"I was sorry to hear of that."

"Thank you, but I have come to terms with it. I miss them terribly—"

"Of course."

"But I have peace about it."

"Your religion believes that Jesus Christ has taken his own to heaven, is that it?"

"That's it."

"I will not pretend that I share that belief, but I respect any comfort the thought may bring you."

Rayford wanted to argue, but he wondered at the advisability of doing what Bruce Barnes would call 'witnessing' to the Antichrist.

"I am not a drinker either," Carpathia said, sipping seltzer water.

"So why didn't you let me come to you?" Steve Plank said. "I would have."

"I need a favor."

"We can trade favors, Buck. Say yes to Carpathia's offer and you'll never have to ask for anything again as long as you live."

"To tell you the truth, Steve, I have too many good stories in the hopper right now to even think about jumping."

"Write them for us."

"No can do. But help me if you can. I want to get in to see those two guys at the Wailing Wall."

"Nicolae hates those two. Thinks they're crazy. Obviously they are."

"Then he shouldn't have a problem with my trying to interview them."

"I'll see what I can do. He's with a pilot candidate today."

"You don't say."

Carpathia and Rayford stepped from the limo outside a huge hangar at Kennedy. Carpathia said to the driver, "Tell Frederick we would like the usual drama."

When the hangar doors opened, the plane was illuminated with brilliant spotlights. On the side facing Rayford were the words *Air Force One* and the seal of the president of the United States. As they walked around to the other side, however, Rayford saw the team of painters high on scaffolding. The seal and the name had been eliminated. In its place was the old logo of the United

Nations but with the words *Global Community* in place of the current name. And in place of the name of the aircraft, painters were putting the finishing touches on *Global Community One.*

"How long until both sides are finished?" Carpathia called out to a foreman.

"It'll be dry on both sides by midnight!" came the answer. "This side took about six hours. Other side will go quicker. Airworthy by Saturday easily!"

Carpathia flashed a thumbs-up sign, and the workers in the hangar applauded. "We would like to board," Carpathia whispered, and within minutes a lift had been jury-rigged that allowed them to enter from the rear of the sparkling new plane. Rayford had toured countless new aircraft and was usually impressed, but he had never seen anything like this.

Every detail was richly appointed, expensive, functional, and beautiful. In the rear were full bathrooms with showers. Then came the press area, large enough for parties. Every seat had its own phone, modem jack, VCR, and TV. A restaurant was midship, fully stocked and with room to move and breathe.

Closer to the front came the presidential living quarters and conference room. One room contained high-tech security and surveillance equipment, backup communications, and technology allowing the plane to communicate with anyone anywhere in the world.

Directly behind the cockpit were the crew living quarters, including a private apartment for the pilot. "You will not want to stay on the plane when we land somewhere for a few days," Nicolae said. "But you would be hard-pressed to find better accommodations anywhere."

Buck was in Steve's office when Hattie Durham dropped in to inform Steve that Nicolae was out for a while. "Oh, Mr. Williams!" she said. "I can't thank you enough for introducing me to Mr. Carpathia."

Buck didn't know what to say. He didn't want to tell her she was welcome. In truth he felt awful about it. He just nodded.

"You know who was in today?" she said.

He knew, but he didn't let on. "Who?"

Buck realized he would have to stay on his toes with her and with Steve, and especially with Carpathia. They must not know how close he was to Rayford, and if he could keep from them any knowledge of his developing relationship with Chloe, so much the better.

"Rayford Steele. He was the pilot the day I met you on the plane."

"I remember," he said.

"Did you know he was up for pilot of *Air Force One?*"

"That would be quite an honor, wouldn't it?"

"He deserves it. He's the best pilot I ever worked for."

Buck felt awkward, talking about his new friend and brother in Christ as if he barely knew him. "What makes a good pilot?" Buck asked.

"A smooth takeoff and landing. Lots of communication with the passengers. And treating the crew like peers rather than slaves."

"Impressive," Buck said.

"You want to see the plane?" Steve said.

"May I?"

"It's in an auxiliary hangar at Kennedy."

"I was just out there."

"Want to go back?"

Buck shrugged. "Someone else has already been assigned the story of the new plane and pilot and all that, but sure, I'd love to see it."

"You can still fly on it to Israel."

"No, I can't," Buck said. "My boss was crystal clear on that point."

When Rayford arrived home that evening, he knew Chloe would be able to tell he was pensive. "Bruce canceled the meeting for tonight," she said.

"Good," Rayford said. "I'm exhausted."

"So tell me about Carpathia."

Rayford tried. What was there to say? The man was friendly, charming, smooth, and except for the lying might have made even Rayford wonder if they had misjudged him. "But there's no longer any doubt about his identity, is there?" he concluded.

"Not in my mind," Chloe said. "But I haven't met him."

"Knowing you, he wouldn't fool you for a second."

"I hope so," she said. "But Buck admits he's amazing."

"Have you heard from Buck?"

"He's supposed to call at midnight his time."

"Do I need to stay up to make sure you're awake?"

"Hardly. He doesn't even know we ate our cookies at the same time. I wouldn't miss telling him that for anything."

FOURTEEN

BUCK Williams was cashing in all his journalistic chips. After trying to sleep off jet lag in the King David Hotel on Saturday, he had left messages for Chaim Rosenzweig, Marc Feinberg, and even Peter Mathews. According to Steve Plank, Nicolae Carpathia had turned down flat Buck's request for help in getting near the two preachers at the Wailing Wall.

"I told you," Steve said. "He thinks those guys are nuts, and he's disappointed you think they're worth a story."

"So he doesn't know anybody who can get me in there?"

"It's a restricted area."

"Precisely my point. Have we finally found something Nicolae the Great can't do?"

Steve had been angry. "You know as well as I do that he could buy the Wailing Wall," he spat. "But you're not going to get close to the place with his help. He doesn't want you there, Buck. For once in your life, get a clue and stay away."

"Yeah, that sounds like me."

"Buck, let me ask you something. If you defy Carpathia and then either turn down his offer or make him so irritated that he withdraws it, where are you going to work?"

"I'll work."

"Where? Can't you see that his influence reaches everywhere? People love him! They'll do anything for him. People come away from meetings with him doing things they never would have dreamed they'd do."

Tell me about it, Buck thought.

"I've got work to do," Buck said. "Thanks anyway."

"*Right now* you've got work to do. But nothing is permanent."
Steve had never spoken truer words, though he didn't know it.

Buck's second strikeout was with Peter Mathews. He was ensconced in a penthouse suite in a five-star hotel in Tel Aviv, and
though he did take Buck's call, he was dismissive. "I admire you,
Williams," he said, "but I think I've given you all the best stuff I
know, on and off the record. I don't have any connection with
the guys at the Wall, but I'll give you a quote, if that's what you
want."

"What I want is to find someone who can get me close enough
so I can talk to these two men myself. If they want to kill me or
burn me up or ignore me, that'll be their prerogative."

"I am allowed close to the Wailing Wall because of my position, but I'm not interested in helping you get there. I'm sorry.
On the record, I think these are two elderly Torah students who
are pretending to be Moses and Elijah reincarnated. Their cos-
tumes are bad, their preaching is worse. Why people have died
trying to hurt them, I have no idea. Maybe these two old coots
have compatriots hidden among the masses who pick people off
who look like threats. Now, I've got to go. You'll be at the signing Monday?"

"That's why I'm here, sir."

"I'll see you there. Do yourself a favor and don't tarnish your
reputation by making a story out of those two. If you want a
story, you ought to tag along with me this afternoon as I tour
possible sites for Vatican involvement in Jerusalem."

"But, sir, what do you make of the fact that it hasn't rained in
Jerusalem since those two began preaching?"

"I don't make anything of it, except maybe that not even the
clouds want to hear what they have to say. It hardly ever rains
here anyway."

Rayford had met the crew of *Global Community One* just a couple of hours before takeoff. Not one had ever worked for Pan-
Continental. In a brief pep talk he had emphasized that safety
was paramount. "That is why every one of us is here. Proper procedure and protocol come next. We do everything by the book,
and we keep our logs and checklists as we go. We look sharp, we
stay in the background, we serve our hosts and passengers. While
we are deferential to the dignitaries and serve them, their safety is

our primary concern. The best airplane crew is an invisible one. People feel comfort and security when they see uniforms and service, not individuals."

Rayford's first officer was older than Rayford and probably had wanted the pilot's position. But he was friendly and efficient. The navigator was a young man Rayford would not have chosen, but he did his job. The cabin crew had worked together on *Air Force One* and seemed overly impressed with the new plane, but Rayford couldn't fault them for that. It was a technological marvel, but they would soon get used to it and take it for granted.

Flying the 757 was, as Rayford had commented to the certifying examiner in Dallas, like sitting behind the wheel of a Jaguar. But the excitement wore off as the flight stretched on. After a while he left the plane in the control of his first officer and slipped into his own living quarters. He stretched out on the bed and was suddenly struck by how utterly lonely he was. How proud Irene would have been of this moment, when he had the top job in the flying world. But to him it meant little, though he felt in his spirit that he was doing what God had led him to do. Why, he had no idea. But deep inside Rayford felt sure he had flown his last route for Pan-Con.

He phoned Chloe and woke her. "Sorry, Chlo'," he said.

"That's all right, Dad. Is it exciting?"

"Oh, yeah, I can't deny that."

They had discussed that the plane-to-ground communications were likely under surveillance, so there would be no disparaging talk about Carpathia or anyone else in his orbit. And they would not mention Buck by name.

"Who do you know there?"

"Only Hattie really. I'm kind of lonely."

"Me too. I haven't heard from anyone else yet. I'm supposed to get a call early Monday morning, your time. When will you be in Jerusalem?"

"In about three hours we land in Tel Aviv and are transported by luxury motor coaches to Jerusalem."

"You aren't flying into Jerusalem?"

"No. A 757 can't land near there. Tel Aviv is only thirty-five miles from Jerusalem."

"When will you be home?"

"Well, we were scheduled to leave Tel Aviv Tuesday morning, but now they tell us that we'll be flying on to Baghdad Monday afternoon and we'll leave from there Tuesday morning. It adds six hundred air miles, about another hour, to the total trip."

"What's in Baghdad?"

"The only airport near Babylon that will take a plane this size. Carpathia wants to tour Babylon and show his people the plans."

"Will you go along?"

"I imagine I will. It's about fifty miles south of Baghdad by bus. If I take this job I imagine I'll be seeing a lot of the Middle East over the next few years."

"I miss you already. I wish I could be there."

"I know who you miss, Chloe."

"I miss you too, Dad."

"Ah, I'll be chopped liver to you within a month. I can see where you and what's-his-name are going."

"Bruce phoned. He said he got a strange call from some woman named Amanda White, claiming to have known Mom. She told Bruce she met Mom at one of the church's home Bible study groups and only just remembered her name. She said it came to her because she knew it sounded like iron and steel."

"Hm," Rayford said. "Irene Steele. Guess I never thought of it that way. What'd she want?"

"She said she finally became a Christian, mostly because of re-membering things Mom said at that Bible study, and now she's looking for a church. She wondered if New Hope was still up and running."

"Where's she been?"

"Grieving her husband and two grown daughters. She lost them in the Rapture."

"Your mom was that instrumental in her life, and yet she didn't remember her name?"

"Go figure," Chloe said.

Buck napped for about an hour and a half before taking a call from Chaim Rosenzweig, who had just gotten in. "Even I will need to adjust to the time difference, Cameron," Dr. Rosenzweig said. "No matter how many times I make the trip, the jet lag at-tacks. How long have you been in the country?"

"I arrived yesterday morning. I need your help." Buck told Ro-senzweig he needed to get closer to the Wailing Wall. "I tried," he said, "but I probably didn't get within a hundred yards. The two men were preaching, and the crowds were much bigger than I ever saw on CNN."

"Oh, there are bigger crowds now as we get closer to the signing of the covenant. Perhaps in light of the signing, the pair have stepped up their activities. More and more people are coming to hear them, and apparently they are even seeing Orthodox Jews converting to Christianity. Very strange. Nicolae asked about them on the way over and watched some of the coverage on the television. He was as angry as I have ever seen him."

"What did he say?"

"That was just it. He said nothing. I thought he looked flushed, and his jaw was set. I know him just a little, you understand, but I can tell when he is agitated."

"Chaim, I need your help."

"Cameron, I am not Orthodox. I do not go to the Wall, and even if I could, I would probably not risk the danger. I don't recommend that you do either. The bigger story here is the covenant signing Monday morning. Nicolae and the Israeli delegation and I finalized everything in New York Friday. Nicolae was brilliant. He is amazing, Cameron. I long for the day when we both are working for him."

"Chaim, please. I know every journalist in the world would love to have an exclusive with the two preachers, but I am the one who will not give up until I get it or die trying."

"That's just what you might do."

"Doctor, I've never asked you for anything but your time, and you've always been most generous."

"I don't know what I can do for you, Cameron. I would take you there myself if I thought I could get in. But you will not be able to get in anyway."

"But you must know someone with access."

"Of course I do! I know many Orthodox Jews, many rabbis. But—"

"What about Ben-Judah?"

"Oh, Cameron! He is so busy. His live report on the research project will be broadcast Monday afternoon. He must be cramming like a schoolboy before a final examination."

"But maybe not, Chaim. Maybe he has done so much research that he could talk about this for an hour without notes. Maybe he's ready now and is looking for something to occupy him so he doesn't overprepare or stress out waiting for his big moment."

There was silence on the other end, and Buck prayed Rosenzweig would yield. "I don't know, Cameron. I would not want to be bothered so close to a big moment."

"Would you do this, Chaim—just call and wish him the best and feel him out about his schedule this weekend? I'll come anywhere at any time if he can get me close to the Wall."

"Only if he is looking for a diversion," Rosenzweig said. "If I sense he is buried in his work, I won't even broach the subject."

"Thank you, sir! You'll call me back?"

"Either way. And Cameron, please don't get your hopes up, and don't hold it against me if he is unavailable."

"I would never do that."

"I know. But I also sense how important this is to you."

———————

Buck was dead to the world and had no idea how long his phone had been ringing. He sat straight up in bed and noticed the Sunday afternoon sun turning orange, the stream of light making a weird pattern on the bed. Buck caught a glimpse of himself in the mirror as he reached for the phone. His cheek was red and creased, his eyes puffy and half open, his hair shooting out in all directions. His mouth tasted horrible, and he had slept in his clothes.

"Hello?"

"Ees dis Chamerown Weeleeums?" came the thick Hebrew accent.

"Yes, sir."

"Dees ist Dochtor Tsion Ben-Judah."

Buck jumped to his feet as if the respected scholar were in the room. "Yes, Dr. Ben-Judah. A privilege to hear from you, sir!"

"Thank you," the doctor managed. "I am calling you from out front of your hotel."

Buck fought to understand him. "Yes?"

"I have a car and a driver."

"A car and driver, yes sir."

"Are you ready to go?"

"To go?"

"To the Wall."

"Oh, yes, sir—I mean, no, sir. I'm going to need ten minutes. Can you wait ten minutes?"

"I should have called before arriving. I was under the impression from our mutual friend that this was a matter of some urgency to you."

Buck ran the strange-sounding English through his mind again. "A matter of urgency, yes! Just give me ten minutes! Thank you, sir!"

Buck tore off his clothes and jumped in the shower. He didn't give the water time to heat. He lathered up and rinsed off, then dragged his razor across his face.

He didn't take the time to find the electrical adapter for his hair dryer but just yanked a towel off the rack and attacked his long hair, feeling as if he were pulling half of it out of his scalp.

He jerked the comb through his hair and brushed his teeth. What did one wear to the Wailing Wall? He knew he wouldn't be getting inside, but would he offend his host if he was not wearing a coat and tie? He hadn't brought one. He hadn't planned on dressing up even for the treaty signing the next morning.

Buck chose his usual denim shirt, dressy jeans, ankle-high boots, and leather jacket. He dropped his tape recorder and camera into his smallest leather bag and ran down three flights of stairs. When he burst from the door he stopped. He had no idea what the rabbi looked like. Would he look like Rosenzweig, or Feinberg, or neither?

Neither, it turned out. Tsion Ben-Judah, in a black suit and black felt hat, stepped from the front passenger seat of an idling white Mercedes and waved shyly. Buck hurried to him. "Dr. Ben-Judah?" he said, shaking his hand. The man was middle-aged, trim, and youthful with strong, angular features and only a hint of gray in his dark brown hair.

In his labored English, the rabbi said, "In your dialect, my first name sounds like the city, Zion. You may call me that."

"Zion? Are you sure?"

"Sure of my own name?" The rabbi smiled. "I am sure."

"No, I meant are you sure I can call you—"

"I know what you meant, Mr. Williams. You may call me Zion."

To Buck, *Zion* didn't sound too much different from *Tsion* in Dr. Ben-Judah's accent. "Please call me Buck."

"Buck?" The rabbi held open the front door as Buck slid in next to the driver.

"It's a nickname."

"All right, Buck. The driver understands no English."

Buck turned to see the driver with his hand extended. Buck

shook it and the man said something totally unintelligible. Buck merely smiled and nodded. Dr. Ben-Judah spoke to the driver in Hebrew, and they pulled away.

"Now, Buck," the rabbi said as Buck turned in his seat to face him, "Dr. Rosenzweig said you wanted access to the Wailing Wall, which you understand is impossible. I can get you close enough to the two witnesses so that you can get their attention if you dare."

"The two witnesses? You call them the two witnesses? That's what my friends and I—"

Dr. Ben-Judah held up both hands and turned his head away, as if to indicate that was a question he would not answer or comment on. "The question is, do you dare?"

"I dare."

"And you will not hold me personally responsible for anything that might happen to you."

"Of course not, but I would like to interview you, too."

The hands came up yet again. "I made quite clear to the press, and to Dr. Rosenzweig, that I am not granting any interviews."

"Just some personal information, then. I won't ask about your research, because I am sure after boiling down three years into a one-hour presentation, you'll explain your conclusions fully tomorrow afternoon."

"Precisely. As for personal information, I am forty-four years old. I grew up in Haifa, the son of an Orthodox rabbi. I have two doctorates, one in Jewish history and one in ancient languages. I have studied and taught my whole life and consider myself more of a scholar and historian than an educator, though my students have been most kind in their evaluations. I think and pray and read mostly in Hebrew, and I am embarrassed to speak English so poorly, especially in an egalitarian country like this. I know English grammar and syntax better than most Englishmen and certainly most Americans, present company excepted I'm sure, but I have never had the time to practice, let alone perfect, my diction. I married only six years ago and have two teenage stepchildren, a boy and a girl.

"A little over three years ago, I was commissioned by a state agency to conduct an exhaustive study of the messianic passages so the Jews would recognize Messiah when he comes. This has been the most rewarding work of my life. In the process I added Greek and Aramaic to the list of my mastered languages, which now number twenty-two. I am excited about the completion of the work and eager to share my findings with the world by television. I don't pretend that the program will compete with anything containing sex, violence, or humor, but I expect it will be controversial nonetheless."

"I don't know what else to ask," Buck admitted.

"Then we can be done with the interview and get on with the business at hand."

"I am curious about your taking the time to do this."

"Dr. Rosenzweig is a mentor, one of my most beloved colleagues. A friend of his is a friend of mine."

"Thank you."

"I admire your work. I read the articles about Dr. Rosenzweig that you have done, and many others, too. Besides, the men at the Wall intrigue me as well. Perhaps with my language proficiency we will be able to communicate with them. So far, all I have seen them do is communicate with the masses who assemble. They speak to people who threaten them, but otherwise, I know of no individual who has spoken with them."

The Mercedes parked near some tour buses, and the driver waited as Dr. Ben-Judah and Buck mounted a set of stairs to take in the view of the Wailing Wall, the Temple Mount, and everything in between. "These are the largest crowds I have seen," the rabbi said.

"But they are so quiet," Buck whispered.

"The two preachers do not use microphones," Dr. Ben-Judah explained. "People make noise at their own peril. So many want to hear what the men have to say that others threaten those who cause any distraction."

"Do the two ever take a break?"

"Yes, they do. Occasionally one will move around the side of that little building there and lie on the ground near the fence. They will often trade off resting and speaking. The men who were consumed by fire recently actually tried to attack them there from outside the fence when they both rested. That is why no one approaches them there."

"That might be my best opportunity," Buck said.

"That was my thinking."

"You will go with me?"

"Only if we make it plain we mean them no harm. They have killed at least six and have threatened many more. A friend of mine stood on this very spot the day they burned up four attackers, and he swears the fire came from their mouths."

"Do you believe that?"

"I have no reason to doubt my friend, though we are several hundred feet away."

"Is there a better time than another to approach, or should we just play that by ear?"

"I propose we join the crowds first."

They descended the stairs and moved toward the Wall. Buck was impressed that the crowd seemed so reverential. Within forty or fifty feet of the preachers were Orthodox rabbis, bowing, praying, sliding written prayers into the cracks between the stones in the Wall. Occasionally one of the rabbis would turn toward the witnesses and shake his fist, crying out in Hebrew, only to be shushed by the crowd. Sometimes one of the preachers would respond directly.

As Buck and Dr. Ben-Judah reached the edge of the crowd, a rabbi at the Wall fell to his knees, his eyes toward heaven, and howled out a prayer in anguish.

"Silence!" shouted one of the preachers, and the rabbi wept bitterly. The preacher turned to the crowd. "He beseeches almighty God to strike us dead for blaspheming his name! But he is as the Pharisees of old! He does not recognize the one who was God and is God and shall be God now and forevermore! We come to bring witness to the Godship of Jesus Christ of Nazareth!"

With that, the crying rabbi prostrated himself and hid his face, rocking in humiliation at the wickedness of what he heard.

Dr. Ben-Judah whispered to Buck, "Would you like me to translate?"

"Translate what? The prayer of the rabbi?"

"And the response of the preacher."

"I understood the preacher."

Dr. Ben-Judah looked puzzled. "If I had known you were fluent in Hebrew, it would have been much easier for me to communicate with you."

"I'm not. I didn't understand the prayer, but the preacher spoke to the crowd in English."

Ben-Judah shook his head. "My mistake," he said. "Sometimes I forget what language I'm in. But there! Right now! He's speaking in Hebrew again. He's saying—"

"Sir, sorry to interrupt. But he is speaking in English. There is a Hebraic accent, but he is saying, 'And now unto Him who is able to keep you from falling . . .' "

"You understand that?!"

"Of course."

The rabbi looked shaken. "Buck," he whispered ominously, "he is speaking in Hebrew."

Buck turned and stared at the two witnesses. They took turns speaking, sentence by sentence. Buck understood every word in English. Ben-Judah touched him lightly and he followed the rabbi deeper into the crowd. "English?" Ben-Judah asked a Hispanic-looking man who stood with a woman and children.

"Espanol," the man responded apologetically.

Dr. Ben-Judah immediately began conversing with him in Spanish. The man kept nodding and answering in the affirmative. The rabbi thanked him and moved on. He found a Norwegian and spoke to him in his native tongue, then some Asians. He grabbed Buck's arm tight and pulled him away from the crowd and closer to the preachers. They stopped about thirty feet from the two men, separated by a fence of wrought-iron bars.

"These people are hearing the preachers in their own languages!" Ben-Judah shuddered. "Truly this is of God!"

"Are you sure?"

"No question. I hear them in Hebrew. You hear them in English. The family from Mexico knows only a little English but no Hebrew. The man from Norway knows some German and some English, but no Hebrew. He hears them in Norwegian. Oh God, oh God," the rabbi added, and Buck knew it was out of reverence. He was afraid Ben-Judah might collapse.

"Ayeee!" A young man wearing boots, khaki slacks, and a white T-shirt came screaming through the crowd. People fell to the ground when they saw his automatic weapon. He wore a gold necklace, and his black hair and beard were unkempt. His dark eyes were ablaze as he rattled off a few rounds into the air, which cleared a path for him directly to the preachers.

He shouted something in an Eastern dialect Buck did not understand, but as he lay on the pavement peeking out from under his arms, Rabbi Ben-Judah whispered, "He says he's on a mission from Allah."

Buck reached into his bag and turned on the tape recorder as the man ran to the front of the crowd. The two witnesses stopped preaching and stood shoulder to shoulder, glaring at the gunman as he approached. He ran full speed, firing as he ran, but the preachers stood rock solid, not speaking, not moving, arms crossed over their ragged robes. When the young man got to within five feet of them, he seemed to hit an invisible wall. He recoiled and flipped over backward, his weapon clattering away. His head smacked the ground first, and he lay groaning.

Suddenly one of the preachers shouted, "You are forbidden to come nigh to the servants of the Most High God! We are under his protection until the due time, and woe to anyone who approaches without the covering of Yahweh himself." And as he finished, the other breathed from his mouth a column of fire that incinerated the man's clothes, consumed his flesh and organs, and in seconds left a charred skeleton smoking on the ground. The weapon melted and was fused to the cement, and the man's molten necklace dripped gold through the cavity in his chest.

Buck lay on his stomach, his mouth agape, his hand on the back of the rabbi, who shuddered uncontrollably. In the distance families ran screaming toward their cars and buses while Israeli soldiers approached the Wall slowly, weapons at the ready.

One of the preachers spoke. "No one need fear us who comes to listen to our testimony to the living God! Many have believed and received our report. Only those who seek to do us harm shall die! Fear not!"

Buck believed him. He wasn't sure the rabbi did. They stood and began to move away, but the eyes of the witnesses were on them. Israeli soldiers shouted at them from the edge of the plaza. "The soldiers are telling us to move away slowly," Dr. Ben-Judah translated.

"I want to stay," Buck said. "I want to talk to these men."

"Did you not see what just happened?"

"Of course, but I also heard them say they meant no harm to sincere listeners."

"But *are* you a sincere listener, or are you just a journalist looking for a scoop?"

"I'm both," Buck admitted.

"God bless you," the rabbi said. He turned and spoke in Hebrew to the two witnesses as Israeli soldiers shouted at him and Buck all the more. Buck and Ben-Judah backed away from the preachers, who now stood silent.

"I told them we would meet them at ten o'clock tonight behind the building where they occasionally rest. Will you be able to join me?"

"Like I would pass that up," Buck said.

Rayford returned from a quiet dinner with part of his new crew to an urgent message from Chloe. It took him a few minutes to get through, wishing she had given him some indication of what was wrong. It wasn't like her to say something was urgent unless it really was. She picked up the phone on the first ring.

"Hello?" she said. "Buck? Dad?"

"Yeah, what's up?"

"How's Buck?"

"I don't know. I haven't seen him yet."

"Are you going to?"

"Well, sure, I suppose."

"Do you know what hospital he's in?"

"What?"

"You didn't see it?"

"See what?"

"Dad, it was just on the morning news here. The two witnesses at the Wailing Wall burned some guy to death, and everybody around hit the ground. One of the last two lying there was Buck."

"Are you sure?"

"No question."

"Do you know for certain he was hurt?"

"No! I just assumed. He was just lying there next to a guy in a black suit whose hat had fallen off."

"Where's he staying?"

"At the King David. I left a message for him. They said they had his key, so he was out. What does that mean?"

"Some people leave their keys at the desk whenever they go out. It doesn't mean anything special. I'm sure he'll call you."

"Isn't there some way you can find out if he was hurt?"

"I'll try. Let's leave it this way: If I find out anything either way, I'll call you. No news will be good news, at least."

Buck's knees felt like jelly. "Are you all right, Rabbi?"

"I'm fine," Dr. Ben-Judah said, "but I am nearly overcome."

"I know the feeling."

"I want to believe those men are of God."

"I believe they are," Buck said.

"Do you? Are you a student of the Scriptures?"

"Only recently."

"Come. I want to show you something."

When they got back to the car, the rabbi's driver stood with his door open, ashen faced. Tsion Ben-Judah spoke reassuringly to him in Hebrew, and the man kept looking past him to Buck. Buck tried to smile.

Buck got into the front seat, and Ben-Judah quietly guided the driver to park as close as possible to the Golden Gate at the east of the Temple Mount. He invited Buck to walk with him to the gate so he could interpret the Hebrew graffiti. "See here," he said. "It says, 'Come Messiah.' And here, 'Deliver us.' And there, 'Come in triumph.'

"My people have longed for and prayed for and watched and waited for our Messiah for centuries. But much of Judaism, even in the Holy Land, has become secular and less biblically oriented. My research project was assigned almost as an inevitability. People have lost sight of exactly what or whom they are looking for, and many have given up.

"And to show you how deep runs the animosity between the Muslim and the Jew, look at this cemetery the Muslims have built just outside the fence here."

"What's the significance?"

"Jewish tradition says that in the end times, Messiah and Elijah will lead the Jews to the temple in triumph through the gate from the east. But Elijah is a priest, and walking through a graveyard would defile him, so the Muslims have put one here to make the triumphal entry impossible."

Buck reached for his tape recorder and was going to ask the rabbi to repeat that tidbit of history, but he noticed it was still running. "Look at this," Buck said. "I got the attack on tape."

He rewound the machine to where they heard gunfire and screaming. Then the man fell and the weapon clattered. In his mind's eye, Buck recalled the blast of fire coming from the witness's mouth. On the tape it sounded like a strong gust of wind. More screaming. Then the preachers shouted loudly in a language Buck couldn't understand.

"That's Hebrew!" Rabbi Ben-Judah said. "Surely you hear that!"

"They spoke in Hebrew," Buck acknowledged, "and the tape recorder picked it up in Hebrew. But I heard it in English as sure as I'm standing here."

"You did say you heard them promise no harm to anyone who came only to listen to their testimony."

"I understood every word."

The rabbi closed his eyes. "The timing of this is very important to my presentation."

Buck walked back to the car with him. "I need to tell you something," he said. "I believe your Messiah has already come."

"I know you do, young man. I will be interested to hear what the two preachers say when you tell them that."

Rayford checked with Steve Plank to see if his people had heard any more about another death at the Wailing Wall. He didn't ask specifically about Buck, still not wanting to let on about their friendship.

"We heard all about it," Plank said angrily. "The secretary-general believes those two should be arrested and tried for murder. He doesn't understand why the Israeli military seems so impotent."

"Maybe they're afraid of being incinerated."

"What chance would those two have against a sniper with a high-powered weapon? You close the place down, clear out the innocent bystanders, and shoot those two dead. Use a grenade or even a missile if you have to."

"That's Carpathia's idea?"

"Straight from the horse's mouth," Plank said.

"Spoken like a true pacifist."

FIFTEEN

RAYFORD watched the news and was certain Chloe had been correct. It had indeed been Buck Williams, not more than thirty feet from the witnesses and even closer to the gunman, who was now little more than charred bones on the pavement. But Israeli television stayed with the images longer, and after watching the drama a few times, Rayford was able to take his eyes from the fire-breathing witnesses and watch the edge of the screen. Buck rose quickly and helped the dark-suited man next to him. Neither appeared hurt.

Rayford dialed the King David Hotel. Buck was still out, so Rayford took a cab to the King David and sat waiting in the lobby. Knowing better than to be seen with Buck, he planned to slip away to a house phone as soon as he saw him.

"In the long history of Judaism," Rabbi Ben-Judah was saying, "there have been many evidences of the clear hand of God. More during Bible times, of course, but the protection of Israel against all odds in modern wars is another example. The destruction of the Russian Air Force, leaving the Holy Land unscathed, was plainly an act of God."

Buck turned in the seat of the car. "I was here when it happened."

"I read your account," Ben-Judah said. "But by the same token, Jews have learned to be skeptical of what appears to be divine intervention in their lives. Those who know the Scriptures know that while Moses had the power to turn a stick into a snake, so did Pharaoh's magicians. They could also imitate Moses' turning water into blood. Daniel was not the only dream-interpreter in the king's court. I tell you this only to explain why these two preachers are being looked upon with such suspicion. Their acts are mighty and terrible, but their message an anathema to the Jewish mind."

"But they are talking about the Messiah!" Buck said.

"And they seem to have the power to back up their statements," Ben-Judah said. "But the idea of Jesus having been the Jewish Messiah is thousands of years old. His very name is as profane to the Jew as racial slurs and epithets are to other minorities."

"Some have become believers here," Buck said. "I've seen it on the news, people bowing and praying before the fence, becoming followers of Christ."

"At great cost," the rabbi said. "And they are very much in the minority. No matter how impressive are these witnesses of Christ, you will not see significant numbers of Jews convert to Christianity."

"That's the second time you have referred to them as witnesses," Buck said. "You know that this is what the Bible—"

"Mr. Williams," Rabbi Ben-Judah interrupted, "do not mistake me for a scholar of only the Torah. You must realize that my study has included the sacred works of all the major religions of the world."

"But what do you make of it, then, if you know the New Testament?"

"Well, first of all, you may be overstating it to say that I 'know' the New Testament. I cannot claim to know it the way I know my own Bible, having become steeped in the New Testament mostly only within the last three years. But secondly, you have now crossed over the line journalistically."

"I'm not asking as a journalist!" Buck said. "I'm asking as a Christian!"

"Don't mistake being a Gentile for being a Christian," the rabbi said. "Many, many people consider themselves Christians because they are not Jewish."

"I know the difference," Buck said. "Friend to friend, or at least acquaintance to acquaintance, with all your study, you must have come to some conclusions about Jesus as the Messiah."

The rabbi spoke carefully. "Young man, I have not released

one iota of my findings to anyone in three years. Even those who commissioned and sponsored my study do not know what conclusions I have drawn. I respect you. I admire your courage. I will take you back to the two witnesses tonight as I promised. But I will not reveal to you any of what I will say on television tomorrow."

"I understand," Buck said. "More people may be watching than you think."

"Perhaps. And maybe I was being falsely modest when I said the program would not likely compete with the normal fare. CNN and the state agency that commissioned my study have cooperated in an international effort to inform Jews on every continent of the coming program. They tell me the audience in Israel will be only a fraction of the Jewish viewers around the world."

Rayford was reading the *International Tribune* when Buck hurried past him to the desk and retrieved his key and a message. Rayford loudly rattled the paper as he lowered it, and when Buck glanced his way Rayford motioned he would call him. Buck nodded and went upstairs.

"You'd better call Chloe," Rayford said when he reached Buck on the house phone a couple of minutes later. "Are you all right?"

"I'm fine. Rayford, I was right there!"

"I saw you."

"The rabbi I was with is a friend of Rosenzweig. He's the one who'll be on TV tomorrow afternoon. Get anyone you can to watch that. He's a really interesting guy."

"Will do. I promised Chloe one of us would call her as soon as I knew anything."

"She saw it?"

"Yeah, on the morning news."

"I'll call her right now."

Buck placed the call through the hotel operator and hung up, waiting for the call that would tell him his party was on the line. Meanwhile he slumped on the edge of the bed and lowered his head. He shuddered at what he had seen. How could the rabbi have seen the same, heard the same, and then imply that these men could just as easily be magicians or seers as from God?

The phone rang. "Yes!"

"Buck!"

"I'm here, Chloe, and I'm fine."

"Oh, thank God."

"Well, thank you!"

Chloe sounded emotional. "Buck, those witnesses know the difference between believers and their enemies, don't they?"

"I sure hope so. I'll find out tonight. The rabbi is taking me back to see them."

"Who's the rabbi?"

Buck told her.

"Are you sure it's wise?"

"Chloe, it's the chance of a lifetime! No one has spoken to them individually."

"Where does the rabbi stand?"

"He's Orthodox, but he knows the New Testament, too, at least intellectually. Be sure you and Bruce watch tomorrow afternoon—well, it would be six hours earlier for you, of course. Tell everybody in the church to watch. It should be interesting. If you want to watch the covenant signing first, you're going to have to be up early."

"Buck, I miss you."

"I miss you too. More than you know."

———————

Rayford returned to his hotel to find an envelope from Hattie Durham. The note inside read:

> Captain Steele, this is no practical joke. The secretary-general wanted you to have the enclosed ticket to the festivities tomorrow morning and to express to you how impressed he was with the service on *Global Community One*. While he may not be able to speak with you personally until tomorrow afternoon on the way to Baghdad, he thanks you for your service. And so do I. Hattie D.

Rayford slid the ticket into his passport wallet and threw the note in the trash.

———————

Buck, still out of kilter with the time change and the trauma of the morning, tried to get a few hours sleep before dinner. He dined alone, eating lightly and wondering if there had ever been such a thing as protocol for meeting with two men sent from God. Were they human? Were they spirits? Were they, as Bruce believed, Elijah and Moses? They called each other Eli and Moishe. Could they be thousands of years old? Buck was more anxious about talking with them than he had ever been about interviewing a head of state or even Nicolae Carpathia.

The evening would be chilly. Buck put on a wool sport coat with a heavy lining and pockets big enough that he wouldn't need a bag. He took only pen and pad and tape recorder and reminded himself to check with Jim Borland and others at the *Weekly* to be sure photographers were at least getting long shots of the two when they preached.

At 9:45 Rayford sat straight up in his bed. He had dozed in his clothes with the television droning, but something had caught his attention. He'd heard the word *Chicago,* maybe *Chicago Tribune,* and it roused him. He began changing to his pajamas as he listened. The newscaster was summarizing a major story out of the United States.

"The secretary-general is out of the country this weekend and unavailable for comment, but media moguls from around the world are corroborating this report. The surprising legislation allows a nonelected official and an international nonprofit organization unrestricted ownership of all forms of media and opens the door to the United Nations, soon to be known as Global Community, to purchase and control newspapers, magazines, radio, television, cable, and satellite communications outlets.

"The only limit will be the amount of capital available to Global Community, but the following media are among many rumored to be under consideration by a buyout team from Global Community: *New York Times, Long Island News Day, USA Today, Boston Globe, Baltimore Sun, Washington Post, Atlanta Journal and Constitution, Tampa Tribune, Orlando Sentinel, Houston . . .*"

Rayford sat on the edge of the bed and listened in disbelief. Nicolae Carpathia had done it—put himself in a position to control the news and thus control the minds of most of the people within his sphere of influence.

The newscaster droned on with the list: Turner Network News, the Cable News Network, the Entertainment and Sports Network, the Columbia Broadcast System, the American Broadcasting Corporation, the Fox Television Network, the National Broadcasting Corporation, the Christian Broadcasting Network, the Family Radio Network, Trinity Broadcasting Network, Time-Warner, Disney, *U.S. News and World Report, Global Weekly, Newsweek, Reader's Digest,* and a host of other news and feature syndicates and magazine groups.

"Most shocking is the initial reaction from current owners, most of whom seem to welcome the new capital and say they take Global Community leader Nicolae Carpathia at his word when he pledges no interference."

Rayford thought about calling Buck. But surely he had heard the news before it had come over television. Someone from the *Global Weekly* staff would have had to have informed him, or at least he would have heard it from one of the hundreds of other media employees in Israel for the signing. But maybe everybody thought everybody else was calling Buck. Rayford didn't want him to be the last to find out.

He reached for the phone. But there was no answer in Buck's room.

A tentative crowd milled about in the darkness, some fifty yards from the Wailing Wall. Remains of the would-be assassin had been removed, and the local military commander told the news media that he and his charges were unable to take action "against two people who have no weapons, have touched no one, and who have themselves been attacked."

No one from the crowd seemed willing to move any closer, though the two preachers could be seen in the faint light, standing near one end of the Wall. They neither advanced nor spoke.

As Rabbi Tsion Ben-Judah's driver pulled into a nearly empty parking area, Buck was tempted to ask if the rabbi believed in prayer. Buck knew the rabbi would say he did, but Buck wanted to pray aloud for the protection of Christ, and that was simply something one would not ask an Orthodox rabbi to pray for. Buck prayed silently.

He and Tsion left the car and walked slowly and carefully, far around the small crowd. The rabbi walked with his hands clasped in front of him, and Buck couldn't help doing a double take when he noticed. It seemed an unusually pious and almost showy gesture—particularly because Ben-Judah had seemed disarmingly humble for one holding such a lofty position in religious academia.

"I am walking in a traditional position of deference and conciliation," the rabbi explained. "I want no mistakes, no misunderstanding. It is important to our safety that these men know we come in humility and curiosity. We mean them no harm."

Buck looked into the rabbi's eyes. "The truth is we are scared to death and don't want to give them any reason to kill us."

Buck thought he saw a smile. "You have a way of knifing to the truth," Ben-Judah said. "I am praying that we will both be healthy on the way back as well and able to discuss our shared experience here."

Me too, Buck thought, but he said nothing.

Three Israeli soldiers stepped in front of Buck and the rabbi, and one spoke sharply in Hebrew. Buck began to reach for his press pass, then realized it carried no weight here. Tsion Ben-Judah moved forward and spoke earnestly and quietly to the leader, again in Hebrew. The soldier asked a few questions, sounding less hostile and more curious than at first. Finally he nodded, and they were able to pass.

Buck glanced back. The soldiers had not moved. "What was that all about?" he asked.

"They said only the Orthodox are allowed past a certain point. I assured them you were with me. I am always amused when the secular military tries to enforce religious laws. He warned me of what had happened earlier, but I told him we had an appointment and were willing to take the risk."

"Are we?" Buck asked lightly.

The rabbi shrugged. "Perhaps not. But we are going to proceed anyway, are we not? Because we said we would, and neither of us would miss this opportunity."

As they continued, the two witnesses stared at them from the end of the Wailing Wall, some fifty or so feet away. "We are headed for the fence over there," Ben-Judah said, pointing to the other side of the small building. "If they are still willing to meet us, they will come there, and we will have the fence between us."

"After what happened to the assassin today, that wouldn't be much help."

"We are not armed."

"How do they know?"

"They don't."

When Buck and Ben-Judah were within about fifteen feet of the fence, one of the witnesses held up a hand, and they stopped. He spoke, not at the top of his voice as Buck had always heard him before, but still in a sonorous tone. "We will approach and introduce ourselves," he said. The two men walked slowly and stood just inside the iron bars. "Call me Eli," he said. "And this is Moishe."

"English?" Buck whispered.

"Hebrew," Ben-Judah responded.

"Silence!" Eli said in a hoarse whisper.

Buck jumped. He recalled one of the two shouting at a rabbi to be silent earlier that day. A few minutes later another man lay dead and charred.

Eli motioned that Buck and Tsion could approach. They advanced to within a couple feet of the fence. Buck was struck by their ragged robes. The scent of ashes, as from a recent fire, hung about them. In the dim light from a distant lamp their long, sinewy arms seemed muscled and leathery. They had large, bony hands and were barefoot.

Eli said, "We will answer no questions as to our identities or our origin. God will reveal this to the world in his own time."

Tsion Ben-Judah nodded and bowed slightly from the waist. Buck reached into his pocket and turned on the tape recorder. Suddenly Moishe stepped close and put his bearded face between the bars. He stared at the rabbi with hooded eyes and a sweat-streaked face.

He spoke very quietly and in a low, deep voice, but every word was distinct to Buck. He couldn't wait to ask Tsion whether he had heard Moishe in English or Hebrew.

Moishe spoke as if he had just thought of something very interesting, but the words were familiar to Buck.

"Many years ago, there was a man of the Pharisees named Nicodemus, a ruler of the Jews. Like you, this man came to Jesus by night."

Rabbi Ben-Judah whispered, "Eli and Moishe, we know that you come from God; for no one can do these signs that you do unless God is with him."

Eli spoke. "Most assuredly, I say to you, unless one is born again, he cannot see the kingdom of God."

"How can a man be born when he is old?" Rabbi Ben-Judah said, and Buck realized he was quoting New Testament Scripture. "Can he enter a second time into his mother's womb and be born?"

Moishe answered, "Most assuredly, I say to you, unless one is born of water and the Spirit, he cannot enter the kingdom of God. That which is born of the flesh is flesh, and that which is born of the Spirit is spirit. Do not marvel that I said to you, 'You must be born again.' "

Eli spoke up again: "The wind blows where it wishes, and you hear the sound of it, but cannot tell where it comes from and where it goes. So is everyone who is born of the Spirit."

Right on cue, the rabbi said, "How can these things be?"

Moishe lifted his head. "Are you the teacher of Israel, and do not know these things? Most assuredly, I say to you, we speak what we know and testify what we have seen, and you do not receive our witness. If we have told you earthly things and you do not believe, how will you believe if we tell you heavenly things?"

Eli nodded. "No one has ascended to heaven but He who came down from heaven, that is, the Son of Man who is in heaven. And as Moses lifted up the serpent in the wilderness, even so must the Son of Man be lifted up, that whoever believes in Him should not perish but have eternal life. For God so loved the world that He gave His only begotten Son, that whoever believes in Him should not perish but have everlasting life."

Buck was light-headed with excitement. He felt as if he had been dropped back into ancient history and was a spectator at one of the most famous nighttime conversations ever. Not for an instant did he forget that his companion was not Nicodemus of old, or that the other two men were not Jesus. He was new to this truth, new to this Scripture, but he knew what was coming as Moishe concluded, "For God did not send his Son into the world to condemn the world, but that the world through him might be saved. He who believes in Him is not condemned; but he who does not believe is condemned already, because he has not believed in the name of the only begotten Son of God."

Suddenly the rabbi became animated. He gestured broadly, raising his hands and spreading them wide. As if in some play or recital, he set the witnesses up for their next response. "And what," he said, "is the condemnation?"

The two answered in unison, "That the Light has already come into the world."

"And how did men miss it?"

"Men loved darkness rather than light."

"Why?"

"Because their deeds were evil."

"God forgive us," the rabbi said.

And the two witnesses said, "God forgive you. Thus ends our message."

"Will you speak with us no more?" Ben-Judah asked.

"No more," Eli said, but Buck did not see his mouth move. He thought he had been mistaken, that perhaps Moishe had said it. But Eli continued, speaking clearly but not aloud. "Moishe and I will not speak again until dawn when we will continue to testify to the coming of the Lord."

"But I have so many questions," Buck said.

"No more," they said in unison, neither opening his mouth. "We wish you God's blessing, the peace of Jesus Christ, and the presence of the Holy Spirit. Amen."

Buck's knees went weak as the men backed away. As he and the rabbi stared, Eli and Moishe merely moved against the building and sat, leaning back against the wall. "Good-bye and thank you," Buck said, feelingfoolish.

Rabbi Ben-Judah sang a beautiful chant, a blessing of some sort that Buck did not understand. Eli and Moishe appeared to be praying, and then it seemed they slept where they sat.

Buck was speechless. He followed as Ben-Judah turned and walked toward a low chain fence. He stepped over it and moved away from the Temple Mount and across the road to a small grove of trees. Buck wondered if perhaps the rabbi wished to be alone, but his body language indicated he wanted Buck to stay with him.

When they reached the edge of the trees, the rabbi simply stood gazing into the sky. He covered his face with his hands and wept, his crying becoming great sobs. Buck, too, was overcome and could not stop the tears. They had been on holy ground, he knew. What he did not know was how the rabbi interpreted all this. Could he have missed the message of the conversation between Nicodemus and Jesus when he had read it from the Scriptures, and again now when he had been part of its re-creation?

Buck certainly hadn't missed it. The Tribulation Force would not be able to believe his privilege. He would not hoard it, would not be jealous of it. In fact, he wished they could have all been there with him.

As if sensing that Buck wanted to talk, Ben-Judah precluded him. "We must not debase the experience by reducing it to words," he said. "Until tomorrow, my friend."

The rabbi turned, and there at the roadside was his car and driver. He moved to the front passenger door and opened it for Buck. Buck slid in and whispered his thanks. The rabbi went around the front of the car and whispered to the driver, who pulled away, leaving Ben-Judah at the side of the road.

"What's up?" Buck said, craning to watch the black suit fade into the night. "Is he finding his own way back?"

The driver said nothing.

"I hope I haven't offended him."

The driver looked to Buck apologetically and shrugged. "No Englees," he said, and drove Buck back to the King David Hotel.

The man at the counter handed Buck a message from Rayford, but since it was not marked urgent, he decided not to call him until morning. If he didn't reach Rayford, he would look for him at the signing of the covenant.

Buck left the light off in his room and stepped out the glass door to the tiny balcony in the trees. Through the branches he saw the full moon in a cloudless sky. The wind was still, but the night had grown colder. He raised his collar and gazed at the beauty of the night. He felt as privileged as any man on earth. Besides his charmed professional life and the gift he had honed, he had been eyewitness to some of the most astounding works of God in the history of the world.

He had been in Israel when the Russians attacked less than a year and a half before. God had clearly destroyed the threat to his chosen people. Buck had been in the air when the Rapture had occurred, in a plane flown by a man he had never met, served by a senior flight attendant whose future now seemed his responsibility. And the daughter of that pilot? He believed he was in love with her, if he knew what love was.

Buck hunched his shoulders and let his sleeves cover his hands, then folded his arms. He had been spared a car bombing in London, had received Christ on the cusp of the end of the world, and had been supernaturally protected while witnessing two murders by the Antichrist himself. This very day he had seen Scripture fulfilled when a would-be killer was thwarted by fire from the throat of one of the two witnesses.

And then, to have heard these two recite Jesus' words to Nicodemus! Buck wanted to humble himself, to communicate to his
Creator and his Savior how unworthy he felt, how grateful he
was. "All I can do," he whispered huskily into the night air, "is
to give you all of me for as long as I have left. I will do what you
want, go where you send me, obey you regardless."

He pulled from his pocket the tape recorder and rewound it.
When he played the conversation he had witnessed that evening,
he was stunned to hear no English. It shouldn't have been a surprise, he realized. It had been typical of the day. But he heard at
least three languages. He recognized Hebrew, though he didn't
understand it. He recognized Greek, but didn't understand that either. The other language, which he was sure he had never heard
before, was used when the witnesses had directly quoted Jesus.
That had to be Aramaic.

At the end of the tape, Buck heard Dr. Ben-Judah ask something in Hebrew, which he remembered having heard in English
as "Will you speak with us no more?" But he heard no response.

Then he heard himself say, "But I have so many questions."
And then after a pause, "Goodbye and thank you." What the
men had spoken to his heart had not been recorded.

Buck took a pen and punched out the tabs, making it impossible to record over his priceless cassette.

The only thing that could make this even more perfect would
to be able to share it with Chloe. He looked at his watch. It was
just after midnight in Israel, making it around six in Chicago. But
when Buck reached Chloe, he could barely speak. He managed to
work out the story of the evening between his tears, and Chloe
wept with him. "Buck," she concluded at last, "we wasted so
many years without Christ. I'll pray for the rabbi."

A few minutes later, Rayford was awakened by his phone. He
was certain it would be Buck and hoped he had not heard the
news of Carpathia's media plans from someone else.

"Daddy, it's Chloe," she said. "I just talked to Buck, but I
didn't have the heart to tell him about the media stuff. Have you
heard?"

Rayford told her he had and asked if she was sure Buck didn't
know. She related everything Buck had told her about his eve-

ning. "I'll try to reach him in the morning," Rayford said. "He's sure to hear it from someone else if I don't get to him first."

"He was so overcome, Dad. It wasn't the time to give him that news. I didn't know how he'd react. What do you think will happen to him?"

"Buck will survive. He'll have to swallow a lot of pride, having to work for Carpathia wherever he goes. But he'll be all right. Knowing him, he'll find a way to get the truth to the masses, either by camouflaging it in Carpathia's own publications or by operating some sort of bootleg production that is sold under the counter."

"It sounds like Carpathia is going to control everything."

"It sure does."

Rayford tried calling Buck at six-thirty the next morning, but he had already left the hotel.

It had been ages since Buck had seen Steve Plank so harried. "This job was fun and interesting until today," Steve said as the entourage at his hotel began assembling for the short trip to the Old City. "Carpathia's got a burr in his saddle, and I'm the one who takes the heat."

"What's up?"

"Oh, nothing special. We just have to have everything perfect, that's all."

"And you're trying to talk me into working for him? I don't think so."

"Well, that'll be a moot question in a couple of weeks anyway, won't it?"

"It sure will." Buck smiled to himself. He had decided to turn the *Tribune* offer down flat and stay with *Global Weekly*.

"You're going with us to Baghdad, right?"

"I'm trying to find a way there, but not with you, no."

"Buck, there aren't going to be too many ways to get there. We've got the room, and for all practical purposes, you work for Carpathia anyway. Just come along. You'll love what he has in mind for New Babylon, and if the reports can be believed, it's already coming along nicely."

"I work for Carpathia? I thought we were pretty clear on that."

"It's just a matter of time, my boy."

"Dream on," Buck said, but wondered about Plank's puzzled look. Buck found Jim Borland organizing his notes. "Hey, Jim," he said. Borland hardly looked up. "Interview Carpathia yet?"

"Yep," Borland said. "No big deal. Right now all he's concerned about is moving the signing."

"Moving it?"

"He's afraid of those weirdos at the Wailing Wall. The soldiers can keep the place clear of tourists, but the guys at the Wall will have an audience of the covenant-signing crowd."

"Pretty big crowd," Buck said.

"No kidding. I don't know why they don't just keep those two homeless guys away."

"You don't?"

"What, Buck? You think those old coots are going to breathe their fire on the army? Get serious. You believe that fire story?"

"I saw the guy, Jimmy. He was toast."

"A million-to-one he set himself on fire."

"This was no immolation, Jim. He hit the ground, and one of those two incinerated him."

"With fire from his mouth."

"That's what I saw."

"It's a good thing you're off the cover story, Buck. You're losing it. So did you also get an exclusive interview with them?"

"Not entirely exclusive and not exactly an interview."

"In other words, no, you struck out, right?"

"No. I was with them late last night. I did not get into a give-and-take, that's all I'll say."

"I'd say if you're going to write fiction, you ought to get a novel deal and go for it. You'd still wind up publishing with Carpathia, but you might have a little more latitude."

"I wouldn't work for Carpathia," Buck said.

"Then you won't be in communications."

"What are you talking about?"

Borland told him of the announcement.

Buck blanched. "*Global Weekly*'s included?"

"*Included?* If you ask me, it's one of the plums."

Buck shook his head. So he was writing his stories for Carpathia after all. "No wonder everybody looks shell-shocked. So, if the signing isn't near the Wall, where will it be?"

"The Knesset."

"Inside?"

"Don't think so."

"Is the outside conducive?"

"Don't think so."

"Listen, Jimmy, are you going to watch Rabbi Ben-Judah this afternoon?"

"If they show it on the plane to Baghdad."

"You got a flight?"

"I'm going on *Global Community One*."

"You've sold out?"

"You can't sell out to your boss, Buck."

"He's not your boss yet."

"It's only a matter of time, pal."

Chaim Rosenzweig came scurrying by and slid to a stop. "Cameron!" he said. "Come, come!" Buck followed the stooped old man to a corner. "Stay with me, please! Nicolae is not happy this morning. We're moving to the Knesset, everything is in an uproar, he wants everybody to go to Babylon and some are resisting. To tell you the truth, I think he would kill those two at the Wailing Wall himself if he had the opportunity. All morning they have been howling about the injustice of the signing, about how the covenant signals an unholy alliance between a people who missed their Messiah the first time and a leader who denies the existence of God. But, Cameron, Nicolae is not an atheist. An agnostic at best—but so am I!"

"You're not an agnostic since the Russian invasion!"

"Well, maybe not, but those are strong words against Nicolae."

"I thought no one was allowed into the area in front of the Wall this morning. Who are they saying this to?"

"The press is there with their long-range directional microphones, and those men have lungs! Nicolae has been on the phone to CNN all morning, insisting that they give the two no more coverage today of all days. CNN has resisted, of course. But when he owns them, they will do what he says. That will be a relief."

"Chaim! You *want* that kind of leadership? Control of the media?"

"I am so tired of most of the press, Cameron. You must know that I hold you in the highest regard. You are one of few I trust. The rest are so biased, so critical, so negative. We must pull the world together once and for all, and a credible, state-run news organization will finally get it right."

"That's scary," Buck said. And quietly he grieved for his old friend who had seen so much and was now willing to surrender so much to a man he should not trust.

SIXTEEN

RAYFORD'S day—and, he felt, his future—were both set. He would attend the gala festivities, then get a cab back to Ben Gurion International Airport at Lod, nine miles southeast of Tel Aviv. By the time he arrived, the crew should have the 757 shipshape, and he would begin preflight safety checklists. The schedule called for an afternoon flight to Baghdad and then a nonstop to New York. By flying west at that time of day, he would go against conventional schedules and wisdom, but for this trip, and maybe for the rest of Rayford's career, Carpathia was the boss.

Rayford would spend the night in New York before heading back home to decide whether it was really feasible to do this job from Chicago. Maybe he and Chloe would move to New York. Clearly the piloting of *Air Force One* for the president was a ruse. His job was ferrying Nicolae Carpathia wherever he wanted to go, and for some reason, Rayford felt compelled to sublimate his wishes, his desires, his will, and his logic. God had laid this in his lap for some reason, and as long as he didn't have to live a lie, at least for now he would do it.

What he had been learning from Bruce and his own study of prophecy indicated that the day would come when the Antichrist would no longer be a deceiver. He would show his colors and rule the world with an iron fist. He would smash his enemies and kill anyone disloyal to his regime. That would put every follower of Christ at risk of martyrdom. Rayford foresaw the day when he would have to leave Carpathia's employ and become a fugitive, merely to survive and help other believers do the same.

Buck saw an American Secret Service agent making a beeline toward him. "Cameron Williams?"

"Who's asking?"

"Secret Service, and you know it. Can I see some ID please?"

"I've been cleared a hundred times over." Buck reached for his credentials.

"I know that." The agent peered at Buck's identification. "Fitz wants to see you, and I've got to be sure I bring him the right guy."

"The president wants to see me?"

The agent snapped Buck's wallet shut and handed it back, nodding. "Follow me."

In a small office at the back of the Knesset Building, more than two dozen members of the press fought for position by the door, waiting to pounce on President Gerald Fitzhugh the moment he headed for the ceremonies. Two more agents—lapel pins showing, earpieces in place, hands clasped in front—stood guarding the door.

"When can we expect him?" they were asked.

But the agents didn't respond. The media were not their responsibility, except to keep them away when necessary. The agents knew better than the press secretary when the president would move from one location to another, but that was certainly nobody else's business.

Buck looked forward to seeing the president again. It had been a few years since he had done the Newsmaker of the Year story on Fitzhugh, the year Fitz had been reelected and also the second time the man had won *Global Weekly*'s honor. Buck seemed to have hit it off with the president, who was a younger version of Lyndon Johnson. Fitzhugh had been just fifty-two when elected the first time and was now pushing fifty-nine. He was robust and youthful, an exuberant, earthy man. He used profanity liberally, and though Buck had never been in his presence when Fitz was angry, his outbursts were legendary among staffers.

Buck's lack of exposure to the presidential temper ended that Monday morning.

As Buck's escort maneuvered him through the throng before the door, the agents recognized their colleague and stepped aside so

Buck could enter. American members of the press corps expressed
their displeasure with Buck's easy access.

"How does he *do* that?"

"It never fails!"

"It's not what you know or how much you hustle! It's who you
know!"

"The rich get richer!"

Buck only wished they were right. He wished he had somehow
talked his way into a scoop, an exclusive with the president. But
he was as much in the dark as they were about what he was doing there.

Buck's Secret Service escort handed him off to a presidential
aide, who grasped his sleeve and dragged him to a corner of the
room where the president sat on the edge of a huge side chair.
His suit jacket was open, his tie loose, and he was whispering
with a couple of advisers. "Mr. President, Cameron Williams of
Global Weekly," the aide announced.

"Give me a minute," Fitzhugh said, and the aide and the two
advisers began to move away. The president grabbed one of the
advisers. "Not you, Rob! How long do you have to work for me
before you catch on? I need you here. When I say to give me a
minute, I don't mean you."

"Sorry, sir."

"And quit apologizing."

"Sorry."

As soon as he had said that, Rob realized he shouldn't have
apologized for apologizing. "Sorry, well, sorry. OK."

Fitzhugh rolled his eyes. "Somebody get Williams a chair, will
ya? For crying out loud, let's get with it here. We've only got a
few minutes."

"Eleven," Rob said apologetically.

"Fine. Eleven it is."

Buck stuck out his hand. "Mr. President," he said. Fitzhugh
gave his hand a perfunctory squeeze, not making eye contact.

"Sit down here, Williams." Fitzhugh's face was red, and sweat
had begun to bead on his forehead. "First off, this is totally off
the record, all right?"

"Whatever you say, sir."

"No, not whatever I say! I've heard that before and been
burned."

"Not by me, sir."

"No, not by you, but I remember once I told you something

and then said it was off the record and you gave me that cocka-
mamie stuff about when it is and when it isn't off the record le-
gally."

"As I recall, sir, I cut you some slack on that."

"So you said."

"Technically, you can't say something's off the record after the
fact. Only before you say it."

"Yeah, I think I've learned that a few times. So, we're clear this
is all off the record from the git-go, right?"

"Loud and clear, sir."

"Williams, I want to know what in blazes is going on with
Carpathia. You've spent some time with him. You've interviewed
him. Word is he's trying to hire you. You know the man?"

"Not well, sir."

"I'm getting pretty steamed by him, to tell you the truth, but
he's the most popular guy in the world since Jesus himself, so
who am I to squawk?"

Buck was staggered by the truth of that statement. "I thought
you were a big supporter of his, sir—America showing the way,
and all that."

"Well, I am! I mean, I was. I invited him to the White House!
He spoke to the joint session. I like his ideas. I wasn't a pacifist
till I heard him talk about it, and by George I think he can pull
this off. But the polls say he would double me in a run for the
presidency right now! Only he doesn't want that. He wants me to
stay in office and be my boss!"

"He told you that?"

"Don't be naïve, Williams. I wouldn't have brought you in here
if I thought you were going to take everything literally. But look,
he weasels me out of *Air Force One,* and now have you seen the
thing? He's got *Global Community One* painted on it and is issu-
ing a statement this afternoon thanking the citizens of the United
States for giving it to him. I've got a mind to call him a liar to his
face and try to turn some of his good press around."

"It would never work sir," the obsequious Rob interjected. "I
mean, I know you didn't ask, but the statement going out makes
it appear he tried to refuse, you insisted, and he reluctantly
agreed."

The president turned back to Buck. "There you go, Williams,
you see? You see what he does? Now am I getting myself in hot-
ter water by sharing this stuff with you? Are you already on his
payroll and going to blow the whistle on me?"

Buck wanted to tell him what he had seen, what he really knew about Carpathia, who the Bible proved he was. "I can't say I'm a Carpathia fan," Buck said.

"Well, are you a Fitzhugh fan? I'm not going to ask you how you voted—"

"I don't mind telling you. The first time you ran, I voted for your opponent. The second time I voted for you."

"Won you over, did I?"

"You did."

"So what's *your* problem with Carpathia? He's so smooth, so persuasive, so believable. I think he's got almost all of the people fooled most of the time."

"I guess that's one of my problems," Buck said. "I'm not sure what he's using for leverage, but it seems to work. He gets what he wants when he wants it, and he looks like a reluctant hero."

"That's it!" the president said, slapping Buck's knee hard enough to make it sting. "That's what gets me too!" He swore. And then he swore again. Soon he was lacing every sentence with profanity. Buck was afraid the man would burst a blood vessel.

"I've got to put a stop to it," he raged. "This is really ticking me off. He's going to come off sacrosanct today, making me look like an overgrown wuss. I mean, it's one thing for the United States to model leadership to the world, but what we look like now is one of his puppets. I'm a strong guy, a strong leader, decisive. And somehow he's succeeded in making me look like his sycophant." He took a deep breath. "Williams, do you know the trouble we've got with the militia?"

"I can only imagine."

"I'll tell you, they've got a point, and I can't argue with them! Our intelligence is telling us they're starting to hoard and hide some major weaponry, because they're so against my plan to join this destroy-90-give-10-to-the-U.N. or Global Community or whatever he's calling it this week. I'd like to believe his motives are pure and that this is the last step toward true peace, but it's the little things that make me wonder. Like this airplane deal.

"We got the new plane, we needed a new pilot. I don't care who flies the thing as long as he's qualified. We get a list from people we trust, but all of a sudden there's only one name on that list acceptable to the Grand Potentate of the World, and he's going to get the job. Now I should care even less, because I guess I've given the plane *and* the crew to Carpathia!" And he swore some more.

"Well, sir, I don't know what to tell you, but it is a pity you're not getting the services of the new pilot. I know him and he's tops."

"Well, great. Wouldn't you think I'd get the best pilot in my own country? No! And I wasn't exaggerating about that new title for Carpathia. There's some resolution in the U.N., excuse me, Global Community, and the Security Council is supposed to vote on it soon. It calls for a 'more appropriate title' for the secretary-general, given that he will soon become the commander in chief of the world's remaining military power and the chief financial officer of the global bank. The worst part is, that resolution came from our own ambassador, and I didn't know a thing about it until it went to committee. The only recourse I have is to insist he vote against his own proposal, withdraw it, or resign. How would that make me look, firing a guy because he wants to give the head of the Global Community, whom the whole world loves, a better title?"

The president wasn't giving Buck an opportunity to respond, which was all right with him, because he had no idea what to say.

Fitzhugh leaned forward and whispered, "And this media thing! We agreed with him that our conflict of interest laws were a little restrictive, along with those of most of the rest of the world. We didn't want to keep the U.N. or whatever from having the right to publish more widely when they were so close to world peace. So we make a little loophole for him and now look what we've got. He'll have bought up all the newspapers and magazines and radio and TV networks before we can change our minds!

"Where's he getting the money, Williams? Can you tell me that?"

Cameron had a crisis of conscience. He had implied to Carpathia that he would not tell about the inheritance from Stonagal. And yet were promises made to devils required to be kept? Wouldn't that be on the same order as lying to an intruder when he asks where your loved ones are?

"I couldn't tell you," Buck said. He felt no loyalty to Carpathia, but he couldn't afford having it get back to Carpathia that he had broken a confidence as significant as this. He had to hold on to his own ability to function—for as long as he could.

"You know what our intelligence people are telling us?" Fitzhugh continued. "That the eventual plan is for the heads of countries represented by the ten members of the Security Council to actually report as subordinates to their ambassadors. That would make those ten ambassadors kings of the world under Carpathia's rule."

Buck scowled. "In other words, you and the Mexican president and the Canadian prime minister would report to the U.N. ambassador of North America?"

"That's it, Williams. But you've got to forget the United Nations. It's the Global Community now."

"My mistake."

"Well, it's a mistake all right, but it's not yours."

"Sir, is there something I can do to help?"

President Fitzhugh looked to the ceiling and wiped his sweaty face with his hand. "I don't know. I just wanted to unload, I guess, and I thought maybe you had some insight. Anything we can get on this guy to slow him down a little. There's got to be a chink in his armor somewhere."

"I wish I could be of more help," Buck said, suddenly realizing what an understatement that was. What he wouldn't give to expose Nicolae Carpathia as a lying murderer, the hypnotic Antichrist! And though Buck would oppose him, anyone without Christ would never understand or agree. Besides, Scripture didn't seem to indicate that even Christ's followers would be able to do more than simply bear up against him. The Antichrist was on a course foretold centuries before, and the drama would be played out to the end.

Nicolae Carpathia was going to swallow up the president of the United States and everyone else in his path. He would gain ultimate power, and then the true battle would begin, the war between heaven and hell. The ultimate cold war would become a battle to the death. Buck took comfort in the assurance that the end had been known from the beginning . . . even if he had known it for only a few weeks.

The aide who had announced Buck to President Fitzhugh politely interrupted. "Excuse me, Mr. President, but the secretary-general is asking for five minutes before the ceremony."

Fitzhugh swore again. "I guess we're through, Williams. I appreciate the ear anyway, and I'm grateful for your confidence."

"Certainly, sir. Ah, it would be really good if Carpathia did not see me in here. He will ask what this was about."

"Yeah, OK, listen, Rob. Go out there and tell Carpathia's people that this room is not conducive and that we'll meet him anywhere else he says in one minute. And get me Pudge."

Pudge was apparently the nickname of the agent who had accompanied Buck in the first place. The moniker didn't fit the trim young man. "Pudge, get Williams out of here without Carpathia's people seeing him."

The president knotted his tie and buttoned his coat, then was escorted to another room for his meeting with Carpathia. Buck was shielded by Pudge, the Secret Service agent, until the coast was clear. Then he made his way to the staging area, where he would be introduced as part of the American delegation.

Rayford's credentials gave him a seat near the front with the American dignitaries. He was one of few people who knew that the witnesses at the Wailing Wall were right—that this was the celebration of an unholy alliance. He knew, but he felt helpless. No one could stem the tide of history.

Bruce Barnes had taught him that much.

Rayford missed Bruce already. He had begun to enjoy the nightly meetings and all the insight he was gaining. And Bruce's intuition was right. The Holy Land was the place to be right now. If this was where the first of 144,000 Jewish converts would come from, Bruce would want to be here.

According to what Bruce had taught Rayford and Chloe and Buck from the Scriptures, the converts would come from every part of the globe and would reap an incredible harvest—perhaps a billion souls. The 144,000 would be Jews, 12,000 from each of the original twelve tribes, but they would be gathered from all over the world, a restoration of the dispersion of Jews throughout history. Imagine, Rayford thought, Jews ministering in their own lands and their own tongues, drawing millions to Jesus the Messiah.

Despite all the mayhem and heartache to come, there would be many mighty victories, and Rayford looked forward to them. But he was not excited about the breaking up and dispersing of the Tribulation Force. Who knew where Buck would land if Carpathia really bought up all the media? If the relationship between Buck and Chloe blossomed, they might end up together somewhere far away.

He turned in his chair and surveyed the crowd. Hundreds were filing into their seats. Security was heavy and tight. At the top of the hour he saw the red lights on the TV cameras come on. Music swelled, news reporters whispered into their microphones, and the crowd hushed. Rayford sat tall and straight, his cap in his lap, wondering if Chloe could see him from their home in suburban Chicago. It was the middle of the night there, and she would not be looking for him as much as for Buck. Buck would be easy to spot. He had a position on the dais directly behind the chair of one of the signers, Dr. Chaim Rosenzweig.

To polite applause, the dignitaries were announced—veteran members of the Knesset, ambassadors from around the world, American statesmen and former presidents, Israeli leaders.

Finally came the second tier, those who would stand behind the chairs. Buck was introduced as "Mr. Cameron 'Buck' Williams, former senior staff writer and current Midwest bureau writer for *Global Weekly,* of the United States of America." Rayford smiled as Buck did at the lukewarm response. Obviously everybody wondered who he was and why he was considered a dignitary.

The loudest applause was reserved for the last five men: the chief rabbi of Israel, the Nobel Prize–winning botanist Chaim Rosenzweig of Israel, the prime minister of Israel, the president of the United States, and the secretary-general of the Global Community.

By the time Carpathia was announced and entered with his trademark shy confidence, the audience was standing. Rayford rose reluctantly and clapped without making a sound, his cap tucked under his arm. He found it difficult to reconcile the appearance of applauding the enemy of Christ.

Chaim Rosenzweig turned to beam at Buck, who smiled at him. Buck wished he could rescue his friend from this debacle, but the time was not right. All he could do was let the man enjoy the moment, for he would not have too many more to enjoy.

"This is a great day, Cameron," he whispered, reaching for Buck's hand with both of his. He patted Buck's hand as if Buck were his son.

For a fleeting instant, Buck almost wished God couldn't see him. Flash units were erupting all over, recording for posterity the dignitaries lending their support to this historic covenant. And Buck was the only one in the picture who knew who Carpathia was, who knew that the signing of the treaty would officially usher in the Tribulation.

Suddenly Buck remembered the Velcro-backed *Global Weekly* patch in his side pocket. As he pulled it out to apply it to his breast pocket, the Velcro caught the flap over the side pocket and held fast. As Buck lifted, his entire jacket pulled up over his belt, and when he let go, the hem stayed up by his shirt. By the time he smoothed out his jacket and used both hands to yank the patch free, he had been photographed a dozen times looking like a contortionist.

When the applause died and the crowd resumed their seats, Carpathia stood, microphone in hand. "This is an historic day," he began with a smile. "While all this has come about in record time, it has been nonetheless a herculean effort to pull together all the resources necessary to make it happen. Today we honor many individuals. First, my beloved friend and mentor, a father figure to me, the brilliant Dr. Chaim Rosenzweig of Israel!"

The crowd responded with enthusiasm, and Chaim rose unsteadily, waving his little wave and smiling like a small boy. Buck wanted to pat him on the back, to congratulate him for his accomplishments, but he grieved for his friend. Rosenzweig was being used. He was a small part of a devious plot that would make the world unsafe for him and his loved ones.

Carpathia sang the praises of the chief rabbi, of the Israeli prime minister, and finally of "the Honorable Gerald Fitzhugh, president of the United States of America, the greatest friend Israel has ever had."

More thunderous applause. Fitzhugh rose a few inches from his chair to acknowledge the response, and just when it was about to die down, Carpathia himself kept it going, tucking the microphone under his arm and stepping back to applaud loudly himself.

Fitzhugh appeared embarrassed, almost flustered, and looked to Carpathia as if wondering what to do. Carpathia beamed, as if thrilled for his friend the president. He shrugged and offered the microphone to Fitzhugh. At first the president didn't react, then he seemed to wave it off. Finally he accepted it to the roar of the audience.

Buck was amazed at Carpathia's ability to control the crowd. Clearly this was something he had choreographed. But what would Fitzhugh do now? Surely the only appropriate reaction would be to thank the people and toss a few bouquets at his good friends the Israelis. And despite Fitzhugh's dawning awareness of the devious agenda of Nicolae Carpathia, he would have to acknowledge Nicolae's role in the peace process.

Fitzhugh's chair scraped noisily as he stood, pushing back awkwardly against his own secretary of state. He had to wait for the crowd to quiet, and the process seemed to take forever. Carpathia rushed to Fitzhugh and thrust his hand aloft, the way a referee does with the winning boxer, and the Israeli crowd cheered all the more.

Finally, Carpathia stepped into the background and President Fitzhugh stood in the center of the dais, obligated to say a few words. As soon as Fitzhugh began to speak, Buck knew Carpathia was at work. And while he didn't expect to witness a murder, as he had in New York, Buck became immediately convinced that Carpathia had somehow caused something every bit as sinister. For the Gerald Fitzhugh speaking to the enthusiastic throng was anything but the frustrated president Buck had met with just minutes before.

Buck felt his neck grow warm and his knees weaken as Fitzhugh spoke. He leaned forward and gripped the back of Rosenzweig's chair, trying in vain to keep from trembling. Buck felt the clear presence of evil, and nausea nearly overtook him.

"The last thing I want to do at a moment like this," President Fitzhugh said, "is to detract in any way from the occasion at hand. However, with your kind indulgence and that of our great leader of the aptly renamed Global Community, I would like to make a couple of brief points.

"First, it has been a privilege to see what Nicolae Carpathia has done in just a few short weeks. I am certain we all agree that the world is a more loving, peaceful place because of him."

Carpathia made an effort to take back the microphone, but President Fitzhugh resisted. "Now I have the floor, sir, if you don't mind!" This brought a peal of laughter. "I've said it before, and I'll say it again, the secretary-general's idea for global disarmament is a stroke of genius. I support it without reservation and am proud to lead the way to the rapid destruction of 90 percent of our weapons and the donation of the other 10 percent to Global Community, under Mr. Carpathia's direction."

Buck's head swam and he fought to keep his equilibrium.

"As a tangible expression of my personal support and that of our nation as a whole, we have also gifted Global Community with the brand-new *Air Force One*. We have financed its repainting and titling, and it can be viewed at Ben Gurion International.

"Now I surrender the microphone to the man of destiny, the leader whose current title does not do justice to the extent of his influence, to my personal friend and compatriot, Nicolae Carpathia!"

Nicolae appeared to accept the microphone reluctantly and seemed embarrassed by all the attention. He looked bemused, as if helpless to know what to do with such a recalcitrant U.S. president who didn't know when enough was enough.

When the applause finally died down, Carpathia affected his humblest tone and said, "I apologize for my overexuberant friend, who has been too kind and too generous, and to whom the Global Community owes a tremendous debt."

Rayford kept a close eye on Buck. The man did not look well. Buck had seemed to nearly topple, and Rayford wondered if it was the heat or merely the nauseating mutual-admiration-society speeches that were turning Buck green around the gills.

The Israeli dignitaries, except Rosenzweig of course, looked vaguely uncomfortable with all the talk of destroying weapons and disarming. A strong military had been their best defense for decades, and without the covenant with Global Community, they would have been loath to agree to Carpathia's disarmament plan.

The rest of the ceremony was anticlimactic to the rousing— and, in Rayford's mind, disturbing—speech of the president. Fitzhugh seemed more enamored of Carpathia every time they were together. But his view only mirrored that of most of the populace of the world. Unless one was a student of Bible prophecy and read between the lines, one would easily believe that Nicolae Carpathia was a gift from God at the most crucial moment in world history.

Buck recovered control as other leaders made innocuous speeches and rattled on about the importance and historicity of the document they were about to sign. Several decorative pens were produced as television, film, video, and still cameras zeroed in on the signers. The pens were passed back and forth, the poses struck, and the signatures applied. With handshakes, embraces, and kisses on both cheeks all around, the treaty was inaugurated.

And the signers of this treaty—all except one—were ignorant of its consequences, unaware they had been party to an unholy alliance.

A covenant had been struck. God's chosen people, who planned to rebuild the temple and reinstitute the system of sacrifices until the coming of their Messiah, had signed a deal with the devil.

Only two men on the dais knew this pact signaled the beginning of the end of time. One was maniacally hopeful; the other trembled at what was to come.

———————

At the famed Wall, the two witnesses wailed the truth. At the tops of their voices, the sound carrying to the far reaches of the Temple Mount and beyond, they called out the news: *"Thus begins the last terrible week of the Lord!"*

The seven-year "week" had begun.

The Tribulation.

SEVENTEEN

RAYFORD Steele sat in a phone booth at Ben Gurion Airport. He was early, preceding the Carpathia delegation by more than an hour. His crew was busy on *Global Community One,* and he had time to wait for an international operator to try to get through to Chloe.

"I saw you, Dad!" she laughed. "They tried to flash names with each shot. They had yours almost right. It said you were Raymond Steel, no *e* on the end, and that you were the pilot of *Air Force One.*"

Rayford smiled, warmed by the sound of his daughter's voice. "Close. And the press wonders why no one trusts them."

"They didn't know what to do with Buck," Chloe said. "The first few times they panned to him, they didn't put anything on the screen. Then somebody must have heard the announcement when he was introduced and they came up with 'Duke Wilson, former writer, *Newsweek.'*"

"Perfect," Rayford said.

"Buck's all excited about this rabbi who's going to be on international CNN in a couple of hours. You going to get a chance to watch?"

"We'll have it on the plane."

"You can get it that far away and that far up?"

"You should see the technology, Chlo'. The reception will be better than we get on cable at home. At least as good, anyway."

Buck felt an overwhelming sadness. Chaim Rosenzweig had embraced him at least three times after the ceremony, exulting that this was one of the happiest days of his life. He pleaded with Buck to come along on the flight to Baghdad. "You will be working for Nicolae in a month regardless," Chaim said. "No one will see this as conflict of interest."

"I will, especially in a month when he owns whatever rag I work for."

"Don't be negative today, of all days," Chaim said. "Come along. Marvel. Enjoy. I have seen the plans. New Babylon will be magnificent."

Buck wanted to weep for his friend. When would it all come crashing down on Chaim? Might he die before he realized he'd been duped and used? Maybe that would be best. But Buck also feared for Chaim's soul. "Will you watch Dr. Ben-Judah on live television today?"

"Of course! Wouldn't miss it! He has been my friend since Hebrew University days. I understand they will have it on the plane to Baghdad. Another reason for you to come along."

Buck shook his head. "I will be watching from here. But once your friend outlines his findings, you and I should talk about the ramifications."

"Ah, I am not a religious man, Cameron. You know this. I likely should not be surprised with what Tsion comes up with today. He is an able scholar and careful researcher, brilliant really, and an engaging speaker. He reminds me somewhat of Nicolae."

Please, Buck thought. *Anything but that!*

"What do you think he'll say?"

"Like most Orthodox Jews, he will come to the conclusion that Messiah is yet to come. There are a few fringe groups, as you know, who believe Messiah already came, but these so-called Messiahs are no longer in Israel. Some are dead. Some have moved to other countries. None brought the justice and peace the Torah predicts. So, like all of us, Tsion will outline the prophecies and encourage us to keep waiting and watching. It will be uplifting and inspirational, which I believe was the point of the research project in the beginning.

"He may talk about hastening the coming of Messiah. Some groups moved into ancient Jewish dwellings, believing they had a sacred right to do so and that this would help fulfill some prophecies, clearing the way for the coming of Messiah. Others are so upset at the Muslim desecration of the Temple Mount that they have reopened synagogues in the same vicinity, as close as they can to the original site of the temple."

"You know there are Gentiles who also believe Messiah has already come," Buck said carefully.

Chaim was looking over Buck's shoulder, making sure he was not left behind when the entourage moved toward transportation back to the hotels and eventually to Ben Gurion for the flight to Baghdad. "Yes, yes, I know, Cameron. But I would sooner believe Messiah is not a person but more of an ideology."

He began moving away and Buck suddenly felt desperate. He held Chaim's arm. "Doctor, Messiah is more than an ideology!"

Rosenzweig stopped and looked his friend in the face. "Cameron, we can discuss this, but if you are going to be so literal about it, let me tell you something. If Messiah is a person, if he is to come to bring peace and justice and hope to the world, I agree with those who believe he is already here."

"You do?"

"Yes, don't you?"

"You believe in Messiah?"

"I said *if,* Cameron. That is a big if."

"If Messiah is real and is to come, what?" Buck pleaded as his friend pulled away.

"Don't you see, Cameron? Nicolae himself fulfills most of the prophecies. Maybe all, but this is not my area of scholarship. Now I must go. I will see you in Babylon?"

"No, I told you—"

Rosenzweig stopped and returned. "I thought you just meant you were finding your own way there so as not to accept any favors from an interview subject."

"I was, but I have changed my mind. I'm not going. If I do wind up working for a Carpathia-owned publication, I imagine I'll tour New Babylon soon enough."

"What will you do? Are you returning to the States? Will I see you there?"

"I don't know. We'll see."

"Cameron! Give me a smile on this historic day!"

But Buck could not muster one. He walked all the way back to the King David Hotel, where the clerk asked if he still wanted information on commercial flights to Baghdad. "No, thanks," he said.

"Very good, sir. A message for you."

The envelope bore the return address of Dr. Tsion Ben-Judah.

Buck trotted up to his room before tearing it open. It read, "Sorry to abandon you last night. Would not have been able to converse. Would you do me the honor of joining me for lunch and accompanying me to the ICNN studio? I will await your call."

Buck looked at his watch. Surely it was too late. He placed the call, only to get a housekeeper who said that the rabbi had left twenty minutes before. Buck slammed his hand on the dresser. What a privilege he would miss, just because he had walked back to the hotel instead of taking a cab! Perhaps he would take a cab to the TV studio and meet Tsion there after lunch. But did the rabbi want to talk before going on the air; was that it?

Buck lifted the receiver, and the front desk answered. "Can you get me a cab, please?"

"Certainly, sir, but a call has just come in for you. Would you like to take it now?"

"Yes, and hold on that cab until I get back to you."

"Yes, sir. Hang up, please, and I will ring your call through."

It was Tsion. "Dr. Ben-Judah! I'm so glad you called! I just got back."

"I was at the signing, Buck," Tsion said in his thick Hebrew accent, "but I did not make myself visible or available."

"Is your lunch invitation still open?"

"It is."

"When shall I meet you, and where?"

"How about now, out in front?"

"I'm there."

Thank you, Lord, Buck breathed as he ran down the stairs. *Give me the opportunity to tell this man that you are the Messiah.*

At the car the rabbi shook Buck's hand with both of his and pulled him close. "Buck, we have shared an incredible experience. I feel a bond. But now I am nervous about informing the world of my findings, and I need to talk over lunch. May we?"

The rabbi directed his driver to a small cafe in a busy section of Jerusalem. Tsion, a huge, black, three-ring binder under his arm, spoke quietly to the waiter in Hebrew, and they were directed to a window table surrounded by plants. When menus were brought, Ben-Judah looked at his watch, waved off the menus, and spoke again in his native tongue. Buck assumed he was ordering for both of them.

"Do you still need your patch, identifying yourself as a reporter from the magazine?"

Buck quickly yanked the patch off his pocket.

"It came off much easier than it went on, did it not?"

Buck laughed.

As Tsion joined in the laughter, the waiter brought an unsliced loaf of warm bread, butter, a wheel of cheese, a mayonnaise-like sauce, a bowl of green apples, and fresh cucumbers.

"If you will allow me?" Ben-Judah pointed to the plate.

"Please."

The rabbi sliced the warm bread in huge sections, slathered them with butter and the sauce, applied slices of the cucumber and cheese, then put apple slices on the side and slid a plate in front of Buck.

Buck waited as the rabbi prepared his own plate. "Please do not wait for me. Eat while the bread is warm."

Buck bowed his head briefly, praying again for Tsion Ben-Judah's soul. He raised his eyes and lifted the delicacy.

"You are a man of prayer," Tsion observed as he continued to prepare his meal.

"I am." Buck continued to pray silently, wondering if now was the time to jump in with a timely word. Could this man be influenced within an hour of revealing his scholarly research to the world? Buck felt foolish. The rabbi was smiling.

"What is it, Tsion?"

"I was just recalling the last American with whom I shared a meal here. He was on a junket, sightseeing, and I was asked to entertain him. He was some sort of a religious leader, and we all take turns here, you know, making the tourists feel welcome."

Buck nodded.

"I made the mistake of asking if he wanted to try one of my favorites, a vegetable and cheese sandwich. Either my accent was too difficult for him or he understood me and the offering did not appeal. He politely declined and ordered something more familiar, something with pita bread and shrimp, as I recall. But I asked the waiter, in my own language, to bring extra of what I was having, due to what I call the jealousy factor. It was not long before the man had pushed his plate aside and was sampling what I had ordered."

Buck laughed. "And now you simply order for your guests."

"Exactly."

And before the rabbi ate, he prayed silently too.

"I skipped breakfast," Buck said, lifting the bread in salute.

Tsion Ben-Judah beamed with delight. "Perfect!" he said. "An international adage says that hunger is the best seasoning."

Buck found it true. He had to slow down to keep from over-eating, which had rarely been a problem for him. "Tsion," he began finally, "did you just want company before going on the air, or was there something specific you wanted to talk about?"

"Something specific," the rabbi said, looking at his watch. "How does my hair look, by the way?"

"Fine. They'll probably comb out the hat line there in makeup."

"Makeup? I had forgotten that part. No wonder they want me so early."

Ben-Judah checked his watch, then pushed his plates aside and hefted the notebook onto the table. It contained a four-inch stack of manuscript pages. "I have several more of these in my office," he said, "but this is the essence, the conclusion, the result of my three years of exhaustive—and exhausting—work with a team of young students who were of incalculable help to me."

"You're not dreaming of reading that aloud in an hour, are you?"

"No, no!" Ben-Judah said, laughing. "This is what you would call my security blanket. If I draw a blank, I pick up the blanket. No matter where I turn, there is something I should say. You might be interested to know that I have memorized what I will say on television."

"An hour's worth?"

"That might have seemed daunting to me, too, three years ago. Now I know I could go on for many more hours, and without notes. But I must stick to my plan to redeem the time. If I get off on tangents, I will never finish."

"And yet you'll take your notes with you."

"I am confident, Buck, but I am no fool. Much of my life has consisted of speaking publicly, but about half the time that has been in Hebrew. Naturally, with their worldwide audience, CNN prefers English. That makes it more difficult for me, and I don't want to compound that by losing my way."

"I'm sure you'll do fine."

"You have just satisfied the requirements of your end of the conversation!" the rabbi said, grinning. "Treating you to lunch is already a profitable proposition."

"So you just needed a little cheerleading."

The rabbi seemed to think about the word for a moment.

Though it was an American term, Buck assumed it was self-explanatory. "Yes," Ben-Judah said. "Cheerleading. And I want to ask you a question. If it is too personal, you may decline to answer."

Buck held his hands apart as if open to any question.

"Last night you asked me my conclusions on the Messiah question, and I told you, in essence, that you would have to wait until the rest of the world heard it. But let me pose the same question to you."

Praise the Lord, Buck thought. "How much time do we have?"

"About twenty minutes. If it takes longer, we can continue in the car on the way to the studio. Maybe even into makeup."

The rabbi smiled at his own humor, but Buck was already formulating his story. "You already know about my being at a kibbutz when the Russians attacked Israel."

Ben-Judah nodded. "The day you lost your agnosticism."

"Right. Well, I was on an airplane, headed for London, the day of the disappearances."

"You don't say."

And Buck was off and running with the story of his own spiritual journey. He wasn't finished until the rabbi was out of makeup and sitting nervously in the green room. "Did I go on too long?" Buck asked. "I realize it was asking a lot for you to even pretend to pay attention with your mind on your own presentation."

"No, Buck," the rabbi said, deep emotion in his voice. "I should be able to do this in my sleep. If I tried to push any more into my head at this late date, I would lose it all."

So that was it? No response? No thank you? No 'you're-a-fool'?

Finally, after a long silence, Tsion spoke again. "Buck, I deeply appreciate your sharing that with me."

A young woman with a battery pack on her hip, earphones and mouthpiece in place, slipped in. "Dr. Ben-Judah," she said. "We are ready for you in the studio for sound check, and ninety seconds to air."

"I am ready." Ben-Judah did not move.

The young woman hesitated, looking doubtful. Apparently she was not used to guests who didn't simply nervously follow her to the set. She left.

Tsion Ben-Judah rose with his notebook under his arm and opened the door, standing there with his free hand on the knob.

"Now, Buck Williams, if you would be so kind as to do me a favor while you wait here."

"Sure."

"As you are a man of prayer, would you pray that I will say what God wants me to say?"

Buck raised a fist of encouragement to his new friend and nodded.

"Want to take over?" Rayford asked his first officer. "I wouldn't mind catching this special CNN report."

"Roger. That rabbi thing?"

"Right."

The first officer shook his head. "That would put me right to sleep."

Rayford made his way out of the cockpit but was disappointed to see that the television was not on in the main cabin. He moved toward the back where other dignitaries and press were gathering around another TV. But before Rayford was completely out of Carpathia's conference room, Nicolae noticed him. "Captain Steele! Please! Spend a few minutes with us!"

"Thank you, sir, but I was hoping to catch the—"

"The Messiah broadcast, yes, of course! Turn it on!"

Someone turned on the set and tuned in ICNN. "You know," Carpathia announced to all within earshot, "our captain believes Jesus was the Messiah."

Chaim Rosenzweig said, "Frankly, as a nonreligious Jew, I think Nicolae fulfills more of the prophecies than Jesus did."

Rayford recoiled. *What blasphemy!* He knew Buck liked and respected Rosenzweig, but what a statement! "No offense, sir, but I doubt many Jews could believe in a Messiah—even if they think he is yet to come—who was born other than in the Holy Land."

"Ah, well, you see?" Rosenzweig said. "I am not that much a student. Now this man," he added, pointing to the TV screen where Tsion Ben-Judah was being introduced, "here is your religious scholar. After three years of intensive research, he ought to be able to outline the qualifications of Messiah."

I'll bet, Rayford thought. He stood in a corner and leaned against the wall to keep out of the way. Carpathia slipped off his suit jacket, and a flight attendant immediately hung it for him. He loosened his tie, rolled up his sleeves, and sat down in front of the television holding a fresh seltzer with a twist. Carpathia obviously considered this a good hour's diversion, Rayford thought.

An off-camera announcer clarified that "the views and opinions expressed on this broadcast do not necessarily reflect the views of the International Cable News Network or its subscribing stations."

Rayford found Dr. Ben-Judah a most engaging communicator. He looked directly into the camera, and though his accent was thick, he spoke slowly and distinctly enough to be easily understood. Most of all, Rayford sensed an enthusiasm and a passion for his subject. This was not at all what Rayford had expected. He would have imagined an ancient rabbi with a long white beard, hunched over some musty manuscripts with a magnifying glass, comparing jots and tittles.

Ben-Judah, however, after a brief introduction of himself and the process through which he and his team did their research, began with a promise. "I have come to the conclusion that we may know beyond all shadow of doubt the identity of our Messiah. Our Bible has given clear prophecies, prerequisites, and predictions that only one person in the human race could ever fulfill. Follow along with me and see if you come to the same conclusion I have, and we shall see whether Messiah is a real person, whether he has already come, or whether he is yet to come."

Rabbi Ben-Judah said he and his team spent almost the entire first year of their project confirming the accuracy of the late Alfred Edersheim, a teacher of languages and Grinfield Lecturer on the Septuagint. Edersheim had postulated that there were 456 messianic passages in Scripture, supported by more than 558 references from the most ancient rabbinical writings.

"Now," the rabbi said, "I promise to not bore you with statistics, but let me just say that many of those prophetic passages are repetitive and some are obscure. But based on our careful study, we believe there are at least 109 separate and distinct prophecies Messiah must fulfill. They require a man so unusual and a life so unique that they eliminate all pretenders.

"I do not have time in this brief hour to cover all 109, of course, but I will deal with some of the most clearly obvious and specific ones. We consulted a mathematician and asked him to calculate the probability of even 20 of the 109 prophecies being fulfilled in one man. He came up with odds of one in one quadrillion, one hundred and twenty-five trillion!"

Dr. Ben-Judah gave what Rayford considered a brilliant example of how to easily identify someone with just a few marks. "Despite the billions of people who still populate this planet, you can put a postcard in the mail with just a few distinctions on it, and I will be the only person to receive it. You eliminate much of the world when you send it to Israel. You narrow it more when it comes to Jerusalem. You cut the potential recipients to a tiny fraction when it goes to a certain street, a certain number, a certain apartment. And then, with my first and last name on it, you have singled me out of billions. That, I believe, is what these prophecies of Messiah do. They eliminate, eliminate, eliminate, until only one person could ever fulfill them."

Dr. Ben-Judah was so engaging that everyone on the plane had stopped talking, moving, even shifting in their seats. Even Nicolae Carpathia, despite the occasional sip from his glass and the tinkling of the ice, barely moved. It seemed to Rayford that Carpathia was almost embarrassed by the attention Ben-Judah had commanded.

Trying not to cause a distraction, Rayford excused himself and quickly slipped back into the cockpit. He put a hand on his first officer's shoulder and leaned down to talk to him. The first officer lifted his left earphone.

"I want this plane to not touch the ground before five minutes after the hour."

"We're scheduled for about two minutes to, Cap, and we're making good time."

"Make whatever adjustments you have to make."

"Roger." He reached for the radio. "Baghdad tower, this is *Global Community One,* over."

"Baghdad tower, go ahead *One.*"

"We're reducing speed a few knots and are setting a new ETA of five minutes after the hour."

"Roger, *Global.* Problems?"

"Negative. Just experimenting with the new plane."

The first officer glanced up at Rayford to see if that was all right. Rayford gave him the thumbs-up and hurried back to the television.

———

Buck prayed as he watched. Other staffers had gathered around monitors. There was none of the usual behind-the-scenes banter. People were glued to the broadcast. To keep from jumping out of his skin, Buck dug out his notebook and pen and tried to keep copious notes. It was nearly impossible to keep up with the rabbi, who rolled on and on with prophecy after prophecy.

"Messiah is not limited to just a few identifying marks," Ben-Judah said. "We Jews have been looking for him, praying for him, longing for him for centuries, and yet we have stopped studying the many identification hallmarks in our Scriptures. We have ignored many and made favorites of others, to the point that we are now looking for a political leader who will right wrongs, bring justice, and promise peace."

Chaim Rosenzweig stepped over to Carpathia and clapped him on the back, turning to beam at everyone. He was largely ignored, especially by Carpathia.

"Some believe Messiah will restore things as they were in the glorious days of Solomon," Rabbi Ben-Judah continued. "Others believe Messiah will make all things new, ushering in a kingdom unlike anything we have ever seen. And yet the prophecies themselves tell us what Messiah will do. Let us examine just a few of them in the remaining time."

Buck was getting a glimpse of what was to come. Jesus was either the Messiah, the chosen one, the fulfillment of God's Word, or he could not stand up to the scrutiny of the record. If only one man could possibly fulfill the prophecies, it had to be Jesus. It didn't appear the rabbi was going to use the New Testament to try to convince his first and primary audience, the Jews. So the prophecies from hundreds of years before the birth of Christ would have to be clear enough to make the point—if indeed that was where Tsion was going.

Dr. Ben-Judah was sitting on the edge of the table where he had displayed the several-hundred-page conclusion to his research study. The camera zoomed in on his expressive features. "The very first qualification of Messiah, accepted by our scholars from the beginning, is that he should be born the seed of a woman, not the seed of a man like all other human beings. We know now that women do not possess 'seed.' The man provides the seed for the woman's egg. And so this must be a supernatural birth, as foretold in Isaiah 7:14, 'Therefore the Lord Himself will give you a sign: Behold, the virgin shall conceive and bear a Son, and shall call His name Immanuel.'

"Our Messiah must be born of a woman and not of a man because he must be righteous. All other humans are born of the seed of their father, and thus the sinful seed of Adam has been passed on to them. Not so with the Messiah, born of a virgin.

"Our Messiah must be born of an extremely rare bloodline. While he must be born of a woman, that woman must be of a bloodline that includes many of the fathers of Israel. God himself eliminated billions of people from this select bloodline so Messiah's identity would be unmistakable.

"First God eliminated two-thirds of the world's population by choosing Abraham, who was from the line of Shem, one of Noah's three sons. Of Abraham's two sons, God chose only Isaac, eliminating half of Abraham's progeny. One of the two sons of Isaac, Jacob, received the blessing but passed it on to only one of his twelve sons, Judah. That eliminated millions of other sons in Israel. The prophet Isaiah years later singled out King David as another through whom Messiah would come, predicting that he would be a "root out of Jesse." David's father, Jesse, was a son of Judah.

"Messiah, according to the prophet Micah, must be born in Bethlehem." The rabbi turned to the passage in his notes and read, " 'But you, Bethlehem Ephrathah, though you are little among the thousands of Judah, yet out of you shall come forth to Me the One to be Ruler in Israel, whose goings forth are from of old, from everlasting.' "

Chaim Rosenzweig was moving nervously, the only one on the plane not perfectly still. Rayford felt the old man had made a fool of himself and hoped he wouldn't compound it. But he did. "Nicolae," he said. "You were born in Bethlehem and moved to Cluj, right? Ha, ha!"

Others shushed him, but Carpathia finally sat back as if he had just realized something. "I know where this man is going!" he said. "Can you not see it? It is as plain as the nose on his face."

I can, Rayford thought. *It should be obvious to more than Carpathia by now.*

"He is going to claim to be the Messiah himself!" Carpathia

shouted. "He was probably born in Bethlehem, and who knows what his bloodline is. Most people deny being born out of wedlock, but maybe that is his history. He can claim his mother was never with a man before he was born, and *voilà*, the Jews have their Messiah!"

"Ach!" Rosenzweig said. "You are speaking of a dear friend of mine. He would never claim such a thing."

"You watch and see," Carpathia said.

A steward leaned in and whispered, "Phone for you, Mr. Secretary-General."

"Who is it?"

"Your assistant calling from New York."

"Which one?"

"Ms. Durham."

"Take a message."

Carpathia turned back to the screen as Rabbi Ben-Judah continued. "As a child, Messiah will go to Egypt, because the prophet Hosea says that out of Egypt God will call him. Isaiah 9:1-2 indicates that Messiah will minister mostly in Galilee.

"One of the prophecies we Jews do not like and tend to ignore is that Messiah will be rejected by his own people. Isaiah prophesied, 'He is despised and rejected by men, a Man of sorrows and acquainted with grief. And we hid, as it were, our faces from Him; He was despised, and we did not esteem Him.' "

The rabbi looked at his watch. "My time is fleeting," he said, "so I want to speed through a few more clear prophecies and tell you what conclusion I have drawn. Isaiah and Malachi predict that Messiah will be preceded by a forerunner. The Psalmist said Messiah would be betrayed by a friend. Zechariah said that he would be betrayed for thirty pieces of silver. He adds that people will look on the one whom they have pierced.

"The Psalmist prophesied that people would 'look and stare at Me. They divide My garments among them, and for My clothing they cast lots.' And later it is prophesied that 'He guards all his bones; not one of them is broken.'

"Isaiah says 'they made His grave with the wicked; but with the rich at His death, because He had done no violence, nor was any deceit in His mouth.' The Psalms say he was to be resurrected.

"If I had more time, I could share with you dozens more prophecies from the Hebrew Scriptures that point to the qualifications of the Messiah. I will broadcast a phone number at the end of this broadcast so you can order all the printed material from our study. The study will convince you that we can be absolutely sure only one person could ever be qualified to be the special Anointed One of Jehovah.

"Let me close by saying that the three years I have invested in searching the sacred writings of Moses and the prophets have been the most rewarding of my life. I expanded my study to books of history and other sacred writings, including the New Testament of the Gentiles, combing every record I could find to see if anyone has ever lived up to the messianic qualifications. Was there one born in Bethlehem of a virgin, a descendant of King David, traced back to our father Abraham, who was taken to Egypt, called back to minister in Galilee, preceded by a forerunner, rejected by God's own people, betrayed for thirty pieces of silver, pierced without breaking a bone, buried with the rich, and resurrected?

"According to one of the greatest of all Hebrew prophets, Daniel, there would be exactly 483 years between the decree to rebuild the wall and the city of Jerusalem 'in troublesome times' before the Messiah would be cut off for the sins of the people.

Ben-Judah looked directly into the camera. "Exactly 483 years after the rebuilding of Jerusalem and its walls, Jesus Christ of Nazareth offered himself to the nation of Israel. He rode into the city on a donkey to the rejoicing of the people, just as the prophet Zechariah had predicted: 'Rejoice greatly, O daughter of Zion! Shout, O daughter of Jerusalem! Behold, your King is coming to you; He is just and having salvation, lowly and riding on a donkey, a colt, the foal of a donkey.' "

Buck leaped from the couch in the green room, standing now, watching the monitor. Others had gathered, but he couldn't help himself. He shouted, "Yes! Go, Tsion! Amen!" Buck heard phones ringing down the hall, and the rabbi hadn't even flashed the number yet.

"Jesus Christ is the Messiah!" the rabbi concluded. "There can be no other option. I had come to this answer but was afraid to act on it, and I was almost too late. Jesus came to rapture his church, to take them with him to heaven as he said he would. I was not among them, because I wavered. But I have since received him as my Savior. He is coming back in seven years! Be ready!"

Suddenly the TV studio was crawling with activity. Orthodox rabbis called, angry Israelis pounded on the doors, studio technicians looked for the cue to pull the plug.

"Here is the number to call to obtain more information!" the rabbi said. "If they will not flash it, let me quote it for you!" And he did, as directors signaled the cameramen to shut down. "Yeshua ben Yosef, Jesus son of Joseph, is Yeshua Hamashiac!" the rabbi shouted quickly. "Jesus is the Messiah!" And the screen went blank.

Rabbi Ben-Judah gathered up his notebook and looked frantically for Buck.

"I'm here, brother!" Buck said, running into the studio. "Where's the car?"

"Hidden around back, and my driver still doesn't know why!"

Executives burst into the studio. "Wait! People need to see you!"

The rabbi hesitated, looking to Buck. "What if they are seeking Christ?"

"They can call!" Buck said. "I'm getting you out of here!"

They ran through the back door and skipped into the employee parking lot. No sign of the Mercedes. Suddenly, from across the road, the driver jumped from the car, waving and shouting. Buck and Tsion sprinted toward him.

"Now *that* was anticlimactic." Nicolae Carpathia concluded. "I would have liked him saying *he* was the Messiah better. This is old news. Lots of people believe this myth. So they have a primo Hebrew rabbi convert. Big deal."

It sure is, Rayford thought, moving back to the cockpit for the landing.

Buck felt awkward in the small home of Tsion Ben-Judah, whose wife embraced him tearfully and then sat with her children in another room, sobbing loudly. "I support you, Tsion," she called out. "But our lives are ruined!"

Tsion answered the phone and motioned for Buck to pick up

the extension in the other room. Mrs. Ben-Judah tried to quiet herself while Buck was listening in.

"Yes, this is Rabbi Ben-Judah."

"This is Eli. I spoke to you last night."

"Of course! How did you get my number?"

"I called the one you mentioned on the broadcast, and the student who answered gave it to me. Somehow I convinced her who I was."

"It's good to hear from you."

"I rejoice with you, Tsion my brother, in the fellowship of Jesus Christ. Many have received him under our preaching here in Jerusalem. We have arranged for a meeting of new believers in Teddy Kollek Stadium. Would you come and address us?"

"Frankly, brother Eli, I fear for the safety of my family and myself."

"Have no fear. Moishe and I will make clear that anyone who threatens harm to you will answer to us. And I think our record is plain on that account."

EIGHTEEN

Eighteen months later

IT was frigid in Chicago. Rayford Steele pulled his heavy parka out of the closet. He hated lugging it through the airport, but he needed it just to get from the house to the car and from the car to the terminal. For months it had been all he could do to look at himself in the mirror while dressing for work. Often he packed his *Global Community One* captain's uniform, with its gaudy gold braids and buttons on a background of navy. In truth, it would have been a snappy-looking and only slightly formal and pompous uniform, had it not been such a stark reminder that he was working for the devil.

The strain of living in Chicago while flying out of New York showed on Rayford's face. "I'm worried about you, Dad," Chloe had said more than once. She had even offered to move with him to New York, especially after Buck had relocated there a few months before. Rayford knew Chloe and Buck missed each other terribly, but he had his own reasons for wanting to stay in Chicago for as long as possible. Not the least of which was Amanda White.

"I'll be married before you will if Buck doesn't get on the ball. Has he even held your hand yet?"

Chloe blushed. "Wouldn't you like to know? This is just all new to him, Dad. He's never been in love before."

"And you have?"

"I thought I had been, until Buck. We've talked about the future and everything. He just hasn't popped the question."

Rayford put on his cap and stood before the mirror, parka slung over his shoulder. He made a face, sighed, and shook his head. "We close on this house two weeks from tomorrow," he said. "And then you either come with me to New Babylon or you're on your own. Buck could sure make life easier for all of us by being a little decisive."

"I'm not going to push him, Dad. Being apart has been a good test. And I hate the idea of leaving Bruce alone at New Hope."

"Bruce is hardly alone. The church is bigger than it's ever been, and the underground shelter won't be much of a secret for long. It must be bigger than the sanctuary."

Bruce Barnes had done his share of traveling, too. He had instituted a program of house churches, small groups that met all over the suburbs and throughout the state in anticipation of the day when the assembling of the saints would be outlawed. It wouldn't be long. Bruce had gone all over the world, multiplying the small-group ministry, starting in Israel and seeing the ministry of the two witnesses and Rabbi Tsion Ben-Judah swell to fill the largest stadiums on the globe.

The 144,000 Jewish evangelists were represented in every country, often infiltrating colleges and universities. Millions and millions had become believers, but as faith had grown, crime and mayhem had increased as well.

Already there was pressure from the Global Community North American government outpost in Washington D.C. to convert all churches into official branches of what was now called Enigma Babylon One World Faith. The one-world religion was headed by the new Pope Peter, formerly Peter Mathews of the United States. He had ushered in what he called "a new era of tolerance and unity" among the major religions. The biggest enemy of Enigma Babylon, which had taken over the Vatican as its headquarters, were the millions of people who believed that Jesus was the only way to God.

To say arbitrarily, Pontifex Maximus Peter wrote in an official Enigma Babylon declaration, *that the Jewish and Protestant Bible, containing only the Old and New Testaments, is the final authority for faith and practice, represents the height of intolerance and disunity. It flies in the face of all we have accomplished, and adherents to that false doctrine are hereby considered heretics.*

Pontifex Maximus Peter had lumped the Orthodox Jews and

the new Christian believers together. He had as much problem with the newly rebuilt temple and its return to the system of sacrifices as he did with the millions and millions of converts to Christ. And ironically, the supreme pontiff had strange bedfellows in opposing the new temple. Eli and Moishe, the now world-famous witnesses whom no one dared oppose, often spoke out against the temple. But their logic was an anathema to Enigma Babylon.

"Israel has rebuilt the temple to hasten the return of their Messiah," Eli and Moishe had said, "not realizing that she built it apart from the true Messiah, who has already come! Israel has constructed a temple of rejection! Do not wonder why so few of the 144,000 Jewish evangelists are from Israel! Israel remains largely unbelieving and will soon suffer for it!"

The witnesses had been ablaze with anger the day the temple was dedicated and presented to the world. Hundreds of thousands began streaming to Jerusalem to see it; nearly as many as had begun pilgrimages to New Babylon to see the magnificent new Global Community headquarters Nicolae Carpathia had designed.

Eli and Moishe had angered everyone, including the visiting Carpathia, the day of the celebration of the reopening of the temple. For the first time they had preached other than at the Wailing Wall or at a huge stadium. That day they waited until the temple was full and thousands more filled the Temple Mount shoulder to shoulder. Moishe and Eli made their way to the temple side of the Golden Gate, much to the consternation of the crowd. They were jeered and hissed and booed, but no one dared approach, let alone try to harm them.

Nicolae Carpathia had been among the cadre of dignitaries that day. He railed against the interlopers, but Eli and Moishe silenced even him. Without the aid of microphones, the two witnesses spoke loudly enough for all to hear, crying out in the courtyard, "Nicolae! You yourself will one day defile and desecrate this temple!"

"Nonsense!" Carpathia had responded. "Is there not a military leader in Israel with the fortitude to silence these two?"

The Israeli prime minister, who now reported to the Global Community ambassador of the United States of Asia, was caught on microphone and news tape. "Sir, we have become a weaponless society, thanks to you."

"These two are weaponless as well!" Carpathia had thundered. "Subdue them!"

But Eli and Moishe continued to shout, "God does not dwell in temples made with hands! The body of believers is the temple of the Holy Spirit!"

Carpathia, who had been merely trying to support his friends in Israel by honoring them for their new temple, asked the crowd, "Do you wish to listen to me or to them?"

The crowd had shouted, "You, Potentate! You!"

"There is no potentate but God himself!" Eli responded.

And Moishe added, "Your blood sacrifices shall turn to water, and your water-drawing to blood!"

Buck had been there that day as the new publisher of the renamed *Global Community Weekly*. He resisted Carpathia's urging him to editorialize about what Nicolae called the intrusion of the two witnesses, and he persuaded the Global Community potentate that the coverage could not ignore the facts. The blood let from a sacrificed heifer had indeed turned to water. And the water drawn in another ceremony turned to blood in the pail. The Israelis blamed the two witnesses for debasing their celebration.

Buck hated the money he was making. Not even an outrageous salary could make his life easier. He had been forced to move back to New York. Much of the old guard at *Global Weekly* had been fired, including Stanton Bailey and Marge Potter, and even Jim Borland. Steve Plank was now publisher of the *Global Community East Coast Daily Times,* a newspaper borne out of the merger of the *New York Times,* the *Washington Post,* and the *Boston Globe.* Though Steve wouldn't admit it, Buck believed the luster had faded from Steve's relationship to the potentate too.

The only positive factor about Buck's new position was that he now had the means to isolate himself somewhat against the terrible crime wave that had broken all records in North America. Carpathia had used it to sway public opinion and get the populace behind the idea that the North American ambassador to the Global Community should supplant the sitting president. Gerald Fitzhugh and his vice president were now headquartered in the old Executive Office Building in Washington, in charge of enforcing Potentate Carpathia's global disarmament plan in America.

Buck's one act of resistance to Carpathia was to ignore the rumors about Fitzhugh plotting with the militia to oppose the Global Community regime by force. Buck was all for it and had secretly studied the feasibility of producing an anti–Global Community website on the Internet. As soon as he could figure out a way to do it without its being traced back to his penthouse apartment on Fifth Avenue, he would do it.

At least Buck had convinced Potentate Carpathia that Buck's moving to New Babylon would be a mistake. New York was still the world publishing capital, after all. He was already heartbroken that Chloe's father was being required to relocate to New Babylon. The new city was palatial, but unless a person lived indoors twenty-four hours a day, the weather in Iraq was unbearable. And despite Carpathia's unparalleled popularity and his emphasis on the new one-world government and one-world religion, there were still enough vestiges of the old ways in the Middle East that a western woman would feel totally out of place there.

Buck had been thrilled at how Rayford and Amanda White had each other. That took pressure off Buck and Chloe, wondering about the future, worrying about leaving her father alone if they were ever to marry. But how could Rayford expect an American woman to live in New Babylon? And how long could they live there before the potentate began to step up his attacks on Christian believers? According to Bruce Barnes, the days of persecution were not far off.

Buck missed Bruce more than he thought possible. Buck tried to see him every time he got back to Chicago to see Chloe. Anytime Bruce came through New York or they happened to run into each other in a foreign city, Bruce tried to make the time for a private study session. Bruce was fast becoming one of the leading prophecy scholars among new believers. The year or year and a half of peace, he said, was fast coming to a close. Once the next three horsemen of the Apocalypse appeared, seventeen more judgments would come in rapid succession, leading to the glorious appearing of Christ seven years from the signing of the covenant between Israel and the Antichrist.

Bruce had become famous, even popular. But many believers were growing tired of his dire warnings.

Rayford was going to be out of town until the day before he and Chloe and the new buyers were to close on the house. He smiled at the idea of buyers securing a thirty-year mortgage. Someone was going to lose on that deal.

With Rayford gone, Chloe would be left with much of the work, selling stuff off, putting furniture into storage, and arranging with a moving company to ship her things to a local apartment and his all the way to Iraq.

For the past couple of months, Amanda had been driving Rayford to O'Hare for these long trips, but she had recently taken a new position and couldn't get away. So today, Chloe would take Rayford by Amanda's new office, where she was chief buyer for a retail clothier. When they had said their good-byes, Chloe would drive him to the airport and bring the car back home.

"So how's it going with you two?" Chloe asked in the car.

"We're close."

"I know you're close. That's obvious to everybody. Close to what, is the question."

"Close," he said.

As they drove, Rayford's mind drifted to Amanda. Neither he nor Chloe had known what to make of her at first. A tall, handsome woman a couple of years Rayford's senior, she had streaked hair and impeccable taste in clothes. A week after Rayford had returned from his first assignment flying *Global Community One* to the Middle East, Bruce had introduced her to the Steeles after a Sunday morning service. Rayford was tired and none too happy about his reluctant decision to leave Pan-Con for the employ of Nicolae Carpathia, and he was not really in the mood to be sociable.

Mrs. White, however, seemed oblivious to Rayford and Chloe as people. To her they had been just names associated with a former acquaintance, Irene Steele, who had left an indelible impression on her. Amanda had insisted on taking them to dinner that Sunday noon and was adamant about paying. Rayford had not felt much like talking, but that seemed not to be an issue for Amanda. She had a lot to say.

"I've wanted to meet you, Captain Steele, because—"

"Rayford, please."

"Well, I'll call you Mr. Steele for now, then, if *captain* is too formal. Rayford is a little too familiar for me, though that is what Irene called you. Anyway, she was the sweetest little woman, so soft-spoken, so totally in love and devoted to you. She was the sole reason I came as close as I did to becoming a Christian before the Rapture, and—second only to the vanishings themselves— she was the reason I finally did come to the Lord. Then I couldn't remember her name, and none of the other ladies from that Bible study were still around. That made me feel lonely, as you can imagine. And I lost my family, too, I'm sure Bruce told you. So it's been hard.

"Bruce has certainly been a godsend though. Have you learned as much from him as I have? Well, of course you have. You've been with him for weeks."

Eventually Amanda slowed down and shared her own story of the loss of her family. "We had been in a dead church all our lives. Then my husband got invited to some outing at a friend's church, came home, and insisted that we at least check out the Sunday services there. I don't mind telling you, I was not comfortable. They made a big deal all the time about being saved.

"Well, before I could get my little mind around the idea, I was the only one in my family who *wasn't* saved. To tell you the truth, the whole thing sounded a little white trashy to me. I didn't know I had a lot of pride. Lost people never know that, do they? Well, I pretended I was right there with my family, but they knew. They kept encouraging me to go to this women's Bible study, so finally I went. I was just sure it was going to be more of the same—frumpy middle-aged women talking about being sinners saved by grace."

Somehow, Amanda White managed to finish her meal while talking, but when she got to this part of her story she clouded up and had to excuse herself for a few minutes. Chloe rolled her eyes. "Dad!" she said. "What planet would you guess she's from?"

Rayford had chuckled. "I do want to hear her impressions of your mother," he said. "And she certainly sounds 'saved' now, doesn't she?"

"Yeah, but she's a long way from frumpy white trash."

When Amanda returned, she apologized and said she was "determined to get this said." Rayford smiled encouragingly at her while Chloe made faces at him behind her back, trying to get him to laugh.

"I'm not going to bother you anymore," she said. "I'm an executive and not the type to insert myself into people's lives. I just wanted to get together with you one time to tell you what your wife, and your mother, meant in my life. You know, I had only one brief conversation with her. It came after that one meeting, and I was glad I got the chance to tell her how she had impressed me.

"If you're interested, I'll tell you about it. But if I've already rattled on too long, tell me that, too, and I'll let you go with just the knowledge that Mrs. Steele was a wonderful lady."

Rayford actually considered saying that they had had a tiring week and needed to get home, but he would never be that rude. Even Chloe would likely chastise him for a move like that, so he said, "Oh, by all means, we'd love to hear it. The truth is," he added, "I love to talk about Irene."

"Well, I don't know why I forgot her name for so long, because I was so struck by it at first. Besides sounding a little like *iron* and *steel,* I remember thinking that Irene sounded more like a name of someone many years older than your wife. She was about forty, right?"

Rayford nodded.

"Anyway, I took the morning off, and I arrived at this home where the ladies were meeting that week. They all looked so normal and were wonderful to me. I noticed your wife right off. She was just radiant—friendly and smiling and talking with everyone. She welcomed me and asked about me. And then during the Bible study, prayer, and discussion, I was just impressed by her. What more can I say?"

A lot, Rayford hoped. But he didn't want to interview the woman. What had so impressed her? He was glad when Chloe jumped in.

"I'm glad to hear that, Mrs. White, because I was never more impressed with my mother than after I had left home. I had always thought her a little too religious, too strict, too rigid. Only when we were apart did I realize how much I loved her because of how much she cared for me."

"Well," Amanda said, "it was her own story that moved me, but more than that, it was her carriage, her countenance. I don't know if you knew this, but she had not been a Christian long either. Her story was the same as mine. She said her family had been going to church sort of perfunctorily for years. But when she found New Hope Village Church, she found Christ.

"There was a peace, a gentleness, a kindness, a serenity about her that I had never seen in anyone else. She had confidence, but she was humble. She was outgoing, yet not pushy or self-promoting. I loved her immediately. She grew emotional when she talked about her family, and she said that her husband and her daughter were at the top of her prayer list. She loved you both so deeply. She said her greatest fear was that she would reach you too late and that you would not go to heaven with her and her son. I don't remember his name."

"Rayford, Junior," Chloe said. "She would have called him Raymie."

"After the meeting I sought her out and told her that my family was the opposite. They were all worried that they would go to heaven without me. She told me how to receive Christ. I told her I wasn't ready, and she warned me not to put it off and said she would pray for me. That night my family disappeared from their beds. Almost everyone was gone from our new church, including all the Bible study ladies. Eventually I tracked down Bruce and asked if he knew Irene Steele."

Rayford and Chloe had returned home chagrined and a little ashamed of themselves. "That was nice," Rayford said. "I'm glad we took the time for that."

"I just wish I hadn't been such a creep," Chloe said. "For hardly having known her, that woman had a lot of insight into Mom."

For nearly a year after that, Rayford saw Amanda White only on Sundays and at an occasional midweek meeting of the larger core study group. She was always cordial and friendly, but what impressed him most was her servant's attitude. She continually prayed for people, and she was busy in the church all the time. She studied, she grew, she learned, she talked to people about their standing with God.

As Rayford watched her from afar, she became more and more attractive to him. One Sunday he told Chloe, "You know, we never reciprocated on Amanda White's dinner invitation."

"You want to have her over?" Chloe asked.

"I want to ask her out."

"Pardon me?"

"You heard me."

"Dad! You mean like on a date?"

"A double date. With you and Buck."

Chloe had laughed, then apologized. "It's not funny. I'm just surprised."

"Don't make a big deal of it," he said. "I just might ask her."

"Don't *you* make a big deal of it," Chloe said.

Buck was not surprised when Chloe told him her Dad wanted them to double-date with Amanda White. "I wondered when he'd get around to it."

"To dating?"

"To dating Amanda White."

"You noticed something there? You never said anything."

"I didn't want to risk your mentioning it and planting an idea in his head that wasn't his own."

"That rarely happens."

"Anyway, I think they'll be good for each other," Buck said. "He needs companionship his own age, and if something comes of it, so much the better."

"Why?"

"Because he's not going to want be alone if we decide to get more serious."

"Seems to me we've already decided." Chloe slipped her hand into Buck's.

"I just don't know what to do about timing and geography, with everything breaking the way it has."

Buck was hoping for some hint from Chloe that she would be willing to follow him anywhere, that she was either ready for marriage or that she needed more time. Time was getting away from them, but still Buck hesitated.

"I'm ready when he is," Chloe told Rayford. "But I'm not going to say a word."

"Why not?" Rayford said. "Men need a few signals."

"He's getting all the signals he needs."

"So you've held his hand by now?"

"Dad!"

"Bet you've even kissed him."

"No comment."

"That's a *yes* if I ever heard one."

"Like I said, he's getting all the signals he needs."

In fact, Buck would never forget the first time he had kissed Chloe. It had been the night he left for New York by car, about a year before. Carpathia had bought up the *Weekly* as well as any of the competition worth working for, and Buck seemed to have less choice than ever over his own career. He could try bootlegging copy over the Internet, but he still needed to make a living. And Bruce, who was at the church less and less all the time due to his ministry all over the world, had encouraged him to stay with *Global Weekly,* even after the name was changed to *Global Community Weekly.* "I wish we could change the last word one more time," Buck said. "To *Weakly.*"

Buck had resigned himself to doing the best he could for the kingdom of God, just as Chloe's father had done. But he still hid his identity as a believer. Whatever freedom and perceived objectivity he had would soon be gone if that truth was known to Carpathia.

That last night in Chicago, he and Chloe were in his apartment packing the last of his personal things. His plan was to leave by nine o'clock that night and drive all the way to New York City in one marathon stretch. As they worked, they talked about how much they would hate being apart, how much they would miss each other, how often they would phone and E-mail each other.

"I wish you could come with me," Buck said at one point.

"Yeah, that would be appropriate," she said.

"Someday," he said.

"Someday what?"

But he would not bite. He carried a box to the car and came back in, passing her as she taped another. Tears ran down her face.

"What's this?" he said, stopping to wipe her face with his fingers. "Don't get *me* started now."

"You'll never miss me as much as I'll miss you," she said, trying to continue to work with him hovering, a hand on her face.

"Stop it," he whispered. "Come here."

She set down the tape and stood to face him. He embraced her and pulled her close. Her hands were at her sides, and her cheek was on his chest. They had held each other before, and they had walked hand in hand, sometimes arm in arm. They had expressed their deep feelings for each other without mentioning love. And they had agreed not to cry and not to say anything rash in the moment of parting.

"We'll see each other often," he said. "You'll rendezvous with your dad when he comes through New York. And I'll have reasons to come here."

"What reason? The Chicago office is closing."

"This reason," he said, holding her tighter. And she began to sob.

"I'm sorry," she said. "This is going to be so hard."

"I know."

"No you don't. Buck, you can't say you care for me as much as I care for you."

Buck had already planned his first kiss. He had hoped to find a reason to simply brush her lips with his at the end of an evening, say good night, and slip away. He didn't want to have to deal with her reaction, or deal with kissing her again just then. It was going to be meaningful and special, but quick and simple, something they could build on later.

But now he wanted her to know how he felt. He was angry at himself for being so good at writing but so incompetent at telling her to her face how much she meant to him.

He stepped back and took her face in his hands. She resisted at first and tried to hide her face in his chest again, but he insisted she look at him. "I don't ever want to hear you say that again," he said.

"But, Buck, it's true—"

He lowered his head until his eyes were inches from hers. "Did you hear me?" he said. "Don't say it again. Don't imply it, don't even think it. There's no possible way you could care for me more than I care for you. You are my whole life. I *love* you, Chloe. Don't you know that?"

He felt her nearly recoil at that first declaration of his love. Her tears rolled over his hands, and she began to say, "How would I—?" But he lowered his mouth to hers, cutting off her words. And it was no quick touch of the lips. She raised her hands between his arms, wrapped them around his neck, and held him tight as they kissed.

She pulled away briefly and whispered, "Did you only say that because you're leaving and—" But he covered her mouth again with his.

A moment later he touched her nose with the tip of his own and said, "Don't doubt my love for you ever again. Promise."

"But, Buck—"

"Promise."

"I promise. And I love you, too, Buck."

Rayford was not sure just when his respect and admiration for Amanda White had developed into love. He had grown fond of her, liked her, loved being with her. They had become comfortable enough with each other to touch each other when they spoke, to hold hands, to embrace. But when he found himself missing her after only a day away and needing to call her when he was gone more than a few days, he knew something was developing.

She actually started kissing Rayford before he kissed her. Twice when he returned to Chicago after several days away, Amanda greeted him with a hug and a peck on the cheek. He had liked it, but had also been embarrassed. But the third time he returned from such a trip, she merely embraced him and did not attempt to kiss him.

His timing had been perfect. He had decided that if she tried to kiss him on the cheek this time, he would turn and take it on the lips. He had brought her a gift from Paris, an expensive necklace. When she did not try to kiss him, he just held her embrace longer and said, "Come here a minute."

As passengers and crew passed them in the corridor, Rayford had Amanda sit next to him in the waiting area. It was awkward with an armrest between them. Both were bundled up, Amanda in a fur coat and Rayford with his uniform coat over his arm. He pulled the jewelry box from the sack in his flight bag. "This is for you."

Amanda, knowing where he had been, made a big deal over the bag, the name of the store, and the box. Finally, she opened it and appeared to stop breathing. It was a magnificent piece, gold with diamonds. "Rayford!" she said. "I don't know what to say."

"Don't say anything," he said. And he took her in his arms, the package in her hands nearly crushed between them, and kissed her.

"I still don't know what to say," she said with a twinkle in her eye, and he kissed her again.

Now, two weeks before his move to New Babylon, Rayford had been on the phone with Buck more often than Chloe had. While she was warming up the car, he sneaked in one last call.

"Everything set?" he asked Buck.

"Everything. I'll be there."

"Good."

In the car he asked Chloe, "What's the status on your apartment?"

"They promised it'll be ready," she said. "But I'm getting a little skittish because they keep stalling me on the paperwork."

"You're going to be all right here with me in New Babylon and Buck in New York?"

"It's not my first choice, but I have no interest living anywhere near Carpathia, and certainly not in Iraq."

"What's Buck saying?"

"I haven't been able to reach him today. He must be on assignment somewhere. I know he wanted to see Fitzhugh in D.C. soon."

"Yeah, maybe that's where he is."

Chloe stopped at Amanda's clothing store in Des Plaines and waited in the car as Rayford hurried in to say good-bye.

"Is he here?" he asked her secretary.

"He is, and she is," the secretary said. "She's in her office, and he's in that one." She pointed to a smaller office next to Amanda's.

"As soon as I'm in there, would you run out to the car and tell my daughter she has a call she can take in there?"

"Sure."

Rayford knocked and entered Amanda's office. "I hope you're not expecting me to be cheery, Ray," she said. "I've been trying to work up a smile all day, and it's not working."

"Let me see what I can do to make you smile," he said, pulling her from her chair and kissing her.

"You know Buck's here," she said.

"Yeah. It'll be a nice surprise for Chloe."

"Are you going to come and surprise me like that sometime?"

"Maybe I'll surprise you right now," he said. "How do you like your new job?"

"I hate it. I'd leave in a New York minute if the right guy came along."

"The right guy just came along," Rayford said, slipping a small box from his side pocket and pressing it into Amanda's back.

She pulled away. "What *is* that?"

"What? This? I don't know. Why don't you tell me?"

Buck had heard Rayford outside the door and knew Chloe
wouldn't be far behind. He turned the light off and felt his way
back to the chair behind the desk. In a few minutes he heard
Chloe. "In here?" she said.

"Yes, ma'am," the secretary said. "Line one."

The door opened slowly, and Chloe turned on the light. She
jumped when she saw Buck behind the desk, then squealed and
ran to him. As soon as he stood, she leaped into his arms and he
held her, twirling her around.

"Shhh," he said. "This is a business!"

"Did Daddy know about this? Of course he did! He had to."

"He knew," Buck said. "Surprised?"

"Of course! What are you doing in town? How long can you
stay? What are we doing?"

"I'm in town only to see you. I leave on a red-eye tonight for
Washington. And we're going to dinner after we drop your dad
off at the airport."

"Yeah, you came only to see me."

"I told you a long time ago to never doubt my love for you."

"I know."

He turned and lowered her into the chair he had been sitting
in, then knelt before her and pulled a ring box from his pocket.

"Oh, Ray!" Amanda said, gazing at the ring on her finger. "I love
you. And for the few years we have left, I will love being yours."

"There's one more thing," he said.

"What?"

"Buck and I have been talking. He's proposing in the next
room right now, and we were wondering if you two might be
open to a double ceremony with Bruce officiating."

Rayford wondered how she would react. She and Chloe were
friends, but not close.

"That would be wonderful! But Chloe might not go for it, so
let's leave it up to her, no hard feelings either way. If she wants
her own day, fine. But I love the idea. When?"

"The day before we close on the house. You give two weeks'
notice here and move with me to New Babylon."

"Rayford Steele!" she said. "It takes a while to get your temperature up, but not long to make you boil. I'll write my resignation before your plane leaves the ground."

"Have you wondered why you never got the paperwork on the apartment?" Buck asked.

Chloe nodded.

"Because that deal's not going to happen. If you'll have me, I want you to move in with me in New York."

"Rayford," Amanda said. "I didn't think I would ever be truly happy again. But I am."

"A double ceremony?" Chloe swiped at her tears. "I'd love it. But do you think Amanda would stand for it?"

NINETEEN

SOMETHING big was brewing. In a clandestine meeting, Buck went to see American President Gerald Fitzhugh. The president had become a tragic figure, reduced to a mere token. After serving his country for most of two terms in office, he now was relegated to a suite in the Executive Office Building and had lost most of the trappings from his previous role. Now his Secret Service protection consisted of three men rotating every twenty-four hours, and they were financed by the Global Community.

Buck met with Fitzhugh shortly after he proposed to Chloe, two weeks before the scheduled wedding. The president groused that his bodyguards were really there to make sure Carpathia knew his every move. But the most shattering thing, in Fitzhugh's mind, was that the U.S. public had so easily accepted the president's demotion. Everyone was enamored of Nicolae Carpathia, and no one else mattered.

Fitzhugh pulled Buck into a secure room and left his Secret Service agent out of earshot. The worm was about to turn, Fitzhugh told Buck. At least two other heads of state believed it was time to throw off the shackles of the Global Community. "I'm risking my life telling this to an employee of Carpathia," Fitzhugh said.

"Hey, we're *all* employees of Carpathia," Buck said.

Fitzhugh confided to Buck that Egypt, England, and patriotic militia forces in the U.S. were determined to take action "before it was too late."

"What does that mean?" Buck asked.

"It means soon," Fitzhugh said. "It means stay out of the major East Coast cities."

"New York?" Buck said, and Fitzhugh nodded. "Washington?"

"Especially Washington."

"That's not going to be easy," Buck said. "My wife and I are going to be living in New York when we're married."

"Not for long you're not."

"Can you give me an idea of timing?"

"That I cannot do," Fitzhugh said. "Let's just say I should be back in the Oval Office within a couple of months."

Buck desperately wanted to tell Fitzhugh that he was merely playing into Carpathia's hands. This was all part of the foretold future. The uprising against Antichrist would be crushed and would initiate World War III, from which would come worldwide famine, plagues, and the death of a quarter of the earth's population.

The double ceremony in Bruce's office two weeks later was the most private wedding anyone could imagine. Only the five of them were in the room. Bruce Barnes concluded by thanking God for all the smiles, the embraces, the kisses, and the prayer.

Buck asked if he could see the underground shelter Bruce had constructed. "It was barely under way when I moved to New York," he said.

"It's the best-kept secret in the church," Bruce said as they made their way down past the furnace room and through a secret doorway.

"You don't want church members to use it?" Buck asked.

"You'll see how small it is," Bruce said. "I'm encouraging families to build their own. It would be chaos if the church body showed up here in a time of danger."

Buck was astounded at how small the shelter was, but it seemed to have everything they would need to survive for a few weeks. The Tribulation Force was not made up of people who would hide out for long.

The five huddled to compare schedules and discuss when they might see each other again. Carpathia had devised a minute-by-minute schedule for the next six weeks that would have Rayford flying him all over the world, finally to Washington. Then Rayford would have a few days off before flying back to New Babylon. "Amanda and I could get here from Washington during that break," he said.

Buck said he and Chloe would come to Chicago then, too. Bruce would be back from a swing through Australia and Indonesia. They set the date, four in the afternoon, six weeks later. They would have a two-hour intensive Bible study in Bruce's office and then enjoy a nice dinner somewhere.

Before they parted, they held hands in a circle and prayed yet again. "Father," Bruce whispered, "for this brief flash of joy in a world on the brink of disaster, we thank you and pray your blessing and protection on us all until we meet back here again. Bind our hearts as brothers and sisters in Christ while we are apart."

Nicolae Carpathia seemed thrilled about Rayford's marriage and insisted upon meeting his new wife. He took both her hands in greeting and welcomed her and Rayford to his opulent offices, which covered the entire top floor of the Global Community headquarters in New Babylon. The suite also included conference rooms, private living quarters, and an elevator to the helipad. From there, one of Rayford's crew could ferry the potentate to the new airstrip.

Rayford could tell that Amanda's heart was in her throat. Her speech was constricted and her smile pasted on. Meeting the most evil man on the face of the earth was clearly out of her sphere of experience, though she had told Rayford she knew a few garment wholesalers who might have fit the bill.

After pleasantries, Nicolae immediately approved Rayford's request that Amanda accompany them on the next trip to the U.S. to see his daughter and new son-in-law. Rayford did not say who that son-in-law was, not even mentioning that the young newlyweds lived in New York City. He said, truthfully, that he and Amanda would visit the couple in Chicago.

"I will be in Washington at least four days," Carpathia said. "Enjoy whatever of that time you can. And now I have some news for you and your bride." Carpathia pulled a tiny remote control from his pocket and pointed it at the intercom on his desk across the room. "Darling, would you join us a moment, please?"

Darling? Rayford thought. *No pretense anymore.*

Hattie Durham knocked and entered. "Yes, sweetie?" she said. Rayford thought he would gag.

Carpathia leaped to his feet and embraced her gently as if she were a porcelain doll. Hattie turned to Rayford. "I'm so happy for you and Amelia," she said.

"Amanda," Rayford corrected, noticing his wife stiffen. He had told Amanda all about Hattie Durham, and apparently the two were not going to become soul mates.

"We have an announcement too," Carpathia said. "Hattie will be leaving the employ of Global Community to prepare for our new arrival."

Carpathia was beaming, as if expecting a joyous reaction. Rayford did what he could to not betray his disgust and loathing. "A new arrival?" he said. "When's the big day?"

"We just found out." Nicolae gave him a broad wink.

"Well, isn't that something?" Rayford said.

"I didn't realize you were married," Amanda said sweetly, and Rayford fought to keep his composure. She knew full well they were not.

"Oh, we will be," Hattie said, beaming. "He's going to make an honest woman of me yet."

Chloe broke down when she read her father's E-mail about Hattie. "Buck, we have failed that woman. We have all failed her."

"Don't I know it," Buck said. "I introduced her to him."

"But I know her too, and I know she knows the truth. I was right there when Daddy was sharing it with you, and she was at the same table. He tried, but we have to do more. We have to get to her somehow, talk to her."

"And have her know that I'm a believer, just like your dad is? It doesn't seem to matter that Nicolae's pilot is a Christian, but can you imagine how long I would last as his magazine publisher if he knew I was?"

"One of these days we have to get to Hattie, even if it means going to New Babylon."

"What are you going to do, Chloe? Tell her she's carrying the Antichrist's child and that she ought to leave him?"

"It may come to that."

Buck stood over Chloe's shoulder as she tapped out an E-mail message back to Rayford and Amanda. Both couples had taken to writing obscurely, not using names. "Any chance," Chloe wrote, "that she will come with him on the next trip to the capital?"

It was seven hours later, New Babylon time, when the message was sent, and the next day they received a reply: "None."

"Someday, somehow," Chloe told Buck. "And before that baby is born."

———————

Rayford found it difficult to take in the incredible change in New Babylon since the first time he had visited following the treaty signing in Israel. He had to hand it to Carpathia and his sea of money. A lavish world capital had sprung up out of the ruins, and now it teemed with commerce, industry, and transportation. The center of global activity was moving east, and Rayford's homeland seemed headed for obsolescence.

The week before his and Amanda's flight to Washington with Nicolae and his entourage, Rayford E-mailed Bruce at New Hope, welcoming him back from his trip and asking some questions.

> A few things still puzzle me about the future—a lot, actually. Could you explain for us the fifth and seventh?

He didn't write *seals,* not wanting to tip off any interloper. Bruce would know what he meant.

> I mean, the second, third, fourth, and sixth are self-explanatory, but I'm still in the dark about five and seven. We can't wait to see you. "A" sends her love.

Buck and Chloe had settled in Buck's beautiful Fifth Avenue penthouse, but any joy normal newlyweds might have received from a place like that was lost on them. Chloe kept up her research and study on the Internet, and she and Buck kept in touch with Bruce daily via E-mail. Bruce was lonely and missed his family more than ever, he wrote, but he was thrilled that his four friends had found love and companionship. They all expressed great anticipation of the pleasure they would enjoy in each other's company at their upcoming reunion.

Buck had been praying about whether to tell Chloe of President Fitzhugh's warning about New York City and Washington. Fitzhugh was well connected and undoubtedly accurate, but Buck couldn't spend his life running from danger. Life was perilous these days, and war and destruction could break out anywhere.

His job had taken him to the hottest hazard spots in the world. He didn't want to be reckless or foolishly put his wife in harm's way, but every member of the Tribulation Force knew the risks.

Rayford was grateful that Chloe had begun getting to know Amanda better by E-mail. When Rayford and Amanda were dating, he had monopolized most of Amanda's time, and while the women seemed to like each other, they had not bonded other than as believers. Now, communicating daily, Amanda seemed to be growing in her knowledge of Scripture. Chloe was passing along everything she was studying.

Between Bruce and Chloe, Rayford found his answers about the fifth and seventh seals. It was not pleasant news, but he hadn't expected any different. The fifth seal referred to the martyrdom of Tribulation saints. In a secured mail package, Bruce sent to Chloe—who forwarded it on to Rayford—his careful study and explanation of the passage from Revelation which referred to that fifth seal.

> John sees under the altar the souls of those who had been slain for the Word of God and for the testimony which they held. They ask God how long it will be until he avenges their deaths. He gives them white robes and tells them that first some of their fellow servants and their brethren will also be martyred. So the fifth Seal Judgment costs people their lives who have become believers since the Rapture. That could include any one or all of us. I say before God, that I would count it a privilege to give my life for my Savior and my God.

Bruce's explanation of the seventh seal made it clear that it was still a mystery even to him.

> The seventh seal is so awesome that when it is revealed in heaven, there is silence for half an hour. It seems to progress from the sixth seal, the greatest earthquake in history, and serves to initiate the seven Trumpet Judgments, which, of course, are progressively worse than the Seal Judgments.

Amanda tried to summarize for Rayford: "We're looking at a world war, famine, plagues, death, the martyrdom of the saints, an earthquake, and then silence in heaven as the world is readied for the next seven judgments."

Rayford shook his head, then cast his eyes down. "Bruce has been warning us of this all along. There are times I think I'm ready for whatever comes and other times when I wish the end would simply come quickly."

"This is the price we pay," she said, "for ignoring the warnings when we had the chance. And you and I were warned by the same woman."

Rayford nodded.

"Look here," Amanda said. "Bruce's last line says, 'Check your E-mail Monday at midnight. Lest you find this all as depressing as I have, I am uploading a favorite verse to comfort your hearts.' "

Bruce had sent it so it would be available to both couples just before they left for their trips to Chicago to meet up with him. It read simply, "He who dwells in the secret place of the Most High shall abide under the shadow of the Almighty."

Rayford shifted in the pilot's seat, eager to talk to Amanda and find out how she was faring on the grueling nonstop flight from New Babylon to Dulles International. She was spending as much of the time as she could in Rayford's private quarters behind the cockpit, but she had to be sociable enough with the rest of the contingent so as not to appear rude. That, Rayford knew, meant hours of small talk.

She had already been asked about the new import/export business she was starting, but then the mood in *Global Community One* seemed to shift. During one of the few breaks Rayford shared alone with her, she said, "Something's up. Someone keeps bringing Carpathia printouts. He studies them and scowls and has private, heated meetings."

"Hmph," Rayford said. "Could be something. Could be anything. Could be nothing."

Amanda smirked. "Don't doubt my intuition."

"I've learned that," he said.

Buck and Chloe arrived in Chicago the night before the scheduled rendezvous with the Tribulation Force. They checked into the

Drake Hotel and called New Hope to leave a message for Bruce, telling him they had arrived and that they would see him the following afternoon at four. They knew from his E-mails that he was back in the States from his Australia/Indonesia trip, but they had heard nothing from him since.

They also E-mailed him that Rayford and Amanda were going to come to the Drake for lunch the next day and that the four of them would travel to Mount Prospect together that afternoon. *If you want to join us for lunch in the Cape Cod Room, we'd be delighted,* Buck had written.

A couple of hours later, when they still had received no response to either the E-mail or the phone message, Chloe said, "What do you think it means?"

"It means he's going to surprise us at lunch tomorrow."

"I hope you're right."

"Count on it," Buck said.

"Then it won't really be a surprise, will it?"

The phone rang. "So much for surprises." Buck said. "That has to be him."

But it wasn't.

Rayford had illuminated the Fasten Seat Belt sign and was five minutes from touchdown at Dulles when he was contacted through his earphones by one of Carpathia's communications engineers. "The potentate would like a word with you."

"Right now? We're close to final approach."

"I'll ask." A few seconds later he came back on. "In the cockpit with you alone after engine shutdown."

"We have a postflight checklist with the first officer and the navigator."

"Just a minute!" The engineer sounded peeved. When he came back on, he said, "Run the other two out of there after shutdown and do the postflight jazz after your meeting with the potentate."

"Roger," Rayford muttered.

"If you recognize my voice and will talk to me, call me at this pay phone number, and make sure you call from a pay phone."

"Affirmative," Buck said. He hung up and turned to Chloe. "I've got to run out for a minute."

"Why? Who was that?"

"Gerald Fitzhugh."

"Thank you, gentlemen, and forgive me for the intrusion," Carpathia said as he passed the first officer and navigator on his way into the cockpit. Rayford knew they were as annoyed as he at the breach of procedural protocol, but then Carpathia was the boss. Was he ever.

Carpathia slipped deftly into the copilot chair. Rayford imagined that along with all his other gifts, the man could probably learn to fly a jet in an afternoon.

"Captain, I feel the need to take you into my confidence. Our intelligence has discovered an insurrection plot, and we are being forced to circulate false itineraries for me in the United States." Rayford nodded, and Carpathia continued. "We suspect militia involvement and even collusion between disgruntled American factions and at least two other countries. To be on the safe side, we are scrambling our radio communications and telling the press conflicting stories of my destinations."

"Sounds like a plan," Rayford said.

"Most people think I will be in Washington for at least four days, but we are now announcing that I will also be in Chicago, New York, Boston, and perhaps even Los Angeles over the next three days."

"Do I hear my little vacation slipping away?" Rayford said.

"On the contrary. But I do want you available on a moment's notice."

"I will leave word where I can be reached."

"I would like you to fly the plane to Chicago and have someone you trust return it to New York the same day."

"I know just the person," Rayford said.

"I'll get to New York somehow, and we can leave the country from there on schedule. We're just trying to keep the insurrectionists off balance."

"Hey," Buck said when President Fitzhugh picked up on the first ring. "It's me."

"I'm glad you're not at home," Fitzhugh said.

"Can you tell me more?"

"Just that it's good you're not at home."

"Gotcha. When can I return home?"

"That could be problematic, but you'll know before you head back that way. How long are you away from home?"

"Four days."

"Perfect."

Click.

"Hello? Mrs. Halliday?"

"Yes. Who's—?"

"This is Rayford Steele calling for Earl, but please don't tell him it's me. I have a surprise for him."

In the morning Buck took a call from one of the women who helped out in the office at New Hope. "We're a little worried about Pastor Barnes," she said.

"Ma'am?"

"He was gonna surprise y'all by comin' down there for lunch."

"We thought he might."

"But he picked up some kinda bug in Indonesia and we had to get him to the emergency room. He didn't want us to tell anyone, because he was sure it was something they could fix real quick and he could still get down there. But he's slipped into a coma."

"A coma!?"

"Like I say, we're a little worried about him."

"As soon as the Steeles get here, we'll head out there. Where is he?"

"Northwest Community Hospital in Arlington Heights."

"We'll find it," Buck said.

Rayford and Amanda met Earl Halliday at O'Hare at ten that morning. "I'll never forget this, Ray," Earl said. "I mean, it's not like carting around the potentate himself, or even the president, but I can pretend."

"They're expecting you at Kennedy," Rayford said. "I'll give you a call later to see how you liked flying her."

Rayford rented a car, and Amanda answered a page from Chloe. "We have to pick them up and go straight to Arlington Heights."

"Why? What's up?"

_____

Buck and Chloe were waiting at the curb in front of the Drake when Rayford and Amanda pulled up. After quick embraces all around, they piled into the car. "Northwest Community is on Central, right, Chlo'?" Rayford said.

"Right. Let's hurry."

Despite their concern for Bruce, Rayford felt a little more whole. He had a four-person family again, albeit a new wife and a new son. They discussed Bruce's situation and brought each other up to date, and though they were all aware that they were living in a time of great danger, for the moment they simply enjoyed being together again.

_____

Buck sat in the backseat with Chloe, listening. How refreshing to be with people who were related and yet loved each other, cared about each other, respected one another. He didn't even want to think about the small-minded family he had come from. Somehow, someday, he would convince them they were not the Christians they thought they were. Had they been, they would not have been left behind, as he was.

Chloe leaned against Buck and slipped her hand into his. He was grateful she was so casual, so matter-of-fact, about her devotion to him. She was the greatest gift God could have granted him since his salvation.

"What's this?" he heard Rayford say. "And we've been making such good time."

Rayford was trying to exit onto Arlington Heights Road off the Northwest Tollway. Chloe had told him that would put them close to Northwest Community Hospital. But now local and state

police and Global Community peacekeepers were directing a snarl
of traffic past the exits. Everything came to a standstill.

After a few minutes they were able to creep forward a little.
Rayford rolled down his window and asked a cop what was happening.

"Where've you been, pal? Keep it moving."

"What does he mean?" Amanda reached for the radio. "What
are the news stations on, Chloe?"

Chloe moved away from Buck and leaned forward. "Hit *AM,*
then try *1, 2,* and *3,*" she said. "One of those should be WGN or
'MAQ.'"

They stopped again, this time with a Global Community peace-
keeper right next to Buck's window. Buck lowered it and flashed
his *Global Community Weekly* press pass. "What's the trouble
down there?"

"Militia had taken over an old Nike base to store contraband
weapons. After the attack on Washington, our boys wiped them
out."

"The attack on Washington?" Rayford said, craning his neck to
talk to the officer. "Washington, D.C.?"

"Keep moving," the officer said. "If you need to get back this
way you can get off at Route 53 and try the side streets, but
don't expect to get near that old Nike base."

Rayford had to keep driving, but he and Buck hollered questions at every officer they passed while Amanda kept looking for
a local station. Every one she tried carried the Emergency Broadcast System tone. "Put it on 'scan,' " Chloe suggested. Finally the
radio found an EBS station and Amanda locked it in.

A Cable News Network/Global Community Network radio correspondent was broadcasting live just outside Washington, D.C.
"The fate of Global Community Potentate Nicolae Carpathia remains in question at this hour as Washington lies in ruins," he
said. "The massive assault was launched by east coast militia,
with the aid of the United States of Britain and the former sovereign state of Egypt, now part of the Middle Eastern Common-
wealth.

"Potentate Carpathia arrived here last night and was thought to
be staying in the presidential suite of the Capital Noir, but eyewitnesses say that luxury hotel was leveled this morning.

"Global Community peacekeeping forces immediately retaliated
by destroying a former Nike center in suburban Chicago. Reports
from there indicate that thousands of civilian casualties have been

reported in surrounding suburbs, and a colossal traffic tie-up is hampering rescue efforts."

"Oh, dear God!" Amanda prayed.

"Other attacks we know about at this moment," the reporter went on, "include a foray of Egyptian ground forces toward Iraq, obviously intending a siege upon New Babylon. That effort was quickly eliminated by Global Community air forces, which are now advancing on England. This may be a retaliatory strike for Britain's part in the American militia action against Washington. Please hold. Ah, please stand by. . . . Potentate Carpathia is safe! He will address the nation via radio. We will stand by here and bring that to you as we receive it."

"We've got to get to Bruce," Chloe said, as Rayford inched along. "Everybody's going to be taking 53 north, Dad. Let's go south and double back."

"It'll be another few moments before Potentate Carpathia comes on," the reporter said. "Apparently the GCN is ensuring that his transmission cannot be traced. Meanwhile, this news out of Chicago regarding the strike against the former Nike base: It appears to have been preemptive as well as retaliatory. Global Community intelligence today uncovered a plot to destroy Potentate Carpathia's plane, which may or may not have contained Carpathia when it was flown to O'Hare International this morning. That plane is now airborne, destination unknown, though Global Community forces are marshaling in New York City."

Amanda grabbed Rayford's arm. "We could have been killed!"

When Rayford spoke, Buck thought he might break down. "Let's just hope I didn't fulfill Earl's dream by getting *him* killed," he said.

"You want me to drive, Rayford?" Buck asked.

"No, I'll be all right."

The radio announcer continued: "We're on standby for a lie feed, excuse me, a *live* feed from Global Community Potentate Nicolae Carpathia. . . ."

"He had *that* right the first time," Chloe said.

". . . Meanwhile, this word from Chicago. GC peacekeeping forces spokesmen say the destruction of the old Nike base was effected without the use of nuclear weapons, and though they regret heavy civilian casualties in nearby suburbs, they have issued the following statement: 'Casualties should be laid at the feet of the militia underground. Unauthorized military forces are illegal to start with, but the folly of mustering arms in a civilian area has literally blown up in their faces.' There is, we repeat, no danger of radiation fallout in the Chicago area, though peacekeeping forces are not allowing automobile traffic near the site of the destruction. Please stand by now for this live feed from Potentate Nicolae Carpathia."

Rayford had finally exited south onto Route 53, snaked his way through an Authorized Vehicles Only turnaround, and was heading north toward Rolling Meadows.

"Loyal citizens of the Global Community," came the voice of Carpathia, "I come to you today with a broken heart, unable to tell you even from where I speak. For more than a year we have worked to draw this Global Community together under a banner of peace and harmony. Today, unfortunately, we have been reminded again that there are still those among us who would pull us apart.

"It is no secret that I am, always have been, and always will be, a pacifist. I do not believe in war. I do not believe in weaponry. I do not believe in bloodshed. On the other hand, I feel responsible for you, my brother or my sister in this global village.

"Global Community peacekeeping forces have already crushed the resistance. The death of innocent civilians weighs heavy on me, but I pledge immediate judgment upon all enemies of peace. The beautiful capital of the United States of North America has been laid waste, and you will hear stories of more destruction and death. Our goal remains peace and reconstruction. I will be back at the secure headquarters in New Babylon in due time and will communicate with you frequently.

"Above all, do not fear. Live in confidence that no threat to global tranquility will be tolerated, and no enemy of peace will survive."

As Rayford looked for a route that would get him near Northwest Community Hospital, the CNN/GCN correspondent came back on. "This late word: Anti–Global Community militia forces have threatened nuclear war on New York City, primarily Kennedy International Airport. Civilians are fleeing the area and causing one of the worst pedestrian and auto traffic jams in that city's history. Peacekeeping forces say they have the ability and technology to intercept missiles but are worried about residual damage to outlying areas.

"And now this from London: A one-hundred-megaton bomb has destroyed Heathrow Airport, and radiation fallout threatens the populace for miles. The bomb was apparently dropped by peacekeeping forces after contraband Egyptian and British fighter-bombers were discovered rallying from a closed military airstrip near Heathrow. The warships, which have all been shot from the sky, were reportedly nuclear-equipped and en route to Baghdad and New Babylon."

"It's the end of the world," Chloe whispered. "God help us."

"Maybe we should just try to get to New Hope," Amanda suggested.

"Not till we check on Bruce," Rayford said. He asked stunned passersby if it was possible to get to Northwest Community Hospital on foot.

"It's possible," a woman said. "It's right past that field and over-the rise. But I don't know how close they'll let you get to what's left of it."

"It was hit?"

"Was it hit? Mister, it's just up the road and across the street from the old Nike base. Most people think it got hit first."

"I'm going," Rayford said.

"Me too," Buck said.

"We're all going," Chloe insisted, but Rayford held up a hand.

"We're not all going. It's going to be hard enough for one of us to get past security. Buck or I will have a better chance because we have Global Community identification. I think one of us with an ID should go, and the other should stay with the wives. We all have to be with someone who can get past the red tape if necessary."

"I want to go," Buck said, "but you make the call."

"Stay and make sure the car is positioned so we can get out of here and get to Mount Prospect. If I'm not back in half an hour, take the risk and come looking for me."

"Daddy, if Bruce is any better, try to bring him with you."

"Don't worry, Chloe," Rayford said. "I'm ahead of you."

As soon as Rayford had jogged through the muddy weeds and out of sight, Buck regretted agreeing to stay behind. He had always been a person of action, and as he watched shell-shocked citizens milling about and commiserating, he could hardly stand still.

Rayford's heart sank as he came over the rise and saw the hospital. Part of the full height of the structure was still intact, but much of it was rubble. Emergency vehicles surrounded the mess, with white-uniformed rescue workers scurrying about. A long stretch of police barrier tape had been stretched around the hospital campus. As Rayford lifted it to duck under, a security guard, weapon ready, ran toward him.

"Halt!" he called out. "This is a restricted area!"

"I have clearance!" Rayford shouted, waving his ID wallet.

"Stay right there!" the guard hollered. When he got to Rayford he took the wallet and studied it, comparing the photo to Rayford's face. "Wow! Clearance level 2-A. You work for Carpathia himself?"

Rayford nodded.

"What's your job?"

"Classified."

"Is he around here?"

"No, and I wouldn't tell you if he was."

"You're all good," the guard said, and Rayford headed toward what had been the front of the building. He was largely ignored by people too busy to care who did or did not have clearance to be there. Body after body was laid out in a neat row and covered. "Any survivors?" Rayford asked an emergency medical technician.

"Three so far," the man said. "All women. Two nurses and a doctor. They were outside for a smoke."

"No one inside?"

"We hear voices," the man said. "But we haven't gotten to anyone in time yet."

Breathing a prayer, Rayford folded his wallet so his ID was facing out. He slid it into his breast pocket. He strode to the makeshift outdoor morgue where several EMTs moved among the remains, lifting sheets and taking notes, trying to reconcile patient and employee lists with body parts and ID bracelets.

"Help or get out of the way," a heavyset woman said as she brushed past Rayford.

"I'm looking for a Bruce Barnes," Rayford said.

The woman, whose nameplate read *Patricia Devlin,* stopped and squinted, cocked her head, and checked her clipboard. She flipped through the three top pages, shaking her head. "Staff or patient?" she asked.

"Patient. Brought into the emergency room. He was in a coma last we heard."

"Probably ICU then," she said. "Check over there." Patricia

pointed to six bodies at the end of a row. "Just a minute," she added, flipping to yet one more page. "Barnes, ICU. Yep, that's where he was. There's still more inside, you know, but ICU was just about vaporized."

"So he might be here and he might still be inside?"

"If he's out here, hon, he's confirmed dead. If he's still inside, they may never find him."

"No chance for anybody in ICU?"

"Not so far. Relative?"

"Closer than a brother."

"You want I should check for you?"

Rayford's face contorted, and he could hardly speak. "I'd be grateful."

Patricia Devlin moved quickly, surprisingly agile for her size. Her thick, white-soled shoes were muddy. She knelt by the bodies one by one, checking, as Rayford stood ten feet away, his hand covering his mouth, a sob rising in his throat.

At the fourth body, Miss Devlin began to lift the sheet when she hesitated and checked the still-intact wristband. She looked back at Rayford, and he knew. The tears began to roll. She rose and approached. "Your friend is presentable," she said. "Some of these I wouldn't dare show you, but you could see him."

Rayford forced himself to put one foot in front of the other. The woman reached down and slowly pulled back the sheet, revealing Bruce, eyes open, lifeless and still. Rayford fought for composure, his chest heaving. He reached to close Bruce's eyes, but the nurse stopped him. "I can't let you do that." She reached with a gloved hand. "I'll do it."

"Could you check for a pulse?" Rayford managed.

"Oh, sir," she said, deep sympathy in her voice, "they don't bring them out here unless they've been pronounced."

"Please," he whispered, crying openly now. "For me."

And as Rayford stood in the bluster of suburban Chicago's early afternoon, his hands to his face, a woman he had never met before and would never see again placed a thumb and forefinger at the pressure points under his pastor's jaw.

Without looking at Rayford, she took her hand away, replaced the sheet over Bruce Barnes's head, and went back about her business. Rayford's legs buckled, and he knelt on the muddy pavement. Sirens blared in the distance, emergency lights flashed all around him, and his family waited less than half a mile away.

It was just him and them now. No teacher. No mentor. Just the four of them.

As he rose and trudged back down the rise with his awful news, Rayford heard the Emergency Broadcast System station blaring from every vehicle he passed. Washington had been obliterated. Heathrow was gone. There had been death in the Egyptian desert and in the skies over London. New York was on alert.

Buck was nearly ready to go after Rayford when he saw a tall form appear on the horizon. From his gait and the slump of his shoulders, Buck knew.

"Oh, no," he whispered, and Chloe and Amanda began to cry. The three of them rushed to meet Rayford and walk him back to the car.

The Red Horse of the Apocalypse was on the rampage.